The Woman Who Walked into the Sea

ALSO BY MARK DOUGLAS-HOME
FROM CLIPPER LARGE PRINT

The Sea Detective

The Woman Who Walked into the Sea

Mark Douglas-Home

W F HOWES LTD

This large print edition published in 2014 by
W F Howes Ltd
Unit 4, Rearsby Business Park, Gaddesby Lane,
Rearsby, Leicester LE7 4YH

1 3 5 7 9 10 8 6 4 2

First published in the United Kingdom in 2013 by
Sandstone Press Ltd

A CIP catalogue record for this book is available
from the British Library

ISBN 978 1 47125 416 1

Typeset by Palimpsest Book Production Limited,
Falkirk, Stirlingshire
Printed and bound by
www.printondema~~nd-wo~~rborough, England

This book is m~~ade entirely of chain-of-cust~~ody materials

For Colette, Rebecca and Rory

CHAPTER 1

A vase of blue African lilies, Diana's favourite, filled the alcove in the church vestibule. Mary Anderson stopped to appreciate it before carrying on to the nave where she selected a prayer book from the oak table by the open inner door. Glancing about her, she expected to find other early arrivals already seated, but the church was empty, despite the lights being on. How fitting, she thought. It would allow her a few moments of private reflection to remember Diana before the family gathered, and to take her seat without having to encounter anyone from Poltown and the unpleasantness that always brought.

As she progressed along the aisle she admired the other displays of flowers: a cascade of reds and burnt oranges beside the pulpit and another, smaller arrangement of similarly rich colours to the left of the altar. She recognised chrysanthemums and dahlias, almost certainly cut from the herbaceous beds on either side of the bench in the walled garden where Diana and Mrs Anderson often used to take tea. Late summer flowers were Diana's preference. If she had to pass away, Mrs Anderson reflected with a tremble at the prospect of her own mortality, then wasn't this the season for it to happen, for dressing up the church with the blooms and colours Diana would have liked? She consoled herself with this thought as she approached the pews near the front to choose a place to sit. The third, or even second, row would be appropriate, in her opinion, considering how close she was to Diana as well as to the family. But across the entrance to each of the front four pews, on both sides of the aisle, was silk rope and hanging from it a printed notice. 'Reserved' was written in black and its boldness and its unexpectedness temporarily threw Mrs Anderson. A gloved hand went uncertainly to her mouth. She turned around in case anyone had followed her in, an usher perhaps, someone of whom she could ask guidance, but she was still alone.

Inspecting each of the front four pews in turn she decided to sit at the aisle end of the last of them, on the left hand side. She lifted the rope off its brass hooks and replaced it behind her. Once seated, she felt relief at having taken the weight off her swollen feet – her shoes were pinching – as well as some satisfaction at the decision she had made. Being where she was, the family would easily be able to move her forwards, as she was sure they would once they saw her. And if it happened late, when the church was full, everyone would witness it. Mrs Anderson felt a brief but enjoyable frisson of pleasure at the prospect of such a public display of favouritism. She settled herself, placed the prayer book with its stiff maroon covers on the wooden ledge by her knees and bowed her head.

After reciting the Lord's Prayer in a whispered undertone, she stared sightlessly at the stained glass window above the altar and became quite lost in memories of Diana; how she was that first weekend at Brae House; already Mr William's fiancée, the romance (if that was the word for it) having taken place over the preceding months in Edinburgh. How Mrs Anderson hadn't pulled her punches when Diana had sought her out in the kitchen on the pretext of offering to help with lunch but really to mine her for information about her husband-to-be. 'He'll bully you,' Mrs Anderson had said in her matter of fact manner, 'because you're a pleaser.' Well, wouldn't it have been obvious to anyone after five minutes in her company? Diana was one of those women who, having been abandoned by one husband, (Mr William had forewarned Mrs Anderson of this fact), settled on smiling compliance as the strategy to prevent it happening again. 'Stand up for yourself, or he'll walk all over you,' Mrs Anderson encouraged her. Didn't Mr William need people to bully him back sometimes? The marriage would be all the stronger and happier for it, she'd advised.

Mr William was forty nine, eleven years older than Diana, and in need of someone taking him in hand for his own good. Not that Mrs Anderson had said so at the time, but hadn't it also been obvious that love didn't come into it? Oh, Diana liked him well enough, but in Mrs Anderson's opinion the partnership had been an unspoken trade-off: financial security for Diana and Alexandra, her six-year-old daughter, and in return Mr William acquired a social secretary, someone presentable and long-suffering who would organise his life in Edinburgh and accompany him to legal parties without making many, if any, emotional demands on him. There were worse foundations for a marriage, as Mrs Anderson used to tell Diana when she rang tearfully from Edinburgh after more of Mr William's fault-finding with her appearance, her weight, the way she laughed, the handbag she carried (there was a green one to which Mr William took particular exception) and her incomplete education (she hadn't attended university).

Under the circumstances, Mrs Anderson liked to think of herself as the glue which held the marriage together. She'd 'done' for Mr William at Brae, his weekend and holiday house, near Ullapool, for so many of his bachelor years that she had learnt to rub along with him despite his preference for distance and to manage his moods. She had passed on her knowledge and experience to Diana. Hadn't she deserved the rewards of making Diana her project? The cottage beside Brae's walled garden, her home now for 35 years, had been one. Diana had persuaded Mr William to let Mrs Anderson move into it soon after the marriage.

But there had been others, presents from Diana as well as innumerable kindnesses in recognition of Mrs Anderson's loyalty and friendship. There had also been the privilege (in Mrs Anderson's view) of belonging to a family like the Ritchies. Sometimes, she liked to think, Mr William and she shared a character trait. Each in his or her different way recognised weakness and took advantage of it. A rich man like Mr William could do it by bullying and temper, a housekeeper by making herself indispensable, and that was what she had become, to Diana.

Mrs Anderson closed her eyes and her head shook a little, a tremor from the past.

How long into the marriage had it been that Diana broke the routine of accompanying Mr William for every weekend at Brae? Eight or nine years, Mrs Anderson thought. By then Alexandra was fifteen and out of control. She was seeing an older boy from Poltown, and Diana had been determined to break it up. The only way of keeping Alexandra from him was for Diana to remain in Edinburgh with her daughter most weekends instead of going to Brae. Mr William would love it, Diana had insisted, having Brae more to himself, Mrs Anderson looking after him, just as it used to be. The truth, as Mrs Anderson knew, was that by this time Diana needed the separation from her husband just as much as she desired to prise Alexandra away from an unsuitable boy. Mr William's irritability with his wife had translated across the years into constant unpleasantness and complaints. Diana thought (or was it hoped?) that weekends apart might improve his temper during the week when she and Alexandra were restored to him on his return to the city. If Mrs Anderson had an opinion on Diana's strategy, she considered it more likely that Mr William would grow to enjoy his solitude, a reversion to bachelordom, and would resent its temporariness as well as Diana when the family was reunited in Edinburgh on Sunday nights. As it happened, both were wrong.

What hadn't entered their thoughts was Mr William's susceptibility to a seductress. Mrs Anderson's neglect of the possibility was mostly practical – that type of woman being as rarely seen in coastal north-west Scotland as pure-blood wild cats – and also conditioned by observation. William Ritchie QC had never been a romantic or a womaniser. By disposition he was comfortable in the company of men, preferably other lawyers like himself. By nature he was a sexless creature who was awkward even at the prospect of social kissing and who adopted all manner of avoidance techniques to keep women out of range. (Diana had confided to Mrs Anderson that intercourse more than once a month when they were trying for a baby was regarded by him as an unreasonable imposition.) Then there was his age, 58, surely too old for a mid-life crisis, especially for a man like that who found pleasure in respectability and routine as well as in disapproving the incontinence and mistakes of others.

Mrs Anderson still referred to that time as his 'madness'. The trouble the affair caused; the agonies, for all of them, while it was on-going as well as in its aftermath; the mess that had to be cleared up; desperate times, difficult decisions to be made. Even after the passage of so many years Mrs Anderson disliked dwelling on it. What was done was done, she said to herself with a wondering shake of her head. Not only Mr William's madness; hadn't insanity infected them all to a greater or lesser degree? Afterwards, Diana had been so frightened he would kill himself she sat all night outside his locked bedroom door. Mrs Anderson remembered his crying. Such emotion, it made her wonder where he'd kept it all this time. Diana forgave him of course, blaming herself for leaving him alone, as a pleaser would. For his part, Mr William appeared as regretful for the distress he had caused as for his moral lapse. From Mrs Anderson's observations, the shell of the man made a better husband; a better man even, certainly a nicer one. Hadn't he and Diana another twenty years together before his death, good years which Mrs Anderson remembered with affection, with each change of the calendar moving her closer to the centre of the family like a leaf caught in a vortex.

Suddenly she was overcome by a sense of loss: Mr William gone; now Diana too. She found a handkerchief in her bag and dabbed it against her eyes.

Of course, she'd offered to go to Edinburgh to nurse Diana but Alexandra had turned her down, saying her mother was too proud to let anyone but a stranger do *those* sorts of tasks for her, and anyway wasn't Mrs Anderson too old and decrepit herself now? Mrs Anderson's reply had been sharp – justifiably so. Then there had also been the hurt over the cremation which had been arranged so quickly and in Edinburgh too. The lack of notice had made it impractical for Mrs Anderson to attend. Alexandra apologised in the breezy, insincere way she had and said neither she nor Matt, that weak creature she had for a husband, thought it mattered. Couldn't people like Mrs Anderson attend the memorial at the church by Brae? Mrs Anderson snapped back that *she* wasn't *people*. Sometimes she wondered how Diana had managed to have such a spoilt, inconsiderate child. *Miss* Alexandra, Mrs Anderson had taken to calling her, though only under her breath and through gritted teeth.

By now the church was filling up behind Mrs Anderson, and one or two mourners were taking seats in the reserved pews, presumably members of Diana's extended family. Mrs Anderson recognised one of them, a man with a florid face and white hair, from Diana's photograph albums. She nodded in polite recognition and he returned the gesture to her.

8

How gratifying, Mrs Anderson thought.

Soon the seats behind her were almost full. Some faces she knew from the general store in Poltown returned her stare but she didn't acknowledge them, nor they her. It was propriety in her case (weren't they gathered in God's house to remember Diana?) but jealousy and resentment she liked to think in theirs. Again she felt the frisson of pleasure at the certain prospect of being promoted to a more desirable seat. After turning back towards the altar, she became aware of a group of people progressing down the aisle past her. It was the family: Matt, Alexandra herself in rustling dark blue silk, and the children Richard and Sophia. Weren't they growing so quickly? Matt's sister was also there, and Diana's nephews and nieces, the children of her brother Malcolm, who was accompanied by his wife. Her name escaped Mrs Anderson who was trying to catch the eyes of some of the family party, any of them really. She'd picked up her prayer book and sat on the edge of her seat, primed to move as soon as she was noticed. How frustrating that no one had seen her.

A family she didn't recognise filed into the pew in front: a mother and father accompanied by two lumpen teenage boys. They blocked her view, rendering it difficult for her to make herself seen, and more to the point, for anyone to see her. She regretted her earlier diffidence about sitting further forward.

Then a little man busied at her elbow, asking to

be allowed into her pew. She didn't know him, nor, it appeared, did he know her, or else he wouldn't have spoken to her in that condescending tone of voice. He lifted the rope and she stood to let him pass, but instead of coming in himself he ushered forwards four others, two middle-aged women dressed (inappropriately in Mrs Anderson's opinion) in bright colours, green and pink, and two teenage girls, one so overweight that mottled flesh protruded between her trousers and shirt. Once they were seated there was no room for the man who said in Mrs Anderson's ear, 'Are you sure you're in the right place?'

How was she supposed to answer? Of course, she wasn't in the right place. She should be further forward but what could she do? She simpered, trying not to take offence at him, when, thank heaven, she saw Matt noticing her predicament and coming along the aisle towards her. 'It's all right Henry,' he said to the man who was still standing beside Mrs Anderson as if he planned to stay there for the duration of the service. Mrs Anderson shrugged at Matt, letting him know that none of this was her fault. He leaned down to her and she could hardly believe what he said, or the abrupt way he said it. 'Would you mind moving further back?'

What could she do? The congregation behind had gone quiet. She felt faces turning towards her, as if she was the cause of this problem. 'Please, Mrs Anderson,' Matt continued. 'We don't want a scene.' He put his hand under her right elbow and suddenly she was being propelled from the pew. She whispered a protest but Matt either didn't hear her or ignored her. He said to Henry, 'Sorry about that old man' and Henry promptly took her place. Before she could explain the misunderstanding to Matt, he tightened his grip on her arm and said angrily in her ear, 'Diana felt obliged to put up with you for all these years God knows why but we're not going to tolerate it anymore.' And then he left her, standing alone half way down the aisle while he made his way back to the front pew. She looked around. People were smiling. They watched her, nudging each other and exchanging whispers. She did the only thing she could. She kept on walking. With every step she was sure her legs would let her down. Instead, her face betrayed her, flushing so red and hot it seemed ready to burst. At the back of the church she found a chair, the last empty one. It was beside the table from which she had gathered her prayer book. No sooner had she collapsed into it than the priest called the first hymn and the congregation rose. Mrs Anderson was too flustered to stand, too dumbstruck to sing. Everything was a whirl of humiliation. The door, only a few steps away, was still open for latecomers.

The next thing she knew she was outside, on the gravel path, short of breath, her heart racing, both it and her legs going faster than was advisable for a woman of seventy seven. In her eagerness to distance herself from her mortification, she stumbled and fell. She pitched the prayer book into the grass at the verge. The pebbles of the path dug into her knees. She cried out, a sound which no-one apart from her heard. The singing from the church drowned it out. 'Land of Hope and Glory': Mr William's favourite. She remained collapsed and broken on the path until the singing stopped. Picking herself up, she looked in bemusement at the pin-pricks of blood oozing through the shreds of her tights and at the fluttering pages of the prayer book in the grass. All she could hear was Matt's venomous whisper, 'Diana felt obliged to put up with you for all these years . . .'

Felt obliged . . .

She let out another little cry of pain and made her way unsteadily past Mr William's grave, averting her face to conceal her tears. She opened and closed the wooden gate in the graveyard wall and followed the path across the moor; the quickest route to her cottage. It took her 20 minutes, longer than normal because of her frequent pauses to wipe her eyes. She was still sobbing when she entered her porch and fell back against her door.

She had never been treated so shamefully, she thought as she removed her gloves and placed them on the hall shelf.

To put up with you for all these years

She had always disliked Matt, disrespected him too, as in general she did all men who described themselves 'dealers' or 'agents' – in Matt's case,

12

property dealer. Now her feelings for him bordered on loathing. And for *Miss* Alexandra.

Still distracted, she picked up a letter which had been pushed through the flap while she'd been out. She recognised the style of envelope: it was the sort Brae used for estate business. She carried it to the sitting room – where the light was brighter – and began to read. A soft mewling sound escaped from her and the letter fluttered from her shaking hands on to an occasional table, a gift for her 60th birthday from Diana. Mrs Anderson stared around the room, at all the photographs there, as though she didn't know these people who were staring back at her, as if she was in the company of complete strangers. Nine matching wooden frames, scenes of her with the family: *her* family she liked to think of them. These photographs which had sustained her for so many years – the proof of her indispensability, of her easy familiarity, even intimacy – now seemed to mock her. Her head turned in an arc as she examined each one, in dazed shock at such betrayal.

Over there, on the chest of drawers, Christmas 2002, the year before Mr William's death: the family and Mrs Anderson assembled for tea in the drawing room. That was the Christmas Diana had given Mrs Anderson a silk scarf, a pretty butterfly pattern of pale yellows and greys, by Hermès. And there, on a Pembroke table behind the door, three more photographs: her 'Easter parade' she liked to call them whenever she showed

13

them off to visitors. She remembered the years, 1998, 1999 and 2001; the family and Mrs Anderson by the front door before the start of the Easter egg hunt, Alexandra's children holding empty paper bags in which to put their finds. Wasn't 1999 the year Sophia ate so many she had to go to bed? Wasn't 2000, the missing year, the Easter Alexandra and the family went skiing and Mr William and Diana took the opportunity to escape to Paris for the weekend? On the mantelpiece, in pride of place, were two other photographs: one taken at Alexandra's wedding; the other at Mr William's 70th birthday party: happy occasions she thought at the time. She turned to examine the group of three photographs on the bookshelves to the right of the fireplace and noticed something to which she had been utterly blind until that moment. For many years now she had regarded her position in every group as unspoken acknowledgement of her importance to the family. Hadn't she been placed on the outside because Mr William stood or sat on the opposite side from her, the two of them like strong supporting pillars? Take one or other away and the edifice would collapse. Now her eyes darted from photograph to photograph and she considered the manner in which Alexandra, Matt and the children held themselves; even Mr William. It was in every one, the turn of a shoulder, the swing of a hip, the slant of a head; away, away, always away from her. She hadn't realised it before and now she could not bear to see it. There was a sign, even then, of what would happen, of what had happened. Why had she been blind to it?

Diana felt obliged to put up with you for all these years . . .

Was it a silent or spoken conspiracy? Had they discussed it before her arrival for lunch, tea, whatever the gathering? She imagined the family laughing at her too: the disdain of duty to a servant, allowing her to think she was one of them when she was nothing of the kind. What a fool she had been? Had there ever been an occasion when she had been invited into the middle of the group? If there had, she could not remember it. 'Pride before a fall', she muttered to herself before going round the room collecting up the photographs, stacking them face downwards so she didn't have to look at them again. She took them to the kitchen and dropped them into the rubbish bin. One slid away and crashed to the floor, splintering the glass. She left it there and returned to the sitting room, stopping by the occasional table. She regarded the letter lying on it as if caught in two minds: should she dispose of it too? She picked it up and read it silently. Her hands wavered at the offence it contained.

Dear Mrs Anderson,
After reviewing the farm accounts following Mrs Ritchie's death, it has come to our notice that you have been occupying Gardener's Cottage on terms enjoyed by

no other tenant on the Brae Estate. I have to inform you that it will no longer be possible for your utility bills or council tax to be met by the estate as was the case when Mrs Ritchie was alive. Also, you will be expected to pay rent at the market rate of £575 a month, all with immediate effect.

Yours sincerely

Matthew Hamilton.

Mrs Ritchie. Not Diana. Matthew. Not Matt. Not even a handwritten signature.

After folding the letter, she put it back on the table. She continued to hover beside it only because she wasn't sure whether she could move without falling. Her hand reached for the back of an arm chair. She had little grip in her fingers so she pushed her bent knuckles against the loose cover for support. Her mouth hung open as her breathing became faster, each exhalation accompanied by a moan. Slowly, she looked around her sitting room, now stripped of the memories which once gave her comfort as well as companionship, and she wondered whether she could afford to go on living there.

Hurt heaped upon hurt.

Her pension was small, the house larger than she could afford on her own. A stab of anxiety went through her, a spasm of pain. Her garden, her hydrangeas – she realised they too might be lost to her. She swayed but managed to stop herself from falling by pressing hard against the chair back.

Hurt upon hurt.

She shook her head. Why had this happened to her? Hadn't she been the most loyal of friends to Diana? What would have become of her without Mrs Anderson?

Put up with you . . .

So Diana only put up with Mrs Anderson because she had to. Because of what Mrs Anderson knew. Because of what Mrs Anderson had done when Diana needed her most.

Diana had always been a pleaser, even with Mrs Anderson it seemed.

Mrs Anderson took a step, and another, finally having the confidence to let go of the chair. She went from her sitting room across the hall to the kitchen where she sat at the square oak table. In the middle of it was an earthenware jar with pens, pencils and scissors. Around about the jar were tidy piles of everyday and useful objects – shopping catalogues, her diary, a pad of paper, envelopes, stamps and the phone book. She reached for a pen and the writing paper. She wrote quickly, two sentences in printed capitals. She read them once before folding the sheet and tucking it into an envelope, the flap of which she had to lick a few times with her dry tongue before it was wet enough to seal. She slid the phone book towards her and found the address she wanted. After copying it, she stamped the envelope and went to the front door, removing her car keys from the hook under the shelf. As soon as she was outside, her ears filled with the sound of sniggering and laughter coming from Poltown, a kilometre away. Whether it was real or imagined she couldn't tell, so she set her face in an expression of indifference, the one she always wore when she went to the post box by the shop.

Going down the drive to the road, she talked to herself about her loyalty to the Ritchies, how she had kept their secrets, how Diana owed her still. Hadn't Mrs Anderson rescued her, getting blood on her hands as a consequence? How the family shouldn't have let her come so close if they planned to abandon her, how they didn't know what they'd done. How they'd pay. Oh, how they'd pay.

CHAPTER 2

Some days there was nothing, others it was like this, the beach at South Bay littered with all kinds of detritus. Duncan Boyd gazed at the sweep of sand with the excitement of a collector at the door of a junk shop. Who knew what he might discover in the next few minutes? Only last week he'd found an old brown bottle buried in seaweed. He realised what it was as soon as he had it in his hands. The lead seal was intact, the documents inside just as they were when Guinness dropped 150,000 like it into the Atlantic in 1959 for a bi-centenary marketing exercise. Thousands floated on to the east coasts of America and Canada, as Guinness intended; others eventually found land in South America, the Arctic, even Europe; and others continued to come ashore, more than half a century and countless thousands of miles at sea later. One of the documents Duncan teased from the bottle, the King Neptune Scroll, was now framed and hanging from a beam in the barn where he did his sorting. He had read the colourful document so often during the past few days he could recite the first long sentence off by heart, and did so then in the voice he considered appropriate for the occasion: deep bass as if emerging from ocean depths.

'To the finder of this document greetings and let it be known to all men (and women) that I, Neptune, Monarch of the Sea . . .' Duncan paused, stuck out his chin and surveyed his imaginary realm with narrowed eyes. Then he began again. '. . . that I, Neptune, Monarch of the Sea, have permitted the House of Guinness to cast in, and/or, upon my Domain the bottle carrying this document – but in precise particular, the Atlantic Ocean – and allow same free passage, without let or hindrance, to convey to you the story of Guinness Stout, as also to further the fascinating hobby of Labology (the collecting of bottles.)'

Immediately the widest grin of sheer delight spread across his face, making his weather-beaten skin a relief of crevasses. He laughed, rubbed his hand across the grey grizzle of his unshaven chin and took the rocky path from the headland to the beach below. Half way down, where the trail descended steeply between perpendicular slabs of rock, he stopped and shouted out, 'I, Neptune, Monarch of the Sea' and cocked his head to one side. When he heard the reverberation, he smiled. 'This,' he said as he negotiated the loose stones, 'is going to be a good day, Duncan.' He smacked his lips in anticipation.

Almost as soon as he stepped on to sand, his prophecy seemed vindicated. A blue mooring buoy was stranded there, a type he hadn't seen before. He turned it over, looking for a manufacturer's name, but couldn't find one. Before lifting it and lugging it across the beach, he checked he was alone. He wasn't expecting anyone. After all, it was late August. The tourists had all but gone and he'd taken his usual precaution of scanning the Poltown road for walkers with his binoculars before venturing out. All he'd seen were cars, lots of them, going to the church for Diana Ritchie's memorial service.

He frowned and pushed out his bottom lip to mark her passing before grinning again at finding he had the place to himself. 'My kingdom,' he announced, trying for a monarch's resonance. The result amused him: more Darth Vader than Roman god of water and sea. He gathered up the buoy and lugged it to the turning circle at the road-end where he'd parked his empty trailer the night before. For a moment he wondered what to do with his find. Should it go with all the other blue buoys in his collection – his general if loose practice was to grade buoys by size and colour – or should it be on its own since he didn't have any others exactly like it? No sooner had the question formulated in his head than he became bored by it and gave the buoy a shove, rolling it to the back of the trailer. His eyes swivelled back to the beach, like a child about to embark on a treasure hunt. What other finds were waiting for him?

Usually, it took a few days for him to collect enough to fill his trailer, but today would be different. If he wasn't disturbed there was a load and more on the beach: the wind and high tides of the last few days had produced a bounty. He liked that word. *Bounty*. He said it again as he decided what to gather next. *Bounty*. A swirl of greens and blues suddenly distracted him. He pounced and exclaimed in pleasure at the rubber ball he produced from its hiding place in the sand. He'd keep it for Pepe, the little dog belonging to the new GP, Dr Bell. Sometimes she walked him at South Bay after her surgery at Poltown.

For the next hour and more, he went backwards and forwards across the sand dragging a net as well as two lobster pots, four lengths of black plastic piping, an assortment of soft-wood planks and other driftwood, a blue fish box, two more buoys (white and orange), broken pieces of polystyrene, an empty oil drum and what appeared to be the blade of an oar. After piling them on the trailer, he stopped to roll a cigarette with the last of his tobacco. He licked the paper, lit it and tried to remember what day of the week it was. If Thursday, his weekly delivery box from the general store would be at the farm gate with another 25g packet of rolling tobacco in it. But he thought it was Wednesday so he limited himself to two puffs before putting out the cigarette by pressing the smouldering end between his thumb and forefinger. He stored the butt away in the breast pocket of his denim shirt and was about to go back to work when it occurred to him he hadn't checked the beach road for a while. After all, he didn't want anyone surprising him.

He climbed on to the trailer and slowly straightened his legs. At first all he saw was the high ridge of hills behind Poltown. Then, as he extended his back and finally his neck, the woods around Brae House came into view followed by the church on its emerald knoll midway between the house and the village. He registered that the cars had gone: the memorial service for Diana Ritchie over. 'God bless her soul,' he said with a sombre expression, before smirking at realising he was a god of sorts so had no need to invoke another deity. By now he was almost upright and most of the beach road was visible. He saw his farm gates, the twin stone pillars, the field which was dotted with old machinery, and further to the right, sheltering below the headland, his house and steading. Just as he stretched to his full height, all six feet, he noticed someone coming out of the open double doors to his barn, and then he saw the bonnet of a vehicle. It was parked inside the steading. Complaining at another intrusion, he ducked down. Whoever it was hadn't seen him. But who was it? His earlier exuberance and excitement at having the beach to himself drained away. Crouching on the trailer he began muttering about it being his land, how he'd never sell, no matter what inducement he was offered or whatever promises they made. He'd never leave. In the few seconds that elapsed since first seeing the stranger, Duncan's

23

features put on a fast evolving display of emotions – panic, worry, love. Love of his house. Love of his field. Love of this beach. His jaw set. His eyes narrowed. His breathing slowed. Finally, defiance: no, he'd never leave.

A plan popped into his head and he smiled at its simplicity. Why hadn't it occurred to him before? He'd paint 'This farm and land is NOT for sale. Turn round here' on the old Ferguson tractor and tow it to the stone pillars at the start of the track to the farm.

Emboldened by this notion, Duncan dared to raise himself up again. He elongated his neck until his barn came into view. A red pickup was moving along the rutted track which went from the steading across the field to the stone pillars. His visitor was going away. Duncan's expression changed again; defiance made way for bemusement. The vehicle looked old and battered and a dent was even visible in the passenger door. The others who had come to talk to him had driven sleek black sports utility vehicles, BMWs and the like. The pickup headed away along the beach road and Duncan waited until it had disappeared over the rise before clambering off the trailer. He loped towards the farmhouse, taking the short-cut through the dunes and climbing the broken-down fence into the field. He paused for breath beside the skeleton of an old horse-drawn cart. His exertion brought back some of his previous exuberance.

'I, Neptune,' he proclaimed in a suitably

triumphal voice, as if a great and bloody battle had taken place, a battle of the gods, from which he had emerged victorious, his enemies in headlong flight. Fired by his conquest, Duncan strode towards home. Only when he was standing between the open doors of his barn did he hesitate. On the packed mud floor was a sheet of paper weighted down by a stone. Its edges fluttered in the draught. Duncan regarded it with alarm and pressed his hands against his ears. Once the pressure subsided, he bent uncertainly to read it.

Dear Mr Boyd,
A friend told me about your discovery of a 1959 Guinness bottle. Like you, I'm a beachcomber and have a large collection of artefacts (though having seen your farm I don't think I'm quite in your league). In my case, beachcombing is part of my research into how and where currents and winds carry objects across the oceans. My areas of interest are the eastern and northern Atlantic, including the Scottish coast. Because of the length of time you've been beachcombing I'd like to pick your brains (and see your Guinness bottle). Could I visit? I've got to go to Edinburgh this afternoon but I'll be back in a few days. My email address is theseadetective@gmail. com. Look forward to meeting you soon, Cal McGill.

His phone number was added as a postscript.

Duncan guffawed at how a piece of flapping paper had made him scared, one moment a fearless sea god, the next a tremulous mouse.

The house was Victorian, semi-detached and built of stone. Cal rang the bell and set off a tumble of descending chimes. As they stopped a pigeon-chested man in his 60s opened the door. 'Hello, Cal. How are you?' Harry Richards was wearing a yellow jersey and an over-solicitous expression. By the look of him, he wanted this to be over as quickly as Cal, and without any bad feeling. 'Good journey?' he inquired when he could have complained about Cal being 40 minutes late. 'Took me six hours the last time I was that far north.'

'Sorry about the delay,' Cal mumbled, not wanting to have his usual discussion with Harry, about routes, roads and short-cuts. It was an odd feeling, being back at the house. The bell had thrown him. He'd expected a monotone ring, not chimes. His face must have betrayed his thoughts because Harry remarked, 'I hope you don't mind. Annabel wanted something more cheerful.' The way he said it hinted at disagreement between husband and wife but, under the circumstances, it was possible Harry was just being diplomatic.

Cal shrugged. *You've bought the house – do what you want with it.*

'Here we are then.' Harry pushed back the door

to show Cal his mother's law books, eight roped stacks on the brown and white tiled floor of the porch. 'Everything's ready for you.' He offered to help Cal carry them to the pickup with a warning to be careful in case the ropes cut into his hand. The job itself they did in silence. When the last stack was on its side on the back seat, Harry said, 'I'm sorry about this.'

'Don't be. It's not your fault. It's nobody's fault.'

'If you're passing and you want to see round the place . . .' Harry placed an avuncular hand on Cal's shoulder. 'Just ring the bell. Annabel will be pleased to see you.'

They looked at each other. On the few occasions Cal had been to the house since Harry and Annabel Richards had become his father's tenants, Harry had always been welcoming; his wife frozen and hostile. Cal had the impression she regarded his unannounced visits as proprietorial or even territorial, the equivalent of scent-marking.

The silence made Harry earnest. 'We'll take care of the place. I promise you that.' His pledge was directed at the house, rather than at Cal.

'I'm sure you will . . .' Cal dangled his spare keys. 'You'd better have these.'

Harry organised his benign features into an expression appropriate for receiving an over-generous present. 'Oh, thanks very much,' he said followed quickly by 'that just leaves the furniture. It's in the garage. I'll give you a hand getting it aboard.'

Afterwards, driving away from the street in Edinburgh's south side, seeing the laburnum tree in whose bark the rope of his childhood swing was still embedded, Cal had the oddest sensation of dislocation. 'I'm twenty-nine years old, for God's sake!' How had he progressed that far into adulthood only to be pole-axed by the sale of a house he'd visited once in the past year, in which he hadn't slept since he was eighteen or nineteen?

Later, he brooded on it in his office, a brick box on an industrial estate three kilometres to the north-east, in Leith. He'd moved there more than a year ago from a studio flat in a converted whisky bond further along Edinburgh's coastline. The box had a monthly rent attached but required little else from Cal, a feature of the place which appealed to him. What had been intended as a temporary move was becoming permanent. Leaning against a shelf, drinking coffee from a red mug, he observed his surroundings, such as they were: the long table cluttered with the paraphernalia of oceanography – dozens of maps, files and books as well as two computers – and at the walls which were papered with charts of ocean currents and newspaper cuttings. There were stories about unidentified bodies washing up on Britain's beaches as well as magazine and newspaper articles about Cal. Many of the headlines had a similar theme: 'Sea detective finds clue in severed head murder hunt'; 'Trawler families make appeal to ocean expert: track down our missing men'; 'Oil tanker implicated in vanishing yachtsman mystery'; 'Sea detective becomes a doctor' and so on. The last of these was about his PhD which he had completed three months ago.

He crossed the office to the kitchenette, walking round the folding camp bed he kept for the nights he spent in town. He topped up his black coffee with water from the kettle until it was brown, before going to the store-room next door, where he'd unloaded the books and furniture from his family home. His fingers passed from one object to the next, from one texture to another: from the corrugations of his mother's roll-top desk to the polished back of the reproduction Chippendale arm-chair with its leather seat on which she used to place her coat and bag after coming in from the solicitors' office where she worked. Now he ran the heel of his hand along the pine chest of drawers from his childhood bedroom, the scars of his wakeful night-time scribblings still visible under an overcoat of white paint. Everything he touched aroused a dormant memory so that in a few seconds of reflection his office store-room became an ante-chamber to a much larger and featureless repository, the one in Cal's head where he filed regrets and hurts.

Almost all of these had to do with the disintegration of his family, an apparently unstoppable sequence of events which began with the premature death of his mother Eilidh from cancer when he was 17 (an age that had seemed grown-up until he kissed her cold forehead). It continued with his father's twin absences. The first was psychological – following his mother's funeral, James McGill suffered a mental collapse. The second was physical and appeared to have no limit of time. For the last eleven years his father had worked abroad, teaching at charity-run schools for orphans. After moving from country to country, he settled in Mozambique where he had set up home with a Swazi woman 12 years his junior and her three children. Even before Cal knew of and welcomed the arrangement, he had grown to understand why his father lived as he did, never returning to Edinburgh. To McGill senior, the city and the house in Newington were places of bitter memories, of loss, where his wife and lover had died, where he had suffered a break-down and might again if he ventured back. In the letter he sent to Cal telling him about the sale (including the contents) to Harry and Annabel, he indicated as much.

Wasn't it time for Cal and him to leave it behind, for it to provide for the future instead of preserving the past, memories which had been happy once but which had become distressing? Cal replied with resignation and restraint. He asked if he could have his mother's books and six pieces of furniture and thanked his father for his 'very generous' division of the money. Cal received £227,000, a quarter of the sale price. He would use it to buy a cottage 'somewhere off the beaten track by the sea; probably without a road or neighbours, not a notion that will surprise you I imagine.'

What he'd felt was something more emotional but he hadn't written it. What would have been the point? The sale had been agreed. It was irrevocable. 'For the first time in my life,' he might have said, 'there's nowhere on a map I can stick a pin and say "this is where I belong". Even though I haven't been living in the house, it has always been *there*. It has always been home.' It was what he thought.

Nothing else had been as dependable, he might have added. Not his mother. Not his father.

He turned out the store-room light, closed the door and sat at his table, waiting for his computer to warm up, glancing at the shelves which displayed his collection of 346 artefacts from beach combing. After drinking some more coffee, he logged on to his email and found he had 17 unread messages. Most appeared to be inquiries from potential clients, more fathers and mothers, husbands or wives wanting him to guide them towards the bodies of their drowned and missing children or lovers. He read the first six. Their tone of desperation was as moving as it was familiar, the burden of expectation too much for him in his present state of mind. He replied with sympathy as well as regrets. He cited pressure of work – 'the disadvantage of being a one-man operation'. He hoped to be 'in a position to take on new cases in a week or two'. He'd be in contact as soon as he could. Then he listened again to the phone message he'd received from Duncan Boyd. 'Neptune Boyd speaking – visit anytime you want.' Cal had seen a King Neptune Scroll so he understood the reference. He rang back but it went to answer.

'I'll be passing in a few days and I'll call in. Look forward to meeting you.'

He shut down his computer, slid his laptop into his backpack and locked the office door. He had to get away, somewhere wild, where the roaring of the sea obliterated everything else.

Dawn. The gale barged into Cal's pickup as if dislodging it was the only purpose for barrelling over hundreds of miles of ocean. Like a thug who wasn't getting his own way, the wind shoved, pushed, threatened and howled. A gust thumped against the front passenger door; another bounced off the cab. The vehicle rocked and shuddered from the ferocity of the assault. Cal opened his window wide enough to slide out his hand. When it was wet with salt and spray, he rubbed it against his face. Zipping his jacket and pulling tight the draw-string on his hood, he experienced excitement as well as melancholy. Was this how it was going to be, he wondered as he opened his door, holding it tight to stop the squall ripping it from its hinges. Would he always be alone and in a storm walking some remote coast?

CHAPTER 3

Anna sat cross-legged under the table putting varnish on her nails; red alternating with black for her toes, glitter pink for her fingers. Her mother had asked her to keep out of the way while she made the bedsit 'half-way presentable'. But the more Violet brushed, wiped and dusted, the more hopeless the prospect seemed to be. At least that was the gist of her exasperated commentary as she went from bed to chest of drawers, to chair, to cupboard. Everything Violet touched or noticed had this wrong with it, or that needing mending or replacing. Her worries about the impression their impending visitor would take away with him extended to her daughter.

'And try not to call me Violet,' she said. Anna had a habit of calling her mother Violet unless she was cross or upset. Then she became Mummy.

'And *try* to call me Violet,' Anna repeated in the opposite.

'And remember to smile.'

'And remember *not* to smile.'

Anna peered out from below the fringe of table cloth as Violet removed jumpers and yesterday's underwear from the chair and shoved them under the bed.

'And if he speaks to you make sure you answer him politely.'

'And if he speaks to you make sure you *don't* answer him politely.'

Violet stopped what she was doing and gave her daughter an anguished look. 'Anna, love, it's serious. Mr Anwar will be here soon.'

'Mr Anwar will . . . *not* . . . be here soon.' Anna began laughing and kicked out her legs knocking over one of the bottles of varnish. It made a little puddle of pink on the bare wood floor.

'Oh Anna, look what you've done.' Violet snatched a dirty cloth and ran to her daughter, wiping the spill with one hand and grabbing at the leaking bottle with another. 'Why are you so naughty?'

As she rubbed at the floor, she noticed a pink stain on her jeans where she'd knelt. Anna saw it too and pre-empted another scolding by sobbing and emitting little gasps of misery. Soon her cheeks were streaked and her nose was running. Violet regarded the wreckage of her daughter and blamed herself. She'd been tense all morning. It was bound to end with someone in tears. She wrapped the varnish bottle in the cloth to prevent it spilling again and placed it out of harm's way on the mantelpiece beside her birthday cards before crouching beside Anna. 'Come here,' she said, pulling on the girl's arm. Mother and daughter leaned into each other. Violet kissed Anna's forehead, stroked away the wetness squeezing from her eyes and brushed back her dark curly hair. She held Anna's hands and blew on her nails to dry them. 'Friends?' Violet offered.

'I suppose,' Anna replied, pulling away to return to her lair under the table just as the door bell sounded. Violet wanted to hug her daughter again, to be certain her crossness had been forgiven, but she couldn't let Mr Anwar see the room like this. What would he think? That she was a bad mother too?

She gathered up the other bottles of varnish and hid them in a drawer in the kitchen alcove along with a dirty pan from the sink. On her the way to the door she diverted by the bed and turned-over the duvet to conceal the rip in the cover. She paused to wonder whether the balloon tied to the bed-head should be removed. The legend 'Happy Birthday' had been reduced by deflation to a mean-ingless jumble of letters, 'Hppitda'. The bell sounded again, this time two rings and Violet left the balloon. She checked herself in the small mirror to the right of the door before glancing back at Anna whose cheeks and nose were smudged from crying. Violet found a tissue in her pocket and ran to her with it. 'Quickly, your face.'

Anna passed the tissue carelessly across her mouth before throwing it behind her. Violet was half way to the door when she turned back to her daughter. 'And remember to smile.'

'And remember *not* to smile.'

Violet made a last despairing inspection of the barely furnished room with its high ceiling and plaster cracks. None of it was as she wanted it to be.

She pressed the entry buzzer, straightened her jersey and combed her fingers through her hair, a habit from when she wore it long. By the time she heard her visitor's footfall on the last flight of stairs she was shaking with nerves. Taking a deep breath, she opened the door.

Mr Anwar it turned out was a small man, balding, with a long face on which perched wire-rimmed glasses. He wore a navy blue jacket, white shirt, and charcoal trousers which were too long for him. 'Miss Wells?' He offered a hand. Violet took it briefly, detaching as soon as it was polite in case he felt her agitation.

'Come in, please,' she said.

After closing the door, she introduced Mr Anwar to Anna, and Anna (*bless her*) did exactly as Violet had asked. She smiled and said, 'Hello, how are you?'

Mr Anwar bent to get a better look at the child. 'Your daughter?' He turned to Violet.

Violet nodded. She'd grown accustomed to the question. 'Anna's father is from North Africa,' she said, explaining the honey-brown colour of Anna's skin. It was all she said: nothing about him deserting her during the pregnancy – she'd heard he'd gone back to Morocco; nothing about the guilt which nagged at her; bringing a child into the world without a father, repeating the cycle.

36

'Anna is a pretty name for a pretty girl.' Mr Anwar addressed the compliment to Violet but he meant it for the child. Violet saw the vomit face that Anna pulled, but she didn't mind. In fact she wanted to embrace her daughter. In that short exchange Anna had won over Mr Anwar. Violet could tell by his expression of amused indulgence.

'And how old is she?'

'I'm four and a quarter,' Anna replied with an indignant note of protest that the question was not directed at her.

'Lovely age, when they're like that,' Mr Anwar said. 'A handful I'm sure, but delightful.'

'Most of the time she is,' Violet replied before offering Mr Anwar a cup of tea, remembering too late the milk in the fridge was past its sell-by. 'Do you mind black?'

'No, not at all; in fact, I prefer it black, thank you.'

She had begun to like Mr Anwar and his courteous ways. As she put the tea bags into the mugs, she indicated the arm chair. 'Please sit down, Mr Anwar.' He hesitated as it was the only chair in the room but Violet reassured him that it was 'fine, really'. She would sit on the end of the bed.

Mr Anwar bowed his head, a gesture simultaneously of obedience and thanks, and perched on the edge of the chair. After Violet brought over the mugs of tea, handing one to him, handle first, she said, 'You have something to tell me about my mother.'

37

'I have, Miss Wells.'

He placed his mug on the floor between his shoes – slip-ons; grey, unassuming and unfashionable like their owner – and brought a white envelope from an inside pocket. 'I hope you didn't mind me contacting Mr Wells . . . I gathered from him that you're not in regular touch . . . that all he has is your email address.'

'It's all right.'

Mr Anwar appeared anxious to reassure Violet there had been no breach of confidentiality. 'I asked him to pass on my details to you: name, phone number and email address. He didn't ask why. Nothing else passed between us.' He paused. 'This address . . .' he looked around the room, '. . . will remain confidential, of course.' While Mr Anwar was talking, Violet watched his forefinger stroking the edge of the envelope.

'We don't have much to do with each other . . .' Violet said apologetically. She glanced up wondering if she needed to explain why she'd drifted apart from her adoptive parents, how they'd never really got on. Mr Anwar read her uncertainty and attempted to put her at ease by bowing his head, letting her know there was no need for her to say more. Violet took a sip of tea. Mr Anwar did likewise and returned his mug to the floor before holding up the envelope. 'This,' he said, 'arrived at our office in Inverness last week.'

Violet stared but said nothing.

'You know what happened after you were born?'

'My parents . . .' Violet said, 'my adoptive parents told me.'

'Well, that makes it easier.' His expression was kindly and understanding. 'For both of us.'

He waited again, glancing at Violet. 'Usually we wouldn't pass on anonymous correspondence, but considering your circumstances, your special circumstances . . .' With that he offered Violet the envelope, holding it in his left hand, stretching across the gap between the chair and the bed. For a while she did nothing. She looked from the envelope to Mr Anwar before taking it from him in both hands.

'My suggestion,' he said, 'would be for you to open it and then we can talk?' His speech was slow and considered, as if he understood the importance of the next few minutes, and the speed at which they should be taken. Such things were best not rushed his tone seemed to suggest.

'Is there a name?'

He nodded. Violet placed the envelope in her lap, rubbed the corners between her fingers and thumbs, and stared at it. Her face showed the hurt of all those years. 'Do you have children, Mr Anwar?'

The question caught him off guard. 'A son . . . yes, a son . . .'

'Could you have done that to him?'

'No. No, I couldn't.' He shook his head to reinforce the point. Violet was struck by the emphatic nature of his response. Mr Anwar added

39

as a softener. 'But not everyone's circumstances are the same. Who knows what was going through your mother's head, what trouble she was in? Perhaps she thought she couldn't look after you.'

A pulse pushed at Violet's neck. 'I've wanted this so much . . . and now I don't know.' She closed and opened her eyes. 'What would you do Mr Anwar?'

He sighed, considering his reply. 'I'd take my time.'

'But would you read it?'

'I think I would, yes.'

'Even though it changes everything.'

Mr Anwar nodded a number of times. Neither spoke for a minute. Then Violet put the envelope on the arm of Mr Anwar's chair and crossed to the other side of the room, as far away from it as she could be. 'What will happen if I don't?'

'It'll be kept for you. When . . . if . . . you change your mind, you'll be able to read it.'

Violet brought her hands in front of her face, as in prayer. Why was she being like this? Didn't she spend part of every day or night thinking about her mother, even now, after all this time?

Mr Anwar let his attention stray momentarily to Anna who was hugging one of the table legs, staring at the envelope, as if her grandmother might suddenly emerge from it, genie-like. He smiled at her and Violet asked, 'If I open it will I have to do anything about it . . . afterwards?'

'Go to see her, you mean?'

'Yes . . .'

Mr Anwar hesitated before replying, forming the answer silently to be sure of his delivery. 'I don't know if this makes things easier for you . . . or more difficult.' He let Violet prepare herself, delaying a beat before continuing. 'I made a preliminary check to ascertain whether this letter had come from the woman named in the letter . . . to be sure it wasn't your birth mother's way of trying to initiate contact with you. Sometimes it happens in cases like these.'

'Was it?'

'No. No, it wasn't.' Mr Anwar shook his head. 'I'm sorry Miss Wells. The woman who is named in this letter isn't alive. She died the day after you were abandoned at the hospital.'

Violet heard it without moving. What transfixed her was not the news of her mother's death, but that she hadn't sensed it, not once, not in all the years of searching for her, of imagining their reunion with such daily regularity that any doubt about it ever happening had gone from her. Not *if*, but *when*: a longed-for moment. 'Oh, she's dead,' was all she managed to say after the first shock had passed. Then, a few seconds later, 'I didn't know.' As if she should have done. As if it was a daughter's duty.

'Gosh.' It was not a word she normally used – it seemed to come from childhood. Ever since she could remember she had felt a living and visceral connection to her absent mother. It had driven

41

Violet to hunt every street, every crowd, certain that her mother would have been doing the same, always on the look-out, always wondering, 'Is this one her?' Sometimes it was simply the way a woman walked, the colour of her hair – the same brown colour, or the style. At others it wouldn't be anything specific, just a feeling, an inexplicable and sudden sensation of affinity. Or, a certain age: someone in their late thirties or early forties, who would have been a teenager when Violet was born, who couldn't have coped, someone too young to understand what she had done deserting a baby like that, someone who hadn't known better. The constancy of her searching hadn't been affected by her living in Glasgow, about 250 kilometres from the hospital where she had been abandoned. As often as once a week, she'd see someone who had something familiar about her. Usually it happened when Violet hadn't even been conscious of looking. She'd lost count of the number of women she'd followed. Some she'd even engaged in conversation, asking directions, anything to detain them for long enough so she could have a sense of them. After each disappointment Violet had lain awake as Anna slept. *One day. One day it will happen.*

How could she have been so wrong?

In the middle of this rush of memories, regrets and recriminations, Mr Anwar dropped another bombshell. He apologised for it but in his judgement it was better she heard it now than find out for herself later. 'According to the records, she took her own life . . .'

Violet gasped and crouched with her back to wall, rocking backwards and forwards.

'I'm sorry, Miss Wells.' Mr Anwar moved further to the edge of the chair, as if preparing to spring to Violet's side should she require support.

'She killed herself . . . after she had held me?' Violet asked.

'I can't say for sure. There's no official record of your birth. We have to assume she delivered you herself or someone unqualified assisted her.' Mr Anwar added. '*If* she was your mother . . .' He paused again. 'Maybe she has brothers or sisters who are still living . . . there are tests you can have done.'

Violet wasn't really listening. 'How could she do that, hold me and then leave me, kill herself?' She was still rocking.

'I don't know, Miss Wells.'

Violet let out a shout of anger and Anna clung tighter to the table leg. She had never seen her mother like this. She didn't know what to do, what she had done wrong. The rocking suddenly stopped and Violet asked, 'Did she kill herself because of me?' Mr Anwar said he didn't imagine she had but nor could he be sure of the answer. 'If only there was more information.'

'You know . . .' Violet's voice trembled. 'I'm so angry with her.' She noticed Anna's frightened face and beckoned to her. The child walked stiffly across

43

the room and crouched against the wall, copying her mother. 'I'm sorry,' Anna whispered, in case she had been to blame for the change of mood. Mr Anwar also apologised for 'managing a difficult situation inadequately, for making bad worse.'

'It's not you. Really, it's not.' Violet replied. She put an arm round Anna and pulled her close. Then she said, 'Will you read out the letter, Mr Anwar?'

'Are you sure?'

'Yes. It doesn't matter anymore, does it?'

Mr Anwar picked up the envelope, opened the unsealed flap and removed a single folded sheet of paper. He looked at Violet offering her an opportunity to change her mind. 'As you'll see,' he said, allowing more time to pass, 'it's hand-written, but there's no signature, sender's address or date.' He coughed, adjusted his glass and began to read. 'A new born baby girl was abandoned at Raigmore Hospital, Inverness, before midnight on September 9 1983. Her mother was called Megan Bates and at the time she lived at Orasaigh Cottage, by Poltown.'

He re-read it to himself before folding the letter and returning it to the envelope. 'Perhaps the anniversary has prompted this – the 9th was two days ago.' He looked at Violet's birthday cards on the mantelpiece. 'Though it's impossible to say for sure . . .'

'Where's Poltown?' Violet asked.

'It's about sixty or seventy miles from Inverness, but on the west coast.'

Violet considered the implication. 'My mother wanted to distance herself from me.'

'You could draw that conclusion but I'm sure there are others if only we had all the facts.'

'How old was she?'

'She was thirty-three.'

Violet shook her head again: another of her presumptions had been confounded. 'So she was old enough to know better.'

'I can't say.'

'Did she have other children?'

'There are no records of any, but there is no record of your birth either.'

Violet pushed back against the wall. Anna copied her. Mr Anwar clasped and unclasped his hands.

'Where is she buried?' Violet asked.

Mr Anwar appeared startled by the question, as if Violet had read his mind. He stammered and coughed. 'I'm sorry Miss Wells. I didn't want to distress you any more than was necessary.' His mouth flinched. 'She wasn't buried.'

'Why not?' Violet turned the question into an accusation.

'Her body was never recovered. She killed herself by swimming out to sea, according to the police inquiry at the time.'

Violet closed her eyes at her mother's final betrayal. Even in death she hadn't wanted to be found by her daughter. Anna pressed closer.

Mr Anwar apologised again for 'being the bearer of such difficult news'. He placed the letter on the arm of the chair and removed a small brown envelope from his inside jacket pocket and put it beside the letter. 'I thought you might like to have these. They're newspaper cuttings about Megan Bates and the search for her body . . . and there's a photograph.'

'Of her?'

'Yes.'

Another shock.

The emotion of the moment affected Mr Anwar too. 'It's not a very good picture, I'm afraid, and it's black and white. Would you like to see it?' He fumbled among the clippings until he found the one he wanted and carried it over to Violet. 'According to the caption it was taken at the Poltown fair the year before you were born.'

All Violet saw was a blur. A woman half-turned to the camera, the wind blowing her long dark hair to make a veil of sorts across her eyes and mouth which was caught open and smiling. A woman captured in a moment of happiness. Her mother. A moment Violet would never share.

'Of course,' Mr Anwar said, 'it's possible you're not her daughter. Whoever wrote the letter might be mistaken . . .'

'They're not mistaken,' Violet replied. 'She is my mother.'

She put her hand into the pocket of her jeans and withdrew a small green box. 'It's the brooch she's wearing in the photograph.' She handed the box to Mr Anwar. 'The nurses found it when they found me. It was attached to a piece of knitting, something cut from a jersey or a cardigan.' She watched as Mr Anwar opened the box and studied its contents. 'The flowers are violets . . . that's why I'm called Violet . . . it was the name the nurses gave me.' She let out a brittle laugh. 'I took it to an expert once but he wasn't able to tell me much except it's made of porcelain and might be worth £60 or £70.'

'Yes, I see.' Mr Anwar closed the box and returned it. 'Yes, I see.' He went back to the chair, where he sat with his head bowed, as usual allowing an interval to pass for Violet to assimilate each new revelation without interruption. 'You have many things to think about,' he said at length. 'And thinking is best done alone.' He stood up. 'So I should leave you now.'

Violet made to move but Mr Anwar insisted she stay where she was. He would see himself out. At the door, he turned back. There was something else he needed to tell her. It was clear from his doleful expression that he was torn about doing it now. 'What is it?' Violet asked.

'There's no mention of her being pregnant in the newspaper cuttings. I don't know why that is because the police report into her death refers to her being close to full term.'

After Mr Anwar's departure, Anna continued to mimic Violet; sitting like her; her back pressed against the wall, legs outstretched, feet together.

She occupied herself by making faces on her finger nails, scratching out two eyes, a nose and a mouth in the dried varnish. Each nail was given a girl's name and was introduced to its neighbour. These formalities included a whispered warning to be quiet because 'Violet is upset'.

'Not with you,' Violet said before examining the photograph again. 'I wish I'd asked if she was married.'

'Don't you *have* to be married when you're thirty-three?'

'No,' Violet said, 'no you don't.'

Anna passed on the news to her 'nail polish' friends, and Violet remembered the day she was told the circumstances of her birth, those few that were known. She had been twelve when Bridget, her adoptive mother, sat her down in the kitchen and explained why a woman might desert a new born baby. 'She'll have been abandoned too, by the father, poor girl. No mother would do that unless she was young, desperate and alone. It must have broken her heart.' Violet recalled every detail of the conversation because Bridget seemed so troubled by it. 'Things are better said, don't you think, so we all know where we are? Even if I'd given birth to you, I couldn't love you more than I do.' Until then she'd thought Bridget was talking about one of their neighbours, or another girl at school. She hadn't liked to ask, because Bridget seemed on the verge of tears. The thing she remembered most clearly about the revelation, once she had understood its significance, was her sense of relief; that and the wave of emotion for her lost mother which had ebbed and flowed ever since. Even before Bridget's 'chat' as she had prefaced it, Violet sensed she hadn't belonged; that Tom and Bridget Wells weren't her real family. After it, she called them by their first names and not mummy and daddy as she had before. Every day she expected her real mother to rescue her, and imagined how extraordinary that would be.

Not her father: though she didn't know why she never imagined him coming.

Never wondered about the way he looked or the way he sounded.

Never wanted his arms around her. She just hadn't, still didn't.

Most likely it was because she accepted her mother's action was dictated by desperation, by circumstances beyond her control, by her father's fecklessness, as Bridget suggested. Was there another possible explanation, one that made any kind of sense? Now Mr Anwar had brought the beginnings of another version of events, one that demolished all her previous assumptions. Megan Bates hadn't been young, a girl, nor had she spent the past 26 years trying to find the daughter she gave away.

A knock at the door interrupted her thoughts: a soft tap followed by another as though the person outside was aware of the sensitivities of the moment; of the tactless inconvenience of wanting to be let in now. Violet and Anna exchanged glances.

'Who is it?' Violet called out. Her question elicited a familiar cough from the visitor on the other side of the door. 'Miss Wells, it's me, Mr Anwar . . . If I might, just for a minute, I won't need to come in, there's something . . .' He sounded so unsure of himself that Violet was concerned for him, of the unsettling effect his visit had had on him too.

'Of course,' she said, going to the door, brushing her hands across her face. 'Please, come in.'

'I won't, if you don't mind.' Mr Anwar stood awkwardly, neither crossing the threshold nor saying why he had returned.

'It's all right Mr Anwar, whatever it is. Really . . .'

Anyway a small man, he seemed smaller still as if shrinking from whatever else he had to tell Violet had shrunk him literally.

'You asked me if I had children.'

'I did, and you said you had a son.'

The repetition of it appeared to cause Mr Anwar anguish. He shook his head and made an expression of contrition. 'I have a daughter too.'

'Oh,' Violet said.

'Shereen – she was very pretty, and clever.' There was pride in his voice; that a daughter of his could be such things; but regret too. Violet registered the tense he used – 'was' – but said nothing.

'I don't see her anymore.' Mr Anwar shrugged. It happened, the shrug said, though he hadn't expected it to happen to him. 'When my wife died . . .' he tried to explain before giving up. 'Shereen found herself another family, I suppose.'

He faltered and Violet stepped towards him, touching his arm lightly with her hand. 'There's no need, Mr Anwar.'

'Please . . .' He sounded cross for not saying what he meant. Violet took her hand back and waited for him to speak.

'She married, too quickly. She didn't know the man well enough and now she might as well be a stranger. His family is rich and I,' he went on, 'well, I am not. I never see her. She has told me never to contact her.' His head dropped, pulled down by the weight of regret. 'Every night for the last four years,' he glanced up at Violet, 'every night before I go to bed, I sit in her room and talk to her.'

From behind his back he produced a carrier bag. 'I couldn't help seeing . . .' His eyes darted around the room and back. It meant he couldn't help noticing the lack of furnishings. 'It's just a book,' he said, sensing her reluctance to accept it.

'There's no need.' She took it because refusing it might hurt his feelings. 'Thank you.'

'Go to where she was, talk to her, like I talk to Shereen. It helps.' He retreated along the landing.

'Thank you, I will,' Violet called after him. As he started down the stairs, she remembered the question she had omitted to ask him before. 'Oh, Mr Anwar,' she shouted, going to the handrail

51

and leaning over it. Mr Anwar seemed apprehensive, as though Violet was about to return his gift.

'Was my . . .' She stopped. 'Was my mother married?'

Mr Anwar shook his head. 'No, no she wasn't. The newspaper reports of the time refer to her as Miss Bates and my information is that the police report also described her as a spinster.'

After the door to the street had shut, Violet opened the bag and removed the book, a travel guide to the Scottish Highlands. Lying flat inside the front cover was a wad of £20 notes and a card from Mr Anwar. She counted out the money, ten notes, more than she had held at one time, ever. Then she read the card.

Dear Miss Wells,

I hope you're able to find your mother's spirit somewhere in Poltown. A word of caution: you might be wise initially to disguise the purpose of your visit and your probable relationship to Megan Bates. It's quite possible, even likely, your father is still alive and that he has family in the area. In my long experience of these kinds of cases, it's better to move slowly and with as many of the facts as possible before declaring who you are. It might save you and others hurt. I hope you don't mind me offering you this small piece of advice.

He had signed it modestly: Anwar.

Violet found the reference on page 192 of the guide book.

'Poltown,' she read aloud to Anna. 'Question: when is a town not a town? Answer: when it's Poltown. This example of misplaced suburban planning was dropped on the unsuspecting West Highlands for the workforce of the Nato refuelling depot which opened here in 1962. The military fondness for acronyms (POL = Petroleum, Oil and Lubricants depot) gave the new settlement its name. Unwisely, those responsible for designing Poltown allowed themselves an evocative flourish, imagining their creation one day becoming notable like the famous dead Scots after whom they called this ugly collection of cul-de-sacs. To save you the bother of going there, there is Thomas Telford Court, Sir Harry Lauder Gardens, William Wallace Drive, Sir Alexander Fleming Rise, David Livingstone Neuk, and Jenny Geddes Walk, after the spirited woman who threw her stool at the head of the Dean of St Giles Cathedral in Edinburgh for having the affront to use an Anglican prayer book. Wouldn't she have aimed another missile at the perpetrators of this more modern heresy had she been alive? If you're still tempted to see it for yourself, there is also a refuelling jetty in the adjacent sea loch, buried fuel tanks in the hill-side behind and a collection of disused military sheds, where visiting forces were trained in the theories and practice of covert mountain warfare. Since Nato's retreat and the departure of the military trainers and depot staff, the cul-de-sacs have been used as overspill social housing from the surrounding towns and villages, the Highland equivalent of a refugee encampment, the residents huddled and forlorn, waiting to return to their lost homelands, all hope gone.'

CHAPTER 4

On the bus from Ullapool Violet studied an Ordnance Survey map of Poltown and the surrounding district. She read again the newspaper cuttings Mr Anwar had given her, though she knew them so well she could recite paragraphs from memory. How Megan Bates had left her cottage on the tidal island of Orasaigh. How she walked the coastal path to the headland by South Bay where she descended to the beach. How it had been a still, sunny day – one newspaper made reference to an 'Indian summer' that year. How 'Miss Bates' had been wearing a loose white dress and a raffia sun hat decorated with broad red ribbon. How she also had a leather bag on a shoulder strap. An unnamed witness, a woman exercising her dog on the beach road 300 metres away, had told the police it was 'unmistakeably Miss Bates because no-one else wears summer dresses in Poltown'. How the witness hadn't thought anything was untoward because the two women often saw each other at a distance on their morning walks. How Miss Bates had stood at the water's edge before wading into the sea.

The witness had been elderly and hadn't paid much attention because it was only 'Miss Bates paddling'. How the hat and bag had been recovered later from North Bay, less than a kilometre up the coast, where they'd drifted ashore. A local farmer by the name of Duncan Boyd had found them. How the witness had come forward the next day. How the police had searched the coast for seven more days waiting for the sea to give up her body. But it never did. How that was unusual in waters like those, with a prevailing south-westerly which brought all kinds of flotsam ashore, including occasionally the bodies of whales and fishermen drowned in The Minch. How the unseasonal and light southerly wind that September might have influenced the natural order of things. How, according to Inspector Robert Yellowlees of Highland Constabulary, the officer in charge of the investigation, there had been 'no suspicious circumstances'. All the evidence pointed to an unhappy young woman killing herself by drowning.

On a ridge three kilometres from Poltown, the bus driver, an obliging middle-aged man called Stuart, pulled into a passing place. He was five minutes ahead of schedule and 'might as well have a ciggie break here' to let Violet 'enjoy the view' considering she was his only passenger and she'd been asking so many questions about the area. As soon as Violet stepped from the bus she realised why he had chosen to stop there. The passing place had a 180 degree view of the coast line, 'a veritable panorama,' Stuart said mockingly, taking on the role of personal tour guide. He lit a cigarette and clamped it in the right hand corner of his mouth. 'Didn't I tell you it'd be worth it?' he said out of the left. Despite his sardonic manner, there was satisfaction that someone ordinary like him could live among magnificence like that.

Violet managed to nod in reply, but her mind was on the map and the cuttings and translating them to this incredible vista of land and sea across which her mother had made her final journey. She identified the features whose names had become familiar in the days since Mr Anwar's visit. There was Orasaigh, the tidal island, at the inner mouth of the sea loch. A band of blue sparkled between it and the mainland: the tide was in. From there Violet's eye was drawn to the north by a scored line a little inland from the coast. This was the trace of the path which Megan Bates had taken that day. At the headland, a distance of half a kilometre, maybe more, she descended to South Bay, a long inviting curve of grassland dunes, sand and sea. Somewhere along its lazy sweep of beach Megan Bates had walked into the water and disappeared. Violet lingered on the view, the scene of her mother's death, before seeking out the final landmark, North Bay, where the hat and bag came ashore. Violet recognised it from its outline on the map, like a mouth that was half-open.

'In case you're interested . . .' Stuart said, his tone suggesting she shouldn't be, 'Poltown is over to the left. It's hidden by the hill. See that grand house?' Violet looked to where he was pointing. 'That's Brae House. And see the church?'

Violet could: a building of grey stone squatting on a hummock of bright green encircled by a boulder wall.

'Well, Poltown's the other side of it, round the shoulder of the hill, out of sight and out of mind . . . best way with Poltown. Bit of a dump to be honest.' He dropped his smouldering cigarette into the swept-up gravel at the side of the lay-by while Violet's attention was drawn back to South Bay.

'Enjoy the view while you can,' Stuart said.

'Yes, it is the perfect day, isn't it?' Violet replied, thinking it might have been similar weather twenty-six years before.

'I wasn't meaning that.' Stuart nodded towards the horizon. 'There's going to be a forest of windmills out there, hundreds of them, a monster of a windfarm or whatever it's called when it's at sea . . . and down there. See that little turn-off to the beach?'

Violet looked at where Stuart was pointing. She guessed it must be the road from which the witness saw Megan Bates. 'Yes.'

'Well, see the field the other side of it?

Violet nodded.

'And the farmhouse and steading . . . across the field, do you see? This side of the headland. They're planning to put up a building the size of a football pitch . . . for converting the electricity for the grid, or something like that. I don't know what. It's all progress, I suppose.' Stuart sounded unsure and kicked at the gravel to emphasise the point. 'But it's causing a rare old stushie between the people who rent out their cottages and make money from the tourist industry and the rest who don't give a tinker's fart about tourism or the environment and just want a house and a job.'

Violet turned quickly away in case Stuart noticed her distress. For the first time in her life she had an address for her mother, geography, a context. She was able to see what *she* had seen; in fact, the last thing she had seen before she died. Now, it was to be spoiled by a 'forest of windmills'.

'Well that's us,' Stuart said, unaware of Violet's mood swing. 'Last stop before sunny Poltown,' he snorted. 'Bet there'll be a cloud hanging over it by the time we get there.'

Violet said, 'I think I'll walk.'

'Suit yourself.' Stuart sounded disappointed. 'Maybe pick you up again some other time.'

'Yes, maybe . . .' she replied.

He loitered, as if hoping she would change her mind. Then he said, 'I'll be off then.'

She nodded without turning, saying 'thanks' after he had shut his door.

Once the bus had gone, Violet remained where she was, the prisoner of conflicting emotions. She yearned to walk in her mother's footsteps but she also had a gnawing fear at the consequences of doing so, at the turmoil it threatened to unleash.

59

She found her mobile phone in the pocket of her backpack and took the opportunity to text Hilary in case there was no signal later at the coast.

'Arrived safely. Love to Anna. Hugs for you and Izzy.'

Hilary lived downstairs from Violet's bedsit in Glasgow. Anna and Izzy were best friends; so were Violet and Hilary who had met as students at the city's School of Art. After graduating they shared the same bed to save money on rent. Hilary worked days as a part-time clerical assistant in an insurance office, Violet nights waitressing in a pizza restaurant. After their daughters were born four months apart, they moved into their own rooms, sharing child care instead of a bed.

'Leave Anna with me,' Hilary had said when Violet told her about Mr Anwar's visit and her decision to go to Poltown. She had 'due days' to take and Izzy always loved it when Anna stayed. Last night, when Violet returned from work, Hilary had hugged her unexpectedly. 'What's that for?' Violet had asked.

'You'll be careful won't you?'

'I'll be fine,' Violet had said. Now she wasn't so sure.

On the road down to the coast, Violet came upon a poster tied to a telegraph pole. It was publicising a public meeting about the wind farm at Poltown community hall in two days. 'Fuck the environment, give us jobs' had been daubed across it in red paint. Despite the bus driver's forewarning, Violet was surprised and unsettled by the angry note it struck in an otherwise harmonious landscape.

Then she had another shock.

She was following the path her mother had taken to the beach. At the headland, it tipped into a gorge between sheer plates of rock. At first the going was firm – compacted peat – but as the path became steeper it became a flight of stone steps. Some were crumbling under the persistent drips of water trickling from an overhang. Others were scattered with loose stones, making it difficult to find a secure footing. Violet leaned forward to pick out the safest descent and her backpack and tent pressed against her shoulders. She feared she was about to topple and let out a cry of surprise. Her voice reverberated in the confines of the gorge, changing into a sound she was sure she had heard before, an age ago. It was the strangest experience, not the sort of fey imagining to which Violet was usually inclined. Yet it had the force of absolute conviction: she *had* been here before. Hadn't she felt that same claustrophobia, heard that same echo?

Now she also knew when. She had been in her mother's womb, not on her last journey, but at some earlier time in the pregnancy. Had her mother also felt enclosed by these rocks? Had she also feared losing her balance, in her case the bulge of pregnancy making negotiation of the stone steps precarious? Had she cried out in frustration? For a moment, Violet believed the echo *was* her mother's voice, travelling back to her through time. Then it was gone. All that remained was the drip-drip of the water and the dankness. Violet was left with a lurching sensation in her stomach, the feeling a child has as soon as it realises it is lost and in peril, its mother nowhere to be seen. She carried on down the remaining steps to the beach, irritated that she'd allowed such a flight of fancy to take hold of her.

As she walked across the sand she reflected on the childhood she had had, instead of the one which should have been hers. Her adoptive parents, Tom and Bridget Wells, were kindly and generous though each had an enthusiasm which (in Violet's slowly developing consciousness) provided adult satisfactions against which a child could not compete. Away from work (as a manager in the council's property maintenance department) Tom's hobby was reassembling old car engines, whereas Bridget's interest was domestic – keeping their 1980s bungalow spotless. Tom's domain was the integral garage; Bridget's the house. Violet went between the two, never feeling she belonged in either or with either. It was a knowledge she kept to herself, aware of its potential for hurt. Perhaps her reticence also owed something to her dim understanding that the differences between her and her parents were parts of a bigger mystery which one day would be revealed. Bridget's disclosure of her adoption provided the single most important piece to the puzzle. Afterwards she remembered over-hearing Bridget worrying to Tom about Violet's non-plussed reaction. Bridget was sure it had been caused by shock which would lead to a delayed and disturbed emotional response; that each should be vigilant for it. Bridget needn't have worried. Violet had never felt more reconciled or more curious about the mysteries still to be revealed.

Violet dropped her backpack on the wet sand, slipped off her trainers and padded towards the retreating water. Despite confiding in her lost mother throughout her teenage years, proximity to her place of death left her without words. She surveyed the sea in accusing silence for being so calm when she was anything but. When she did speak, all she could say was, 'How could you leave me?'

Cal McGill watched her through his dirty windscreen. There was something compelling about her stillness, about the length of time she had been standing there, square-shouldered, erect, staring out to sea, like an Antony Gormley figure waiting for another of its cast-iron tribe to emerge from the waves. By his calculation, she hadn't moved for ten minutes, not a stretch of an arm, a twist of the shoulders, a turn of the head – nothing. What brought her here, he wondered? Just as he began to guess at some of the possibilities she turned around, collected her backpack and continued further along the beach, towards North Bay.

Her imminent departure caused him an unexpected pang of regret followed by the whimsical notion that this young woman, whom he had never met, whose face he had never seen, of whom he had been aware for no more than a dozen minutes, might be a companion spirit, someone who found refuge by the sea, as he did. For as long as she remained in view, he let himself be distracted by the possibility of an unexplored affinity between them. The thought was accompanied by a wistful smile. A beach was where he met his wife, Rachel. The divorce wasn't quite six months old. If he had learned anything by the experience surely it was to be wary of a combination of wide skies, an empty beach and the chance appearance of an unaccompanied young woman? Still, it was a bitter-sweet sensation as this newest encounter climbed the headland and began to descend towards the next bay. He followed her progress until all that was visible of her above the horizon was her bobbing head, and then he closed his eyes. The cab of the pickup was warm, the afternoon sun making it soporific. He dozed for ten, perhaps fifteen minutes. When he woke the statue from the beach was coming towards him through the dunes, and the path she was following led her to the turning circle on the beach road where Cal had parked. He reached for a file, opened it and pretended to read, while tracking her approach out of the corner of his eye. She was taller than he'd imagined: 5'8" or so, almost his height, and slender too. He feigned surprise when she tapped on his door, taking in her boy's-cut short brown hair, the two silver rings in her left ear, and an impression of pale skin on a small face.

'Do you live here?' she asked before he'd lowered his window, repeating the question as it was sliding down. He shook his head and she seemed disappointed, pulling her mouth to one side and looking around as if hoping to see someone else. 'Try me,' he said.

'The island in the sea loch . . . I'm trying to find out who owns it.'

'Orasaigh?'

'You know it?' Her voice lifted.

'No not really.' He'd walked there earlier in the day.

She sighed and apologised for bothering him. She made to leave but changed her mind. 'You don't know when low tide is, do you?' He took his mobile phone off the pickup's dashboard. 'In exactly one hour and 42 minutes, at 17.54, and the next one is at 06.36 tomorrow morning.'

'How do you know that?'

'Just do.'

She raised a hand in thanks and went along the beach road. 'Hi, my name is Cal McGill,' he said quietly to her retreating back.

★   ★   ★

A knee deep stream of retreating water covered the causeway. After removing her trainers, socks and jeans and clutching them to her, Violet waded across the 80 metres to Orasaigh Island. She went ashore at a gravel ramp at the side of which was a wooden notice board nailed to a post. 'Beware of the changing tides,' it warned. 'This causeway is impassable either side of high water. If you find yourself trapped, please have consideration for the inconvenience of others before attempting to summon help. An hour or two passes surprisingly quickly and enjoyably on Orasaigh.'

After brushing sand and grit from her feet, Violet dressed. She left the ramp and climbed uphill on a grassy track which wound through a plantation of spindly alder, ash and birch. Wherever she looked she asked herself the same question: had it changed since her mother lived there?

Where the trees gave way to bracken and grass, a pitched roof appeared above the sky-line. In her impatience to see where her mother had lived, Violet broke into a run. Soon she found herself standing before a two up, two down 19th century cottage. It was surrounded by a mossy wall which enclosed twin patches of lawn and between them a path edged with narrow borders of lavender. Violet lifted the latch of the gate and went uncertainly down the path. Knocking at the outer door of the porch, she noticed a card in one of the side windows. She read it while she knocked again. 'For letting inquiries, ring Brae Estate

Office.' The phone number was printed in fading letters. She shouted out 'Hi, hello.' After waiting for a response, she crossed one of the patches of lawn to what turned out to be the sitting room window. She peered through the glass onto another life. Her mother's, she wondered?

The room was dark but neat with two arm chairs either side of an open fire framed by matching bookshelves. Violet took it all in, noticing there was none of the clutter that went with occupation. It seemed no-one was in residence. She made her way back to the letting notice and tapped the number into her mobile. It went straight to message. Violet left her name and number and a request for her call to be returned. Then she looked in the window on the other side of the porch, at a small dining room with a circular table and four chairs. It, too, was neat and gloomy. Going back to the porch, she rattled at the locked door in frustration. Having waited so long to discover her birth-place, she found her patience gone. With a regretful backward glance, she left the garden and carried along the track towards the middle of the island until she found a sheltered area of grass beside some rowan trees. She took off her backpack and unfolded a small tent.

After putting it up, she rang Hilary, who regaled her with the exploits of the two girls. Typically, she ended one story with a burst of laughter before launching into another, until Violet's silence prompted her to ask, 'Are you all right?'

'I think I've found my mother's house.'

Hilary relayed the message to Anna. Violet heard the child cry out with excitement. 'Would you like to speak to her?' Hilary asked.

'I can't,' Violet replied.

'Why what's wrong?'

'Nothing's wrong. I'll cry and I don't want Anna to think I'm upset.'

Hilary sounded put out. 'Well, ok, if that's what you want.'

Violet could still hear Anna's excited squeaks. 'Ask her if she will paint me a cottage with two windows upstairs and two downstairs with a door in the middle? Ask her,' she added, 'to paint her granny's house.'

Cal had seen something similar on Texel, the largest of the Dutch Frisian Islands. Strategically positioned between the North and Wadden seas, Texel had a long history of being journey's end for cargoes lost overboard in collisions or storms and an equally long tradition of beach-combing. Cal had visited it because he'd heard of beach-combers there who kept dated records of their finds. He'd matched their logs of high value flotsam – Burberry bags from Britain, the wooden components of kit houses from Germany, cases of wine from Italy – with the ship-owners' reports of losses. Comparing where they'd gone overboard with where they'd beached, he was able to calculate actual speeds of travel for different weights, shapes and sizes of flotsam against his computer program predictions and to make adjustments. The beachcomber who provided the most useful data went by the name of Olaf, a merchant seaman from Norway who had also washed up on Texel after a shipwreck. His bungalow had been constructed from the spoils of beach-combing – when Cal paid him a visit he found it hard to be certain what was dwelling and what his collection of flotsam.

Duncan Boyd's farm had the same feel about it, Cal thought, as he bumped along the rough track to the house and steading, past the old tractor with 'This Farm and Land is NOT for sale', through a field littered with other derelict farm machinery and piles of flotsam. Despite the appearance of chaos, on his previous visit Cal had detected a semblance of order, as there had been at the Texel farmstead. In Olaf's case, flotsam was stacked by date, a new pile for a new year. In Duncan Boyd's, the piles were colour coordinated as well as sorted by type. Blue buoys were gathered together in one pile; orange in another nearby. Ditto ropes of different colours. Cal detected method where others might have seen mess, a judgement which was reinforced by the sight of footwear of all shapes and sizes nailed to a barn wall. There were fishermen's boots, brogues, sandals as well as trainers. Scrawled at the top of the barn in white paint was 'The Wall of Lost Soles'. Cal found it funny even on second viewing: wit as well as method.

He parked outside the steading entrance. The dilapidation of the buildings struck him for the first time – roofs sagging and bowing as if close to collapse; intermittent and forlorn heaps of broken slates and fallen masonry at the bottoms of the walls. Entering the courtyard, he came upon three men with ill-fitting suits and office pallors. Two leaned against a car, their arms folded; the other, a big, balding man, stood separately smoking a cigarette. 'You don't know where he is by any chance?' He sounded weary with waiting.

Cal shook his head.

'Mr Boyd isn't expecting you?'

'Not really. This evening or tomorrow morning, one or the other. Nothing firm.'

The smoker's brow creased in mild irritation. 'Well?' He directed the question at his two colleagues. 'What'll we do?'

'It's up to you,' one with a sharp face said. The other, a younger man, shrugged in bored agreement.

'Another five, then,' the smoker said before introducing himself to Cal. 'Alastair Henderson. I'm the councillor for this area.'

Cal nodded. 'Hi.'

'We were hoping to speak to Mr Boyd about the windfarm.' He studied Cal on the off chance he could be of assistance. 'See if he's open to persuasion at all.'

Cal wished he could help but he didn't know

anything about it. Since there was a queue for Duncan, he'd try again in the morning.

Driving away, Cal looked back and noticed a movement at a skylight in one of the barns. He had the impression of a disembodied head, grey hair and a goofy broken-toothed grin.

CHAPTER 5

Mary Anderson's hands were clasped around a mug of tea which had become lukewarm since her last sip. Her eyes were staring vacantly at the wall opposite, at the space between the cooker and the kitchen clock. On the table beside her was a collection of seven letters, which she had been re-reading for the first time since she found them in Mr William's dressing room at Brae House after his death six years ago. They had been in his chest of drawers, concealed under his jerseys and wrapped around with two rubber bands. At Diana's request, Mrs Anderson had been sorting through his clothes, separating what could be given to charity and what should be burnt. Diana had said she would find the task too distressing but it had to be done, or else the room would become 'William's mausoleum'. Would Mrs Anderson be 'an absolute dear', while Diana removed herself to Edinburgh?

Mrs Anderson hadn't told Diana about her discovery, a correspondence from Mr William to Megan Bates, nor had she burnt any of the letters. After reading them she had locked them away in her bureau, considering them to be a form of insurance, evidence should she ever require it of Diana's motive in wanting rid of the child, of Diana being the instigator.

It was 2.23 in the morning. The kitchen was in shadows. The only light was from a lamp on the table, which cast a pale glow on Mrs Anderson's face, as if she had seen a ghost. And, in a manner of speaking, she had. On re-reading the letters, she had not only disinterred the remains of Mr William's affair with Megan Bates, but also those of Mrs Anderson's own marriage which ended when Robert, her husband of eight years and an instructor at the Poltown base, abandoned her for another woman. What made the memory bitter, and the letters poignant, was that Mrs Anderson was pregnant when Robert abandoned her, as was Megan Bates by the end of the correspondence. Mr William's transformation from surprised lover to terse negotiator when the affair cooled still had the capacity to create a whirlwind of emotions in Mrs Anderson. Like her husband, Mr William appeared to consider a promise of continuing financial support sufficient to resolve 'an impossible conflict' in his responsibilities to two women. The significant difference in the behaviour of the two men was which woman they attempted to placate with money. In Mr William's case, it was his mistress Megan Bates – in his letters he promised the child would be his heir; the mother would be given a house and an allowance. In Robert's,

73

it was Mrs Anderson, the soon-to-be-abandoned wife. As was usually the case with Robert, it was an offer made in drink, late at night, circumscribed and grudging. It was limited to maintenance for the child and to 'keeping a roof over *its* head'. A final similarity: in neither case did the man honour his commitment.

As the storm of emotion subsided, it left Mrs Anderson with a legacy of anger: at the casual and capricious trail of destruction left by men in pursuit of their desires and at women who conspire with them, women like Megan Bates and Alice Forsyth, her husband's lover who became his wife and the mother of his three children. Most of all Mrs Anderson reserved her bitterness for the loss of her baby daughter, still-born at eight months, her death the consequence she would always believe of the stress she suffered when Robert finally deserted her.

Hadn't that been the story of her adult life: her loyalty always rewarded by betrayal of one kind or another?

As usual, the thought was quickly followed by a spasm of self-pity and by tears which welled at the corners of her eyes. Her hands began to shake and she placed the tea cup back in its saucer. She continued to hold it, and every time her hands trembled the cup rattled against china, a noise like a distant chiming clock marking the passage of time. She appeared deaf to it: at any rate she didn't change or release her grip. And so the distant chiming continued as she rehearsed for the umpteenth time since Diana's memorial service the injustices she had suffered. Having run through those, she fretted about the precariousness of her position, at the household bills which would eat into her savings and pension, at the first rental demand for £575 which was due in a few days, at the lawyer's reprimanding tone in response to her written protests. Finally, there was the nagging worry that her anonymous letter concerning Megan Bates's daughter was lying crumpled and discarded in some official's waste bin.

In one combination or another, these ghosts and fears assailed her throughout the night, until at 4.20am, exhausted, she went to bed, having set her alarm for nine to have sufficient time to be dressed and ready for Jim Carmichael who would deliver her order from the shop in Poltown around eleven. She would encourage him to divulge all the local news, the comings and goings, in the hope he would tell her whether any young woman had been in the shop asking questions about Poltown. A slice of Mrs Anderson's chocolate cake and a cup of tea were usually enough encouragement to get Jim talking. Sometimes he became so carried away she had to remind him that others were still waiting for his deliveries and to chivvy him, either in mid mouthful or mid-story, often both. That was something she wouldn't be doing later that morning. She'd let him talk for as long as he wanted and she'd listen to his ramblings for any mention of a last minute B&B booking, for a stranger walking the beaches, a young woman in her mid-20s. If Mrs Anderson had been the daughter of Megan Bates, she would start the search in the shop, either there or at Boyd's Farm though she'd get no sense at all out of poor Duncan Boyd. Just before she fell asleep, Mrs Anderson wondered how Duncan would react to hearing the name of Megan Bates again.

Cal woke before seven, his shoulders and neck stiff after sleeping uncomfortably in the pickup's cab. He'd dozed off six hours earlier to a radio discussion about the banking crisis and had come round to another memory altogether. During the night when he'd barely been conscious he'd heard a short news item about the search being abandoned for a five year old boy who had been swept off a pier in the south of England by a freak wave. The pained dignity of the parents as they thanked the emergency services for trying to find their child's body had stuck in his mind. He could picture their faces – the sucked-in cheeks, dulled eyes and grey skin, the sudden and silent tumble of tears, the gnawing of despair. Hearing their agony as well as their tenacity – they would keep looking for their boy's remains for as long as it took – had forced Cal to think about an issue which had nagged at him uncomfortably for a few months now. Avoiding it had been one of the reasons he'd taken off to the coast; that, and a dislocated feeling of not quite belonging anywhere else.

Did his success at tracking and finding bodies lost at sea offer people at their wits' end, like the mother and father of that dead boy, false hope?

Recalling his cases he couldn't think of any where he hadn't. It wasn't intentional. It was just the nature of the work. Either he'd draw a blank – a matter of regret even though Cal warned in advance about his area of expertise being an 'imprecise science' and the sea having its own unwritten rules – or the body he led them to would be bloated, disfigured or half-devoured by scavengers of one sort or another. The media usually described these as 'astonishing discoveries' which provided 'closure for the parents'. It was a phrase and a concept Cal had come to loathe. It was why he'd started to fob off those who emailed him with emotional pleas for him to take on their cases too, to help them find their relative's body. If all that Cal could do was lead them to putrefying flesh had he helped them at all? Better, he thought now, that their memories survived intact – their dead child or spouse smiling, happy and living – than having them replaced by the stuff of continuing nightmares.

Would the mother and father of that missing five year old boy contact him too?

He rubbed his face, his stubble rasping under his fingers. He swore, pushed open the driver's door, and ran across the beach, escaping his demons. At the high tide mark, he stripped off his shirt and jeans. He walked the remainder of the way to the sea and waded out until the water was up to his armpits. He let the waves wash past him before ducking his head. Splashing back through the shallows, he remembered Rachel, his ex-wife, complaining about his habit of removing himself to a distant coast instead of discussing what was wrong with their marriage. She had accused him of using his work as an avoidance technique. He couldn't keep on running away, she'd said. In that, as well as other things, she had been wrong.

Back at the pickup, he put on a blue shirt, cotton trousers, thick socks and walking boots. After eating breakfast – a cheese sandwich left over from the day before and a swig from a carton of milk – he drove to Boyd's Farm. As on the previous evening, he parked at the entrance to the steading. Unlike it, there was no-one to be seen when he entered the courtyard. His progress past the Wall of Lost Soles was witnessed by two stray cats from the slate roof of the back porch and, as it turned out, by Duncan Boyd who spied on him from an upstairs window in the farmhouse, a habit it seemed. Only when Cal shouted out who he was and why he was there did Duncan emerge into the sunlight, grinning shyly, wearing baggy black trousers and a creased off-white shirt with frayed collar and cuffs which was tucked into his waistband at the front but not at the back.

'Good morning, lovely day,' Cal said.

His greeting caused Duncan to indulge in a succession of facial expressions, from amusement to panic to vulnerability, as if he was trying out each one in an attempt to discover which felt appropriate to the day. He settled on amusement.

'Wall of Lost Soles . . .' He nodded towards the rows of shoes nailed to the barn.

'Yes, I saw it.' Cal said. 'It's funny.'

Duncan grinned at Cal's reaction. 'I stole it,' he said, 'from a woman who lives on the Pacific coast of America. She has a Wall of Lost Soles too.'

'I wouldn't call that stealing,' Cal shrugged, 'and anyway the world's big enough for two.'

Cal's answer again seemed to please Duncan who began to hum, turning this way and that before beckoning to his visitor and leading him from one barn to the next. Duncan kept up a continuous commentary about his beach-combing finds, selecting examples for inspection, until Cal was taken to see the Neptune Scroll. Though it was squint and in a damaged frame, Duncan ushered Cal into its presence with all the comic formality of a fawning courtier. Making admiring comments, Cal cast his eye over Duncan's table of special discoveries. He wondered aloud whether he could spend some time picking through the barns. He was sure they would reveal all kinds of interesting information. In case he hadn't explained properly, he said he researched 'anything that floats really'. His particular area of interest was the

North Atlantic, discovering all the quirks of the wind and currents, discovering where things washed up, tracking back to find out where they'd originated.

Duncan shot Cal the same half-mad grin he'd seen at the skylight the previous evening. Without thinking, Cal said, 'By the way who were those men?'

The grin faded. Duncan picked at the sleeve of his shirt and muttered about his land not being for sale, about the public meeting, about people taking sides against him. He wouldn't look Cal in the eye.

'I'm sorry,' Cal said, seeing his distress. 'It's none of my business. I shouldn't have said anything.'

The tide was out, Duncan said, changing the subject. It was time he went to South Bay.

'You're ok if I have a look around?' Cal said as Duncan turned and walked away.

Duncan stooped but not low enough – at fifty-seven, he wasn't as supple as he imagined. The effect was the exact opposite of the one he intended. Instead of keeping himself hidden by the dune until he had checked the identity of the woman on the beach, he broke the sky-line. She saw him and changed direction.

He cursed his bad luck and lit a cigarette. The thought of another angry confrontation made him jumpy. He talked to himself, a nervous undertone, like someone psyching himself for a challenge:

reminding himself how it was *Boyd's* Farm, how he was a Boyd, how he could do what he wanted. It seemed to help because he added 'I, Neptune, Monarch of the Sea' grinning and peering through the tall grass. The figure was still too distant to tell whether she was friend or foe. Duncan hoped it was Dr Bell, who walked her terrier, Pepe, at South Bay. But Duncan couldn't see any sign of the little dog. He prepared for a stranger, turning his back, raking his fingers through his unruly and brittle hair and brushing down his clothes. When, eventually, she was close enough to try 'hello' he pretended not to hear her.

'Hello,' she tried again, louder, and walked round him until she was beside him, looking up into his face. 'Hi.'

He indicated with a nod of his head the pile of flotsam he had collected. He picked up a lobster pot, followed by a buoy, which he turned around so that she could see all sides of it. 'I'll be busy sorting out this lot for a while I imagine.' The remark was boastful in a juvenile way and his demeanour also that of a self-satisfied child expecting a compliment for his hard work.

'I'm sure you will,' Violet said. She tried to summon up sufficient enthusiasm. 'It must have taken you ages. Haven't you done well?'

Duncan pulled a piece of torn netting from the pile and then a plastic pipe.

'Wow, so many different items,' she said, getting the hang of things.

After Duncan had shown her a length of blue rope, Violet asked, 'I was wondering whether you might know who lives at the farm house?'

'Depends,' he replied, squinting at her to see her reaction.

'On what?'

'Why you might want him?'

'Just to ask him about someone who used to live near here.'

'Not about the windfarm?'

'*Definitely* not about the windfarm . . .'

'Good.'

'You don't like the windfarm?'

He shook his head. 'I won't sell, you know.'

'So you own the farmhouse,' she said. 'I saw the notice.' She referred to the old Ferguson tractor parked at the farm gate. 'Land NOT for sale,' she repeated. 'Good for you,' She laughed a little at another strange turn in the conversation.

'I've told you I won't.' He puffed out his chest.

'Yes, you have, haven't you?' She laughed again.

Instead of replying he pulled something else from the pile of flotsam, some wire netting, and started humming.

'Are you Duncan Boyd?'

The humming stopped. 'I am.'

'Hi, my name is Violet . . . Violet Wells.' She extended her right hand. 'I'm visiting, just here for a day or two.'

Duncan busied himself rolling up blue rope and

eyed the outstretched hand with suspicion until Violet withdrew it.

'I was wondering,' she carried on, 'if you ever came across someone who used to live here, a friend of my mother's . . . Her name was Megan Bates.'

Duncan dropped the rope. He pressed his hands to his ears. Violet noticed his head was shaking.

'Mr Boyd, are you all right?'

'I want you to go now.' He sounded petulant, as though Violet had spoiled a game and her punishment was to be banished.

She said his name again and touched him on the arm to let him know she hadn't intended to provoke him.

'I want you to go now . . . I want you to go now.' With every repetition he said it louder. Violet thought her departure was the only thing that would calm him. She retreated through the dunes to the beach road where she stopped and looked back. Duncan was half-running, half-walking towards North Bay, where her mother's hat and bag had drifted ashore.

A little unnerved, she wondered if he was having a fit of some kind and whether she should tell anyone. Going along the road, by the stone gate pillars of Boyd's Farm, she was relieved to come across a blue van. A man in work overalls was getting out of the driver's door holding a cardboard box which was full of groceries.

'Hello,' Violet said. 'Can you help me?'

The man was balding, red-faced and with a friendly expression He pretended to be surprised by her sudden appearance. 'Oh, you gave me a fright.' He clutched his spare hand to his heart, coughing and spluttering before giving up the pretence. 'What can I do for you, Miss?'

'You know Mr Boyd?'

'Indeed I do, I've been delivering the same order of groceries to this farm for more years than I can remember.' He noticed Violet's worried expression, the way she kept looking towards the beach. He thought he understood what had happened. His tone changed, becoming confiding. 'Duncan's not quite like everyone else if you know what I mean . . . But there's no harm in him, no harm at all.'

Violet said, 'I think I've upset him. He's run off towards North Bay.'

'Did he now? He must be out of sorts then.' He put down the grocery box in the shelter of the pillar. 'Always leave it here.'

'We were just talking,' Violet said. 'I didn't mean anything.'

'I'm Jim, by the way.' He held out his hand after wiping it on his overalls. 'Jim Carmichael.'

'Violet . . . Violet Wells.'

'Nice to meet you Violet.' He glanced in the direction of North Bay. 'Now don't you worry yourself about Duncan. We're used to his ways. He'll be up there, standing on the beach like he does, and in an hour or two he'll come back, right as rain.' He looked at Violet. The same confiding voice. 'He's been a bit overwrought recently about this windfarm business.'

Jim drew Violet's attention to the 'NOT for sale' sign on the old tractor through the gate. 'People trying to get him to sell . . . The electricity's coming ashore over there.' He looked toward the bay. 'And see this field . . .' Jim nodded past the tractor. 'They're going to cover it with a shed, massive so they say.' He glanced up the coast, frowning as though Violet might have reason to worry. 'Still he hasn't gone up there for a while. Usually sticks around South Bay, does Duncan.'

They were where he was standing now: the raffia sun hat with its broad band of red ribbon, and her leather shoulder bag. Duncan had gone from one to the other, not wanting to pick them up, fearful of what they signified. He'd looked behind him, hoping it was a practical joke of some kind, willing her to be hiding among the boulders which tumbled down to the little beach. Hoping it was a game and she would suddenly jump from behind a rock laughing. Knowing it had been a portent of something else.

The tide was beginning to ebb. The hat and the bag beside each other, both wet. He looked up hoping against hope to see her swimming in the bay, knowing she wouldn't be there. She didn't like North Bay because of all the rocks, and because the beach shelved away too quickly. She preferred the wide and flat expanses of South Bay. He touched the hat and then the bag, feeling them with his outstretched fingers, as nervously as if he was touching her flesh. He hadn't picked them up or taken them away. Later the police asked him why not. He could tell from their faces he hadn't been able to provide a satisfactory answer.

He backed away, until he was among the rocks. Scrambling across them, he fell and cut his hands and knees, and then he ran to Megan's. Her cottage on Orasaigh, the tidal island inside the mouth of Poltown Loch, was the other side of Duncan's farm. He waited at the causeway calling for her, cursing his inability to swim, waiting for the ebb to quicken, for the narrow channel separating Orasaigh from the mainland to be shallow enough for him to cross. He went up to his waist wading it, still shouting her name, so by the time he arrived at the cottage he knew she wouldn't be there. He banged on the door before going inside. The cottage was still, still and empty, her spirit gone. He pressed his hands to his ears and closed his eyes tight When he calmed down, he went round the sitting room touching the places he remembered she'd been, the arm chair, the rug at the corner of the coffee table where she'd poured the tea, feeling again the brush of her fingers when she'd told him he was 'a sweet man' for offering to look after her and her baby if the father didn't. If she felt she had no other option but to leave Orasaigh so that she wasn't living under a roof owned by him. She had kissed him too, on the cheek. He told the police he'd been there half an hour or so. He judged it by the causeway when he left. By then the water was only at his knees.

Later the police asked him why smears of his blood had been found on her desk, the arm chair and the rug. He said he'd cut himself on the rocks at North Bay. They asked whether he loved her and he said he did; whether he was jealous of the other man and he said he was, a little; whether he'd killed Megan, whether he'd been destroying evidence when he'd been in her cottage, whether he'd taken her things to North Bay to make it look like she'd gone into the sea. Hadn't there been two sets of footprints in the sand, both his from when he carried her things there, and when he departed? Didn't he have a reputation for being, no offence intended, unlike other people? In his case, they weren't dealing with a criminal mastermind but someone who'd been caught up in the emotion of the moment, who didn't have the 'resources shall we say' to resist male impulse, who wouldn't have the guile to cover his tracks, who would make elementary mistakes because he wasn't 'overly blessed in the intellect department'?

A crime of passion, one of them said. Yes, the other had agreed. A crime of passion.

He went to the corner of the interview room, facing the wall. 'I love her,' he said.

'Did she love you?'

'I love her,' he repeated.

They registered the tense. One wrote down 'love', underlined it and added a big question mark. His colleague glanced at it, raised an eyebrow and tapped an index finger against his temple. *Screw loose.*

The interrogation continued. 'Did you have sex with her?'

'No.'

'Did you hate her for carrying another man's baby, because she'd let another, older man thumb his prick into her, like you wanted to?'

'No.' He wailed at the sudden crudeness. 'No.'

'You knew you'd lose her as soon as the baby was born, so you killed her didn't you? You took her somewhere and killed her. Did you put her into the sea, Duncan? Did you bury her? What did you do with her, Duncan?'

By then his hands were over his ears and he was stamping on the floor. He told them to stop talking about her like that, about the woman he loved. Later, when they persuaded him to sit at the table with them, to have some tea and a cigarette, they said they had always believed him, in their hearts they had, but they had to be sure, they had to test him. It wasn't personal, it was routine. They were sorry if he felt they'd been rough with him. They didn't like coming on strong like that. But the job was the job. Was there anything he could tell them about Megan that would help them with their inquiries? When had he last seen her?

Two days before.

Where?

In her cottage.

Had she asked him over?

No.

What time was it?

The middle of the afternoon. He'd gone then because it was low tide.

Had he washed beforehand? Had he put on clean clothes? Had he wanted to look his best for her?

He agreed he had.

They smiled. They would have done so too their expressions seemed to suggest. Pretty woman like that.

What was the purpose of his visit?

He'd wanted to tell her something.

What?

He told them how he'd promised to look after her, her and the baby, if the father didn't. She could have lived with him at the farm.

A happy family, they said, and he smiled and repeated it. 'Yes, a happy family.'

And what happened?

'When?' he asked suddenly confused.

When you said that to her, about her living with you, being a happy family?

She'd said he was sweet.

They looked at each other and smirked. Sweet, they said.

Yes, sweet, he replied.

Bit of a kick in the teeth, they said. For a man

who'd gone to all that trouble, smelling nice and getting all dressed up, laying it on the line like Duncan had done. 'Sweet? I'd have slapped her,' one said. 'Me too,' the other agreed. Sweet, they both said in unison. For fuck's sake, they said. It was as if they had a script.

'I'd have smacked her, no question.'

'Wouldn't blame anyone, not after that. Sweet. What an insult. What kind of woman would treat you like that?'

They were speaking so quickly, one then the other, that Duncan wasn't able to say anything. It confused him and worried him that these two policemen were taking his complicity for granted.

'No question Duncan; I'd have done the same.'

'She had it coming,' the other said.

By then Duncan's hands were shaking so much he spilt his tea over the table. They let him fuss over it, covering it with a newspaper, but when he looked at them again their faces were hard.

'Afterwards, when you left the cottage, you met a fisherman, didn't you?'

He had or thought he had. He wasn't sure.

'What did you say to him?'

He couldn't remember, he said. He was upset, he remembered that.

'Do you remember if you were crying?'

He thought he had been.

'Do you remember what you said?'

He shook his head.

One of them read from a notebook. 'Duncan

said, "Megan's gone" and when I asked him where she'd gone he said he didn't know. He told me about the hat and bag and I returned to Poltown to raise the alarm.'

'Why didn't you call the police, Duncan?'

He didn't know, he said.

'Where did she go Duncan?' one of his interrogators asked.

'After you'd killed her?' the other added.

'Where did you put her, Duncan?'

Tweedledum and Tweedledee again.

'I loved her.'

Each looked at the other, significance in their expressions. They had noticed the change of tense.

'Loved her, Duncan?'

'That's better Duncan. Now we seem to be getting somewhere.' Then they started up another conversation, how people like Duncan didn't have the control panel 'up top or down below', how the police and the courts knew that, how he'd get psychiatric help and maybe that would be a relief to him, because 'old mother nature' hadn't played fair with him, giving him urges and no mechanism for keeping them under control.

Duncan slammed his hands on the table and told his questioners he wouldn't talk anymore because they confused him, made his head muddled, twisting his words. 'I love her,' he said and turned his back on them.

Silence was the same as an admission of guilt, they told him, then they left him alone. He spent the night in a cell. In the dead of night, when no-one was at his door listening, he talked to her. Hadn't he shown her the strength of his love? Hadn't he kept her secret? Hadn't she said she would leave something behind, something for him, something to let him know she would return? One day. Hadn't that been the hat and the bag? You're a sweet man, Duncan. He felt her soft lips on his skin.

He was released the next morning by the custody sergeant who said more evidence had come to light. The police were following a new and positive line of inquiry.

When he returned to the farm in a police car 'for his own protection' he discovered they'd searched everywhere, all through the house and the farm buildings. As he walked around, unable to settle to anything, unable to feel anything except Megan's kiss and the bitter contrast of what had happened since, his two interrogators dropped by to see how he was, to let him know they'd be watching, every minute of every day, until they got him for what he'd done to Megan Bates.

'Sticks in here,' one said, pointing at his throat.

'And mine,' added the other.

'Out there,' the first one said with a sweep of his hand which encompassed the landscape beyond his few fields, 'is hostile territory for a wee shite like you.'

CHAPTER 6

A chocolate sponge cake was on the table. Two places had been laid, at each a plate decorated with a brown quail pattern, matching cup and saucer and an ivory-handled knife. The tea pot was warming beside the kettle which Mrs Anderson would bring back to the boil as soon as Jim Carmichael's blue van turned up the road to the cottage. She waited by the window watching for it, beginning to fret. Usually he delivered to her by half past eleven but it was already twenty to twelve and she was worried he wouldn't be able to stay more than a few minutes, long enough to take a swig of tea and cram some cake into his mouth. It was typical of him. When she didn't want him cluttering up the kitchen, spilling crumbs on her floor and telling her his gossip he had all the time in the world. When she had some use for him he was late. Her anxiety betrayed itself with sighs, muttered complaints and restlessness. Twice she'd left the window to bring the kettle back to the boil, as if the steam coming from its spout or the click of the switch as it turned itself off would act as a summons to Jim, making him hurry.

When, finally, the van did appear it was almost noon and Mrs Anderson had the beginnings of a headache. She attended to the kettle, checked she had put away her bottle of 'medicinal' whisky – it wasn't fair to Jim otherwise – and called out 'come on in' when she heard the latch on the door. She put three tea bags into the pot, poured in water and as she took the tray to the table Jim backed into the kitchen, pushing against the kitchen door with his left thigh, holding Mrs Anderson's grocery order in a cardboard box.

'You're late, Jim.' There was a note of reprimand.

'Morning, Mrs A.' It was the name he'd called her ever since he began working part-time at the general store, fitting his deliveries around odd jobs and the demands of his small-holding at the far end of the sea loch. He'd been in his twenties then and Mrs Anderson, in her forties, was the housekeeper at Brae House. Calling her 'Mrs A' was as familiar as Jim thought he dared to be. The same still applied. Mrs Anderson enjoyed the respect and status the abbreviated form of her name implied.

'Is this right, Mrs A?' Jim had swung the door shut behind him with his foot, leaving a muddy mark on the paint (Mrs Anderson wished he wouldn't do that), and placed the box on the worktop by the kettle. 'It's not your usual is it?'

The remark caught Mrs Anderson on the raw. Under normal circumstances she would have

94

snapped at him, saying something chilly like 'If I had wanted more I would have ordered more'.

Instead she said, 'Have I missed out a few things? I must be getting forgetful.'

'Oh, not you, Mrs A.'

Mrs Anderson was listening for any sign Jim had heard talk about her having to pay rent and her other bills, of her finding it harder to make ends meet from now on. But he didn't appear to be that interested: his attention had turned to the table. 'You're not in a hurry, Jim, are you?'

'Not in a hurry at all, Mrs A,' he replied, looking at his watch, the prospect of cake and conversation taking precedence over the other deliveries he still had to make.

Mrs Anderson poured his tea and inquired whether it was strong enough before inviting him to sit down. Usually he stood with his back to the cooker, a cup in one hand, biscuit or piece of cake in the other, his flow of chat hardly stopping for a sip or a bite. However, the invitation to sit threw him, as if it required forewarning as well as a different standard of behaviour. He inspected his overalls and apologised for the state they were in. Unzipping them, he let them drop to his feet, saying something about not wanting to leave any marks on 'Mrs A's chairs'. Then he examined his hands and decided they needed to be washed. He asked if he could use her bathroom but she directed him instead to the kitchen sink, taking a clean towel from a cupboard and placing it beside the soap tray which she pushed closer to the taps. Standing back to make way for him, she began to wish she hadn't laid the table after all as he waddled past her duck-like, his overalls threatening to trip him.

'Come and sit down, Jim.' She sat herself, wanting to get on with things. 'Shall I cut you a piece of cake? It's your favourite.'

'Please, Mrs A.'

She removed a big wedge and put it on his plate. Then she cut a slither for herself. While he shuffled back round the table, falling into his seat with a thud and a groan as he took the weight off his feet, she asked, 'How are you keeping, Jim?'

In her experience, it was a question guaranteed to start him talking. Normally he'd say something like 'I'm fine but have you heard about so and so?' and he'd launch into the details of some other person's misfortune. However, on this occasion, he pulled a face, followed by a frown and wiped the back of his hand across his mouth. 'I don't mind telling you Mrs A that I've been better.'

The last thing she wanted to say was, 'Why, what's wrong?' but form seemed to demand it so she did, adding, 'It's not like you to be under the weather'. She hoped that might deter a lengthy flow of personal revelation.

'The thing is Mrs A,' he scratched his head, looking uncomfortable. 'I've made a bit of a mess of things recently.'

He wrung his hands and shuffled in his seat. She hadn't seen him like this for a long time, since his troubles with the bottle, so she looked interested. 'Go on, Jim, you know you can trust me.'

He nodded, agreeing with her. 'I can Mrs A and there's not many you can say that about nowadays.'

Mrs Anderson acknowledged the compliment as well as his meaning. Ever since Nato's withdrawal from Poltown and the sale of surplus MoD houses to charities, the village had changed. Few of the older residents stayed on after the base closed. The exodus was accelerated by empty houses in the cul-de-sacs being allocated to anti-social tenants and the homeless from fifty miles around. 'It's not the place it was,' she agreed.

'I've borrowed from the Turnbulls.' Jim blurted, shaking his head in agitation and wonder that he'd done such a stupid thing. All Mrs Anderson could manage in reply was a lament, 'Oh Jim'.

His shoulders drooped, and he gave a long deflating sigh.

'Oh, Jim,' she repeated. 'What will you do?' If she sounded hopeless on his behalf it was because of the reputation of the Turnbulls, and also because of Jim's previous experience of borrowing money from the family. He had been badly beaten up. According to village rumour, Diana had rescued him, paying off his debt in return for Jim doing odd and ends of carpentry in the big house and helping out at lambing.

'Oh Jim . . .' She fell into silent contemplation.

'I don't know what to do.' Jim pushed his plate away.

'You can't repay them?'

Jim shook his head and accompanied it with the baleful expression of a condemned man awaiting his fate.

'I wish I could help,' Mrs Anderson said with feeling.

He shook his head again, this time to let her know he wasn't asking for money.

'£2000 that's all it was, to fix the van so it would pass the MOT. Suspension, brakes, new tyres . . .' He threw his hands up in exasperation at this simple shopping list leading to such trouble. 'I'd be sunk without the van.' The irony of it brought a fleeting smile: he was sunk with it.

Mrs Anderson sympathised but the sight of Jim's transformation from ebullience, his usual mood, to emasculation reminded her of her own fragility and financial predicament: was this the fate that awaited her too? The thought unnerved her. 'There's no good in the Turnbulls,' she snapped, as if trying to ward off an encroaching evil. 'There never has been, and there never will be.'

Afterwards, the heat of the moment past, she realised her outburst wouldn't have helped Jim's frame of mind. 'I'm sorry but those wretched girls . . .' She didn't have to say anymore because Jim knew the story. In the 1980s, eight or nine years after Mrs Anderson had moved from Poltown to Gardener's Cottage, the military asked her to be a 'wise head' for the young women on the base, to pass on her experience of setting up home in a remote corner of Scotland, with a husband away on training exercises for days at a time. She'd agreed as much for the extra money as for having something to do during the week when Mr William and Diana were in Edinburgh. Until then she'd known of Alec Turnbull, the depot's head store-man, only through his son, Ross. She remembered Diana's dismay when he and Alexandra started going out together. Hadn't she told Diana every teenage girl tested her mother with an unsuitable boy?

She grew to dislike the father every bit as much as Diana disapproved of the son. Alec, she discovered from her counselling work, bombarded the base's lonely wives with presents and flattery and, after submission, with blackmail threats. Given her head Mrs Anderson would have reported him to the base authorities but for the tearful pleas of his victims who were terrified of exposure and of their husbands.

As a result he continued his campaign of conquest and blackmail until a snap audit in the stores uncovered how he funded his seductions. He'd been skimming military rations and clothing and selling them. The scandal was hushed up and Turnbull summarily dismissed. The village found it harder to rid itself of his malign influence since he also ran a money lending business (at one time or another at least half of Poltown had been in debt to Turnbull). The profits were laundered through a portfolio of other businesses. There was a taxi company, the static caravans which were rented out to backpackers and the fleet of mobile cafes which patrolled the West Highlands in summer selling burgers and ice creams to holidaymakers and locals alike. Even a car accident, in which Alec Turnbull's spine was crushed, didn't release the village from his grip. Though confined to a wheelchair, he carried on running his operation. He was the brains, the muscle he hired from elsewhere. And so it continued until a stroke rendered him all but helpless. Rather than let the father's hired hands take over the business, Ross had returned to Poltown six months ago to claim his inheritance. Despite the intervening years of working and living abroad, and the impression Ross tried to give of being different from his father, in Mrs Anderson's opinion the apple hadn't fallen far from the tree.

'You've thought about the police, have you, Jim?'

Jim grimaced and Mrs Anderson was thrown back to all those pitiable young women who let Alec Turnbull have a hold over them and to Jim's battered and bruised face after he'd missed a repayment the last time he was in debt to him. 'Someone should stop them,' she said. 'Someone must.'

What then passed between them was a look of understanding. Each had heard similar stories about the Turnbulls, how anyone making a report to the police had always suffered retribution and how the family seemed to enjoy protection from the authorities, both council and legal. For as long as Mrs Anderson could remember there had been talk of bribery or blackmail, but it was speculation that stayed within Poltown. From bitter experience, the villagers knew what was good for them.

'I'm sorry, Mrs A, shouldn't have bothered you with it.' He looked forlornly at his cake. 'Eyes bigger than my stomach, I'm afraid.' He pushed against the table and stood up. Mrs Anderson said, 'Jim, do you mind my asking what's going to happen?'

'I'll be running errands in the van I imagine . . . whatever Davie tells me.'

Davie's name brought another exclamation from Mrs Anderson. Davie White had been Alec Turnbull's enforcer for two or three years. There had been talk of friction when Ross had returned, of Davie running freelance operations while Ross negotiated for concessions from BRC, the consortium behind the windfarm proposal. These included the ferry service which would shuttle personnel between the land base and the windfarm site. Ross had been involved in something similar offshore in Nigeria, though in the opinion of many people, Mrs Anderson's included, it would be a front behind which the Turnbulls operated and expanded their criminal activities.

'Not drugs. You won't be carrying drugs will you?' Mrs Anderson asked

'I don't know.' She could tell he was thinking that too. They'd heard the same stories about Davie White.

'Oh, Jim . . .'

'Ach well,' he sighed, saying he'd better be off because he was poor company and anyway he had other deliveries to make. As he pulled up his overalls and fastened them, Mrs Anderson had the presence of mind to ask about Duncan Boyd, whether Jim had seen him recently. 'Poor Duncan.' She said it so Jim wouldn't think it odd. It was what she usually said whenever Duncan's name cropped up.

'Funny you should mention him,' Jim said. 'He was a bit upset this morning, up at North Bay.'

'Is all the fuss about the windfarm getting to him?'

'I don't know if it was that. A young woman had been speaking to him and he'd just gone off. She thought it was her fault but I told her not to worry. Nice girl she was, brown hair, short like a boy, and a couple of ear-rings.' Jim touched his left ear. 'Pretty name too, Violet Wells I think she said.'

Violet followed instructions. At the bridge over the stream, she took the right fork and right again by the stables. She was skirting Brae House, approaching from the side, but she managed occasional glimpses of it through gaps in the trees and bushes along the driveway. Brae, it seemed, was a house of many parts: the main building an elegant square of three-storeys with matching pavilions at right angles to it and a floor lower. For all Brae's beauty and the drama of its situation – a pine wood sheltered it and a rock crag appeared to overhang it – Violet was more taken with the contrast between the refinement of the property and the bad manners of its owner. If her telephone conversation that morning had been any guide, Matt Hamilton was rude and bad-tempered. It was an impression the man himself did nothing to dispel when Violet appeared in the open door of the estate office and he shouted at her, 'You're five minutes late.'

He was a big man, not only tall but large framed and overweight with a florid face, slicked black hair and a loud voice which he directed without a change of tone or volume at Violet and then at a woman with blonde hair and an impatient expression who was searching through a pile of papers at the desk he was hovering beside.

'How many nights did you say?' he barked at Violet, then at the woman: 'Alexandra, for goodness sake I can do that.'

'I'm not sure,' Violet replied. 'It depends . . .'

Alexandra ignored him and carried on shuffling papers.

Matt looked from one to the other with a perplexed frown as though having to deal with two women at the same time was too much of an imposition.

'Darling,' he addressed Alexandra, 'why don't you sort out this and let me do that?'

Alexandra gave her husband an exasperated look and surrendered the desk with parting shots about him never being able to find anything and always surrounded by chaos.

'I'm sorry,' she directed at Violet, who was still standing just inside the door. 'As you can see, we are in a bit of a muddle.' Violet assumed the 'we' referred to Matt, because Alexandra gave the impression of being anything but disorganised. She wore a white shirt and black jeans with a thin belt, and she walked the length of the room with a click of heels that seemed to indicate purpose. 'Hello, I'm Alexandra, Mrs Hamilton,' she said. She rolled her eyes at Violet, inviting feminine collusion at the hopelessness of men.

'I just wanted to know,' Violet said, 'whether you rent Orasaigh Cottage by the day and how much you charge?'

Alexandra was about to answer when an eruption of complaint from her husband distracted her. 'Not those, Matt,' she said, 'I've already hunted through those.' He responded with a frustrated growl. She turned back to Violet. 'Well, we don't really have a day rate; didn't Matt . . . my husband . . . explain that to you when you rang this morning?'

'No, he didn't. He appeared to have other things on his mind once he'd told me how to get here.'

'Yes, he can be rather short on the telephone.' She looked apologetic, pressing her lips together.

'You were saying you don't have a day rate . . .'

'Normally we only let it out for a week or more.'

The implication hovered between them until Violet said, 'Well your husband could have told me that on the phone, couldn't he?'

An exclamation came from the desk and once again Alexandra's attention drifted. 'Don't say you've found it?'

'No thanks to you,' he answered and left the room flicking over the stapled pages of a document. When quiet had been restored, Alexandra said, 'Well, there isn't a tenant at the moment so I don't see why we shouldn't let it for a day or two, however long you want really, since it isn't booked next week either.'

She accompanied the offer with an emollient smile. 'How does £50 a day sound or,' she paused, 'in view of everything, why don't we say £40?'

Three days would be good, Violet replied. While she peeled off six of Mr Anwar's £20 notes, she said, 'A friend of my mother's used to stay in the cottage. It was a long time ago, you probably wouldn't remember her.'

'Lots of people have stayed there . . .' Alexandra searched a wire basket on the table beside her. 'It's a popular cottage . . . Ah, here it is.' She brandished a note-book and asked Violet for her name, address and mobile phone number.

Violet gave her details and handed over the rent money. 'My mother's friend,' she said, 'was called Megan Bates.'

'Megan?' Alexandra said, tucking the money into the notebook and returning it to the wire tray. 'Megan Bates.' She repeated the name and shook her head. 'No, but as I say so many people pass through.' She selected a set of keys from a small tin that seemed to be full of them. 'Yellow for Orasaigh,' she said, referring to the coloured tag and handed it to Violet. 'And you'll need these . . .' She picked up two sheets of paper from the wire tray. 'The house rules, the 'dos and don'ts' as well as some useful numbers,' she said handing over the first sheet. 'And most important of all . . .' She passed over the second. 'The tide times.'

Violet thanked her and asked if the cottage had recently been done up. 'I had a look through the front windows and it looked smart inside.'

'My mother had the place gutted,' Alexandra replied, 'when my step-father died six years ago.'

'Was the furniture replaced?'

'Oh everything was chucked out as far as I can remember.'

Violet held up the keys, said 'thanks' and made for the door, before turning. 'I don't suppose you know Duncan Boyd?'

'Yes,' Alexandra looked puzzled. 'Why?'

'Yes, of course you would.' Violet made it sound as though she had made a silly mistake. 'I suppose you've been neighbours for years.'

'Yes. He was here when I first came to Brae as a child.'

'How long ago was that?'

106

'Oh, I don't know, must be thirty-five years . . .' She still had the puzzled expression.

'You must have been very young.'

'I was six, but why did you ask about Duncan Boyd?'

'Oh it's just that he remembers her, Megan Bates I mean. By the way he reacted to hearing her name, I think he remembers her quite well.' Violet paused. 'I'm surprised you don't since you would have been, what, fourteen or fifteen, when she lived at Orasaigh Cottage?'

With that Violet went out. She walked slowly giving Alexandra the opportunity to come after her, to remember Megan too. Where the drive led into a copse of yew and holly, Violet looked back over her shoulder. Mrs Hamilton was watching her through the estate office window. They regarded each other for a moment, neither quite sure what the other was thinking.

The skull was large with a deep hollow above the slope to its beaked jaw. Cal had found it among a pile of recovered bones which Duncan Boyd had left in a disused stable. Coming across it Cal wondered at first if a horse had died of neglect and its broken skeleton was all that remained. Then, he noticed the skulls – three of them – and recognised two as porpoises. He'd found similar examples on his own beach-combing forays. The remaining skull was the one that interested him. He hadn't seen anything like it before but he had read about a creature whose description seemed to match the bony structure. Not only the hollow, but the size of the head – 70-80cms from point of beak to the back – and, most of all, the two cylindrical teeth which were still embedded in the bottom jaw, near the tip. He was more or less certain it was the skull of a Cuvier's, an elusive type of beaked whale which inhabited deep water and dived for squid. This detail had lodged in his memory because he had watched a YouTube clip of American scientists opening up a beached and dead Cuvier's and removing from its stomach twenty-two carrier bags. Apparently the bags – the way they hung in the water, how light played on them – confused the whales and they mistook them for their staple food.

Cal held the skull in both hands and wondered if that was how this one met its fate too. Thinking Duncan might be interested, he carried it to where he'd left another piece of flotsam which caught his attention. It was a cylinder of wood, more than a metre long, a pole perhaps or a section of mast, and it had been colonised by goose barnacles. Cal had come across barnacles of this type before but never in such concentration on a single object. There were so many than none of the pole was visible, except at one end. The wood there was still saturated, indicating recent recovery from the beach. He thought Duncan might like to know it could have floated a considerable distance before ending its journey at South Bay. Given the sheer number of barnacles it had certainly been at sea for some time. He put the skull down beside the pole as a post van appeared in the yard driven by a middle-aged woman with a white face and curly red hair turning grey at the temples. She drove up to Cal and asked through her open window, 'Is he about?'

'Duncan?' Cal asked, shaking his head. 'He's on the beach.'

'Would you sign for these then?' The postwoman retrieved four letters from the passenger seat and followed them with a pad and pen for Cal's signature. 'One for each letter if you don't mind,' she added.

Cal examined the envelopes: each was addressed to Duncan Boyd and each had 'Final Warning' stamped in red on it. He screwed up his face in apology and handed them back. 'Don't know what I'd be signing for.'

She sighed. 'I'll just have to bring them back tomorrow. As likely as not there'll be a couple more by then.'

'Sorry I can't help,' Cal said.

'Someone's got to.' A frown of concern wrinkled her brow. 'Have a look in there.' She nodded towards a lean-to, its door closed. 'Someone's got to,' she said again with more emphasis before turning and driving away.

Cal watched the van go, glanced at the closed door and decided to have a quick look. It opened half-way before sticking. He pushed with his shoulder and it gave some more. After going inside, he found himself looking at another pile – this time of paper. The difference was it hadn't been collected from the beach. It was a mound of letters and packages of different shapes and sizes. There were so many that Cal wondered if this was where Duncan routinely dumped his post. The notion took further hold when Cal noticed some envelopes like the ones he had handed back to the postwoman. They bore the same blood-red warnings.

Cal picked up a few of them. They hadn't been opened but others on the mound had. Cal examined the closest to him, scanning a few lines before straying to the next letter. Either they were about the windfarm, or about Duncan being in breach of environmental or building safety regulations of one kind or another. The common denominator, as far as Cal could tell from his fleeting sample, was a threatening tone warning of legal or other enforcement action. One letter which impressed itself particularly on Cal was from lawyers acting for BRC. It threatened compulsory purchase and compensation for Duncan of 'a nominal sum considering our client's potential liabilities arising from your reckless negligence of many years'. The only response by Duncan that could prevent 'imminent' court proceedings would be 'immediate and unconditional acceptance of our clients' existing offer to purchase Boyd's Farm in its entirety'.

Three weeks had passed since the letter had been written and, presumably, ignored by Duncan.

Muttering 'bastards' Cal went out into the yard. He collected the whale skull and the barnacle-encrusted pole and lugged them to the barn where the Neptune Scroll was hanging. He put them by the table on which Duncan displayed his prized finds and tore a sheet from the small notebook he kept in his pocket. He wrote about Cuvier's, telling Duncan how rare it was to find a beaked whale skull like that, and also about the barnacles, speculating how they might even have travelled from the tropics on the North Atlantic Current. He thought about adding something about the windfarm, an indication of his outrage, but instead asked Duncan to ring him.

I'm leaving my phone number in case you've mislaid it.

While he was writing he prepared a speech to deliver when Duncan contacted him, how he was right to stand firm against BRC, against big business extending its realm over the sea, in this case 362 square kilometres, using the cover of global warming, the false promise of jobs and an over-promoted technology to fool people into allowing the oceans to be industrialised. When Cal turned round to leave, Duncan was standing in the doorway. His expression was morose, his skin grey, eyes cloudy. He seemed drained of life.

The speech stayed unsaid. Thinking now that too many people were telling Duncan what to do,

Cal thanked him instead for letting him look around.

Duncan neither reacted nor spoke.

'I've left you a note about these . . .' Cal indicated the skull and the encrusted pole. Then he said, 'Look, I know people who might help you – marine scientists, guys I studied with, experts on offshore windfarms, how they disrupt currents and so on. They could raise objections, delay things until BRC loses patience and walks away.'

Duncan didn't even blink. It felt to Cal as if his offer had also been consigned, unopened, to a dump, just like all those threatening letters. 'Of course, it's up to you,' he added, wishing he'd said nothing. 'I'll be around for a few days if you change your mind.'

Violet wandered from room to room, imagining the daily routine of Megan Bates's life.

Did she rise early? Did she make coffee while running a bath? Was it her habit to bathe in the morning? Did she listen to the radio? Did she read? On which side of the fireplace in the sitting room did she sit? Did she light the fire? Did she cook? Was she tidy? Did she talk to herself? Did she go to bed early or late? Was she in love?

Orasaigh cottage, Violet discovered, was like a sullen stranger. It gave nothing of its past away. The effect was demoralising. Within an hour of turning the key on the front door and entering the porch in high excitement, she had retreated to the kitchen and was standing with her back to the sink, her jaw locked in disappointment. The house was empty of personality. Nothing of her mother remained and for a brief mad moment brought on by distress Violet saw the span of the last twenty-six years, starting with her birth, as a continuing and deliberate conspiracy. It began with a calculated act: her mother walking across a beach and abandoning her daughter forever. It continued with the sea refusing to give up her body. Another part of the plot had taken place in this cottage where Violet was standing: anything which might hold her mother's memory had been stripped from it and still the conspiracy continued. Duncan Boyd had shut his ears to the sound of her name. Alexandra Hamilton said she hadn't even heard of her.

Later, when she was calmer, Violet understood the hurt she felt was that of a child who yearns for a sighting of her mother, even if she has to make do with the dim memory of someone who met her long ago. She longed to know how she *was*, whether she had been extrovert or introvert, whether she'd been kind, whether she'd laughed loudly or softly. The answer to any one of these Violet would treasure, and once she had knowledge of it she would look for it in herself and then in her own daughter Anna.

In the sitting room, she found a telephone directory. She started at the back, going through the 'Y's, searching for 'Yellowlees', the name of the detective in charge of the investigation into Megan Bates's death.

On the bus to Poltown she had rung police headquarters in Inverness. Her inquiry caused the switchboard operator some amusement because 'Mr, rather Chief Superintendent, Yellowlees retired nine months ago'. Violet found four Yellowlees in the book: two in Inverness, one in Ullapool and the last in Mallaig. She rang the first Inverness number. There was no reply. The second was answered by a man and Violet asked if his name was, by any chance, Mr Robert Yellowlees. He replied that he was Iain but had a brother called Robert. Had she confused the two? Violet said the Robert Yellowlees she was attempting to contact had been a doctor and lived in Glasgow until his retirement.

'Oh,' Iain Yellowlees replied, 'that couldn't be my brother because he was a policeman, a chief superintendent, and he's never lived in Glasgow, never lived in a big city, not even one the size of Inverness. No, he always liked the great outdoors when he wasn't apprehending villains. He lives in a cottage at Ullapool now.'

Violet apologised for taking up his time. In the dimming evening light, she found Yellowlees again, circled the Ullapool entry and dialled it. A man who sounded cross answered and Violet said, 'That's not Tom is it?' The man said no and Violet replied, 'Sorry, wrong number.' Hanging up, she ripped the page from the phone book and went

114

to the kitchen where she had left the information leaflet given to her by Alexandra Hamilton. Half way down the list of useful numbers she found what she was looking for: 'Turnbull's Taxis'. The woman who answered her call said a return trip to Ullapool with a wait of an hour would be £36. Before confirming the booking, Violet checked the tide tables. 'So that's 8.30 tomorrow morning at the causeway to Orasaigh,' the woman repeated. 'Cash up front, mind . . .'

Violet collected her backpack from the porch and locked the door behind her. She shuddered as soon as she was outside, a reaction to the cottage's gloomy spaces. Going along the path to her small tent, she watched black clouds gathering to the west. She wondered where her mother's remains were lying, what little of them were left. Were her bones buried by sand and seaweed? Were they lying together or dispersed across the sea bed, scattered over the years by storms like the one that was gathering? The thought of them kept her awake, that and the showers which thrummed on the sides of the tent.

Beyond North Bay, there was no path, just the worn tracks of deer and sheep. The rain slanted in from the sea. The wind drove it hard against the left side of Cal's face until he was numb. He walked quickly, his pace determined by exhilaration at heading out into wildness, of being alone, of a storm breaking around him. He had another five kilometres to go before he reached the part of the coast where he would wake up at dawn and look out over sea to south, west and north. Or if the storm was as spectacular as it promised to be he would sit through the night and enjoy its raging.

CHAPTER 7

Intermittent squalls of rain rattled against the bathroom window in Orasaigh Cottage. Violet had showered to wash away the overnight chill of the tent, and was dressed and running her fingers through her wet hair when a knock sounded at the front door. It made her jump. She was on edge anyway, being back within those four walls, on edge as well as in a hurry to meet the taxi which would soon be arriving on the other side of the causeway. She crossed the landing to the front bedroom – its window overlooked the porch and garden – and on the gravel path below was a woman wearing a waterproof hat which covered her face. She had on a rain-jacket, a skirt which flapped in the wind and wellington boots. Violet backed away into the room hoping her visitor, whoever she was, would go away, but instead she knocked again, once then twice more. 'What does she want?' Violet said irritably before going to see.

When she opened the door, the woman lifted her head. Under the hat Violet recognised Alexandra Hamilton from Brae. 'Oh, hello,' Violet said, 'I was just getting ready to go out. A taxi's coming for me . . .'

A squall blew against the cottage. Alexandra turned sideways to it, the rain striking her back. Reluctantly, Violet stepped back to allow her into the shelter of the porch, and apologised for having to abandon her there while she went upstairs for her coat and bag. Coming back down, Violet found her visitor in the sitting room. She had taken off her hat and was peering out at the weather, warning Violet the worst was still to come. They would be better waiting for it to pass. Violet protested weakly about her taxi, aware she had time to spare, a quarter of an hour, and it wouldn't take her more than five minutes to go along the track and cross to the mainland. Her objection was more about having to talk to Alexandra, even if it was a confinement lasting only a few minutes.

An uneasy silence followed until Alexandra asked Violet if she was comfortable in the cottage. Violet let her think she'd spent the night in it. 'Fine,' she said, and added a compliment, the only one which occurred to her, about the shower and the hot water. Alexandra inspected the room, as though it might prompt a topic of conversation, and Violet checked in her bag for her purse. Neither looked at the other. 'I really have to be going,' Violet insisted.

'There's something I need to tell you,' Alexandra countered, now examining the fireplace. 'I should have said it yesterday. A woman called Megan Bates did live here.'

Violet watched her.

'I'm sorry. I shouldn't have pretended otherwise but there was a reason for it.'

Violet waited, her heart thumping.

'I did meet her a few times. I didn't know her very well,' she went on, now looking at Violet. 'I didn't acknowledge her name yesterday because it was just such a shock to hear it after all this time . . . it's a name from the past and to be honest I'd have preferred it to stay that way.'

'Why?'

The question hung unanswered for a while.

'Do you really want to know?'

Violet nodded.

'Because Megan Bates made my mother's life hell. She was unscrupulous. She was manipulative. She was dishonest. She liked to take what wasn't hers. She didn't have any family of her own and tried to take someone else's.' She paused and looked around the room as if some trace of her might have survived. 'And yes, my father . . . my step-father . . . allowed her to live in this cottage and for the three years she was here there was never a second my mother didn't wish her gone. As far as I'm concerned drowning herself was the only decent thing she ever did.'

For the last sentence she held Violet's stare, and when it was finished Violet said quietly, 'I'd like you to leave now.' She turned away from Alexandra, trying to conceal the dreadful shock she had received.

The porch door banged shut, but Violet barely heard it. Nor did she move. In all her many imaginings about her mother, she had never considered the possibility of her being as Alexandra described. Part of her wanted to rush to her mother's defence – to run after Alexandra and protest that it was lies. Another part of her was apprehensive: what if other people told Violet the same; what if it was true? She was still immobilised when her phone rang. She dug into her bag to answer it. 'Would you be planning to cross this low tide or the next?' It was a man's voice, her taxi driver, sounding impatient at having to wait.

'This,' she said, resenting yet another intrusion.

The taxi turned out to be a silver people carrier. The driver was a middle-aged man wearing trainers, white socks, olive green shorts and a Celtic shirt stretched across a prodigious belly. He said his name was Graham and as he opened the rear sliding door for Violet he explained that such a big taxi was useful for picking up parties of hill walkers at the end of a day and returning them to their cars. 'The state some of them are in after a few hours on the hill being eaten by midges,' Graham exclaimed, wiping a fat hand across his face, 'Oh my goodness me.' His belly carried on wobbling jelly-like after his mirth had died away. Graham, it seemed, was the talkative kind so Violet asked whether he would mind if she sat at the very back because she had a phone call to make. A private phone call was her implication. Graham shrugged as if to suggest it was her loss, missing out on his patter. 'You sit wherever you like love; the taxi's all yours. Sit at the back going this way and at the front on the return journey. It's up to you.'

After this speech, he made a little bow. Violet rewarded him with a fleeting smile. No sooner had she sat at the back than he asked if she was car sick 'at all' because the road was nothing but twists and turns. 'There's more swing at the back,' he said. Graham, she gathered, would prefer to have her company in the front, but she wasn't in the mood. She'd never been car sick, air sick or sea-sick, she assured him, and immediately concentrated on her phone, keying in Hilary's number. Graham, she prayed, would take the hint; a hope that was accompanied by a wash of indignation. Why did every ugly middle-aged man imagine he was irresistible and interesting to any young woman travelling alone?

When Hilary picked up her call, Violet made her promise to stay on the phone 'forever' or else, she whispered, 'a fat bloke in his fifties will try to have his way with me'.

Hilary laughed. 'How are you?'

Before Violet could answer Hilary told Anna 'it's Mummy' and handed over the phone. 'I've painted the house but it's got a crooked door,' Anna announced.

'That doesn't matter, darling,' Violet replied. 'Will you paint another picture for me?'

121

'Not a house.'

'No, not a house, what about painting Granny?'

Anna considered the new commission. 'Was she very pretty?'

'Yes, I think she was . . . don't you remember the photograph of her?'

'Kind of,' Anna said before asking, 'what clothes should she have?'

'Let me see,' Violet said. 'What about a summer dress, a white one, and she should have a raffia hat which is sort of like a straw hat? And the hat must have a big brim, wide enough to shade her face from the sun and with a broad red ribbon around it.'

After Anna had gone to tell Izzy, Hilary asked, 'Well, how are you really?'

'Frightened that the more I discover about my mother the more I might dislike her.'

'Wow, where did that come from?'

Violet sighed. She told Hilary about Duncan Boyd's reaction to Megan Bates's name and about Alexandra Hamilton's description of her – 'unscrupulous and dishonest'. Hilary tried to cheer her up, saying, 'God, I wish my mum had had a fling.'

As they were saying goodbye Violet asked Hilary to put the phone where Anna and Izzy were, so she could listen to them for a while. Hilary made Violet promise to ring again at any time of the day or night.

Violet heard Anna telling Izzy what a 'pretty woman' looked like. She had long brown hair which shone in the sun, big eyes which were as big as the moon, and lips as red as a tomato.

'You'd better come in.'

Robert Yellowlees was tall and stooped. He had steel grey hair, brushed neatly and parted on the left, a large fleshy face and the put-upon expression of a man who had something better to do. 'Before the wind takes this door off,' he added.

Violet apologised for dropping by unannounced but she was only in Ullapool for an hour or two and it seemed like an opportunity. He raised an eyebrow (*an opportunity for whom?*) and led her along a broad corridor with beige carpets and bare white walls. 'Well, you've certainly brought the bad weather with you.'

They passed a sitting room in which there was a large screen television. The sound was off but the picture showed a golfer on a fairway somewhere lush and sunny. Violet said she hoped she hadn't disturbed his viewing.

'I don't imagine a short break from it will do me any harm.' He put the emphasis on 'short'. By the time they reached the kitchen at the end of the corridor, Violet had formed an unfavourable impression of retired Chief Superintendent Robert Yellowlees.

She sat at the chair he pulled out from the table for her and refused his offer of coffee, tea or biscuits. She didn't want to put him to any trouble.

'Any more trouble,' he corrected her and stood

across the table from her, his back to the cooker. He had only caught half of her story at the door. The remainder was lost in the wind. 'So, what is it you want?'

Violet explained again how her mother was a childhood friend of a woman called Megan Bates, how Violet had grown up hearing stories about her, how she had become fascinated by her life and, more particularly, the manner of her death. She had read in old newspaper cuttings references to an Inspector Robert Yellowlees and had found this address in the phone book. Had she got the right Yellowlees?

'You have,' he replied with a resigned look, as if he knew from experience where this was going and how it would end.

'I was wondering,' she carried on, 'if you remembered the case and whether there was any clue why a woman who had gone through nine months of pregnancy would kill herself and her baby. Didn't you think it odd at the time, Mr Yellowlees?'

He let out a single snort of laughter at her naivety. 'I don't remember thinking it odd, Miss Wells. Policemen spend their entire careers seeing and dealing with things that don't make any sense at all.' He shrugged. The gesture meant there was nothing much else to say. In case she hadn't understood it, he added, 'You'd be better advised speaking to force headquarters about this. I am retired, after all.'

But he didn't do what she'd been expecting, end

the conversation and ask her to leave. He kept watching her, trying to work out why she was really there, his policeman's instinct for possible trouble still strong. What else could it mean when an old case turned up unexpectedly on your doorstep? So he waited for Violet to say something.

'Do you remember the investigation?' she asked while she still had his full attention.

His eyes narrowed but he didn't answer.

'I've seen the newspaper reports,' she went on, 'but there's nothing in them to explain why the police decided there were no suspicious circumstances.'

'From memory,' he spoke slowly, still watching her, 'Megan Bates wrote a suicide letter.'

'She left it in the cottage where she was living?'

'No,' Mr Yellowlees replied in a despairing tone which suggested she was beginning to exhaust his patience. 'She posted it. If I remember correctly, it arrived a day or two after she was reported missing.'

'Who was it addressed to?'

Mr Yellowlees let out another snort. 'Oh come on Miss Wells, you don't honestly expect me to remember the name do you?'

'Well, can you remember what it said?'

'As far as I can recall it was addressed to her married lover, who was the father of her unborn child. In the letter she expressed her distress at what she regarded as his betrayal. Apparently he couldn't make up his mind whether to abandon his wife. Megan Bates threatened to make it impossible for him to see her or the child.' He paused. 'I think that answers why she did it, don't you?'

Violet said, 'I don't know.'

'What more would you like, Miss Wells?'

'A body, I suppose.'

'Well, we'd all have liked a body, but there was an eye witness who saw her going into the sea, and some of her possessions were washed ashore later.'

'A hat and a bag, yes.' Violet reached into her pocket for Mr Anwar's newspaper cuttings. She found the one she wanted and read it out. 'Inspector Yellowlees said all the evidence pointed to a terrible tragedy, an unhappy young woman who felt she had nothing left to live for.' She looked at the former policeman. 'Do you still think that?'

'Well, I haven't thought about it at all for many years, but since you ask, yes of course I do.'

'You considered every possibility?'

'Yes.'

'Did you at any time consider whether Megan Bates might have given birth to her child and *then* killed herself?'

He shook his head as she spoke but she carried on. 'Let's say she abandoned the child at a hospital somewhere and then returned to Poltown where she drowned herself. If your memory of the letter is correct isn't that possible? That way she would have deprived the father of the child – wasn't that what she said? – as well as carry out her threat to kill herself.'

Mr Yellowlees said, 'There were no records of Megan Bates having given birth to a baby. We checked.'

'What if she delivered the baby herself or someone helped her?'

'What if, what if . . . where's the evidence? We had evidence. She was seen going into the sea. We had her letter. We had her hat and bag from the beach.'

'What if . . . ?'

Mr Yellowlees threw back his head in exasperation. 'Enough, enough Miss Wells. This is fantasyland.' He went towards the kitchen door, opened it wide and stood beside it. 'Now if you don't mind,' he added unnecessarily. 'As I said you'd be better speaking to someone at police headquarters.'

She held his glare. 'Why won't you even consider it?'

Instead of answering he pushed back against the door, opening it wider. She stayed where she was. 'I won't go until you've answered me.'

'I'll put you out myself if you don't leave now.'

Something snapped in Violet. She took the letter from her anorak and slapped it on the kitchen table. 'Why don't you read it?' she said, her voice trembling.

'What does it say?' he asked.

'It was brought to me by a social worker. It had been sent anonymously to his office in

Inverness. It says Megan Bates gave birth to her daughter.'

Mr Yellowlees walked from the door back to the table. He picked up the letter. As he was reading it, she said, 'That's the date I was abandoned at Raigmore Hospital in Inverness. I am Megan Bates's daughter.'

What had she done? In the taxi back to Poltown, she sat in the front passenger seat beside Graham and flipped between his discourse on the wind-farm (*like winning the Lottery if you want my opinion*) and the one that was going on in her head.

What had she done? Every time she repeated the question, she felt elation and then seeping doubt followed by nausea. What had she done? Snatching the letter from Mr Yellowlees, she had bolted for the front door. 'Wait,' he barked, the habit of command still ingrained. When she looked back he was striding after her, telling her how mistakes happened, honest mistakes, how it was every policeman's nightmare, a case coming back to haunt him. She recognised it for what it was, an attempt to keep her there. She slammed the door and ran along the side path to the wooden gate on to the street where Graham's taxi was waiting. She got in beside him because it was quicker than opening the sliding back door. She didn't look round again. 'Can we go?'

Graham glanced at her. As he pulled away he

128

must have seen Mr Yellowlees in his mirror because he asked, 'Problem?'

'No problem at all.'

'To my way of thinking,' Graham was saying now, 'we've got enough wilderness and mountains for the eagles or whatever, all the stuff the conservationists shout about, but what we don't have are jobs. Right enough . . .' After a few kilometres, Violet realised he punctuated the ending of his sentences with the same two words and in the same loud voice.

At first Violet thought he was asking for her agreement. But when she didn't offer an opinion Graham carried on regardless and she concluded he must be used to his own company and conversation. 'If you're asking me,' he said. She hadn't. 'Without the windfarm, people will be the endangered species around Poltown. Right enough . . .' He broke off to criticise another driver for going too slowly and to speculate about the weather now that some blue sky had appeared. 'There'll be another storm along later. Like buses, you wait for one then two come along together. Right enough . . .'

Violet had been too preoccupied to notice the rain had stopped. 'How much further?' she asked.

'Ten . . . eleven kilometres, maybe more,' Graham replied.

'Would you let me out here?'

'The fare'll be the same because the car still has to travel the distance, right enough.' It was his way of saying she might as well stay for the ride because she'd paid for it anyway.

'I just need a long walk.' It was an apology of sorts. She said it had been interesting hearing all about Poltown and the windfarm. She hoped she didn't sound insincere.

'It's what makes this job enjoyable,' Graham said. 'Meeting people.' The taxi slowed and stopped. Violet thanked him and waved as he drove away. What had she done? She recalled Mr Anwar's warning 'to move slowly and with as many of the facts as possible before declaring who you are'.

Whatever she had done could not be undone.

CHAPTER 8

12.15, early afternoon. The next low tide was ten hours away. She had time to kill. It was one of the reasons she had decided to walk. The other was a disconcerting feeling of being out of control. Too much was happening too quickly and Violet wished it would slow down. If only she had Mr Anwar's instinct for an appropriate speed. In the space of a few hours she had heard distressing testimonies about both her parents: a mother who had been deceitful and immoral; a father unable to choose between his wife and his mistress, who hadn't cared sufficiently for his baby. In this her biological parents appeared well-matched.

As Violet made her way towards Poltown she tried to understand why they'd behaved as they had, whether there was ever a pressure sufficient to excuse a parent from the obligation to a child. It was Violet's open wound. Anna's father, Hassan, had disappeared when Violet broke the happy (she thought) news of her pregnancy. She hadn't forgiven him so how could she forgive her mother or father?

Walking also gave her time to work out why she was being pulled back to Poltown and the inevitable revelations to come, why she wasn't returning home to Glasgow and to Anna. Only when she reached the top of the ridge from which she'd first seen Orasaigh, South Bay and North Bay did she find an explanation in her emotional response to the landmarks of her mother's life and death. It reminded her of her unbreakable and possessive love for Anna; how she was always on guard to fight her battles for her. Now, it seemed, she was doing the same for her mother.

Violet rested where Stuart, the bus driver, had described the view as 'a veritable panorama'. If anything it was more dramatic now. The wind was strong and picking up speed, a second storm chasing in on the tails of the one just gone. Clouds jostled against each other over the sea, a disorderly and looming procession, and here and there the landscape was lit by diagonal shafts of sunlight creating intense pools of colour where they fell: the rust-red of dying bracken behind Brae, sparkles of silver from a stream flowing to Violet's right; and emerald green surrounding the church to her left. Violet looked from one to another until a movement on the pale sand of South Bay caught her attention. A small black figure was gathering up debris, going backwards and forwards across the beach.

It took her ten minutes to arrive at the beach road and a few more to find Duncan. She followed the smell of cigarette smoke and found him sitting against a dune. At first she wasn't sure it was him. Could it be the nerdy owner of the pickup she'd met two days before? Then she saw Duncan's unruly hair, like wind-blown stalks of dried grass. She walked close to him before sitting cross-legged and looking out to sea, instead of at him. She began to talk as if she'd been speaking to him for ages and this was just the continuation of a conversation, one in which he'd been taking part.

She told him how clever he'd been, how hard-working, how lucky it was someone like him was prepared to keep the beach clean, how exciting it must be, never knowing what he would turn up from one day to the next, his own Tombola, how Tombolas had been her favourite things when she'd been a child. Had they been his too? She told him the objects she would like the sea to wash up: jewellery, a necklace, diamonds. Wouldn't that be something? Had he ever found anything like that? A message in a bottle: had he ever come across one? She bet he had; someone as resourceful and experienced as him. Oh, wouldn't it be extraordinary to find a love letter written a century ago or a message from someone ship-wrecked? Had he found any like those? When she was a child she made a raft and launched it and often wondered where it drifted. Maybe it had even come ashore on South Bay. Had he ever found a little wooden raft with an upturned yoghurt pot for a wheelhouse and a pencil for a mast? She laughed. No, she guessed he hadn't, or if he had, it wouldn't have been hers. Hers would hardly have drifted at all; probably it came back on the next tide. She kept her voice the same pitch and speed, and she punctuated some of what she said with sighs of self-deprecation. She knew he was listening. She knew he was watching her too, but she didn't look at him. She just kept talking.

She had a daughter, she said. Her name was Anna. She was sweet and lovely, with curly hair the colour of black chocolate, and glossy too. Her skin colour was somewhere between honey and brown. If he ever met her she was sure he would find her adorable; everyone did. In case he was wondering, and she was sure he must be, Anna was half-African; well, North African. Her father was Moroccan, a visitor to Scotland, an economic migrant. Weren't economic migrants rather like flotsam too; different but the same? In their case, poverty, wars or politics drove them to other shores instead of winds and tides; but sometimes winds and tides helped them on their way, didn't they? What was it about men, she asked?

She dared to look at Duncan. Since their first encounter deep folds had formed on his face; one traversed the thick stubble of his right cheek, another the left. His eyes were pink-rimmed and blood-shot. His appearance was dishevelled, even more so than before. He wore stained blue track-suit bottoms, probably scavenged from the beach, and an old denim shirt worn open over an old-fashioned vest which had long since turned grimy. She was shocked by the deterioration in his appearance but she didn't show it. As she looked away he glanced at her and she wondered whether this was working, whether she was closer or further away from finding a way to him.

She was still talking.

Sometimes, she said, she was glad Anna's father upped and went; sometimes she wasn't. What was wrong with men that they would run away from a child? A woman wouldn't; couldn't. If Violet had to she'd kill to be with Anna, to keep her safe; the bond was that strong. She interlocked her fingers and tried to pull her hands apart. Men seemed to have a choice; women didn't. As soon as a woman held her baby, that was that, for life. It was the strongest tie. It was like that with her and Anna. The love of a mother was the fiercest thing. Sometimes it frightened her. What she would do to protect her child; what wouldn't she do? She knew women who would abandon a husband or a lover as quickly as they would discard a cigarette butt, but none who would abandon a child. Not one. She imagined he'd heard stories to the contrary just as she had. But, in her opinion, they were stories put about by the kind of men who would desert a child, selfish, horrible men. Now that she was on the subject she might as well say it, she didn't believe a story people had been telling her. The story was about Megan Bates. No woman could carry a child in her womb for nine months, feel it wriggling and kicking, and not be overwhelmed by love. It happened long before the baby was born. Ask any woman. No way could Megan Bates have drowned herself and her baby. No way, she said again. Then she fell silent.

She gazed over the beach at the rolling waves and she waited.

At least he was still there. 'What do you think, Mr Boyd? Could Megan Bates have done that?' She risked another glance at him.

He started a little and said, 'I've been looking after this beach for years.' The boy was back. So was the expression of childish expectancy.

'Isn't that good?' she replied. 'I bet you've found some amazing stuff.'

He didn't reply and Violet said, 'You were neighbours weren't you? You must have known her well.' His expression was one she hadn't expected, of sadness. 'I think she was lucky to have you as her neighbour.' Her voice wavered because she could tell that he was about to tell her something. He had the look of someone who had carried a secret for so long and who had longed for an opportunity to share it.

'Yes,' he said simply. 'She was lucky.'

She gave him another fleeting look. He was smiling. 'Did you like her?' she asked

'Yes.'

She smiled too. Now they were like children exchanging secrets.

'She was very pretty wasn't she?'

'Yes.'

Violet gave an appreciative murmur, impressed that he had managed to make a friend of Megan, maybe more than a friend.

'She said I was sweet.'

'Did she? Why did she say that?'

'Because I said I would look after her and the baby.'

'Did you say that?'

'I did.'

Violet's heart was beating so loudly she was worried Duncan would hear it. 'You're a good man,' she said.

'I am,' he agreed

'Were you the father?'

'No.'

'Hm.' She was even more impressed: a man offering that to a woman when the child wasn't his. 'Did she love the father?'

'Yes.'

'Did *he* love her?'

'Not as much as I did.'

'Did you love her?'

'I did.'

'Did you know the father?'

'Mr William Ritchie QC.' He boomed it, like a master of ceremonies announcing a guest arriving at a party.

'Does he live around here?'

'He did.'

'Oh.'

'He used to live at Brae House.'

Violet tried to hide her surprise. *That* house. Despite her shock, she managed to ask, 'Where does he live now?'

'For the last six years Mister William Ritchie QC has lived in the graveyard.'

Violet listened to the announcement of her father's death and waited to feel some emotion. There was nothing. 'In the graveyard here . . . ?'

'Yes.'

Still nothing. She changed the subject. 'Did Megan love the baby?'

'She did.'

'Did she say that to you?'

'She did.'

'When did she say that to you?'

'Just before she disappeared.'

'Did she love the baby more than she loved the father?'

'Yes.'

'Did she say that?'

'Yes.'

'She must have trusted you.'

'She did. We trusted each other.'

'Good friends then?'

'Yes.'

'I would have looked after her and the baby.'

'I know you would.'

'They could have lived here with me.'

'Did you tell her that?'

'I did.'

'What did she say?'

'She said I was sweet.'

'Yes, I remember.'

'I didn't kill her.'

'She killed herself didn't she?'

'I don't know.'

'Why do you say that?'

'The police thought I'd killed her but I love her.'

'I know.'

'I love her.'

'Did you tell the police that?'

'I did.'

'Did they believe you?'

'I don't know.'

'You found her hat and bag didn't you?'

'I did?'

'In North Bay?'

'Yes.'

'That must have been upsetting.'

'It was. I love her.'

'I know. You said.'

'I didn't tell the police.'

'What didn't you tell them?'

He glanced at her. 'That she'd gone away . . . she said she would.'

Duncan's expression seemed fearful. Violet decided not to press him. She'd come back to it. 'What did you love about her?'

'She was kind.'

'Was she?'

'She was always kind to me.'

Violet smiled. 'That's nice to hear. And what else?'

'She had nice hair.'

'Did she?'

'Yes. It was brown.' He grinned again. 'She let me brush it once.'

'Did she?'

'I keep the beach clean for her. I always have.' He was pumped up with pride again.

'Why?'

He shook his head. 'I can't tell you.'

'Yes, you can.'

He shook his head again. 'No I can't.'

He stood up and she looked away, fearing what was about to happen, hoping he would stay. When she turned back he was walking slowly back towards Boyd's Farm.

Violet lay flat in the grass to shelter from the strengthening wind. The sky was black and lowering. *Mister William Ritchie QC and Megan Bates*: for the first time she knew both her parents' names. She said them out loud, practising the unfamiliar sequence of shapes her lips and mouth had to make, as if repeating them would compensate for time lost, would bring them to life or summon the missing story of their affair and project it image by image on the underside of the chasing clouds she was watching. She experimented with the names. *William Ritchie and Megan Bates, Megan Bates and William Ritchie,* but reverted to *Mister William Ritchie QC and Megan Bates* because it better described the little she knew of their relationship; that it was an unequal one. Mister William Ritchie QC had been a man of position, with property and a wife. Megan Bates was a woman who seemed to have spirit and prettiness but little else, not even a family. Yet it was Megan Bates who lost everything: her lover, her baby, her life.

Spirited *and* kind, she reminded herself of Duncan's comment. *She was always kind to me?*

She distracted herself with these and other speculations about her parents while putting off the next thing she had to do, to find her father's grave in the churchyard. She'd been delaying because she was worried about what might happen. When Duncan Boyd told her about his death she had heard the news with indifference. The clocks didn't stop, her heart didn't miss a beat, her breathing didn't quicken, nor did a tear form. Her father was dead: the father who abandoned his pregnant lover; the father who deserted his unborn child. Hadn't he always been dead to Violet? But, as she wondered about her mother and father, she experienced a nagging curiosity about him. When she was standing in front of his grave, reading his name carved into the stone, what would she feel? Would she experience a daughter's love for the father she never knew? Would it be a betrayal of her mother if she did?

As it turned out, she needn't have concerned

herself. She walked up the broad gravel pathway to the front of the church, her face and her heart as stony and as cold as her surroundings. The headstones on either side of her were all tilting and ancient with inscriptions that had been worn away after long exposure to wind and rain. Looking around, she saw more graves arranged in neat rows behind an old yew tree. They appeared to be more modern and some were decorated with flowers. She was approaching them when she noticed a grave apart from any others. It was under the wall which surrounded the churchyard. The headstone was white marble with black engraving and legible from a distance.

In memory of William Ritchie, QC, beloved husband to Diana and darling stepfather to Alexandra 1925-2003.

The brevity of it kept her rooted to the spot. More should have been written down: another woman and another child to acknowledge. She looked away at the wrought iron gate in the wall beside the headstone. Through its bars Violet spied the sheltering woods around Brae, and it occurred to her that William Ritchie QC had chosen his burial plot with care. Wasn't he interred to provide him with an everlasting view of God's as well as his own house? The headstone was another reminder of the inequality between Mister William Ritchie QC and Megan Bates: he was buried, she was not. He had a headstone; she did not. He had recognition; she did not.

For all her worry about having an emotional reaction to his grave, Violet was at her most composed since arriving in Poltown. Striding alongside the grave to reach the gate, she decided to show it the same cold disregard it displayed for her mother. She was almost past when a flutter of paper caught her eye. She glanced down and saw a book, its torn pages turning in the wind. She bent to pick it up and at that moment the grave and its inscription were as close as an arm's stretch away. She turned her head away, stood and walked from the churchyard. Only when she was beyond the stone wall did she examine what was in her hands.

It was a Scottish Prayer Book, its maroon covers soggy from the wet. As she turned its pages, an idea took hold of her. She flicked past 'Morning Prayer', 'Evening Prayer', 'A Catechism' and 'The Order of Confirmation' not quite sure what she was looking for. Prayers and religion had not been part of her life. She was hurrying now, turning the pages fast, past 'The Visitation of the Sick' and 'The Communion of the Sick' until she came across 'At the Burial of the Dead.' She read snippets of text, tasting them for suitability, liking the sound of 'We commend into thy hands, most merciful Father, the soul of this our *brother* departed, and we commit *his* body to the ground, earth to earth, ashes to ashes, dust to dust . . .' The italics encouraged her to think she could change brother to sister, and his to her. She looked at the two footnotes below the prayer and the second of them concerned the alterations that should be made for a burial at sea. Violet gave a little yelp of triumph.

She stood with her back to the stone wall, her father's grave on the other side, and directed her reading of the prayer towards the sea. 'We commend into thy hands, most merciful Father, the soul of this our sister departed, and we commit her body . . .' she checked the note and substituted 'to the deep' for 'to the ground' and went on: '. . . in sure and certain hope of the general resurrection in the last day and the life of the world to come; through our Lord Jesus Christ, who shall fashion anew the body of our low estate that it may be like unto his glorious body, according to the mighty working whereby he is able to subdue all things unto himself.'

She closed the book.

Later, walking the road into Poltown, she told Hilary about her day and her discoveries: her father had been seventy-eight when he died, so he must have been fifty-nine when Violet was born. The gap between him and Megan had been twenty-six years. 'He was married,' Hilary said wearily, adding without waiting for Violet to reply, 'of course.'

'Yes, to a woman called Diana.'

'Children?'

'A step-daughter,' Violet said. Alexandra Hamilton, the woman who had rented her Orasaigh

Cottage. 'Darling stepfather to Alexandra' was on her father's headstone.

'The bitch who told you that Megan Bates made her mother's life a hell?'

Violet ignored the question. She had other more important news. 'She loved me, Hilary. My mother loved me.' She told Hilary about Duncan Boyd, how he'd fallen for Megan, how he'd offered to look after her and the baby. Her mother had said he was sweet. She had told him she loved the baby.

'When?'

'Just before she died,' Violet replied.

'So why would she kill herself?'

'I don't know,' Violet sighed, 'except there was the letter.'

'Saying what she planned to do?'

'According to the police, it was a suicide letter.'

'I wish I was there with you.'

'It's ok.'

'Well, at least you've now got God on your side.'

They laughed. Violet had told her about the prayer and how emotional it had made her. She'd be fine, she told Hilary, once she had something to eat. She was on her way to the shop in Poltown to buy some food, bread and milk, anything she could find really. Then, she'd wait at the causeway for low tide or perhaps she'd go to the public meeting in the community hall.

In the event, the decision was taken out of her hands by the first spatter of rain and by an elderly woman with white hair stopping her car and asking

Violet whether she was on her way to the meeting. If so, would she care for a lift? 'It's about to pour.' No sooner had Violet closed the door and put her carrier bag of shopping at her feet than the rain beat against the windscreen and bounced off the road.

'Wow, I'd have been completely soaked.' Violet laughed at the narrow escape she'd had. 'Look at that . . .'

The car moved off slowly and the woman asked, 'Are you staying locally, in Poltown?'

'Just outside,' Violet replied, a smile of gratitude replacing her wonder at the violence of the storm. 'The cottage on Orasaigh . . . do you know it?'

'Ah, yes. Well at least you'll have a good roof over your head.'

Violet turned back to look at the rain.

'On account of my age,' the woman said after a pause, 'people seem to think my name is Mrs Anderson or Mrs A, anything but Mary. You may choose which you call me.' There was a prompting tone to her voice and Violet realised her omission.

'Oh, I'm sorry. I'm Violet. Violet Wells.'

'Violet,' replied Mrs Anderson, 'I haven't come across that for a while, but what a pretty name.'

CHAPTER 9

Mrs Anderson parked close to the community hall and suggested to Violet they stayed put.

'There's no point in us getting soaked until we have to.'

While they waited for a break in the rain, Violet ate crisps and a bread roll because she was 'so hungry' and Mrs Anderson reminisced about her childhood, about a game she used to play with her mother whenever it rained, 'and it rained a fair bit'. Most languages had different names for the different varieties of rain, she said. For example, English had shower, drizzle, downpour, and deluge (Violet suggested 'torrent') but Mrs Anderson's mother had only ever used sound and volume to differentiate between types of rain. So drizzle was 'rain' said in a whisper. A shower was 'rain' said in an ordinary speaking voice. Prolonged precipitation was 'rain' said like an extended yawn. A sudden brief deluge or thunderstorm was 'rain' spoken abruptly and loudly like a dog barking, but this was 'RAIN'. She attempted a shout and immediately apologised for her croakiness.

Whenever it rained like this, she carried on, she and her mother would scream 'RAIN' over and over, and the house would reverberate with their voices and with the water drumming on the slates until they became hysterical with laughing. Her father would come in from the fields complaining about a racket that could be heard from 'here to Ullapool'. Mrs Anderson's chortle trailed away into a sigh of sadness at the silent, embittered woman her mother had become. Violet said she'd tell the story to her daughter. 'She doesn't like rain very much but she does like shouting a lot.'

'Oh, you have a daughter . . .' Mrs Anderson sounded wistful. 'Not having children is the thing I regret most; and not having grandchildren. Tell your mother she's very fortunate.'

Violet didn't know what to say. Mrs Anderson peered short-sightedly through the windscreen and remarked on bleary groups of people running to the door of the community hall, coats over their heads. 'I suppose we'd better brave it, or there won't be any seats left near the front and I won't be able to hear.' Violet should leave her bag of shopping in the car because there was no point in it getting soaked too. 'Would you be kind enough to reach into the back seat for my umbrella?'

After retrieving it, Violet pulled up the hood of her anorak. 'Wait there a minute,' she said, letting in a blast of wind. She ran round the front of the car, opened the driver's door and held the umbrella low over Mrs Anderson as she got out. 'Oh my

148

goodness,' Mrs Anderson said as the storm buffeted at her and the umbrella blew inside out. 'Hold on to me, Violet dear, or else I will be blown away.'

Violet gripped the older woman's arm and guided her across the tarmac to the awning by the entrance to the community hall. Others were hurrying to the same destination from all over the car park. Two teenage girls screamed as they splashed through the puddles. A man overtook Violet and Mrs Anderson arriving at the door ahead of them. He held it open while he wiped the rain from his face.

'Oh, hi,' he said, 'the statue from the beach.'

Violet looked up. 'I'm sorry?'

'I'm Cal. We met the other day at South Bay. You asked me about the tides.'

'Yes, I remember.' She gave him a puzzled look. 'Why statue . . . ?'

'Just that when I first saw you, you were standing by the sea and you were so still you reminded me of one of the Gormley statues on the beach near Liverpool.'

Before she could reply Violet found herself being carried along into the foyer by others pressing behind her. '*They're* all men,' she shouted back at Cal who was wedged against the door by the newcomers. He signalled he couldn't hear above the noise of the wind and Violet went to join Mrs Anderson. She was talking to the man who had delivered Duncan Boyd's box of groceries.

Jim Carmichael nodded at Violet. 'Hello again.'

'Of course, you two have met,' Mrs Anderson said. 'Jim had a cup of tea with me yesterday and told me you were worried about poor Duncan. He'd run off or something, hadn't he Jim?'

Jim appeared ill-at-ease at Mrs Anderson relaying his gossip. 'Duncan and Mrs Anderson here are first cousins,' he explained anxiously to Violet, the implication being it hadn't been loose talk on his part, more a case of keeping it in the family. 'Mrs Anderson grew up at Boyd's Farm.' He reinforced the point.

'Poor Duncan,' Mrs Anderson sighed in a wandering way, still oblivious to Jim's difficulty. Her attention had turned to the hall and the speed with which it was filling up. They should claim their seats or else there wouldn't be any left, she said to Violet, deliberately excluding Jim by turning her shoulder. Mrs Anderson led Violet away and Jim remained where he was, looking uncomfortable. Violet managed a reassuring smile.

The incident reminded her of school, of the competition to befriend a popular girl, and once she had been won the snubs that had to be delivered to keep rivals away. Violet puzzled at why Mrs Anderson should treat her as some kind of playground conquest. All she could think was that old people often became selfish, and a jealous nature was one of the signs. Another possible explanation came soon after when Mrs Anderson asked Violet if she smelt whisky off Jim because she thought she had. 'I do hope he hasn't started drinking again.'

The hall was bright, busy and noisy with the storm providing conversation for the gathering crowd as well as a background rumble, like a growling predator. Mrs Anderson found two seats by the central aisle and while she settled herself Violet said, 'So you were brought up on Mr Boyd's farm?'

'A long time ago, when it was a proper farm with livestock, sheep and cows,' she replied tartly. Mrs Anderson's tight mouth and pinched white cheeks discouraged further inquiry. Instead, Violet mentioned Brae House, how impressed she had been with the building when she'd visited it to book Orasaigh Cottage. Mrs Anderson asked if she'd noticed the walled garden to the right of the drive because she lived on the far side of it, in what used to be the gardener's cottage. 'Indeed, it still has that name.' Violet said she thought she'd seen chimney pots. 'It must be a nice place to live,' she added politely, and Mrs Anderson said, 'It is or rather it *was*.'

Again, Mrs Anderson's sharpness put Violet off from prying further so she inquired about Brae House in the hope of finding out something about her dead father. 'I met the owners when I collected the cottage keys . . . Matt and Alexandra Hamilton.'

Mrs Anderson rolled her eyes. 'Some people deserve good fortune, and others certainly do not.' Clearly, Mrs Anderson believed the Hamiltons belonged in the latter category. 'People,' she said after a pause, 'with little instinct for their responsibilities'. She was clipped and disapproving.

151

'Did Mr Hamilton buy the property?' Violet asked, pretending to ignorance.

'He did not,' Mrs Anderson replied abruptly. Brae, she went on to explain, had been passed down from Mrs Hamilton's step-father, a lawyer 'and a gentleman, though sometimes a difficult one' called William Ritchie. She had got to know him well because she had been his housekeeper for many years.

'He was your employer?'

'He was and for the most part he was a good one too.'

Violet mentioned seeing a grave with the surname Ritchie when she'd been wandering around the churchyard. 'Would that have been him?'

'It would,' Mrs Anderson shook her head in sadness. 'A child was the only gift missing from Mr William's life . . .' She glanced at Violet.

'On the gravestone,' Violet continued quickly, 'it says husband to Diana. So she was Alexandra Hamilton's mother?'

'Yes.'

There was a stir behind them. 'Talk of the devil,' Mrs Anderson said.

Violet turned as Alexandra appeared in the hall, followed by Matt. She also noticed the man who'd likened her to a Gormley statue. He was sitting at the other side of the hall, a little further back than Violet and Mrs Anderson, by a pillar. He acknowledged Violet with a tilt of his head and Mrs Anderson spotted the exchange. 'Who is that?' she said, as if she should know him.

'I don't really know, except his name is Cal,' she answered. 'I've only met him twice, once at South Bay on the day I arrived and just now.'

Violet considered him quickly as he stood to let two women into his row. Short dark hair, black or dark brown: hard to tell which since it was still wet; deep set eyes; his mouth almost smiling; his nose slightly skewed to the right. She looked away before he caught her. An interesting face rather than a handsome one, she decided on second acquaintance.

By now, the Hamiltons were going past. Violet felt the swish of their clothes; the rustle of prosperity. Mrs Anderson sensed it too because she tutted and sniffed at fortune 'always favouring the unworthy'. The land which had been earmarked by BRC for extending Poltown – industrial units, the site for the new store, the school and housing – belonged to Brae. Without the prospect of development it was worthless bog. With it, according to gossip in the village, the Hamiltons would be £1.75m richer.

The Hamiltons' progress to the front of the hall was also being monitored by a woman in a floral print dress, who emerged from the group of people standing in front of the speakers' table. She left the stage, all bonhomie and bustling efficiency, and greeted the new arrivals by touching their forearms and with a broadening smile on her face. 'Gwen Dixon,' Mrs Anderson said. 'At least she's got a good heart . . . which is more than can be said for those two.'

As Violet was discovering, a compliment from Mrs Anderson wasn't always what it seemed. In Gwen Dixon's case, it turned out to be more a plea of mitigation to set against her crimes. 'One of those interfering women who sits on committees and thinks she knows what's best for other people,' Mrs Anderson said before drawing Violet's attention to a side door at the front right of the hall. Coming through it was a man in his mid-forties with cropped hair and wearing black jeans with a white shirt which stretched and strained as he moved giving an impression of a muscled chest and arms. He pushed a wheelchair in which sat an elderly man, his head hanging, his face haggard and lined, left side drooping. Mrs Anderson and Violet weren't the only ones watching their slow entrance. Others in the hall were beginning to stare too, the volume of chattering voices suddenly reducing. It was as if an open coffin, the corpse decaying, was being brought into the room. 'That's Alec Turnbull,' Mrs Anderson whispered. 'Not many people have seen him since he had his stroke . . .' As an afterthought she said, 'If ever a man deserved to lose his looks it's him.'

'Who's that pushing him?'

'His son, Ross,' Mrs Anderson replied without affection. 'He runs Poltown just as his father did before him.' There was no choosing between them in her opinion. 'One as bad as the other . . .' She warned Violet of 'the charade' she was about to witness: 'Ross Turnbull pretending he's interested

154

in jobs for Poltown when everybody knows he supports the windfarm and the expansion of the village because of the concessions he hopes he can get from the developers.'

Violet said she had taken a taxi which had Turnbull's name on the side. Was it his? Yes, Mrs Anderson replied, and there were holiday caravans and ice-cream vans during the summer season. But most of their money came from drugs and money-lending. The father's rackets were being run by the son, whatever he might pretend to the contrary. 'Inheritance is a way of life around here,' Mrs Anderson said. 'The land-owners pass on their acres, the Turnbulls their scams.'

As Ross Turnbull settled his father at the end of the front row of seats, the babble of conversation started up again. Mrs Anderson drew Violet's attention to a group of thuggish-looking men standing at the back of the hall. 'Turnbull's I wouldn't wonder,' she said. The speakers began to take their seats and the atmosphere in the hall changed. There were competing jeers for one side of the argument and the other. Someone shouted, 'Poltown scum' and suddenly it was tribal and menacing: the dispossessed against the propertied.

Gwen Dixon scowled in disapproval at the uproar as Ross Turnbull took his seat on the platform. He was the last to do so: with him was a city type in a blue suit, a crop-haired woman in shirt, skirt and sandals and a middle-aged man in a yellow jersey and pink corduroys.

Gwen Dixon called the meeting to order with a voice made for filling halls. Like a thunderclap, it silenced the hecklers. She was 'merely the umpire', she insisted. Her role was to ensure courtesy was shown to all the speakers, whatever their views. She glowered meaningfully at the back of the hall where a woman dared to comment loudly, 'Ooh, courtesy is it?'

'This,' she said, 'is a most important decision for the community of Poltown and beyond, a chance to make our feelings known.' She looked round the audience. 'I don't need to tell you that BRC has a policy of only putting its footprint in communities where it is welcomed.'

She suggested ground rules in a tone which discouraged discussion. The main contributors would be limited to five minutes each, the invited floor speakers to two and each member of the audience to one question or point of order as time allowed. A murmur of agreement rose from the hall. 'In that case,' Gwen Dixon said, 'we'll start with BRC, followed by Ted Russell for the Stop campaign, Ross Turnbull for the Poltown Action Group and finally Johnnie West, representing environmental charities. First,' she paused, glancing sideways at the woman, 'Joanna Dilmott for BRC . . .'

Violet smiled at the crop-haired woman in sandals turning out to be the corporate player and the city type in a suit being the environmentalist. Ms Dilmott's hand-knitted look wasn't the only surprise. After thanking the chair, she descended from the stage to the floor of the hall, talking as she went.

Who liked being spoken down to? She didn't, and she didn't imagine the people of Poltown liked it any more than she did.

'In case you're wondering . . .' Now she was standing in the aisle between the two front rows, 'how my accent ended up east of mid-Atlantic, it's because I was born in Ireland, raised and educated in England, and found success in America.' She scanned the audience. 'Yes, I'm doing ok, but that's not what this is about. It's not about people like me getting rich by ruining your environment, as some of our opponents like to say. This is about you, whether you want jobs, opportunity, prospects for your families, whether you'll let me and the other companies in the consortium give that to you, or whether you'll make us go elsewhere.' She frowned, looking towards the left of the hall where a single detonation of pent-up protest had greeted her last sentence.

'Honestly? I'd rather it was here,' she said trying to identify her opponent. 'Why?' She looked for him again. 'Because you people need it the most. Yes there'll be a cost. You'll lose some scenery, but not much.'

Giving up the search, she addressed the hall again, 'Hell, this is a great opportunity for you. Don't turn this one down because nothing like it is going to come this way again soon.' She paused to consider what she'd said. 'Correction. Ever. Don't let anyone take this from you.' She waited before finishing: 'And you know who I'm talking about.'

Her last remark drew another outburst, the same shout as before, the same expression of anger. Violet didn't hear it clearly because Mrs Anderson was wondering aloud if the speaker had been referring to Duncan Boyd. A family behind was coming to the same conclusion since 'Boyd was the big problem'. Violet strained to see who had bellowed in protest and noticed people shifting their chairs away from Cal. Others were staring at him. 'It's your friend,' Mrs Anderson said, spotting it too. 'Does he know Duncan?' she asked doubtfully, 'because people who know him generally don't speak up for him.'

Violet did not answer and anyway the speaker had started again. 'I imagine you expected me to come here this evening and talk about the project, how much it'll cost, the timetable, how you'll be saving the world, and so on. But you know all of that, and anyway it's beside the point. What you've got to decide is whether you want a future, whether you're going to save yourselves.'

She placed her hand on her heart. 'D'ye know something, I think you will.' She bowed before going back up the steps, her sandals flapping against the treads, pursued by warm applause. Violet half-expected another protest from Cal. She glanced around. He was sitting stony-faced with his arms folded while around him people were clapping.

Ted Russell, in corduroys, was next. He rose to his feet with a piqued expression as though he expected a respectful quiet to descend on the hall. Instead there were cat-calls and, around Violet and Mrs Anderson, a gathering undertone of hostile comment about Duncan and the risk his opposition to the windfarm posed to the village's future. Mr Russell's face became as livid as his trousers as he struggled to make himself heard. At one point he warned about the threat of unrestrained development and the lasting damage it would do to 'our wonderful west coast way of life not to mention the tourist industry that sustains us all'. The remark brought more jeers; and a deeper shade of red to the speaker's cheeks and neck. The hecklers didn't seem to regard his 'wonderful west coast way of life' to be the same as theirs. Russell's response was to start shouting back. 'Might I remind you,' he boomed with patrician superiority, 'that we're custodians of this ancient landscape and history won't be kind to us if we sacrifice it for a technology which is both inefficient and unproven.' Despite Gwen Dixon's calls for quiet, he gave up the unequal battle and sat down, his face glowing like embers in a draught.

'The only things that are inefficient and unproven around here,' a man shouted, 'are incomers like you.'

159

The jibe brought a counter from Russell's supporters of second home owners and B&B proprietors. They clapped their man out of loyalty until Ross Turnbull got to his feet. The hall fell silent, apart from Russell's bad-tempered complaint to Madam Chair about unfair treatment.

Turnbull spoke quietly. 'My definition of unfair is different to Mr Russell's.' The hall strained to hear him. 'Unfair is growing up in Poltown and having to leave because there's no work and no prospect of any work. It's families being broken up . . . it's what our children will always have to put up with if we don't back this development.' He spoke, he said, for those without a job or a decent home. The *forgotten* he called them. 'Those of you who have been held back for too long by people with a selfish interest in keeping the landscape as it is – this is your moment.'

Mrs Anderson tutted with impatience, rather too loudly for Violet's liking. Heads swayed to identify the source of the complaint, and Violet turned too, trying to deflect them. She picked out Cal. He was muttering to himself and shaking his head in disagreement with what had just been said.

'Well? What are you going to do?' Ross Turnbull carried on. 'Grab the opportunity for God's sake.' The applause was deafening as he left the stage to attend to his lolling father.

The final platform speaker, the suited environ-mentalist, talked fluently but drily about the impact of windfarms on bird-life in particular (the area around Poltown being important for Sea Eagles and Peregrine) and biodiversity in general. 'You are lucky enough to have miles and miles of wild land and seascape but it's disappearing globally. It's important to protect what's left. You are its guardians.'

It was an unfortunate echo of Ted Russell's speech and elicited another chorus of boos.

No sooner had he sat down than Gwen Dixon stood up. 'Quiet, quiet,' she boomed but even her voice failed to silence an argument that had broken out in the wings of the hall. Violet craned her neck to see what was going on. Two young men in tee shirts, Turnbull supporters Mrs Anderson said, were arguing with a young farmer type with swept back blond hair and a tweed jacket. A punch was thrown. Violet wasn't sure whose. The young farmer lunged forward. Suddenly men were running to take sides. The two tribes shoved at each other, the preliminaries to a skirmish. The rest of the audience sat transfixed until the crack of a head butt on the bridge of the farmer's nose. A collective gasp of shock sounded in the hall. It was followed by more fists flying and a scraping of chairs and people hurrying for the door.

Violet grabbed at Mrs Anderson's arm, 'I think we'd better go, don't you?'

Worse violence happened most Saturday nights in Sauchiehall Street, Cal thought. The punches and the head-butt gave way to insults and shouting but the audience still rushed for the exit. There was a yell for a missing child. A woman cried out. Cal caught a glimpse of an elderly man toppling. A shout of 'Don't push' went up. Gwen Dixon strode down the aisle towards the crush at the doors, her shoulders and hips rolling together, her elbows bent; a practical woman prepared for action. The speakers were on their feet, wondering at what had happened, finding themselves the audience to a drama, all apart from Ross Turnbull who was wheeling his father towards the side exit. Cal noticed him look back at the melee and grimace, a combination of worry at the crush of bodies and disappointment at the turn of events. Not quite the show of overwhelming support he'd called for or that BRC had demanded.

'Stop pushing.' Gwen Dixon was working her way into the throng. She scolded and shouted, calling for common sense, telling everyone to take a step back, to take their time. Heads turned towards her: the pressure on the door relaxed. 'One by one please, and no pushing. Everyone will get out safely if you take your time.' Cal joined the back of the queue that was forming. He nodded towards Gwen Dixon as he passed her, acknowledging her efforts. She glowered back, communicating disapproval of his interventions.

Outside, the rain was still falling and the wind blowing. Groups of distressed and crying people huddled together to exchange stories. A woman

Cal's age went from cluster to cluster inquiring about cuts or other injuries. He watched for the statue and her white-haired companion. He'd come to the conclusion they were granddaughter and grandmother. Then he saw the old woman by a car. She'd dropped her keys. The wind was shoving at her, almost tipping her over, as she bent to pick them up. Cal ran over to her, steadied her, retrieved her keys and placed them in her hand. 'Are you all right?' he said.

She blinked at him. 'Where's Violet?'

'Don't worry. Everything's fine.' He looked around the car park. 'Where did you last see her?'

'At the door . . .'

After helping her into her car he said she should drive home in case trouble flared again and he would look for Violet. Then he headed off across the car park, calling out her name and asking if anyone had seen her, describing her appearance. Having drawn a blank, he tried the hall. As he passed the side of the building, he heard a scream. The light cast by a small window lit up two struggling figures. 'Hey,' he called out, running towards them. 'Hey stop that.'

The light fell across Violet's face as she was pushed to the ground. A small, burly man looked back at Cal. His face was hidden by shadow and a hood. Cal shouted again. The man held out his right hand as a warning to Cal to keep his distance before turning and disappearing into the blackness.

Cal knelt beside Violet and helped her sit up. 'He's gone. Are you all right?'

She held her hands to her face and nodded. 'Yes,' she said uncertainly.

'God, what was all that about?'

He must eat. He must drink. He must ring his son Rahim. They were the reasons for leaving Shereen's room; reasons for going downstairs, for picking himself up. He *must*. Why must he? Muhammad Anwar tried to remember. Slowly it dawned on him. It wasn't so much that he must do these things. It was just that they were all he had left to do.

No case files to read.

No shirt to iron.

No trousers to press.

No sandwiches to make for his lunch break.

No need for wakefulness in the night, fretting over this or that boy or girl and whether the right decision has been made.

No alarm clock to set.

No flask of tea to prepare.

No emails or texts to read before work.

No diary to consult.

Not tomorrow, not the next day, not next week. For the time being he had no work. 'Until further notice,' Mr Hunter had said. 'You are suspended and I must ask you to leave these premises immediately.'

Eat, drink, ring Rahim: except Mr Anwar was

not hungry or thirsty (despite having had no food or water since he left the office at midday), and he couldn't (wouldn't) ring Rahim. So he remained where he was, watching the light fade to dark, the pink draining from Shereen's duvet cover and the skin of a Bollywood starlet's airbrushed face becoming translucent in the streetlight which illuminated the poster hanging beside the door. Did he have a reason for leaving his daughter's bedroom? Not to eat. Not to drink. Not to ring Rahim.

Rahim, he sighed. Rahim was all he had left. Rahim, in his final year at Edinburgh University, would soon be a doctor. Dr Rahim Anwar. How could he admit to Rahim that he had a stupid old man for a father?

Instead he told Shereen, as he used to do when she was a baby, as he had done these past four years, an account of his day, the same theme usually recurring: how a man like him (a man of colour is what he meant), also an unassuming man, had to accustom himself to disappointments; how he had become wiser as a result and kinder; how kindness was under-rated; how some people confused it with weakness, in particular Mr Hunter.

You shouldn't judge the man until you know the pressures bearing on him, he told Shereen, in case he sounded disparaging of Mr Hunter.

Always step into the other man's shoes before criticising him, he advised Shereen, with a rueful tilt of his head. Even before she left home the only shoes she was prepared to step into were peep-toed, sparkly and high-heeled and well beyond her father's pocket. He imagined that nothing had changed except that Shereen's taste for glittering extravagance was being indulged by her wealthy husband.

Sighing again, he returned to the subject of Mr Hunter. As director of the department, his shoes were necessarily big ones, he told Shereen. Mr Anwar held his hands wide apart to show her just how big. There was the inquiry into the death of Charmaine Hislop, the fostered toddler who was killed by her baby-sitter. There was the claim for unfair dismissal by Gillian McKay, Mr Hunter's demoted deputy. There was the work-load that was growing like Topsy: important work. Very important work, he emphasised in case Shereen hadn't grasped the seriousness of the situation.

Mr Hunter didn't have his troubles to seek.

If your father was sounding regretful, he told Shereen, it was because he was. Regretful at the inconvenience he had caused Mr Hunter, regretful at being disobedient, though not regretful at what he had done.

You see, he said with a degree of caution, Mr Hunter was unmarried. (The circumspection was because Mr Hunter was gay.) Mr Hunter didn't have children. He had no experience of the heartbreak when parents and children lost touch with each other. Mr Anwar shook his head, his expression one of resigned endurance. He wouldn't say more; he didn't need to. Shereen had heard it before, often: how the ache never diminished. Mr Anwar's silence was a long one, lasting many minutes. Jagged edges of pain stabbed his heart, rendering him speechless, as it always did. It was twenty-two years since his darling Meera died; Meera, his wife; Meera, the mother of his two children; and four years since he had last seen or spoken to Shereen. The spasm passed.

He sighed again.

How could your father have carried out Mr Hunter's instructions, your father of all people?

He told Shereen about the letter he had taken to Mr Hunter. 'It was a mistake, Shereen. Your father is stupid.' Mr Hunter had said, 'Anonymous letters about something that may or may not have happened twenty-six years ago can wait. Can we just focus on what we *have* to do today please Mr Anwar?'

He breathed in. 'Shereen, if you had been abandoned as a baby and didn't know your mother's name, wouldn't you want to see that letter?'

Another silence: this time because Mr Anwar was unsure of Shereen's receptiveness to the question. Meera had died when Shereen was only a few months old, the pregnancy accelerating the cancer which killed her. All through Shereen's childhood, Mr Anwar kept Meera's name alive by telling stories about her. But round about the age of 16 Shereen had asked him to stop. He didn't know why. At different times he favoured different explanations. The kindest to Shereen, the one he reverted to at times like this, was that his daughter carried the guilt of Meera's death. To escape, she had to run away.

Mr Anwar stared again at the poster, at the starlet's flawless face. Suddenly he felt a foolish and deluded old man. What his heart knew his head would not admit: glamour not guilt carried Shereen away.

He closed his eyes and tried to remember where he was, the place in the story. Had he told Shereen about the inquiries he made with the police, about his visit to Violet Wells, the abandoned baby, now a mother with her own little daughter? In case he hadn't, he would tell her anyway.

He wondered whether to tell Shereen about his gift of £200 or the guide book, but decided against.

As he'd expected, Violet Wells went looking for Megan Bates, looking for information about her. 'Your father doesn't have all of the details but it appears that Miss Wells tracked down the officer in charge of the original investigation. Your father hadn't told Miss Wells about Mr Hunter's instruction *not* to pursue the case, so Miss Wells cannot be blamed for the repercussions. Anyone in Miss Wells's position would have done exactly the same.'

Nor was he surprised the retired police officer complained. Not surprised either by Mr Hunter's reaction or his suspension for going against his manager's instructions.

He glanced again at the starlet, and her face brought to mind his wife, Meera, and how he used to talk to her in the dark. He would sit on his side of the bed, as if readying to swing his legs in beside hers, but instead he would turn off the light and he would tell her all his ambitions, fears and secrets, the atmosphere of the night becoming so charged with intimacy that when he lay down beside her they would make love.

CHAPTER 10

O ne moment Mrs Anderson was fast asleep, the next wide awake and startled at being jolted from unconsciousness. Her eyes strained against the pitch dark of her bedroom, and her head shifted on the pillow so that she could listen with both ears. She picked out familiar sounds, those that had accompanied her for her thirty-five year occupation of Gardener's Cottage: the hollow tick of her alarm clock; the rustle of mice or tumbling mortar in the sealed chimney at the foot of her bed – she had never been sure which; the movement of a floorboard; the murmuring and rattling of the pipes which told her it must be past six because the boiler had started to heat the water.

What kept her on edge was a sound she couldn't hear. She listened for the noise that woke her, of someone banging at her front door accompanied by a shout; a woman. She waited for it to be repeated before deciding whether she'd had a vivid dream or whether there really was someone outside.

The seconds ticked away. The fug and confusion

of waking from a deep sleep began to clear and with it the uncertainty. Mrs Anderson had heard the noise before; the first time when Diana brought the baby and thereafter at odd occasions like this when she was deep in sleep and the room was dark and still.

'So much blood,' she whispered. It was what she always said.

Diana at the door, holding a new-born baby, drenched in blood; the baby covered in it too, a girl.

Mrs Anderson rolled on to her side and turned on her bedside lamp. Her clock showed it was 06.23. At seven her alarm would ring. She watched the second hand's circular journey.

Then, she'd have done anything for Diana.

Violet's head was pressed against the sitting room window. Her slow breathing made a plume of condensation on the cold glass; its expansion and contraction the only movement inside or outside Orasaigh Cottage, as far as Cal could tell. From the armchair in which he had spent the night, he saw she was as motionless as the branches of the trees behind her.

'Did the storm go in the night?' Cal asked, stirring, pretending he'd only just woken when he'd been watching her for a while.

His voice startled her but she attempted to conceal it.

'Would you like coffee?' she asked. 'I found a jar

of instant in the kitchen. The milk I bought is still in Mrs Anderson's car – do you mind black?'

She was talking quickly as if she was worried about what he might say if she gave him an opportunity. He played along. 'Black's fine.' He stretched and yawned. 'No sugar,' he called after her.

When she returned, holding a single mug of coffee, he said, 'Aren't you having one?' She shook her head, barely looking at him. 'Not at the moment.' She put it beside his chair and made for the door again.

'Violet, we've got to talk about this.'

She stopped with her back to him.

'I know what I saw last night,' he continued.

She seemed to slump in resignation. She knew what he was going to say, or thought she did.

Cal hoped she would turn round. 'Well, you know what I think.'

She replied in the same weary tone of the night before. 'There are creeps like him everywhere. There's always some guy . . .'

'It wasn't like that, Violet. You know it wasn't.'

She grunted in exasperation, as if Cal didn't understand, as if any man could. 'That's *exactly* what it was like.' She sounded impatient with Cal for doubting what she was saying, but the emphasis was forced. Cal could hear it. She was trying to persuade herself as well as him.

The night before, driving to the causeway in Cal's pickup and then crossing it on foot, Violet had

172

been more concerned about Mrs Anderson than about herself. Despite Cal's reassurances about her having reached her car safely, the first thing Violet did inside Orasaigh Cottage was to find the old woman's number and ring her. While they talked, Cal went round the cottage checking the windows were locked and wondering at Violet's behaviour, at how odd it had been. Perhaps it was shock. Perhaps she found it easier to worry about Mrs Anderson than to confront what happened to her. After checking upstairs, he joined Violet in the sitting room. She had been sitting in the dark. Cal suggested drawing the curtains and turning on the light. She told him not to bother. She felt tired – no, much more than tired, exhausted, as if she hadn't slept for a week. He wasn't surprised, he told her. She had had a nasty experience. She was bound to have a reaction, anyone would.

He sat in the chair opposite her. What, he asked, had Mrs Anderson said?

'About what?'

'What happened to you.'

'I didn't tell her,' she said. 'I was arranging to meet her tomorrow, to collect my shopping.'

He took the opportunity to question her some more, asking whether she had seen the man before, whether he'd said anything to her, if she knew of any reason for him to do that to her. Shouldn't she involve the police?

Her replies were clipped, her voice strained. She couldn't really remember the man. It was like trying to recall a dream, the detail kept slipping from her it had happened so quickly. She hadn't really looked at him. One second he was there at her side, gripping her, forcing her to go with him; the next he was gone. She hadn't seen his face; it was dark and he had a hood pulled over his head. He might have spoken but the wind had been howling and there was so much noise anyway. She had no recollection of a voice. The police? What did she have to tell them? A man grabbing at a woman: it happened. It wasn't pleasant but nor was it uncommon.

'Can't we just leave it for now?' She moved in her chair making herself more comfortable, letting him know she had had enough for one day.

'I'm sorry,' he said, 'Maybe I should go, leave you alone if that's what you'd prefer.'

She didn't reply, and he listened to the wind wailing outside until she dropped off to sleep. Then he went upstairs to find blankets to cover her, puzzling why she was downstairs in an uncomfortable chair when there were bedrooms upstairs. Was she afraid to be alone?

Eventually he dozed off too, wondering if rest would make her more receptive in the morning.

About that, he had been mistaken. Sleep didn't appear to have altered her mood. He was suddenly irritated by her behaviour, by the stupidity of it. 'For Christ's sake Violet, I'm only trying to look after you.' He regretted his outburst immediately, not only what he'd said but the manner of it, the unexpected emotion he invested in it. Now she would know he minded about her. He swore silently. He expected her to leave the room but she stood there, quite still, as if caught between opposing forces: wanting to hear what he had to say; not wanting to; wanting his company; not wanting it.

Cal sighed. 'Look, I'm sorry. I don't know what's going on or why . . . maybe it's none of my business.' She stood with her head bowed, arms folded. At least she was listening. 'Violet, what you're saying doesn't make any sense – some bloke just trying it on. Stuff like that doesn't happen in a place like this.'

He watched the rise and fall of her shoulders.

'All I'm saying is that you should take it seriously. Just in case. Go to the police. Tell them what you can.'

She shook her head. 'We've already talked about this, and I told you I didn't have anything useful to tell the police.'

'Ok, so why don't you move on? Go somewhere else. Go home. Why stick around when there's some guy out there . . . ?'

'I've still got things to do,' she insisted. 'Things I want to see.'

'What happens if he finds you on your own, when you're walking a beach?'

She sighed again. Cal going over the same ground frustrated her. Without turning, she said, 'I'm going to have a shower, all right.'

Do what the hell you want, he thought.

While she was upstairs, Cal made another cup of coffee and took it to the front garden. He leaned against the gate, letting the sun warm him. His clothes were still damp from the rain, his bones chilled by the cold and airless atmosphere inside Orasaigh Cottage. He checked the time on his phone: not quite 8am. Low tide was three hours away. Until then he was stuck on an island with someone who would prefer him to shut up or leave. He remembered seeing Violet for the first time and thinking she might be a companion spirit, someone who was like him, who found refuge by the sea. How wrong he'd turned out to be. The thought accompanied him uneasily as he wandered along the track. 'Fuck,' he groaned. Had he made it obvious he was attracted to her? Perhaps that's why she was being difficult. Was that why she kept a distance between them?

On his return to the cottage, he saw her before she saw him. She was coming out of the porch into the garden. Her hair was still wet from the shower. She had on jeans, a white vest and a blue and white check shirt which she wore loose.

'What a difference a day makes,' he said, stopping by the gate.

'Hard to imagine it's even the same place,' she replied, smiling and squinting as the sun caught her eyes.

He wondered if it was her way of making amends:

176

a new beginning for them too after the disagreements of the last twelve hours.

'Can I get you coffee now?' he asked.

'No thanks.' She glanced at him and away. 'I'm sorry.'

'Sorry for what?'

'For getting cross when I should have been grateful.'

'It's ok.'

'No . . . No it isn't.' Her mouth twisted. 'This cottage . . .' she looked behind her. 'It's so depressing inside.'

Cal nodded.

'Are you in a hurry?' she said, a look of anxiety in her eyes.

'No.'

'Could we do something?'

Mrs Anderson's morning walk usually took her over the moor path to the churchyard where she sat and rested her feet if the weather was sufficiently clement. Today, however, she skirted the walled garden and joined the main driveway. Turning left, away from the big house, she settled into her stride and prepared for the possibility of an encounter with Alexandra or Matt Hamilton. Should either of them drive by she would carry on regardless, neither stepping on to the verge, nor looking up. She fixed her face accordingly – it drained from milky pink to pallid grey to suit the dourness of her expression – and stared at the potholed tarmac ahead of her. Yet in her breast there was a flutter of excitement at what had been set in train, at its potential.

There she was walking the driveway of the people she would destroy, tramping across their property just as surely as she was tramping on their hopes and ambitions, just as they had trampled on hers. Yet, if they were to drive past her now what would they make of her, she wondered? Would they see the resourceful and dangerous adversary who had arranged the return of Mr William's only child, the rightful heir to Brae, or the dry husk they had discarded, a woman barely worth the bother of reviling or pitying, let alone fearing? She assumed the latter and wished one or other of them would happen by and glance up at her in condescension. Just for the joy of it: Alexandra or Matt Hamilton being taken in by the illusion she was creating, of a woman brought low by her expulsion from the family she had served beyond duty for all these years.

Where the drive met the Poltown road, she turned right, crossing over to the paved footpath on the other side. She walked slowly, enjoying the sun and the unexpected warmth, until she reached the turn-off to South Bay. She forked left and, after 150 metres or so, stopped beside a slatted bench with a decorated iron frame. She put down her bag and glanced at her watch. Low tide wasn't for another hour. She had time to while away and where better to waste it than there, where she could see the long crescent sweep of the bay, where she could watch for Duncan? She sat and made herself comfortable, the only sign of any restlessness the frequency with which she lifted her eyes towards the north-west, towards the bay. Where was Duncan? Where was the idiot?

While she waited for him to put in an appearance, she occupied herself with memories. Nowadays her head was filled with so many bitter recollections that she wondered whether she had ever been happy for anything more than fleeting or long-forgotten periods of her life. So preoccupied did she become in resuscitating past insults, slights and grudges that it seemed no time at all before she noticed a figure moving quickly through the dunes. Mrs Anderson checked her watch. It was 10.53. Fifty minutes had passed. She opened her bag, removed a tissue from its packet, dabbed at her eyes and blew her nose. She waited a while longer until Duncan was busily clearing the beach of its latest debris before stirring. Just to be sure.

She walked quickly along the road, her childhood knowledge of the folds in the land being put to good use. Only when she reached the stone pillars at the gateway to Boyd's Farm did she rest. There, with the dunes rising between them, she could no longer see Duncan, nor was there the risk of him seeing her as long as he was working the high tide line.

Her exertions had made her short of breath and she reached out to the stone pillar at her side. As usual, its touch stirred up vivid memories. She sniffed at the air, a reflex response, her head tilting one way, then another, just as it used to when she'd been a girl, following the wafts and trails of smoke from her father's pipe as the two of them spent early summer evenings watching over the sheep. Her father's habit had been to lean against the gate while Mary Boyd (as she was then) perched on the stone pillar from which he would lift her and send her running across the cropped grass to move a ewe that didn't 'seem right', to let him cast his expert eye over it. She examined the pasture now: not only was it no longer lush and dark green, the field was colonised by docks and rushes as well as old and rusting machinery. The nearest wreck to her was her father's Ferguson tractor. 'This farm and land is NOT for sale. Turn round here' was emblazoned across it. A 'pah' of annoyance erupted from her. Everywhere her eye settled, she saw neglect, chaos or madness. Was it any wonder it tore at her soul?

The emotion of the moment acted as a goad and she set off along the farm track. Before she had gone half way to the farmhouse and steading, her eyes welled up and her breathing became laboured. Her transformation had been brought about by a notion so unexpected and compelling that it almost choked her. For as long as she had dwelt on the misfortunes which accompanied her in adulthood – since the day of her marriage forty-seven years before – she had regarded herself as the guileless victim of other people's selfishness. If she had been guilty of anything it was of giving her loyalty too easily and too well. Yet now, on these acres where she'd spent her childhood, another narrative insinuated itself into her thoughts. Following her humiliation at Diana's memorial service, she saw the course of her life as a repeating pattern: one in which she had invested unwisely in people who repaid her trust by abandoning her and – this, the deadliest realisation of all – of her complicity in it. Was there any other explanation possible when someone time and time again laid themselves open to the same injustice?

It happened here first.

Wasn't this where she learned about sheep and cattle, about hay and silage, about the growing seasons, about the business of farming in the expectation that one day Boyd's Farm – its name for three generations – would be hers? Wasn't this where she suffered the worst of her betrayals, the one that would set the pattern for all the others?

Her childhood at Boyd's Farm had been content. It marched along to the seasons and with a growing understanding of her place in the world. Being the only child of Archie and Catherine Boyd, she imagined the farm would be where she lived out her life. A shepherd's expression used by her father explained it best. The sheep, he used to remark, were 'hefted' to the place: in other words they belonged to Boyd's Farm, and so in her view did she. She was 'hefted' too, knowing the farm's character and moods better than her own, believing there to be an unbreakable bond between her and its acres and animals, her bloodline and theirs. She'd assumed her father knew it too, since there was no sibling for there to be rivalry over the legacy. Yet, she had been wrong, as she had continued to be wrong thereafter on the question of bonds, belonging and the giving of unconditional love.

Boyd's Farm was where it had begun, with her father, a man who was as knowledgeable about the whims and wiles of nature as he was ignorant of the jealousy and competition that was conducted daily between Mary – once she became a teenager – and her mother. By the time Catherine Boyd died, Mary was forty-five and divorced, but still she remembered the frisson of excitement at having her father to herself at last. The sentiment had been short-lived. When Mary had suggested moving from Gardener's Cottage to Boyd's Farm to take her mother's place, her father appeared troubled, inquiring why she would want to give up her home when he wouldn't be alive for long – his heart was failing and his lungs filling with fluid. Didn't she know the house and the farm would soon belong to his brother's younger son, Duncan? The farm had always gone to a Boyd. Farming was a man's business. Who else but Duncan could it be? Surely she had known, and anyway why would she have expectations of the farm when she wasn't a Boyd? She had become an Anderson by marriage. Despite divorcing, didn't she call herself by that name still?

Mary had fallen silent with hurt and rage and he'd shuffled off to find his will among the papers on his desk. Returning with it, he'd shown her the paragraphs detailing how he intended her to have 15% of the farm, a share that Duncan would purchase from her once he'd turned a few years of profit. Her father had looked at her with hurt bewilderment. He had provided for her better than any Boyd had provided for a daughter. Her charge of unfairness had been unjust. Didn't she owe him an apology?

Beginning with her father she had always loved jealously. It was true of her husband, who left her after eight years of marriage, two miscarriages and a still birth. It had also been true when Mr William brought Diana to Brae. How Mrs Anderson relished the time the two women spent together over morning coffee in the kitchen or tea by the east wall of the garden or at South Bay where Diana liked to swim (Mrs Anderson following later with the picnic basket and tartan rug and watching Diana's athleticism admiringly). It had never been enough. Mrs Anderson would have contemplated anything to secure Diana for herself.

Mr William's affair with Megan Bates had given her that opportunity.

At the open gateway to the steading Mrs Anderson looked around her at the gaudy and untidy hillocks of buoys, rope, piping, plastics and pots, and at the 'Wall of Lost Soles', hardly believing how much it had extended since her last visit six months before. She carried on into the steading courtyard, on three sides of which were barns with sagging slate roofs. Despite knowing what to expect, she was astonished at the sheer volume of rubbish, astonished and upset. 'And all for what?' she muttered angrily, 'The ruination of my farm.' Under Duncan's thirty year stewardship, there had never been a profit and her share remained at 15%.

On the fourth side of the quadrangle was the back door to the house. When she'd lived there with her parents it had been the only entrance they used. It was the same with Duncan, possibly the only tradition that had remained unchanged. As she crossed to it, two black and white cats stirred from the porch roof. They stretched, arched their spines and raised their hackles. One after the other they jumped down on to an old kitchen chair beside the back step and went careering, back legs askew, as if blown by a gale, across the yard. Mrs Anderson took a deep breath, preparing herself for the shock of what she would find inside. It was always a shock. Every time she came.

The door was unlocked as she expected. It had been the joke of the village for years: how Boyd's Farm was an open invitation to thieves; how none had ever accepted it because the house contained nothing worth stealing. The boys of the village regarded it as a rite of passage to run in and scrawl their names on the wall of the attic room before running out again.

Mrs Anderson closed the door behind her.

She went from dusty corridor to dirty hallway, from chaotic room to still more chaotic room, satisfying the urge that every so often drove her to visit the farm and to wander the house. As usual, she chewed at her cheeks at the evidence of her father's wickedness in preferring a man like Duncan over his only child. If anything, with each succeeding visit, the case against Archie Boyd grew along with the increasing decay she witnessed. And so it was today. Ten minutes after going indoors she was back in the yard, her face white, her mood sour, the creeping tendency of a daughter to blame herself and to exonerate her father laid to rest for another while. Usually she would hurry away to the Poltown road to avoid an encounter with Duncan on his way back from the beach. On this occasion, however, she took the old kitchen chair from the back door and placed it in the shade against the wall by the steading entrance. There she waited for Duncan, for the cousin she hadn't addressed since he took up residence at Boyd's Farm. She sat erect, and with her hands folded on her lap, her demeanour composed even when she saw him approaching across the field.

'Hello Duncan,' she said before he realised she was there. Her voice startled him. He lifted his face, the first time she had looked on it in three decades. She could hardly find anything remaining of the good-looking young man she recollected.

185

The creature before her now resembled a scarecrow. His clothes were nothing but rags and his face scored with deep fissures as well as being blotched with stubble. His eyes were red-rimmed and sunken, his nose bigger than it should be and oddly bulbous at the end, his face somehow smaller. While he gathered himself, she examined him as a pathologist would a corpse, looking for cause and effect. How, she wondered, could a man's skin be so lined? What limit was there to the degradation of a living human body?

Duncan peered at her. 'Is that you Mary?'

No-one had called her by her first name for years; it caught her by surprise to find she was still known by it at Boyd's Farm.

'Yes, it is,' she replied. 'How are you Duncan?' She looked him with disapproval and Duncan seemed at a loss to know what to say next. He coughed and fidgeted and looked at the sky.

'I hear you've had a visitor,' she said.

'I have?' His eyebrows arched as though confused by which of his many visitors she might have meant.

'Yes.'

'About the windfarm?' he asked. 'I told them not to come back.' He pointed towards her father's old tractor. 'This land is NOT for sale.' He smirked at his cleverness.

She had heard this about him, that he was just a boy at heart, a show off. 'No, not about the windfarm,' she said. 'A young woman, a pretty young woman.'

A worry frown formed across his forehead. Mrs Anderson found it surprising there was room given the competition from all the other lines and wrinkles.

'Her name is Violet Wells, Jim tells me. At least I think it was Jim. Well, someone told me . . .'

Duncan held his head to one side, listening

'. . . that she's been asking you about Megan Bates. You remember Megan don't you Duncan? Didn't you take quite a fancy to her?'

Instead of answering the question, he fidgeted some more, one moment picking at his fingers, the next becoming side-tracked by the cats which had reappeared to welcome him. They rubbed against his legs, tails raised, and made a chorus of meows.

'You're not very forthcoming, are you?' she scolded. 'Well, Duncan, has Violet Wells been asking you about Megan Bates or has she not?'

Duncan picked at his teeth, rubbed at his lips and blinked. She could tell he wanted to run away – *so* like a child.

'I wonder why, after all this time. How long would it be, Duncan? Twenty-five years, more? A long time anyway.'

Duncan had folded his arms. He hugged them to his chest. 'I didn't kill her. I didn't kill her.' He shouted it at her, his eyes angry, his neck bulging. After his outburst, he seemed anxious at what he had done as if he hadn't meant to say anything, certainly not that.

Mrs Anderson raised her eyebrows. 'My goodness Duncan. Where did that come from?'

There was silence for a moment.

'Poor Duncan, you didn't really know what you were getting into, did you?' she said eventually. 'I do hope Violet Wells doesn't start it up all over again, all that nastiness with the police. Oh, I do hope not Duncan, for your sake.'

She scowled at him, then stood up and brushed down her coat. 'Well, I must leave you, Duncan. A lovely day like this deserves a good walk.'

Examining the field in front of her she said, 'What a mess you've made of the farm.' Then, looking back over her shoulder: 'I always knew you would.' She took a few steps. 'If you want my advice, you should sell up while you have the chance, before the police come searching through Megan's things again, before they come looking for you, Duncan.'

His head was still shaking.

'Duncan,' she snapped. 'Are you listening to me?'

'Yes Mary,' he replied, a chastened boy.

'I hope you are because this land will never be worth anything again if BRC takes its money elsewhere.'

Without further ado she started back across the field. When she passed the gate-pillars, her hand reached out to touch the smooth curve of the stone. She read the sign: *Boyd's Farm*, her farm. She'd had to bear its loss. Why shouldn't Duncan suffer in the same way? Returning along the Brae driveway, she appeared a figure revived, her head high and defiant. She had found other uses for Violet Wells. Alexandra's nemesis could also be Duncan's torment and, just possibly, Mrs Anderson's salvation. By all accounts, BRC had raised its 'final' offer for Boyd's Farm to half a million. Her share would be £75,000, sufficient to sustain her in Gardener's Cottage for her life-time. If only Duncan would sell.

CHAPTER 11

The northwest tip of Orasaigh Island overlooked the narrow entrance to the sea loch. Cal leant against a large boulder which stood sentry at the shore. From force of habit he watched the lethargic progress of seaweed floating on the ebb tide. Not even two knots, he estimated, maybe only one. Violet was nearby on a little gravel beach, gazing towards distant mountains. His assessment of her had changed in the time it had taken to traverse the island. He'd started out imagining she might be having some sort of personal crisis, that she'd escaped to the west coast (why else would she rent an isolated cottage on a tidal island?) only to find trouble had followed her. He didn't know precisely what form trouble took: he imagined an ex-lover or an ex-husband, maybe a stalker, something of that kind. Whatever it was, he'd assumed she was the one being pursued.

Now he wasn't so sure.

When they set off along the track, Cal said, 'Don't worry. I'm not going to say another word about last night.'

She sounded relieved. A rest from it would be good, she replied. It would be nice just to enjoy the day.

'So what should we talk about?' he asked.

'Anything,' she said. 'Anything apart from me.'

The track narrowed and he hung back to let her go first. When he caught up again, she said, 'Tell me. How do you always know when the tides will be?'

It was his business to know, he said. But it was also his interest. As a boy, he had always been mad on everything to do with the sea. He had studied oceanography at university and had recently completed a PhD. His enthusiasm had never left him, though sometimes it got the better of him. That was why he'd shouted when the woman from BRC was speaking at the public meeting. He didn't believe in big corporations being handed large areas of sea. Nor did he like what happened to people like Duncan Boyd who got in their way.

She nodded, seeming to agree with him, and asked, 'Is it what you do for a living, science of the seas, that sort of thing?'

'When I was studying it used to be that but now most of what I do is ocean tracking – using tide and wind data and computer programs to calculate where all kinds of flotsam originated, where it will go.'

She asked him if he worked for the government or a laboratory. Neither, he told her; he was self-employed. He had a variety of clients – from environmental organisations who hired him to identify ocean polluters to distraught parents, husbands or wives desperate to recover the body of a drowned and missing relative or spouse. The balance of his work had changed in the last year or two: more of it was bodies lost at sea, less of it environmental work. The change happened because he had been involved in some high profile missing body cases which had attracted media attention. People had got to know his name. Also, because of the recession, fewer marine charities had spare money to mount investigations. His business was called Flotsam and Jetsam Investigations because of his environmental work but he was thinking of changing the name. The media dubbed him 'The Sea Detective', so he was toying with *The Sea Detective Agency*.

'I've already changed my email but I'm not sure about it. Maybe a name with detective agency in it would attract more cranks and hoaxers.'

Violet thought it was a good name, easy to remember. 'Do you prefer environmental work to tracking bodies?'

'Yeah,' Cal said. 'I suppose I do, or did. Identifying the tanker that has spilt oil or the container ship that has lost cargo overboard and hasn't bothered to alert anyone. There's a satisfaction in that. Finding the guilty . . .'

As they walked on Cal said that missing bodies cases were 'well, a bit different.'

192

'How different?'

'Oh, just about in every way. The clients for a start.'

It was his rule, he said, to emphasise that nothing was certain. All he could provide were possible search areas. A few metres of sea could make all the difference to where a body would beach, *whether* it would beach.

'More often than not all that's keeping people going is the hope of finding a body.' He sighed, a long exhalation. 'I don't know what's worse anymore, finding a body after it has started to decompose or *not* finding a body.'

Those were the only outcomes possible by the time he was called in. Either he found a horror story and destroyed someone's happy memories of their child, spouse or lover, or he drew a blank and robbed them of hope.

'I didn't realise that at first. Now I do, I dread the effect, one way or the other. I suppose that's why I'm here.' He glanced at her again, checking her reaction. 'Avoiding the issue . . . running away.' He hoped this would give her an opening to talk about herself.

She went quiet after that and they walked on. He assumed he'd lost her until she asked, 'How does it work, tracking things I mean?'

Normally he wouldn't take on a job, he explained, unless he had three pieces of information: the 'what, where and when'. He needed a description of the target object. For example, if it was a body, whether it was wearing a life jacket or not; if it was a boat or a yacht, what type and size, whether it had a sail up; and so on. Knowing exactly where the target – he apologised for using the word – went into the sea or where it was last seen was also crucial. Finally, he needed to know the time: when it went into the sea. Having the precise position and time allowed him to work out the tides and the winds.

'What happens if you know 'what' but you only have an estimate of where and when?' she said.

'There's more risk of error. Otherwise there are too many variables. Where things go and at what speed depends on the strength and direction of the currents and the wind, on the size and shape of the object you're tracking, how much of it is above the water, how much below. The Coastguards will tell you wind has a bigger influence on where things go than the current.'

He looked at her to check she was still interested. She was.

'Go on,' she said.

'Well, very few things go straight down the wind. A lilo does because it has no traction in the water. But something with traction will go off at an angle to the wind. The divergence can be 5 degrees to 90 degrees. Once an object starts to diverge it will continue on that course until the wind changes speed or direction.'

He gave her the example of an oil tanker with a wall of steel above and below the water going off at anything up to 80 degrees, and described how at the opposite end of the scale small differences had significant consequences on an object's destination.

'What about a person?' she asked.

'You mean a body?'

'Yes.'

'It's a small target for the wind, even a body that's wearing a life jacket and bobbing up and down. It'll tend to go with the current though that doesn't mean one with a life jacket will end up in the same place as one without. Look at shoes. A left shoe will beach in a different place to a right. It's because of the different curve of the soles and the way the sea works on it.'

They had arrived at the tip of the island and Violet peeled off to the pebble beach. Cal stood by the boulder, watching her. He felt he'd been taking a test and was in the unsatisfactory position of not knowing how well he'd done; whether he'd passed or failed.

Whether trouble was pursuing Violet or whether Violet was pursuing it.

After a while, she came to join him, following a sheep's trail through low bracken, apparently deep in thought. He registered the easy way she moved, the white curve of her neck, the billow of her shirt. When she was close he said, 'The tide's out now, if you want to cross the causeway.'

She looked up and smiled. The tension seemed to have dropped from her. Perhaps it was just getting away from the gloomy atmosphere of the cottage.

'We've got half an hour haven't we?'

'About that, yes.'

She held up her right hand. In it there was a smooth white stone. 'My daughter paints them,' she said. 'She gives them to me as presents. She's called Anna. She's a sweetie. Her father ran off when I was pregnant.' She looked across the loch. 'I've never seen him again.'

He said nothing.

'Anna's being looked after by my friend Hilary. Her flat is below mine. Hilary's daughter is called Izzy. She's Anna's best friend. What else should you know? I live in Glasgow. I went to the art school and stayed on. I was brought up in Inverness. I don't have any brothers or sisters. My mother is dead . . .' She paused. 'Oh, and I have a night job in a pizza restaurant so my education paid off big-time.' She smiled. 'That's some of the important stuff. Most of it really . . .'

Her smile faded. 'Actually, there's more. But you're better off not knowing it.'

Cal watched the reflection of the hills in the loch and wondered at the significance of the last few minutes, of Violet telling him the day-to-day details of her life. Had he passed the test? What did it mean when a woman volunteered her life story when not so long before she had been monosyllabic and resentful. If he asked her about last night would she revert to resentful silence?

'Last night . . .' He risked it. 'Was that Anna's father?'

'No. Absolutely not.' She answered easily and without umbrage. 'He's never even seen Anna. She's four. He's gone. I don't know where he is and he doesn't know where I am. Last night . . . I don't know who that was.'

'Do you know what it was about?'

She shook her head. 'No. No I don't.'

'Not some guy trying it on . . .'

'I don't know. It might have been. I don't think so.'

'What else is there?'

'Something to do with why I'm here . . .'

'Which is?'

She glanced quickly at him again, as if weighing up whether she should tell him or not. She shook her head. 'I can't.'

Cal waited. 'Ok, so what now?'

Violet said she had something to ask him. 'What you were saying . . . about things floating on the sea . . . I hadn't thought about it before . . . how likely is it that a hat and a handbag would come ashore together . . . a raffia sunhat with a broad brim and a shoulder bag, quite compact, leather, with a zip-up container?'

'They went into the water together?'

'Yes.'

'Did they come ashore at the same time?

'Yes, I think so.'

'Was there a wind?'

'I don't know.'

'Were they near each other or just in the same general area?'

'They were close.'

'Where?'

'In North Bay.'

'Do you know the time and date?'

'I know the date.' She studied him. 'They were found on Sunday September 11. Late morning . . . I don't have an exact time.'

'Last week, you mean?'

'No.' She hesitated. 'You'll think I'm weird. It was 1983.'

'Not weird. Unusual,' he replied. The temptation was to say more. Pretty. Attractive.

'It just never occurred to me,' she said. 'Not until the walk over here and listening to you, the stuff about objects with different shapes following different courses.'

'I don't suppose you have the hat and bag.'

'No.'

'Do you know where and when the hat and the bag went into the water?'

She appeared relieved at the question, at him taking her seriously. 'Not precisely. Somewhere in South Bay. When? Around 8am on September 10 . . .'

'And you're sure about 1983?'

'Yes.'

'So you want to know how likely it is these two objects would turn up together?'

She nodded.

'You're not going to tell me why?'

'No.'

'But you will if there's any more trouble, if you're in danger?'

'I don't know.'

He wanted to hold her, to kiss her.

'Ok,' he said. 'I'm going to need my laptop, and some oranges.'

At Violet's request, he stopped the pickup at the entrance to Brae. She said she would walk the rest of the way. The driveway was pretty and anyway she was early – her appointment to pick up her shopping wasn't for another twenty minutes. She might only have met Mrs Anderson the day before but she was certain she knew this much about her: she preferred visitors to be punctual. 'And she disapproves of everyone given the opportunity.'

'You'll be all right?' Cal asked.

'With Mrs Anderson?' She misunderstood him deliberately.

'You know what I mean.'

She did, she said. 'I'll be fine . . . Really I will.'

He considered offering to stay with her but instead said 'ok' and told her he planned to drive to the general store. Then he would try out a few things at North Bay, to get a feel for the way the sea worked. He would buy something for lunch while he was shopping in Poltown. They could have a picnic on the beach, light a fire, whatever.

'I'd like that,' she answered, climbing out and shutting the door.

'Give me a call,' he shouted through the open window.

A smile lit up her face, a look of happiness, the first he'd seen. He was still working out what it meant when she disappeared into the shadows of an avenue of ash trees.

Driving into Poltown, he reminded himself of Rachel, his ex-wife, how similar in looks if not character she was to Violet. He banged his open hand against the steering wheel. Why didn't he learn from his mistakes? There had been enough of them. The names came to him like a parade of failure. Apart from Rachel, there were Lydia, Maria and Kate. He remembered Rachel writing bitterly to him before their divorce, saying he was just another geek with a hobby, that girls knew what to expect when they got involved with a train-spotter or some dumb bloke who boosted his testosterone by watching repeats of Top Gear, but with Cal ocean-ography and all his 'crap about the sea' was a masquerade. It made him out to be some kind of romantic hero when he wasn't. As soon as he was in a relationship he tried to escape from it. It wasn't deliberate on his part, she had conceded, but still, breaking up with him had left her with a nasty after-taste of deceit. 'Whoever wrote no man is an island clearly hadn't met you.'

At that stage, she hadn't even known about his affair.

Cal turned left, into Poltown's first cul-de-sac, and pulled up outside the shop which used to be twin garages – another architectural misapprehension inflicted on the populace. For the most part the residents had little use for garages since few were prosperous enough to own cars. 'Run by the community for the community' was the legend underneath the sign which proclaimed 'Poltown General Stores'. The opening hours were painted in white on the door, along with an indecipherable scrawl of luminous pink and yellow graffiti which extended across the plate glass window. All that was missing was a metal grille, Cal reckoned, and it could be dropped into any big city sink estate without it seeming out of place.

Cal noticed a group of teenagers sitting on a front step opposite. They were watching him in silence. He took the precaution of locking the pickup.

Inside, the shop was a cross between a small warehouse and a car-boot sale. The floor was concrete and the walls lined with a type of shelving Cal associated with DIY stores. The centre of the shop (the car boot sale) was filled by end-to-end trestle tables on which were trays of bread, rolls, fruit and vegetables, boxes of crisps, bags of dried dog food, stacks of cat food tins and, incongruously, a collection of red and gold 'Santa Claus Crackers' (whether relics of Christmas past or stocked too early for Christmas to come Cal wasn't sure). The bread was white only, he noticed in passing, and the selection of fresh fruit and vegetables beside a display of Pot Noodle and packet soups.

Cal's other impression was of a group of people gathered at the back of the shop. There were half a dozen of them, four men and two women. One of the women sat behind a till around which newspapers were arranged. The others stood leaning against the counter or shelves, talking.

'Hi,' he offered in their general direction. He took a wire basket from the stack at the door and began to search for the ingredients of a picnic. He put rolls into a paper bag, three over-ripe tomatoes into another and rejected two droopy lettuces before selecting a third. Snatches of conversation drifted over to him. It was about the meeting the night before, who had hit whom, who had been hurt, who had thrown the first punch and who had seen what.

'Excuse me.' The discussion stopped. Six faces turned to Cal. 'Are there any oranges?'

'I took them off this morning,' the woman at the till replied, 'because they'd gone a bit soft.'

'Just like you then, eh Helen,' a man leaning back against the counter growled. He had a thin, stubbly face and a mocking expression. Cal recognised him from the night before. In all the panic and commotion, he'd been the odd one out. Instead of running for the door, he'd stayed in his seat observing the melee with detached interest. Cal hadn't paid him much attention – his concern then had been Violet.

Cal ignored the remark. 'Have you still got them?'

Helen glanced nervously at Cal and then at the man who had joked at her expense. 'Aye,' she said uncertainly, 'they're on the floor, by me.'

'Can I see?'

'You wouldn't want to eat any of them.' She bent down to lift up the box and showed it to Cal who was approaching the counter, 'Well I wouldn't at any rate.'

He saw what the woman meant: they were discoloured and shrunken, like collapsed old faces. 'Those are perfect,' Cal said, ignoring the surprised reactions of his audience. 'Can I have them?'

'All of them?'

'Yes.'

The woman peered at them again in case she'd made a mistake about their condition. 'Are you sure, son?'

'Yeah, they're good.' Cal went to the other side of the shop to buy juice and bottles of water. While he was away from the counter he heard Helen wonder what she should charge since the oranges were 'five minutes away from the bin.' She asked nervously, 'What should I do, Davie?'

'Why do you want them?' Cal recognised Davie's growl. It had a distinctive and hard edge.

'Nothing interesting . . .' Cal picked up a packet of biscuits.

'You were at the meeting last night.' It was less an observation, more an accusation.

'I was there, yes.' Cal returned to the counter with his basket, feeling Davie's eyes on him. After Helen began recording his purchases, Davie said, 'I always remember a face.'

Cal shrugged and extracted a £20 note from his pocket and unfolded it.

'So what brings you to Poltown?' Davie persisted.

'The sea, the scenery, usual things . . .' His answer was off-hand. 'Isn't that why everyone comes here?' He put his money on the counter, while Helen worried aloud about the unresolved problem of charging for the oranges.

'Half price? What do you say?' The others mumbled in agreement. 'Half price is fine,' Cal reassured her.

'Full whack,' Davie said. 'He pays full whack.'

'For them?' Helen asked doubtfully, holding one up, inspecting it, glancing at Davie, wondering what was going on, what she had missed. 'I wouldn't feel right charging 35p for that.'

Cal was aware of a change in the atmosphere, as were the others. They were looking at Cal and then at Davie as if they expected something to happen.

'Don't worry about it,' Cal said. '35p is fine.' He'd rather pay £3.50 for 10 oranges than argue about it.

'I'll put them in a carrier for you,' Helen said helpfully.

'Make him pay for that too,' Davie ordered, '50p a bag.'

Helen glanced nervously at Cal. *That's all right,* he nodded back and handed over £10. She shot another anxious look at Davie. Her face showed concern at the bewildering turn of events, at her inadvertent role in what was happening, at Davie turning this into a confrontation. Cal had the impression she'd witnessed similar scenes before and that she knew what might be coming next.

Once Helen has finished packing Cal's groceries, she counted out his change, dropping it into his open hand. When Cal lifted up the full carrier bag in his other hand, Davie asked, 'Is that your vehicle outside?'

'It could be,' Cal replied without looking up.

'Didn't I see it at South Bay the other day?'

'It's possible.' He might as well have told him to mind his own business. Cal walked deliberately and slowly towards the door. He lingered for a few moments beside the community notice board to show he wasn't in any hurry before going outside. As he drove away he glanced in his wing mirror and saw Davie standing in the doorway of the shop, legs apart, mobile phone at his ear. Cal opened his window, extended his arm, and raised his middle finger in the air. 'Fuck off, Davie.'

Along the west wall of the garden Violet found a place where she could not be seen from the drive or from the track leading to Mrs Anderson's house. She could kill time there without the complication of the Hamiltons or anyone else noticing her and prying into what she was doing. Having ten minutes to waste gave her the chance to ring Mr Anwar, a duty call that had been on her conscience. Usually she was slow to make judgements about peoples' characters. About Cal, for example, she had yet to make up her mind, an indecision which had a number of causes: caution about involving him in something she did not yet understand, reticence about divulging her purpose, wariness about romantic entanglements (she suspected Cal's interest) and his recent habit (in so far as she could tell his habits) of impetuousness, of saying aloud what he thought. About Mr Anwar, by contrast, she had made a decision quickly. As soon as she had met him, she'd warmed to him. At the time she thought it was his good manners which won her over. On reflection she realised it was his consideration, the trait which he displayed again once she started to explain who she was and why she was ringing. 'Do you remember? I gave you tea without milk and you met my daughter Anna.'

'Miss Wells, my dear, I was thinking about you, wondering how you were getting on. How are you?'

His quiet civility brought an end to her gabbling. She made a little sound in appreciation. 'I'm well, thank you, Mr Anwar. And you?'

'Oh, it doesn't matter about me,' he replied after a hesitation which Violet noticed, a stumble she regarded as uncharacteristic. She found herself saying, 'You matter very much Mr Anwar, after the kindness you have shown me. Very much indeed.'

Immediately, she worried that Mr Anwar would be offended by her effusiveness. To her surprise, it affected him in a different way altogether. Instead of the polite deflection she expected, he told her he'd been foolish and he mentioned people he had wronged in some way or other. Someone called Mr Hunter cropped up a few times. Then there was Meera, and, the only one she recognised, Shereen. When she heard it, she interrupted him. 'Shereen's your daughter isn't she Mr Anwar?' He talked through her question, raising his voice, which was so untypical of the unassuming Mr Anwar she knew that she said, 'Where are you Mr Anwar? Are you at work?' She heard his breathing and then a different sound, a distant muttering, as though he had put the phone down and he was pacing around the room. Then she heard a noise like paper being torn.

'Mr Anwar, Mr Anwar,' she said. 'Mr Anwar? Are you all right?'

'Shereen will be angry with me.'

'Why?'

'I've torn her poster.'

'Mr Anwar, are you in Shereen's room?' She heard him take a deep breath.

'Should I be somewhere else?'

'At work?' Violet tried.

'Ah, work,' he replied.

'What's happened, Mr Anwar?'

'I'm sorry Miss Wells . . .'

'What have you got to be sorry about? You've

been wonderful to me.' She almost mentioned the money but worried it might offend him. Then she said, 'It's something to do with me, isn't it?' His silence made her think she was right. 'What's happened? Please tell me? I couldn't bear it if it's something I've done.'

'It's nothing you've done, dear Miss Wells.'

She could hear he was trying to protect her. 'It's better I know Mr Anwar, really.'

'I suppose it is,' he conceded. 'You've been to see a police officer.'

'Yes, a retired one. He was the man who led the inquiry into my mother's disappearance.'

'He reported your visit to the police authorities and they passed it on to my employers.'

'What has happened?'

'I have been suspended.'

'That's awful. Because of me?'

'Because I was stupid, Miss Wells. Because I disobeyed my superior. Not because of you.'

'I'm so sorry Mr Anwar.'

'You must go now, Miss Wells. You must carry on. But be careful. It pains me to say this but sometimes people prefer to let things lie than to suffer the discomfort of unearthing the truth.'

'Who, Mr Anwar, who? The police? Tell me, Mr Anwar.'

The phone went dead. Mr Anwar had gone. She rang again but there was no answer. She left a message, promising to visit him as soon as she had discovered the truth about her mother. She'd bring

Anna too. 'We'd love to do that,' she said, 'and look after yourself . . . please Mr Anwar, dear Mr Anwar.'

She stared at her phone, impotent in the face of the havoc she had wreaked on his unassuming life. She had an unsettling feeling that forces were gathering against her, the police, the threatening man at the end of the public meeting – and that her clumsiness had been the cause. Standing there, hidden in the shelter of Brae's walled garden, she suddenly felt exposed. In Poltown, she realised, nothing went unnoticed, herself included. She was two minutes late for Mrs Anderson.

At South Bay, Cal opened his laptop and called up the Admiralty's tide prediction website, EasyTide. A map appeared on his screen: green for land, blue for sea, and a scattering of yellow dots around the UK coast. The dots represented ports. He scrolled across the map to the north-west of Scotland. As he hoped, there was a yellow dot in Poltown Loch. He put the cursor on it and a small rectangular box appeared with the name 'Nato jetty' on it, a legacy from before its closure when allied navies needed to know the best times for approaching and leaving the loch.

He clicked on the box and the website asked him whether he wanted historical data or a tide prediction. He opened the calendar icon and selected the year Violet was born, and a week either side of September 10th. According to Violet, that

209

was the day the hat and bag went into the sea. Two 7-day graphs filled his screen, one above the other, separated by grids of numbers. Each graph appeared as a series of blue finger-like spikes. The peak of each spike represented high tide: the base, low tide. On the first graph, the spikes grew longer day by day, the high tides climbing higher, the low tides becoming lower, and the cycle advancing towards the highest and lowest tides of all, Spring tides. On the second graph they did the opposite as the relative positions of the moon and the sun changed; as they moved out of alignment, as their gravitational influence on the sea lessened. The 10th was the first day of the second graph. At 8am, the time the hat and the bag went into the water, the tide was already flowing, building to a peak one hour and 50 minutes later. According to the graph, it reached a height of 5.2 metres.

Cal started an up-to-date search for the next seven days, this time selecting prediction. When the graph displayed, he studied that day, the 15th. The next high tide was at 17.17. It would reach 4.6 metres, lower than he'd hoped. Still, it would give him an idea. It was past noon now: he'd wait for exactly the same stage, until one hour and 50 minutes before its peak. It'd mean kicking his heels until 15.27.

Next, he called up his ocean database for information about the wind. He had columns of figures going back a century; wind speeds and directions for the entire North Atlantic. He searched back 26 years to September 10. There had been a southerly breeze on the coast around Ullapool, 10mph becoming 15 during the afternoon and moderating to 5 by nightfall. According to his live weather feed, the breeze today was a few degrees more to the west and lighter at 5mph. Cal studied a large scale map of the Poltown area. If anything, he thought, the wind direction today was more likely to push a hat or a bag ashore in North Bay than the one more than quarter of a century before.

He checked the forward tide data: the New Moon was in three days. At 07.14 that morning there would be another high tide of 5.2 metres, the same as the one in 1983. He brought up the weather. The forecast was unchanged for the rest of the week, an Indian summer they were calling it: highs of 17 or 18 degrees in the middle of the day; long sunny periods; clearing skies at night, the temperature falling sharply after sunset; light winds, between 5-15mph; shifting from south to south-south-west and back again to south. If the forecast was right, there would be three days of similar conditions. If he needed to, he could test the currents again.

His phone rang.

'Cal.' Violet dropped her voice to a whisper. 'Mrs Anderson has just started making me lunch, I'm going to be here for ages. I'm sorry.'

'Don't worry,' he said. 'Violet, I need some information from you.'

'Ok.' She sounded wary.

'How did the hat and the bag get into the water?'

'Someone put them there.'

'How far out?'

'I don't know. Whoever it was probably went deep enough to swim.'

'Is there anything else you can tell me?'

'Only that it was a woman . . .' She hesitated. 'Sorry Cal, I've got to go.'

Cal wasn't sure if Mrs Anderson had come back into the room or if Violet was protecting her secrets.

CHAPTER 12

On the map, North Bay resembled the profile of a human gargoyle. Its northern headland was ridged and hooked and had the appearance of a large, bony nose. The southern jutted out like a protruding and sharp chin, and the bay itself took the form of a toothless mouth which could no longer open wide. Standing on the hooked nose, Cal estimated the channel between the tip of the northern headland and the protrusion of the chin at less than 60 metres, a narrow opening for flotsam travelling north-east with the flow tide and returning on the ebb. In this and other respects, North Bay couldn't have been more dissimilar to its southern neighbour. Not only was it sheltered, exposed only to westerlies, it had a small beach which sloped into the sea and was protected on the landward-side by a collar of boulders. South Bay, by contrast, was open to the elements, vulnerable to any wind between south-south-west to north-north-west, with a beach which was wide, flat and long. Instead of boulders, its sweep of sand was bordered by low-lying dunes.

A length of blue rope caught Cal's attention. It

was marooned in a stagnant pool among the rocks below him. He looked around for more debris. A section of white plastic piping protruded from a tangle of seaweed by the shore but otherwise the northern headland appeared to be almost flotsam and litter-free. He skirted the bay, followed the high water mark across the beach, treading on a blue and black mosaic of broken mussel shells, until he was among the boulders by the southern shore. He noticed a detergent bottle, some bleached wooden planks, sections of rope, the remains of a lobster pot, an orange buoy (which was half-buried under seaweed) as well as two white carrier bags. Considering Duncan Boyd only cleared the neighbouring beach, there was little enough. Still there was more debris at that part of North Bay than any other: support for Cal's theory about the possibility of a slack water eddy spinning into the open mouth and of the breeze nudging flotsam ashore where the eddy's tail brought it closest to land, near to where he was standing. He made a mental note to quiz Duncan about whether North Bay had altered much in the last 26 years; whether the headlands had eroded significantly; whether there had been any other changes affecting the flow of the tides; whether it would have been more likely for flotsam to wash up on the small beach then than it was now. (Now was unlikely in his opinion.)

He made his way up a chute of loose stones to the top of the south headland, a plateau of grass interspersed with grey slabs of rock. His new vantage point provided a view of South Bay, the dunes and the road-end where he had left his pickup. Another vehicle was parked there too and three men were walking from it. As he watched, they spread out. One stayed on the dune path, the other two on the beach but fifty metres apart. By the way they were walking – their intent – he knew they were coming for him. It was like watching the closing of a net. Rather than going to meet them or attempting an escape, he stayed where he was. It gave him an advantage of sorts, if only psychological. His inactivity seemed to unnerve the two beach-walkers. They came together and parted again; and the man on the path waved at them and shouted. At least Cal knew who gave the orders, who led this little gang. He crouched and picked at the grass, as if he didn't really have a concern about the confrontation to come. Out of the corner of his eye he saw the two from the beach climb the slope of the headland.

By then his only escape was the sea.

Cal kept pulling at the grass, and throwing it into the air as if he was still more interested in the strength of the wind than his uninvited companions. Only when the leader stopped ten metres away did Cal look up.

'Mr Turnbull wants you out of Poltown,' he said.

Cal glanced at the owner of the voice; then at his side-kicks who were drawing closer. They were all of similar age and appearance; Poltown's version of rent-a-thug. Cal had seen similar at the public

215

meeting. The two to his right sported muscled necks and sloping shoulders; the one in front of him, the leader, was taller, leaner and bow-legged. His hair was short, another feature of the breed, and his face was flushed. Not, Cal guessed, from exertion but from an adrenalin rush.

'Mr Turnbull?' Cal shrugged, as if to say *who is he to tell me whether I can stay or leave?*

The leader stared past Cal, out to sea. Cal wondered if it was a pose he'd been practising in the mirror: studied nonchalance. 'You know who he is, and he knows who you are, Mr McGill.'

Cal tore at more grass. How had Turnbull discovered his name? Only Violet and Duncan Boyd knew anything about him. He'd heard triumph in the leader's voice. Had someone checked out his vehicle number, someone with friends in the police? He thought of Davie at the shop. Had it been him?

'Mr Turnbull knows the kind of work you do. He doesn't want you here, doesn't want you meddling in something that isn't your business.' He nodded to his side-kicks. 'Tam, you tell him . . .'

The thug closest to Cal swaggered, as though he'd become a favoured son. 'People do what Mr Turnbull tells them.' He tried for menace but his light voice let him down.

The leader shouted again. 'That's it Tam. Now you show Mr McGill that we don't want to come across him again.' Tam screwed up his right fist and punched it into the palm of his left hand.

'You've been watching too many bad films,' Cal said. Tam took a step towards him.

'Not now, Tam,' the leader shouted. 'Later. You'll get your chance later.'

'Violet, it's Cal. Ring me when you leave Mrs Anderson's.' Should he warn her to stay away from the Poltown road, in case Turnbull was looking for her too? Perhaps he had already found her – had it been his thug who attacked her? It seemed to be Turnbull's form.

He waited for Tam and Co to drive away before dropping down the flank of the headland to South Bay. Apart from worrying about Violet, he was also concerned about the pickup, whether his departing visitors had taken the opportunity to show him something of their capabilities. But, when he arrived at the road-end, the vehicle seemed to be untouched. Looking through the windows, his laptop, cameras, binoculars and other equipment were as he'd left them on the back seat. He checked the tyres but none had been slashed or damaged. By now it was after 3pm. In less than half an hour the tide would be perfect.

Among the disorderly jumble in the pickup, he found a waterproof bag with a strap hanging from one corner. He filled it with the oranges he'd bought. By pressing them in, he managed to pack eight, leaving two behind. Stripped to his boxers, he crossed the beach to the sea. When he was in the shallows he stopped and put his right foot through the bag's strap, pulled it above his knee, and made it tight. He removed two oranges, clipped it shut and carried on into the water until it was lapping his thighs. In case the woman discarded her hat and bag straight away, he dropped one orange there and the next in water a little deeper. The first gave an impression of a nervous child on a swimming lesson. It moved closer to Cal. The other orange was already drifting, parallel to the shore.

How far did she wade before swimming? How far did she swim? How strong was she? What distance could she have gone? The last two were questions he never asked his clients, not any more. When he used to, when he was new to missing body cases, they caused too much distress. As soon as he'd asked them, his clients imagined their son, daughter, husband or wife fighting for life, swimming until their strength was spent, dying from exhaustion and in despair. Now he tried to find out the answers in other ways. He asked if the missing person could swim and whether a life jacket had been worn. Other factors affecting the distance someone might travel before death he researched for himself: water temperature, weather and the strength of tidal currents. Also, he tended to avoid discussing what might happen after death. In his experience, his clients imagined the body floating, the water lapping round it: peace at last. When often it sank, and sometimes remained sunk. Mostly, it returned to the surface some days or weeks later, the gases of decomposition making it buoyant again. On this detail, Cal generally said nothing.

He swam breast stroke, then a slow crawl. He counted to 50 before stopping. Treading water, he reached for the bag and removed two more oranges. He released them one after the other, letting them bob to the surface. He drifted with them wondering at the woman, what she was doing, why she'd put her hat and bag into the sea. What was Violet's interest?

He swam, counting once more to 50 before releasing two more oranges: one beside him, the other thrown a little way ahead of him. And counting to 50 again, he did the same. He turned and swam back to the beach, trying to recall when he'd last used oranges. A year or two before he'd studied oceanography at the Scottish Marine Institute near Oban, he thought. He'd been reading an American school text about ocean currents and a formula for measuring their speed by using oranges. They were cheap, biodegradable as well as visible, all of which appealed to him at that age and stage. And they worked.

Back ashore, he removed the bag from his leg, and walked up the sand. He was dry by the time he opened the pickup's back door. Finding his binoculars, he scanned the bay. Despite the distance, he spotted two oranges: one close in, and in danger of beaching, another 100 metres offshore and drifting towards North Bay. He put on jeans, a cotton shirt and trainers. Clutching his binoculars, he went back towards North Bay. On the way he worked out how long the oranges should take to reach the gargoyle's mouth.

The distance was about a kilometre. He estimated the tidal current at between two to four knots. In theory one of the oranges could be off North Bay in eight minutes or so. But there'd be eddies on the way and other invisible obstacles. Back on the headland he found a rock to sit against. He spotted two oranges, both a few hundred metres away, still off South Bay. He marked them against rocks at the end of the point and watched their progress. Another sweep with the binoculars located one more, nearer to the shore than the others. It looked as though it was on course to pass close by the headland. Cal checked the time. It was 16.47. He was hoping one orange would be off the point at 17.17, just after the tide had reached its peak and the volume of water piling up against the head-land had reached its maximum. It was then an eddy might curl into the bay, carrying any flotsam with it. His phone beeped, his screen lit up. Violet had sent a text. She was on her way. Apologies, she added. She'd left Mrs Anderson and was calling on Duncan Boyd. She was crossing the field to his farm. Cal wondered why, but he was thankful she hadn't run into Tam and the gang.

He messaged back, 'I'm at North Bay. Text when you're leaving Boyd's Farm. I'll look out for you.'

★   ★   ★

The lunch was still on the table; the spoon in the cottage pie, the gravy congealed on Violet's dirty plate as well as Mrs Anderson's; the glasses of water where they'd left them, one half-empty, the other hardly touched. The napkins too: Violet's folded and placed beside her clean knife; Mrs Anderson's sitting like a collapsed tent where she'd dropped it as Violet abruptly excused herself. Mrs Anderson watched her go and hadn't moved since, apart from the tremor of a pulse in her neck, an occasional flicker of her eyelids and her left hand kneading its companion on her lap. Like good food, some things were best savoured slowly; the thought of Violet Wells claiming back her mother's belongings, of her taking them from Duncan, being one.

So Mrs Anderson remained in her seat while her mind fluttered restlessly, reviewing her encounter with Violet, teasing at it for errors. Could she have phrased things better? Had her tone been right? Had she sounded sufficiently surprised at Violet's interest in Megan Bates; sufficiently credulous at Violet's 'mother' being an 'old friend' of Megan's; appropriately reticent but yet matter-of-fact about Mr William's affair? Should she have broached the subject of Megan's clothes and her other possessions in the way she had?

Violet had wondered what Megan Bates was like. What kind of woman was she? Mrs Anderson deflected the question. 'Why don't you ask Duncan about her?'

'I have,' Violet replied.

'Did he show you her things?' Mrs Anderson put on a disapproving frown, somewhere between shame at passing on tittle-tattle and an apology for being so dim-witted as not to have mentioned it earlier.

'What things?' Violet asked.

'Her clothes, other possessions; furniture and some books I think.' Mrs Anderson sounded unsure.

Violet looked shocked at this revelation.

'Oh dear have I said something wrong?'

'No, not at all . . .' Violet said quickly. Then, after a pause, she asked in a puzzled voice, 'Her clothes? Why would he have those?'

'Apparently, Duncan cleared Orasaigh Cottage after Megan's death,' Mrs Anderson continued. 'I don't know whose idea that was. Diana's I suppose.' She pursed her lips in disapproval.

'Go on,' Violet urged.

Mrs Anderson sighed, as though Violet was dragging it out of her. 'Well, you know Duncan was suspected of killing her?'

'No, I didn't!' Violet had said.

'That was before the police announced she'd committed suicide.' Mrs Anderson made a face.

'You don't think she did.'

'Oh, I don't know if she did or not.' Mrs Anderson stopped to stare out of the window, as though someone might be there, listening. 'There were whispers about suicide being a convenient

222

outcome for the Turnbulls. They didn't want police taking Poltown apart in a murder inquiry, especially not police from out of the area, detectives from Inverness who wouldn't have known the set-up here.'

'Because the police would have found something?'

Mrs Anderson closed and opened her eyes. That's what people were saying, the gesture meant.

'Could Duncan have killed her?' Violet asked.

'I can't imagine he did,' Mrs Anderson replied. 'Though . . .' She'd waited long enough. The time had come to tell Violet.

'What?'

'It's one matter keeping her things if he could make use of them . . .' She glanced at Violet letting her see her distaste, watching for her reaction. 'But her clothes, the hat and bag, what would he want with those?'

'What hat and bag?'

'The ones that came ashore, the ones Duncan said he found in North Bay.'

'He's got *those*.'

'Yes, that's what I mean.'

'How?'

'The police didn't need them anymore, once they'd *decided* on suicide.' Mrs Anderson loaded 'decided' with cynicism. 'Megan didn't have any next of kin so they brought the hat and bag to Brae – they knew Mr William was the father of the child Megan had been carrying. Diana answered the door. I don't think she ever told Mr William about it, but she took the hat and bag and gave them to Duncan with all of Megan's other possessions.'

Violet stared at her. 'He's still got them?'

'I don't know, but I imagine so.' She paused and looked at Violet. 'According to people in the village,' she continued hesitantly, 'he keeps a room upstairs in her memory. Her things are there. Apparently some boys were in the house for a dare and they found the room . . . all neat and tidy.' Mrs Anderson sniffed. 'The only part of the house that is, I dare say.'

Violet put down her napkin, said 'excuse me' and hurried to the door.

The last time Violet had been in Mrs Anderson's house, she had been a tiny baby, her face screwed up and crying, blood smeared on her, and on Diana. 'So much blood,' Mrs Anderson said quietly as Violet ran along the track beside the walled garden.

CHAPTER 13

The clap and clatter of pigeon wings resonated around the courtyard. The birds had burst from a broken skylight and were flying in frantic loops and circles above Violet's head. 'Mr Boyd. It's Violet.' She spun around, directing her shouts at one side of the steading, then at another. 'Duncan . . . Mr Boyd.'

'Where are you?' she said.

Meeting him, he'd seemed so guileless, a 'poor soul' as her friend Hilary might say. Harmless, Violet had thought, even sweet in his way. Looking about her, at the dereliction and disarray, she questioned why a man like Duncan Boyd had kept her mother's clothes and possessions for 26 years; what he wanted with them, what seedy purpose. Like a chill, the atmosphere of the steading seeped into her bones and made her think its owner capable of anything, even murder. The place was sinister, she decided, and so was the man who brought it to such a state of ruination. Like Poltown, she thought, where nothing was what it seemed.

'Where are you?' she said again as though she was

playing hide and seek with a malevolent child. She backed across the yard towards the farmhouse door. It was ajar. 'Duncan?' she inquired into the gap between door and jamb and stepped away, as if expecting him to jump out and surprise her.

She jumped instead, in anticipation.

'Where are you?' she asked again softly, the sound of her voice keeping her companion.

'Hello.' Her knuckles rapped on the wood of the door. 'Duncan. It's Violet. Are you there?'

She pushed open the door and went inside.

The smell was what assailed her first – cats – and then the mess. She cupped a hand over her nose to stop herself gagging and picked her way across the porch. The floor was strewn with old and muddy boots of all kinds and lined with scuffed newspapers on which were three chipped enamel plates covered with stale and smelly scraps of food. A black and white cat was lying on an old kitchen chair. It watched her, blinked and started to purr as Violet disappeared into the gloom of a passageway. She took a deep breath. Stale air: it tasted of decay and dustiness. She imagined white bones. 'I love you Anna,' she whispered, wishing she was back in Glasgow with her daughter, wishing she was anywhere but here.

She emerged into a rectangular hallway, slowly, a step at a time, letting the passageway provide cover and the prospect of escape until she was sure she was alone. She looked at the chipped flagstone floor, at broken lumps of plaster scattered across it, at the peeling and cratered walls, the cracked ceiling, at the stairs to her right.

Mrs Anderson had said the room was upstairs.

She crossed the hall and climbed them two at a time. At the top, she experienced something approaching exhilaration. Across the landing, against the far wall, under a faded watercolour of a fishing boat on a stormy sea, was a chest of drawers. Violet glanced to its left, at the closed door.

A name was stencilled on it. Megan.

She gasped.

Until then, her mother's name had belonged in the past – in the conversations Violet had had, in the yellowing newspaper cuttings given to her by Mr Anwar. Seeing it on the door was the first time she'd encountered it in the present. How hope waited for just such a thing, how quick it was to flare.

She had to remind herself, *she's dead, she's dead, she's dead,* and crossed the landing to the unpainted wooden door. Cracks ran up and down the grain and one was wide enough for Violet to see daylight through it and to feel the faintest puff of fresh air on her cheek. Turning the knob, the door swung open onto a tidy and well-furnished room. What would be normal and unremarkable in any other house was a shock among the chaos of Boyd's Farm. Violet stood in the doorway transfixed, her eyes skipping from one item of furniture to the next. Pretty floral curtains flapped in the draught from an open window. Below, there was a mahogany dressing table, bleached by the sun on which were laid out a hair brush, hand mirror, scent and nail varnish bottles as well as an open box of tissues. To the left of the dressing table was a wardrobe, and on the opposite wall an iron bed-stead with a patterned cover. A teddy bear reclined against the bulge of a pillow. A book was on the bedside table. A fabric book-mark extended from its pages. Was it hers? 'She's dead,' Violet repeated. Everything in the room suggested otherwise, that her mother had gone out but would soon be coming back.

After stepping inside, she shut the door quietly but grabbed at the handle as soon as she'd let it go because she had to support herself on something. Behind the door was a cot, its mattress sealed in the manufacturer's polythene wrapping. A large brown paper parcel tied with string rested against the headboard. Someone had written across it 'for baby'. Violet reached for the side of the cot. Her fingers slid over the tail board to the side rail. Then she touched the parcel again before lifting it and putting it on the bare planks of the floor and kneeling beside it. Instead of wasting time undoing the knot, she slipped off the string and exposed the dark brown of the paper which it had covered. The remainder was bleached and pale, indicating how long ago it had been wrapped, how long it had been there. After peeling away three layers of paper, Violet laid the contents around her: six old-fashioned cotton nappies, two sleep suits, two white cot sheets. Everything in white, she imagined, because when her mother bought them she hadn't known whether her baby would be a boy or a girl.

Looking under the cot, Violet found an upturned baby bath and a nappy bucket.

She stared about her, her face set in an expression of puzzlement, her fingers kneading the soft fabric of the sleep suits. She was looking for an explanation for this room and why it was clean and aired, the bed made, everything neat, tidy and welcoming, as though Megan Bates lived there. Why, Violet asked again, when the rest of the house was falling down?

She got to her feet, approached the wardrobe and turned the key. The dark-wood doors opened together. Violet let them swing wide on their hinges. On the left was a series of drawers with half-moon hand holds; on the right, a rail on which hung a modest collection of dresses and jackets. She was surprised by how few there were, and by their muted colours, a mixture of creams, greens and browns. Not only had she expected her mother's wardrobe, if that was what it was, to be full to bursting but also for her to have a collection of brightly coloured clothes to match her reputation. Violet's impression of her mother had been formed by snatches of information – the white dress and the sun hat she had worn the day she disappeared and the eye-witness's comment to the police about her being sure it was Megan Bates because 'no-one else wears summer dresses in Poltown'. Neither of these suggested to Violet that her mother had been anything other than showy.

What was in the wardrobe lent a different impression and left Violet confused as well as ashamed of her previous rush to judgement.

She touched a dress, then another and another until she had stroked them all, her fingers sampling the fabrics, this one silk, that cotton, another wool. From habit she registered which was which, though her thoughts were on another attribute of these clothes, how once they would have touched her mother's skin, how her fingers were a slither of fabric away, how it was as close as she would ever come to her flesh and blood.

She lifted out a cream silk dress. The style, like the colour, was restrained: a full skirt and a high buttoned neck. Violet held it against her, trying to imagine her mother wearing it, looking in the mirror on the back of the wardrobe door to see whether it suited her too, whether it fitted. She checked the label before returning it to the wardrobe. It was size 10, and the discovery led Violet to examine the labels of the other skirts and dresses. Apart from two maternity dresses which she uncovered in the search, her mother's clothes were Violet's size.

Having entered the room imagining mother and daughter to be different from each other, she found with every discovery her opinion moderating until she arrived at the conclusion that, perhaps, they weren't dissimilar after all. A voice warned her of the emotional danger of veering from one impression to another on such flimsy evidence. But despite its cautionary effect, Violet experienced a deep-seated and, under the circumstances, odd sensation; one which was close to happiness. In every child there was a desire to belong: in Violet's case it had stayed into adulthood.

She let her hand run along the clothes, feeling again the different textures, the hangers knocking against each other on the rail, before turning to the part of the wardrobe which had drawers. She removed shirts and cardigans, finding folded away jeans and underwear, none of it immodest or lacy, and she experienced another shift in her emotions, to anger. She was hurt for her mother whose mistake had been to fall for a married man and to have become pregnant by him, and to have lived on the fringes of a small community which had an appetite for gossip.

She wandered over to the bed, touched the teddy bear and noticed the slight wear around its ears and nose. She speculated on its age, whether it would have been her mother's companion from childhood, whether it would have been in worse condition if it had been. She glanced at the bedside table, at the book there. As with everything else she'd seen, her preference was to observe and only afterwards to touch, to acclimatise herself to her mother's possessions a sense at a time. The book's title, written in ornate gold lettering, was *The Far*

Pavilions by M.M. Kaye. Violet had heard of it but hadn't read it. The illustration gave the impression of it being an eastern romance, accurately as Violet discovered when she read the cover blurb: 'The famous story of love and war in nineteenth-century India – now a sumptuous screen production.' She opened it at the book-mark which had been left on page 564, the start of chapter 39. She scanned the text before turning back a page and reading the last three paragraphs of the previous chapter and wondering if they had been the last her mother had read. Another impression of her mother formed, of a woman with a romantic streak, who chose to live in isolation. Why?

Violet crossed to the dressing table and sat at the stool. She picked up the hand-mirror and watched her reflection, imagining her mother doing the same. She examined the bristles of her mother's hair brush, looking for stray hairs, disappointed to discover there weren't any. Next, she investigated one of the dressing table's two drawers, observed the tidy array of jars, tubes and bottles, before opening the other. It contained a hair dryer, and tortoise- shell hair clips. For a time she was distracted, looking around the room. Then she stood on the stool and felt along the top of the wardrobe. It wasn't level as she'd thought but recessed. Her fingers touched what felt like a cardboard box. She lifted it down and put it on the bed before getting back on the stool. Reaching up again she found another box, bigger and squarer than the first. Placing it on the bed beside its companion she noticed how little dust there was on them. Either Duncan must have put them on the wardrobe recently or else he must take them down regularly to clean them.

She took a deep breath.

The lid of the bigger box slid off easily. Inside was a raffia sun-hat. It had a red ribbon tied around its broad rim. In places, where the ribbon was stained with water marks, the red had turned to pink streaked with brown. Violet removed the other lid. Lying in that box was a leather shoulder bag, the strap still attached, the leather blackened and cracked.

All she could think about now was Megan dying and these *objects* surviving. She lashed out at the lids, the boxes and their contents sending them hurtling from the bed and crashing on to the floor.

Afterwards, shocked at what she had done, she stared at the boxes, at the bed-cover and at the new creases in it. She straightened it, smoothing it with her hands, and checked to make sure the door was still closed. Next she removed her mobile phone from her pocket and took photographs of the hat and the bag. Then she went around the room, tidying it, packing up the boxes, returning them to their hiding place, carrying the stool to the dressing table, pulling at the wardrobe door to make sure it was locked. She crossed the room and checked everything again. The stool looked to be too far from the dressing table and at wrong angle. So she adjusted it. At the door she turned the handle and paused, listening. She pushed it wider and slipped from the room on to the landing.

She crossed to the stairs, descending them slowly, checking the floor below as it came into view. When she was sure she was alone, she ran across the hall to the back corridor. She stopped by the rear porch. The cat had gone from the chair. Did that mean Duncan was back? Did it mean anything? She ran again, across the steading courtyard and out into the field. She imagined Duncan pursuing her, shambling and lumbering like a creature in a horror movie. At the stone pillars, safe at last, she stopped and looked back.

'Oh my God,' she whispered. 'You were there all the time.'

Duncan stood at the entrance to the steading, watching after her.

CHAPTER 14

At Violet's request, Cal pulled off the road below the crest of the ridge, where Stuart, the bus driver, had introduced her to Orasaigh Island, South Bay and North Bay, the landmarks of her mother's life and death. She'd be five or ten minutes, she said, opening her door. Her meaning was clear. She'd rather be alone.

'Take as long as you want,' Cal answered. He watched her in his wing mirror. She stopped at the edge of the passing place: a slight figure against a huge vista of land, sea and sky. An appropriate backdrop, he thought, since Violet had the demeanour of someone taking on the troubles of the world.

When she had appeared at South Bay, after her visit to Boyd's Farm, she seemed worried and withdrawn. He had asked if she was all right. She confessed to feeling 'a mess'. Could they go somewhere else for a while, away from Poltown? She needed time to think. Cal wondered whether she'd also had an encounter with Turnbull's thugs or whether the farm's perilous state had affected her. Under the circumstances getting her away from Poltown had seemed like a good idea.

Now he checked his mirror again. She hadn't moved. Cal opened his door and walked towards her. She glanced back at him and shook her head, as if to stop his questions.

'While you were with Mrs Anderson, I had a visit,' he said, carrying on anyway.

'Who from?'

'Three men. They told me to leave Poltown.' He waited before adding, 'I was just wondering if they're acquaintances of your friend from last night. Do you remember him? The guy who was just trying it on . . .'

She closed her eyes. 'I didn't want this to happen.'

'Well, it's a bit late for that.' He sounded impatient, his way of letting her know he wasn't prepared to put up with her secrets forever. 'So what did your guy want?'

She sighed with resignation. 'He told me to stop asking questions about things that didn't concern me. Then you chased him away.' She wiped her hand across her mouth, remembering the spray of saliva. 'He spat. Ugh.'

Cal looked at the view. 'So, what questions have you been asking?'

'You know.'

He pulled a face. 'About a woman who went into the sea and a hat and a bag that turned up the next day on a beach further along the coast, in 1983.' He glanced at Violet. 'Is that it?'

'The woman was my mother,' she said. 'She was never seen again. She died.'

236

'Did she take her own life?' he asked after a pause.

'I don't know. I just don't know.'

'Tell me what you do know.'

She pointed out the faint continuous line of the coastal path from Orasaigh, her finger following it across the grass behind Boyd's steading to South Bay. She indicated the headland, where the path seemed to end. The path went into a gully there, she said, between two sheets of rock, before descending to the beach.

'Around 8am on Saturday 10th September, 1983,' Violet continued, 'my mother went along that path. She was wearing a white dress and the sun hat – it had red ribbon around the rim – and she had the leather shoulder bag over her shoulder. It was a route she took every morning, whenever she could, whenever the tide allowed her to leave the island.'

'She lived on Orasaigh?'

'Yes. In the cottage . . .' She looked away, before he could catch her eye. Cal nodded, as though things were beginning to make some kind of sense.

'What was her name?'

'Megan Bates.'

'Ok.'

'She was seen on the path by a woman who was walking her dog on the Poltown road.' The same woman saw her again a short time later. By then Megan was on the beach, standing at the edge of the water. When the woman turned for home

Megan was walking into the sea. She told the police she didn't think it unusual. She'd seen Megan there often. It was quite normal for her to paddle or swim. Her hat and bag turned up the next day. Duncan Boyd found them. At first the police thought he'd had something to do with her disappearance. A day or two later the witness and a letter Megan had written came to light. It had been posted just before she died. According to the police, it showed her to be suicidal. The officer in charge of the investigation told newspapers she had taken her own life 'on the balance of probabilities'. All the usual checks had been made to see if she'd taken her passport, money, make-up, clothes, 'things like that'.

'She hadn't?'

'Her passport and purse were found in her bag.'

Violet studied the panorama in front of her as if it concealed the clue to solving the mystery. 'She'd been pregnant, almost full-term,' she said. 'The letter was to the child's father. His name was William Ritchie, a big shot lawyer who worked in Edinburgh during the week and spent weekends here. He owned Brae House and Orasaigh Cottage. Megan was his tenant as well as his lover.' She broke off before adding, 'He was married. Of course. He's dead now, buried in the graveyard.' She directed Cal's attention to the church.

'Pregnant,' Cal repeated it, trying to understand the consequences. 'So she killed the baby too?'

'That's what the police thought.'

'You don't?'

'No. She'd already given birth. The night before my mother was seen at South Bay her baby had been abandoned at Raigmore Hospital in Inverness. The child was left at the main door, just before midnight, in a cardboard box, wrapped only in towels. There was no note, nothing to identify the child apart from an envelope taped to the side of the box. Inside it was a small rectangular section of a cardigan or a jersey, knitted from green wool, and a brooch.'

'So the baby was your brother or sister?'

She put her hand into the pocket of her jeans, removed a small flat box and took from it an oval brooch. She watched him examine it. 'The baby was me. The nurses called me Violet because of this – the flowers are violets.'

She told Cal about Mr Anwar, about the anonymous letter and the newspaper photograph of Megan Bates wearing the brooch and about the shock of discovering her mother's name, discovering what she looked like, discovering she was dead. 'All my life I thought I'd find her; sooner or later, if I kept looking. I never thought she was dead. Not ever. Not once.' A smile faded on her lips, as though she'd been a fool. 'I got into the habit of taking the brooch with me. I used to put it on if I was going out into a crowd or shopping, or if I saw someone I thought might be her. I'd walk towards her so she'd be able to see the brooch. I thought I'd be able to tell by her reaction whether

239

she'd seen it before.' She paused. 'You see I was so certain she was alive. Some days I could feel her.' She pressed her right hand against her stomach; 'Here.'

'Did she leave you at the hospital, come back to Poltown and walk into the sea?'

'It's possible.' Her voice broke. 'Perhaps she did. Perhaps she was just waiting for me to be born before drowning herself, so she didn't kill me too . . .'

'Why would she though?'

'Revenge,' she said. 'At least the police thought so. William Ritchie had told her he wouldn't leave his wife. In her letter she talked about depriving him of her and the baby. Perhaps that's what she had in mind.'

'She thought killing herself was the only way she could escape.'

'She was wrong though wasn't she? Anyway, how did she know her body wouldn't be washed up?'

'What do you mean?'

'Because if it had come ashore, the police would have known she wasn't carrying a baby. They would have looked for me. They would have found me.'

For a while, neither spoke. Violet looked at the brooch and Cal retraced Megan Bates's route from Orasaigh Island to South Bay. Eventually, he said, 'On a day like this it's hard to imagine anything bad happening here.'

Violet let out a bitter laugh. 'That's what I

thought when I saw it first. I thought it was heaven.'

She told him about her meeting with former Chief Superintendent Robert Yellowlees, who had been an inspector at the time of her mother's disappearance. 'I made a mistake. I thought if I showed him the letter Mr Anwar brought me, he would realise something terrible had gone wrong, that he'd want to put it right.'

'What did he do?'

'He made a complaint about Mr Anwar, about me harassing him. Mr Anwar has been suspended. Mrs Anderson told me some people thought the police closed down the inquiry into Megan Bates's disappearance as quickly as they could because a murder inquiry would have disrupted the Turnbulls' business operations. The way Mr Yellowlees behaved made me think there was something in that.'

'The local police were being paid off?'

'If it had been a murder inquiry, detectives would have come from Inverness.'

'Did she say anything else?'

'She said Duncan Boyd had fallen for Megan Bates.' Violet repeated this with distaste. According to Mrs Anderson, her mother seemed fond of Duncan too. And Duncan had offered to let her stay at Boyd's Farm because she hadn't wanted to continue living under a roof owned by William Ritchie. This was why the police suspected Duncan at first, before the witness and Megan's letter turned up. 'Have you been into Duncan's house?'

241

'No. Just the barns,' Cal replied.

'It's like the rest of the place, falling to pieces, except for one room, a bedroom. It's upstairs. Megan's name is on the door. All of her things from Orasaigh Cottage are there; furniture, her clothes, her make-up, even the cot she bought. For a heartbeat, I actually thought she was still alive.' She hesitated. 'Cal?'

'What?'

'Duncan has the bag and the hat.'

'The ones that washed up in North Bay?'

She folded her arms and shuddered. 'Why has he still got them Cal? Why has he kept her clothes, everything?'

'He's odd. Maybe it's no more than that.'

She had thought that too but now she had changed her mind. She'd never felt so frightened leaving the farm, Duncan staring after her. Every time she thought about it she imagined his childish smirk. She'd believed it was harmless until then. Didn't small boys smirk like that when they were pulling the legs from a frog or piercing a living butterfly with a pin or throwing a kitten into a pond and watching it drown? Was that what he did to her mother? At school there were boys with grotesque collections of sad little corpses, boys who recorded the deaths of their victims, in diaries, private inventories of suffering. Was that why Duncan had kept her things?

'Don't you see,' she said to Cal. 'That's why he smiles the way he does. He's smiling because he's fooled everyone. Duncan, the idiot, has taken everyone in. He keeps her room like that because he's a cruel little boy cleaning his private trophy cabinet.'

Cal considered what she had told him and whether he should explain his sympathy for Duncan, one beach-comber's affinity for another, his instinct for underdogs. Instead he said, 'Well, someone knows what happened. Whoever wrote that letter Mr Anwar gave you, and it wasn't Duncan, not if he killed your mother. Why would he want you back here asking awkward questions?'

'But who then and why write it after 26 years?'

'Guilt, bad conscience, somebody sick or old putting things right before they die. There could be any number of reasons. The anniversary . . .'

'Maybe it is as simple as that.' She sounded as though she hoped so.

'But you don't think it's any of those.'

'I've been brought here for a reason. I just don't know what it is.'

'Ok,' Cal said, 'So where now?'

'I have to go back.'

'I thought you wanted to get away for a bit.'

'I thought I did.'

'If you go back you know what's going to happen.'

'Some guy's going to be waiting for me.' She shrugged. 'I have no choice.'

Cal said, 'Haven't you forgotten to ask me something?'

'What?'

'When's the next low tide?'

'Sometime tonight?' she guessed.

'It's at 23.45. So what are we going to do until we can get back on to the island?'

A blue van waited at the bottom of the track to Gardener's Cottage. Jim Carmichael rubbed the steering wheel and debated whether or not to call in on Mrs Anderson. In all the time he'd known her, he had never just dropped by. The welcome he'd received on his last visit encouraged him to think it would be all right. Indeed, Mrs Anderson might even be grateful to see him since he knew how much she disliked waste and she had a chocolate cake beginning to go stale. Maybe she would be glad of the opportunity to take it from its tin, he thought, banishing from his mind the blackface ewe he called Mrs A because of her truculent nature and haughty airs.

Having convinced himself it would be all right, he drove up the track thinking how much things had changed since his last visit. It might only be two days but it seemed like a lifetime. Then, he'd been apprehensive about the Turnbulls and what they would require of him to pay off his debts. So far all he had had to do was drive around putting up posters in support of the windfarm and removing those of the scheme's opponents. Since Jim had become a convert to the windfarm cause, it wasn't an imposition at all. In fact he rather liked the involvement, hearing the chat when he collected posters from the back of the shop, which had become the campaign's headquarters. It had also opened his eyes to the advantages of keeping in with Ross Turnbull. Jim had heard yesterday about BRC awarding Ross the concession to run the new shop that would be built as part of the expansion of Poltown. Ross said local suppliers like Jim would be able to showcase their produce.

Far from debt being his downfall and ruin as he'd feared the last time he approached Mrs A's door, now he thought it might even be his salvation if Ross Turnbull was true to his word. Maybe Jim would at last be able to enlarge his flock of sheep, or increase his bee hives from two to five, to supply the shop with honey. After he'd paid off the Turnbulls, maybe he'd be able to put money aside for a polytunnel. He'd pitch the idea to Ross, of Jim becoming the local supplier of tomatoes, cucumber, peppers and lettuce.

Despite this unexpected turn of events, Jim's expression was rueful, if a little distracted. As ever, no sooner had one worry departed than another arrived. It was this which brought him to Mrs Anderson. So when he pulled up at her door, an undertow of anxiety prevented him from enjoying the prospect of chocolate cake and a refreshing cup of tea. He knocked and when there was no reply he tried again, two short raps. He peered through the side window. Although the external door was locked, the inside one was open as usual, and Mrs Anderson's walking shoes were beside the boot scrape; signs of occupancy. Still there was no reply and he wondered what to do, his conviction about the wisdom of this visit draining away.

Perhaps she'd seen him coming. Perhaps she didn't want a visitor after all.

Just as his nerve was about to fail him, it occurred to him she might have fallen and hurt herself. Emboldened by this idea, he went to the window on the right of the front porch. It was Mrs A's lounge (sitting room, he could hear her correct him), a room into which he had never been invited. He had only managed glimpses of it when he carried Mrs A's box of groceries into the kitchen across the hall. Looking through the quartered pane he was surprised to see the mantelpiece and tables empty of photographs. They'd been such a feature of the room, though he'd always thought it rather peculiar Mrs A having so many photographs of William Ritchie, Diana and Alexandra when she had relatives of her own, and living close by too. Hamish Boyd, who farmed on the other side of the ridge, and his brother Duncan were her first cousins. From the bits and pieces Jim had picked up from Hamish or Duncan over the years, it seemed Mrs A had no time for either of them. In Duncan's case, Jim could understand the antipathy. Not only was Duncan odd, but Mrs A had had to suffer in silence as he wrecked Boyd's Farm. If Jim had grown up there, as Mrs A had, he would also have found it hard to be civil to the perpetrator of such destruction. In Jim's opinion now, and the opinion of the villagers, the only thing the land was good for was the shed BRC wanted to build on it.

Mrs Anderson's frostiness with Hamish was less understandable. Once or twice he had asked Jim about her: whether she was well; whether she needed anything; whether he could help. On each occasion the conversation had ended with Hamish wondering why his offers of hospitality had always been refused. How could she live so close by and yet never have met his two children, Margaret and Graeme? Jim had thought it might be rubbing salt into Hamish's wound ever to mention the proprietorial way Mrs Anderson spoke about 'Mr William', Diana and 'Miss Alexandra' or how many of their photographs she displayed in her home, as though they were her real family.

Jim put his hands to the sides of his face, to shelter the window from the sunlight, to let him see inside more clearly. He turned his head one way then the other to make certain Mrs A hadn't had an accident, that she wasn't lying immobile on the floor. He noticed the wing chair by the fireplace, the newspaper folded over the arm and the tapestry stool in front: more evidence of Mrs A being there. Puzzled as well as concerned, he went to the other side of the front porch to look in the kitchen window. To his surprise he saw the table had dirty dishes on it, and when he cupped his hand to his face and pressed closer to the pane he saw Mrs A sitting at the table, quite still, looking straight ahead. He wondered why she hadn't either responded to his knocking or to his appearance at the window which surely she must have noticed. He became more convinced that something awful had happened, that she had suffered a stroke or some other trauma, so he knocked gently on the window, called out her name saying 'it's only Jim', in case she was confused, in case the knocking frightened her.

At first she didn't react. Then she turned her head slowly, her expression altering as it travelled. By the time she was looking directly at Jim, she had a glower of irritation. Jim was taken aback to see it, but he was still worried about her so he waved and asked if she could let him in. A scowl crossed her face as she rose from her chair and Jim realised he'd done the wrong thing. He returned meekly to the door and awaited her arrival with trepidation. It had been a while since he'd felt the edge of her tongue – it had happened often enough when she'd been housekeeper at Brae. He knew what to expect.

From the other side of the door he heard a series of terse exclamations, none of which he could make out though he imagined he was the butt of them. In anticipation of the ordeal to come, he took a step backwards as Mrs A opened the door. She asked crossly what on earth he wanted and why he was bothering her at this time in the evening. Her mood was so at odds with his last visit that he became awkward and apologetic and hopped from foot to foot.

'Stand still, Jim, and tell me why you're here.' She swiped at a loose filament of cobweb the setting sun had illuminated. Jim imagined he would have been her target had he not been prudent enough to stay out of range.

'I was just passing – I'd taken a delivery to the big house,' he attempted to explain. 'I thought I'd just check how you were.' Jim knew it was another mistake. Nothing was more likely to put Mrs A in a bad mood than someone taking an interest in her, uninvited. 'And I've got some news,' he added uncertainly, hoping for salvation.

Her face suggested such a possibility was most unlikely.

'You know that young woman I told you about?' Jim blurted.

Mrs Anderson chewed at her lip. 'What of her?'

'She's called Violet Wells.'

'I know Jim. You've told me already.'

'Wait,' Jim said. 'You know I'm doing some work for Turnbull . . .'

Mrs Anderson shrugged as if to imply it wasn't a concern of hers.

'Well, there was talk today about this Violet Wells being the daughter of Megan Bates.' Jim looked at Mrs Anderson, hoping the revelation would soften her attitude, might even tempt her to share whatever she had heard about the young woman, what she was doing in Poltown. 'She told some retired policeman. He passed it on. The boys were saying Megan Bates mustn't have killed herself after all, that she must have faked her death and gone off somewhere to bring up the baby.'

Mrs Anderson rubbed at a mark on window sill, as though it was more deserving of her attention than Jim and his tittle-tattle about Violet Wells. 'I can't imagine you're right, Jim,' she said, still rubbing. 'She was here this afternoon and didn't say anything of the kind to me. Now if you don't mind, I've things to be doing.'

After Mrs Anderson had closed the door with a firm bang, Jim returned to the van and made a mental note never to drop in unexpectedly again. He felt the gap in his stomach where anxiety had been gnawing at him, a gap on any other occasion that cake would have filled. Driving away, he thought of Duncan, and wondered whether Violet Wells had told him why she had come to Poltown now, whether that was why he'd run away from her, as he suspected.

Mrs Anderson cleared the table with practised efficiency. The dirty plates went into the Belfast sink to soak, the used glasses put straight into the dishwasher, the leftovers scraped into an ovenproof dish for reheating for lunch tomorrow. Anything clean, the cutlery and the side plates, she placed on a tray over which she draped a clean dish towel. Her habit was only to eat one proper meal a day, usually lunch, unless she had been awake for most of the night and had slept in. Then she'd have breakfast late and high tea as she liked to call it: scrambled eggs and baked tomatoes followed by toast and jam with a cup of tea. This evening, she'd probably make do with biscuits – fig rolls were her favourite – and a cup of leaf tea, Indian for preference. She found it more soporific than China. She put the teapot beside the kettle, followed by a cup and saucer, then the milk jug and the biscuit tin. The sugar bowl was added as an afterthought and she covered the ensemble with another clean dish towel to keep the flies away. Then she went to the window, as she did when a storm was approaching, to wait for a drama to unfold.

CHAPTER 15

Cal told Violet about the oranges, how some of them would have come ashore by now. Where they'd beached would give him a clue to the currents and eddies, to the forces in play the day her mother went into the sea. He climbed into the back of the pickup, talking to himself and, occasionally, to Violet. One minute he was searching for his laptop, the next asking Violet to hold on to his spare mobile phone 'just in case'.

'Just in case what?' she said.

'The battery should last two or three days,' he said as though he hadn't heard her. 'Keep it on you.'

'I've already got a phone.'

'I know.'

He turned on his laptop and, between complaints about how slow it had become, he told her that smart phones could be adapted for all sorts of unexpected purposes nowadays. For example, he used the one she held in her hand for tracking currents. He sealed it in a waterproof box, attached a drogue so that it had traction in the water and then launched it. Although he had access to data collected by drifters and gliders, the sophisticated and expensive ocean monitoring equipment deployed by marine institutes, more often than not he needed precise information about particular stretches of coastal water. A friend of his had devised a phone app for that purpose.

'How does it work?' she asked.

'It lets me know where it is. It texts its position.' He passed his laptop to her. 'Do you see the map? See the dot flashing?'

'Yes.'

'That's it. When the phone moves so will the dot. It means I can watch where currents take it. I can calculate speed, direction and so on.' He put the laptop in his backpack and rummaged around on the back seat, addressing Violet as well as the objects of his search as though coaxing them into being discovered. 'Where are you water bottles?' Having found them, he started another search for the carton of long-life milk he'd bought and the carrier bag in which he had bread, cheese and biscuits. One by one he put them into his backpack and concluded that it shouldn't be too heavy. 'Are you ready?' he asked.

'Yes,' she replied. She nodded too, letting Cal know she understood why he had been talking all the time. She realised he was trying to divert her from what he had just said about the phone, the implication of it; of him being able to track her every move, should she go missing.

'Not,' he said, making light of it, 'that I'm planning to let you out of my sight.'

He returned to rummaging, finding his camera and binoculars, putting one into a pocket of his anorak, the other around his neck.

'I don't have a choice, do I?'

'Not really,' he said.

'But you do?'

'Well, I've chosen.' He backed out of the pickup. 'Are you coming?'

They walked in single-file and in silence, South Bay giving way to North Bay, the forestry on the hill looming at them, until Violet asked where they were going.

'There's something I want to show you,' he said. 'Further up the coast. If we hurry we should be back here by dusk.'

They came to cliffs and Cal stopped to scan the shore below. He moved on and did the same, and again. 'There,' he said eventually. 'See that sandbar.' He handed Violet the binoculars. 'There's an orange on it.' As she searched, he explained how he'd put it into the sea in South Bay along with seven others. He'd expected some to come ashore where they were looking. If they carried on for a bit he was sure there would be more, because of the curve of the land, because of its exposure to the wind, light though it was, because of the flow of the current which swept up close to that stretch of coast.

After spotting two more oranges, they returned

to North Bay. Scrambling over its rock-strewn collar, he asked if she knew precisely where the hat and the bag came ashore.

'On the beach, I think. That's what I've been told.'

Cal showed her how small it was, how far back from the bay's mouth, how clean of debris, even sea-weed, and why. He pointed out the narrow sea entrance, the way the high headlands provided shelter from every wind apart from a westerly, and even that had a small target to hit, how the tidal current passed by the bay at between 2-4 knots, fast enough to carry debris beyond it before any wind-assisted divergence could occur.

'What are you saying?' she asked.

'Just that it's unlikely a raffia hat and a leather bag would drift ashore on this beach and even more unlikely they'd end up together. Come and see.'

They picked their way through the boulders going to the bay's protruding chin. After a while Cal began to point out a few pieces of flotsam, rope, some netting and a buoy. 'Stuff like this comes ashore here because a slack water eddy spins into the bay after high tide. Flotsam gets carried on it.' While Violet watched, he clambered among the rocks, lifting loose sea-weed, searching the sea pools. Suddenly he tossed an orange into the air, shouting 'catch' to Violet.

'That's what I mean,' he said as she caught it. 'The eddy brought it to this side of the bay, but on the day your mother disappeared, the wind had more south in it. Most likely the hat wouldn't have come in here at all. The wind would have taken it further up the coast.'

'What about the bag?'

'The bag, different weight and lying lower in the water . . . it would have gone more with the tidal current. If it passed close by the mouth of the bay around high tide it might have got caught in the eddy. If it did, this is the place it would most likely have beached, where we're standing now.'

'So they wouldn't have come ashore together?'

'In all probability they wouldn't have come into the bay. The bag might, but both together. That's the most improbable.'

'So how did they get here?'

'Someone could have left them to make it look as though they had floated ashore.' He didn't know the answer. 'It's also odd her body was never found.'

'Why do you say that?'

'In these waters, at these depths, you'd expect a body to be recovered, if not straight away then after a couple of weeks, once decomposition had brought it back to the surface. Out in the ocean you might not see it again, but in here, you'd anticipate it turning up along the coast somewhere.' He looked at Violet. 'It might take a few days, or even a few weeks. It might travel a fair distance but sooner or later it would catch in an eddy. When your mother went missing, it was settled weather like this.

Afterwards, there were gales on and off, south-westerlies as well as westerlies and north-westerlies. She'd have come ashore, more likely than not she would.'

The right-hand side of Violet's face glowed golden in the setting sun. Her mouth pulled at the corners. At length she said, 'What you're saying doesn't necessarily prove anything?'

'No.'

Violet lobbed the orange into the sea. It splashed before bobbing to the surface.

'Although . . .' Cal began.

'Go on,' Violet said.

'Well, If Duncan had been involved in her disappearance he wouldn't have tried to cover it up by leaving her hat and the bag on the beach over there.'

'Why do you say that?'

'He knows where things come ashore. Even back then, he was collecting flotsam. He'd have known how little came into North Bay.'

Violet wandered off, picking up stones for Anna, turning over shells, reflecting on what Cal had said. On the beach, she crouched and dug into the sand with her fingers, as if trying to disinter its secrets.

When Cal joined her, she said, 'Who then?'

A few weeks before, Jim had watched a television documentary about the flowering of a desert. The location was in Africa or America, he couldn't remember which. Duncan's face reminded him of it now: his cracked and dry skin like the baked earth before the rains; his patchy white stubble like shrivelled stalks of vegetation; his tears like insistent rivulets which pushed out across the arid desert landscape following a thunderstorm in the hills, the trail of wetness colouring Duncan's deadened flesh a pinky-grey. Jim noticed how the tears from Duncan's right eye criss-crossed the wrinkled contours of his cheek, going off in one direction then back in another, whereas those from the left eye dropped vertically into a crevasse beside his nose before splitting into a mini-delta of channels at his mouth. Jim became mesmerised by the slow motion progress of Duncan's silent misery. He could not look away because he felt responsible for it. He could not hold Duncan's hands, as he might a distressed woman's, or put his arms around him. He could not leave, not while Duncan was like this.

As he observed the rivulets of tears it occurred to him that this was the first time he had been confronted by a sobbing man, indeed, the first time he had made a man cry. Both these 'firsts' had left Jim feeling uncomfortable and hoping that Duncan would pull himself together soon. To Jim's dismay, the opposite seemed to happen. Duncan reached out and grabbed Jim's forearms and held them tight, in the manner of a supplicant or beggar.

'It's all right Duncan,' Jim found himself saying, 'I'm not going anywhere.'

He hoped the reassurance would simultaneously calm Duncan and encourage him to loosen his grip. Once again, the contrary happened. Duncan stiffened his hold, his tears flowed more freely and he began a mumbling commentary, only some of which was intelligible. When Jim managed to make sense of a few words, he attempted to engage Duncan in conversation which, after all, had been his purpose for visiting. At one moment, for example, Duncan rebuked Megan Bates for misleading him and Jim asked, 'How did she mislead you Duncan?'

At another, Duncan mentioned a 'signal' and Jim inquired, 'What signal?'

At another still, Duncan appeared despairing and repeated 'not coming back, not coming, not coming back' and Jim said, 'Who's not coming back?'

Duncan looked perplexed, as if he could not understand why Jim asked such a question.

'Megan,' he answered, as if it was obvious. 'Megan isn't coming back.'

Duncan's puzzlement reminded Jim of the conversations he used to have with his father, James senior, in the weeks leading up to his death. Much of their time together at hospital visiting time would be spent sorting out whether Isobel, Jim's mother, would be joining them or not. Jim would start by changing the subject or saying he didn't know when his mother would be visiting, but he would always end up telling the truth because his father became enraged at his evasiveness. 'Mum is dead,' he would say. Then he would watch his father's anger subside to be replaced by a silent and inconsolable grief. It was why Jim started out being evasive: each time he hoped he would be able to avoid announcing his mother's death and each time his father reacted as though it was his first time of hearing it.

'Megan died 26 years ago, Duncan,' he said.

'I didn't know,' he said.

'You must have forgotten.' Jim lapsed again into the rhythm of conversation he used to have with his father.

'I didn't know. I thought she would come back.'

'It's why Violet Wells is here. She's Megan's daughter and she's trying to find out what happened to her mother. Don't you remember talking to her?' Jim tried to probe further. 'What did she ask you, Duncan? When she spoke to you?' But Duncan's grip on Jim tightened again.

'She isn't coming back.'

'I'm afraid not, Duncan.'

'She promised.'

'What did she promise?'

'She said she would go away and . . .' Duncan stared into Jim's face with disconcerting intensity.

'And what, Duncan?'

'She said she would go away,' he repeated, 'where he couldn't find her and then some day she'd come back.' Duncan pumped Jim's arms. 'She promised.'

'She did go Duncan. She went for a swim in the

sea, don't you remember? Don't you remember finding her hat and bag in North Bay?'

Duncan regarded Jim as though he was the idiot now. 'She left them there. She knew I would know.'

'Know what Duncan?'

'I would know she had put them there. I would know she was alive.'

Jim asked, 'Was that the signal?'

'Yes, yes, the signal,' he said with animation. 'The signal that she'd gone away . . . only I would know.'

The turn of the discussion made Jim wonder whether Duncan had understood anything he'd said. 'You've met Violet, haven't you?'

Duncan's face registered confusion. 'She was here?'

'Yes, she asked you questions about Megan. She upset you. She told me you ran off to North Bay, where the hat and the bag came ashore, where you go when you're upset.'

Duncan nodded. He remembered.

Jim continued, 'She's asking questions because she wants to know how her mother died all those years ago, how her mother is dead when she is alive; why everyone thought her mother had drowned and the baby with her.'

'Megan loved her baby,' Duncan said. 'She wouldn't have killed her baby.' Then, sounding betrayed, 'She promised.'

'What did she promise, Duncan?'

'One day she'd come back with her baby.'

'But her baby's come back without her, Duncan.

Her baby hasn't seen her since the day she was born.'

At last Duncan let go of Jim. 'Megan's not coming back.'

'No.'

'Not coming.'

'No.'

Jim patted Duncan on the knee, withdrawing his arm before it became Duncan's prisoner again. 'You've had a shock,' Jim said. 'It's confusing for you.'

'I loved her,' Duncan said.

Jim stood. 'Well, I'd better be getting back to my rounds and I've my sheep to feed.'

He put his hand on Duncan's shoulder. Later he would remember how bony it felt, how lifeless, as though Duncan's body was already preparing for what would happen, as though Duncan was dying from the feet upwards and all that remained alive were his neck and head.

She stood at the corner of the table, her hands clasped together across her midriff, her skin suddenly translucent in the evening light, her breathing quickening, her eyes flicking from one part of the kitchen to another as if searching for something but not knowing what. Ever since Violet's arrival in Poltown she had been having these turns. Before, they were confined to the emptiness of the night. Now they assailed her at quiet moments during the day too, with memories so vivid she was temporarily paralysed, memories so distressing she felt her chest constrict until she could barely take a breath.

Each time it had happened it was as if she was turning the page of a photograph album. Yesterday, for example, the image which filled her head was of Diana: blood on her hands, face and blouse, her eyes flashing with hatred. Today, it was of the baby, lying naked on the kitchen table, the stump of the umbilical cord milky-grey against the pale white of the child's washed skin, the cardigan in which she had been wrapped beside her, where Mrs Anderson had let it drop.

As Mrs Anderson struggled for breath, the image disappeared and she unfolded her hands and rested her knuckles against the table to steady her. Even now, so long after, it had the power to stun her. She remained standing, the scene rolling forward, that stark image providing a prompt for the next: Mrs Anderson dripping glucose and water into the child's mouth; dribbles of it forming into a sticky pool on the table; Diana ranting on about Megan Bates; her face contorted by loathing; how detestable the child was; how she wished it had died like its mother.

Mrs Anderson had removed the cardigan in which the baby was wrapped and swaddled her in a white towel. After placing her in a cardboard box, she stroked her cheek with the back of her fingers and said, 'There you are. You're safe now.' Then she took

Diana to the bathroom and removed her blood-stained clothes and shoes. While Diana washed, Mrs Anderson went to look for the hand-me-downs she'd had from Brae House over the years. When she returned to the bathroom Diana was standing naked in front of the mirror. She dressed her in black trousers and a pale yellow shirt and Diana protested about yellow not suiting her. Mrs Anderson put Diana's jersey and skirt into a plastic bag, intending to put Megan's bloodied cardigan into it too.

After going downstairs she peered in the baby's box and the child was fast asleep. She was so small, so defenceless. It was already a miracle she had survived. How many more hardships were to come? She remembered her own childhood, how much comfort her little blue blanket had given her. In moments of worry or trouble how she had always sought it out. She spread out the cardigan and used the kitchen scissors to cut a rectangle from its back, where it wasn't blood-stained. That was when she found the brooch. She unfastened it, took it to the sink and washed a smear of blood from it. Thinking it pretty, she pinned it to the piece of cardigan and put it into an envelope which she taped to the side of the box. She couldn't send the child out into the world with nothing. Mrs Anderson said a prayer then went upstairs to tell Diana she was taking the baby away. She stroked Diana's forehead, reassuring her. She was safe now, she said, leading her to the spare bedroom. She told Diana to sleep if she could, to rest if she couldn't, to relax now because her torment was over.

Mrs Anderson took the baby to her car and drove to Inverness. When she returned, she found Diana gone. A note was on her bed: *I won't ever forget. D.* Mrs Anderson cleaned the floor, and wiped the table. She put the mop, the cleaning cloths and the bag with the bloodied clothes on her garden fire. The note she kept in case she ever had need of it. Later, she and Diana had spoken again, Mrs Anderson, as usual, doing what had to be done. Once the fuss had died down, she sought Diana's 'absolute assurance' of secrecy. Giving it, Diana asked Mrs Anderson never to raise the subject again or to inquire how Megan Bates died or where her body was. They never broached it thereafter, except with their eyes, one providing the other with reassurance or understanding. It was a silent bond between them, one which acted as a spur to greater intimacy in other matters, Diana relying on Mrs Anderson, or so she said, more and more.

CHAPTER 16

Cal sat against a slab of rock, Violet nearby on a shingle bank, the closing-in of night making an exchange of intimacies possible. Violet was explaining why she hadn't been in a relationship since Anna's birth, how she'd been formed by 'the hours, days, months, years' she'd spent yearning for her mother, then by the desertion of Anna's father.

'I don't want any of that: being in a relationship, breaking up, starting again, Anna wondering who'll be next, whether I'll still love her as much when Mr Right comes along; *if* Mr Right comes along.' She screwed up her face, finding even the notion objectionable. 'I don't want her to grow up with that insecurity, with that influence. I don't want her to see me . . .' She glanced at Cal. His face was in shadows. She stared into the gloom, trying to make out his expression. 'I don't want her to see me searching for something she can't give me. That's it, I guess.' She picked at the stones around her, feeling their shapes, selecting one, letting it drop, choosing another until she found one small and round enough to fit her hand. She threw it, the movement making the shingle under her shift and rattle, like a drum roll heralding the splash of the stone in the sea.

Violet glanced again at Cal. 'Having Anna has changed everything.'

'I shouldn't have asked. I'm sorry.' He spoke quickly and quietly. 'It's not my business.'

'It's fine, really it is. I'm glad you did.' She smiled. 'Anyway,' she said, 'it was me. I started it.'

They were waiting for dark, watching its shadows creep across the bay, keeping out of the way of Tam and Co. As the colours of the day drained away, she asked him about his childhood fascination for the sea. What had inspired it?

'I suppose you could blame my grandfather,' he replied. 'He died in World War Two, lost overboard, his body never recovered, or so I'd thought. I spent hours, days, trying to work out where he'd gone.'

At one point he had become convinced his grandfather had been preserved in Arctic sea ice. Aged nine, he wrote to Norway's government providing some possible coordinates and requesting an immediate search. 'And all the time he'd been buried on a Norwegian island called Moskenesoy and had been since his death. There'd been a mix-up over identities – it's a long story. Nobody had known it was him until I found the grave a year or two ago.'

She made a sound which let him know she was impressed.

'So you see my grandfather's to blame for

everything, for me becoming an oceanographer, for me doing what I do.' He'd never even considered another field.

Recently he had been questioning the direction of his work – he'd said as much to her on the island. He'd always had an academic interest in where and how bodies floated, but dealing face to face with the relatives had become draining. He didn't think he could do it anymore. The last few days had given him time and space to make a decision. He'd reply to 'those poor, distressed parents' who wanted him to track down their missing children. It would be hard to say no to them.

He apologised for being so serious. Then, his voice lifting with enthusiasm, he said, 'The rest of it . . . all the other stuff . . . yeah, I still get a kick from knowing that in three days there'll be a new moon, that the sun, the moon and the earth will be aligned, that it's called syzygy. That the combined gravitational pull of the sun and the moon will make the high tide higher than normal and the low tide lower.'

He laughed. 'Rachel . . . she was my wife . . . used to say I was just another train-spotter, stamp-collector, or the guy who played computer games at 3am because he was a loner, because it was his escape. With me it was the sea.' He stopped to consider the accusation. 'Yeah, she might be right.'

'You were married?'

'I was, yes.'

'Children?'

'No.'

She hadn't meant to pry, she said.

'It doesn't matter, he answered. 'And you? Were you married to Anna's father?'

'No, nothing like that,' she said.

Usually she'd have left it at that but in the circumstances she thought it an opportunity to say more. She'd seen the way he looked at her. She didn't want him to have a false impression. 'I wouldn't marry now. There's no chance of that. I don't even do relationships.'

'Why not?'

She attempted an explanation, awkwardly. Being a good mother was the only thing that mattered to her. That meant 'never letting Anna think she isn't sufficient for me, never letting her think I might love someone else more than her, never loving anyone else, never taking that risk.'

After a while and with night settling in, he said, 'Shall we go now?' She heard a difference in his voice, or thought she did, and she wondered if he was bruised by what she had said, if the difference was disappointment.

They walked back among the dunes, Cal in front, Violet following; going from dip to gully. The sand of South Bay lay to their right. 'Did you see the buoys and the driftwood?' Cal said when they reached the scrub of bushes where the pickup was parked for concealment.

'No,' she said.

He pointed across the sand. 'See?'

She screwed up her eyes. 'I think so.'

'It's an oil drum. Duncan hasn't been out today. He hasn't been collecting. That's not like him.'

A beech tree reared up from the slope by the back door to Brae. Its lower limbs drooped and hung so that anyone standing close to its trunk was rendered invisible by the murk of evening. Yet, inside the tree's shroud of branches, it was possible to see out and in particular to observe Brae's large kitchen, as Mrs Anderson had been doing for more than twenty minutes.

She was watching Alexandra Hamilton moving between the Aga and the table with occasional forays to the pantry – so far she'd brought back a bowl of cooking apples, flour and a joint of meat, venison or leg of lamb. Mrs Anderson observed Alexandra's comings and goings with something approaching glee. To think she had produced the ingredient which could wreck this scene of rural domesticity. As tantalising to Mrs Anderson was the increasing frequency with which Alexandra scowled at the windows from which pools of yellow light spilled across the back courtyard. It was as if she knew she was being watched, as if she had a sixth sense for impending disaster. Alexandra had been peeling an apple at the table when suddenly her head jerked up. She searched the three windows in turn before Matt came into the kitchen disturbing her. He took a tray of glasses from the sideboard – for the drinks cupboard in the sitting room, Mrs Anderson guessed – and departed by the swing door. As soon as Alexandra was alone again, her eyes flashed back to the windows. It brought a smirk to Mrs Anderson's face.

'All in good time, *Miss* Alexandra,' she said. 'All in good time . . .'

Mrs Anderson wondered what would happen next. Would Alexandra go to one of the windows to stare out into the darkness? Would she go to the back door, open it and stand in the yard? Mrs Anderson decided to wait and see. After all, she was in no hurry to move things on. She was warm in the tree's shelter. It was dry underfoot and quite apart from considerations of comfort, she was enjoying the capriciousness of power, her ability to decide when to exercise it. In fact she expected this part of the evening to be just as enjoyable as the next.

There. It happened again. Alexandra interrupted rolling pastry to stare at the middle window. Her face was flushed and fuller than it used to be, Mrs Anderson decided. On its own this was a source of some satisfaction, the thought that Alexandra's looks were going. As Mrs Anderson watched, Alexandra's expression changed from watchfulness to worry. She walked hurriedly to the back door. Mrs Anderson heard the old lock turn, a noise which brought back her days as housekeeper, when she had been custodian of the same key. The outside light came on and Alexandra appeared beneath it. She glowered in the direction of Mrs Anderson without seeing her before going back indoors. At the kitchen table again, she draped the pastry over a pie dish and trimmed the edges with a knife. When she had finished, she glanced at the window again. A smile fluttered across Mrs Anderson's thin lips. 'It's time,' she said.

She moved away from the shelter of the tree and crossed the grass to where steps led to the drive. She proceeded with care, feeling for each mossy tread with one foot before taking her weight off the other. When she reached the bottom she looked up. Her face shone in the beam of the backdoor light and the movement caught Alexandra's eye. By her expression – turning from shock to anger when Alexandra saw who was there – Mrs Anderson realised she was unlikely to be asked inside, even into the kitchen. She had imagined Alexandra sitting her down in the hall or the drawing room and Mrs Anderson having the pleasure of telling her about Violet Wells surrounded by the most precious artefacts of her inheritance from Mr William. But it was clear from Alexandra's opening salvo that would not happen.

'What are you doing creeping about out here?' she demanded imperiously pulling the back door open to intercept Mrs Anderson. 'What do you want?' Alexandra stood with hands on hips. 'Well?

Mrs Anderson did her best to look as though some terrible and unjustified wrong was being done to her by such an ungracious welcome. 'If I'd known this was how I was going to be treated I would have had second thoughts about coming out at night.'

Alexandra laughed; short and bitter. 'Oh please, Mrs Anderson, do me a favour.'

Mrs Anderson thrust out her chin in turn and addressed the black sky above Alexandra's head. 'I refuse to repay your ingratitude with disloyalty. It is not my way.' Her head gave a little tremble of repressed pride, as well as excitement.

Alexandra snorted again. 'I'm bored by this, by you, always trying to interfere. If you don't say what you want I'm going back inside.'

Mrs Anderson glowered. How she wished Alexandra was still small enough to be put across her knee and smacked.

'Jim told me this evening that the young woman who is renting Orasaigh Cottage . . .'

'You mean Violet Wells?'

'I am only telling you what Jim said because of the implications . . . for you, the family, for Brae. I thought you'd want to know.'

'Oh, ever the loyal and faithful servant,' Alexandra sneered. 'What implications?'

'Violet Wells's mother was Megan Bates. She's Mr William's daughter . . . his flesh and blood.' For dramatic effect, Mrs Anderson waited before carrying on. 'His only child . . . his heir.'

Anyone else wouldn't have noticed the flicker in Alexandra's eyes, a slight widening. But Mrs

Anderson was watching for it and knew what it meant. 'Oh go away, Mrs Anderson. Go away.' Alexandra collected herself and strode back across the courtyard. 'Go away. Go away. Go away.'

The door slammed shut. The outside light snapped off, leaving the yard lit only by the light from the kitchen windows. Alexandra extinguished that too by closing the kitchen shutters, leaving Mrs Anderson in the dark.

One noise after another entered the darkness of her bedroom. If it wasn't the wind pushing breathily at the window or mortar chips tumbling down the chimney, it was the hollow tick of her alarm clock. With each interruption Mrs Anderson shifted in her bed. To prevent the wind disturbing her, she turned her back to the window. To block out the intermittent skittering from the chimney, she rolled on to her right side, her left ear being the duller of the two. To muffle the tick of the clock, she pushed it to the furthest edge of her bedside table. Every competing sound banished, she lay in the dark, her eyes closed, revelling in the memory of Alexandra's discomfort, in the wound she had inflicted, and listening as the fluttering in her breast grew ever louder. For Mrs Anderson, vengeance was an overdue visitor and it did not come as a horned, horrible creature but as a glorious butterfly.

Jim Carmichael's hands shook. A mug of tea was in his left and a bottle of 12-year old Macallan, a

Christmas present, in his right. He was attempting to top up his brew with whisky but neither the mug nor the bottle remained steady enough for any kind of accuracy. The result was a splatter on the kitchen floor followed by a lucky splash of whisky into his tea. He brought the mug to his mouth and gulped at it before taking a swig from the bottle. He washed the alcohol down with more tea and banged the mug on the table. He was as careless letting go of the whisky bottle. It toppled and spewed the rest of its contents across his paperwork – over his calculations of the previous night, over his ruined plans – before tumbling on to the flag floor with a crash. Jim leaned back in his chair and listened to Tommy, his collie, howling. The sound expressed a little of what Jim was feeling too: fear and a sense that something irrevocable had happened even though it was only 7.30 in the morning. Tommy, who was shut up in the tractor cab, only knew about the missing blackies. He didn't know the half of it; he didn't know the worst of it.

Jim put his head in his hands and rubbed his unshaven face, groaning and cursing. He berated himself either for his stupidity or for his naivety and followed it up with: 'What did you think would happen, Jim? Well?' The question went unanswered because Jim's elbow knocked against his mug of tea, tipping it over. The remaining liquid spilled across the table and Jim stared at the mingling pools of whisky and tea and then at the damp papers on which he had been estimating the costs of acquiring a polytunnel to supply the new village store as well as his projections of cash flow. Splashes of tea or whisky or both stained the page on which he had made a clean copy of his calculations the night before.

He had retired to bed with an intoxicating sense of optimism, of opportunity finally seeking out his remote corner of the world and rewarding his years of uncomplaining hard work. Unusually for him, he'd even thanked God before going to sleep. Now the sodden page seemed to mock him and he tore it up, scattering the pieces on to the floor. His mug went flying too, as did a pottery vase of dried flowers, a bottle of ketchup and another of mustard. After a cacophony of discordant crashes and bangs the kitchen fell quiet, apart from Tommy's intermittent howling and the clock above the stove. Tick. Tick. Tick. So often it had been Jim's reassuring companion. Now it was a sound filled with menace. In an hour and a half, Davie would be returning. Then Jim would be told what job he had in mind for him.

He had wakened before sunrise to a ruckus in the front field: sheep calling out in distress and Tommy going mental yapping and growling. Jim had jumped from his bed and gone to the window. In the grey light of early morning he saw a collie rounding up his blackface sheep. It wasn't Tommy, who was where he always spent the night, on the tractor seat. Jim pulled down the window and shouted, 'Hey. Hey.' The dog stopped its herding and looked at Jim who shouted, 'Away with you, go away.' *Devil*, he muttered under his breath and banged on the window frame to frighten the animal. He imagined the dog to be a stray from Poltown or perhaps it belonged to a camper and had escaped. Just as he wondered whether it might have been abandoned, he heard a man's confident voice instructing the dog to carry on. Jim went downstairs, threats issuing from him, and he put on his boots and pulled up his overalls, only managing to hang one strap over his shoulder while struggling to open the door. As soon as he was outside he shouted again. 'Hey, hey. What do you think you're doing?' By now the gate was open and the collie was going backwards and forwards behind the sheep driving them towards it. A man holding the gate didn't even bother to look up.

Jim shouted again. 'Hey. Hey.'

He had started down the path when a voice seemed to come from behind him.

'Morning, Jim.'

Jim stopped and looked round. Davie White was leaning against the corner of the house. 'What's going on?' Jim shouted.

Davie waved his arm airily. He had a cigarette in his hand. 'Don't you find it's always so rewarding to get out of bed early,' he said looking across the glassy water of the loch towards Poltown. 'Best part of the day don't you think, Jim?'

'What are you doing with my sheep?'

'Your sheep, Jim?' He sucked on his cigarette and blew the smoke out of the side of his mouth. 'I don't think so, Jim, not anymore.'

By now the sheep were on the track, running. Davie held up his hand and the other man instructed his dog to get ahead of them and to hold them where they were.

Tommy was going demented in the tractor cab. His claws were scrabbling against the plastic sheeting which covered the broken window. 'Tell your dog to stop that,' Davie ordered.

Jim looked at Davie and then at the tractor which was parked beside the hayshed. 'Settle down now Tommy lad,' Jim shouted. 'Settle down.' The dog whimpered and fell silent.

'That's better. We can talk.' He wandered over to Jim and threw his cigarette stub at his feet, as if throwing down a challenge. 'You know why we're here?'

Jim said nothing.

Davie shrugged. 'Interest soon builds up on £2,000, doesn't it Jim?' Davie glanced at the house and the sheds. His expression suggested he didn't see much of any value. '£428 interest after five weeks,' he'd said, shaking his head. 'I thought it might assist you if I took a payment in kind now before things got out of control.'

Jim's world was falling around him. He felt winded. Words wouldn't come without a struggle. 'I've been driving around doing the posters for Ross.'

'So you have, Jim and Mr Turnbull is very grateful. Thing is, the money you borrowed is mine.' Davie put his arm round Jim. 'Lovely here isn't it?' He looked at the view. 'Tell you this – I wouldn't mind a place like this myself one of these days.'

He went towards the garden gate and waved to his colleague. The sheep started bleating again as the collie resumed its herding. Tommy barked and scratched at the tractor windows. Davie looked back at Jim. 'Next time it'll have to be the van or the tractor. The dog too.' He tried to look concerned. 'You don't have much of value do you, Jim? I can't see you having anything left at all in six months.'

Davie started along the track, hesitated and stopped. 'Tell you what,' he called back. 'There's a job that needs doing.'

'What?' Jim said.

'What about you making some coffee later and we'll have a chat?'

'When?'

'Let's say nine o'clock. That's when I like to have my breakfast.'

The first thing Jim did on returning indoors was to open the store cupboard, grab the coffee jar and throw it across the kitchen. The glass smashed against a wall; the granules spilled on to the floor. He drowned his sorrows in tea and whisky and added to the breakages and mess. Looking at the disarray all around him – soaked and shredded paper, shards of glass, fragments of pottery, and coffee – Jim shook his head, his anger turning to resignation, the impotent gesture of a man who was already finding reasons to choose appeasement over defiance. Jim had sometimes wondered if his aversion to confrontation, of his inability to go 'toe to toe' at the drop of a hat like some men do, would disappear if his life or someone or something dear to him was under threat; whether he too would stand his ground. In the last few minutes the answer had gradually made itself known to him. He wouldn't; he couldn't. He let his head drop and closed his eyes. The dog's howling provided a distraction from his thoughts about cowardice.

'I'm coming, Tommy lad,' he said, going to the open door. 'You hold on there.'

Tommy cocked his head, lifted his ears in expectation as Jim took the side path from the house. When he opened the tractor door, the dog leapt out and ran backwards and forwards in excitement. It curled its body around the back of Jim's legs and lifted its nose towards Jim's searching hands.

'There you are Tommy boy. Did you think I wasn't coming to get you?'

Jim patted the squirming dog's neck and ears. 'I wouldn't leave you, Tommy boy. Course I wouldn't.' He knelt, and buried his face in the dog's hair. 'I won't let them take you from me Tommy boy. Course I won't.' Jim let the dog slobber over him then stood up to slam the tractor door.

In the half second his back was turned Tommy sprinted along the stony track. The dog jumped the wall into the field and began searching for the sheep. Without any commands from Jim, he went through his morning routine, running into the corners in case one of the ewes had slunk off on her own, quartering the grass as the flock was brought to the gate where Jim would be waiting and watching, checking to see if any had gone lame overnight. In his bewilderment at the empty field, Tommy added a few tricks. The dog lay still in the grass as if a recalcitrant ewe was standing its ground, stamping its foot, Mrs A more than likely. Then he squirmed forward, legs bent, belly flat to the grass, ears pricked. Jim contemplated Tommy's performance, wishing he had a fraction of the collie's courage. He called out to the dog. Tommy obeyed quickly, running across the field and jumping on to the stone wall. The dog looked back at the empty field, as if the missing flock might suddenly have reappeared. Jim did the same, wondering whether he'd ever see sheep in it again.

'Come on, Tommy boy,' he called sadly. In a few bounds the panting dog was lying at his feet. Jim knelt on one knee and Tommy rose to meet him, licking his hands and face.

'What are we going to do Tommy, eh?' Tommy's breath was hot on Jim's face. 'What are we going to do?'

When Jim had gone back inside, Tommy slunk away to the hen coop by the hay shed. He lay beside it, his neck and head flat in the grass, his eyes following every movement of the clucking mother hen and her chickens behind the wire mesh. Meanwhile his master set about tidying the kitchen for Davie White's second visit of the morning.

Luckily for Jim, only some of the shattered coffee jar's contents had scattered across the floor. The rest had settled into a heap, like a miniature mole hill, at the base of the wall. Jim scooped up half a dozen spoonfuls into a mug before taking it to the safety of the store cupboard. He placed it carefully on a shelf, the exact place where the coffee jar had been, before searching other shelves for the pot of marmalade he'd been given by Mrs Youngson in exchange for two boxes of eggs, but it didn't seem to be there. Instead he found a jar of honey, from his own bees, and a damaged packet of digestive biscuits from the bargain box at the store. He felt through the packaging and was reassured to discover a few intact. Putting the honey and the biscuits on the sideboard, he lifted the bread-bin lid and checked the loaf for mould. Then, he sniffed the butter dish. Surprisingly, it was all right, if sweating a little. He picked up the broom and started sweeping, its stiff bristles causing broken bits of glass and pottery to skitter across the slab floor. While he gathered it all into a tidy pile, something that Davie said came back to him. 'Business, after all, is business.'

Jim crouched beside the rubbish and picked out the torn sheets of paper. He studied each one before either binning it or saving it. The half dozen or so that he kept were laid out on the slab floor. Bending over them, he tried to decipher his writing, some of which had smudged or lost definition. Three fragments of paper more or less fitted together. Apart from a jagged tear at the bottom, Jim managed to reassemble the sheet – the top copy with his polytunnel calculations – while dishing out muttered reprimands about his impetuosity.

In the kitchen table drawer by his right shoulder, he found a clean sheet of paper. He placed it beside the one he had reassembled and retrieved a pencil from the bib pocket of his overalls. He wrote down the figures and put the sheet of paper for safe-keeping on the kitchen table.

By the time he had cleared away the rubbish, washed the dirty dishes left over from his meal the night before and laid the table for breakfast, he had rehearsed 'a proposition' which he would put to Davie. At first, it did little to lift his spirits but mulling it over, speaking it out loud so that he was word perfect for his visitor, he persuaded himself of its good common sense and he managed, too, to resuscitate a notion that had shrivelled and died round about the time Jim last saw his flock of sheep. Briefly stated, it was that the events of earlier that morning had been a misunderstanding, a failure of communication. The proof, Jim told himself with increasing certainty, lay in Ross Turnbull's proposition – there, that word again – for Jim to grow salads and vegetables for the new village store. Ross had even suggested a supplier of polytunnels in Inverness and had told Jim to mention his, Ross's, name to be certain of being quoted the company's 'best price'. As Davie White worked for Ross Turnbull, an accommodation must surely be possible.

Jim put the sheet of figures in front of the table placing he'd laid for Davie. With ten minutes to go, he rehearsed his pitch. He would tell Davie he had a business proposition. If Davie would provide seed capital for a new polytunnel business, Jim would hand over all the projected profits for the first two years (he slid the paper closer towards the seat where Davie would be sitting) – a figure of £10,000, sufficient to pay off his enlarged debt if they could agree a lower interest rate. In subsequent years they would share the profits 50-50. Jim was still undecided whether to conclude by holding out the prospect of expansion – say three polytunnels by year five – when Tommy started to bark. Jim looked at the clock. Davie was seven minutes early. He flicked the switch of the kettle, checked that he'd put coffee granules into the mugs and went to the door. As soon as he saw Davie – he had changed into jeans and a short-sleeved tee shirt revealing tattoos on his arms – Jim's confidence began to drain away. It disappeared altogether when Davie barked at Jim to get his dog to 'shut the fuck up'. He shoved

Jim from his own front doorstep out into the garden. 'Well, what the fuck are you waiting for?'

The sight of his master being manhandled startled the dog. Instead of yapping and howling, Tommy emitted a rumble of growls and rose to greet Jim, but with none of his usual exuberance. The dog knew something was badly wrong. Jim grabbed him by his scruff and led him to the toolshed, opening the door and closing it, whispering in Tommy's ear that he must be good and quiet. Retracing his steps, Jim felt a stab of fear at the pit of his stomach. His breathing quickened so that by the time he had returned to his kitchen and saw Davie lolling back in a chair, legs splayed, he was panting. He swallowed, thumped at his chest as though he had something in his throat and coughed. What made everything worse was the way he started jabbering. A jumble of words emerged from his mouth and 'proposition' wasn't one of them, nor 'partnership', nor 'profit', nor even 'polytunnel'. Jim heard himself begging for another chance, promising to do whatever Davie wanted of him, if only . . .

'If only, what? Davie sneered.

'If I can have my sheep back. They're my livelihood. I'll do anything.'

Davie smirked. 'You don't get it do you Jim?'

'No,' he agreed, hoping even now that conciliation might help.

Humiliation followed humiliation. His bladder let him down next. He felt the wet and warm urine spread out from his groin and run down his right leg. He cried out, 'Oh God, leave me alone.'

An expression of disgust crossed Davie's face. 'See all this,' he said. Jim lifted his head and looked around the kitchen with Davie. 'This house, this place . . . you're going to lose it, Jim.'

Then, from nowhere Jim found his voice, the one he'd rehearsed. 'I've been working on a proposition, a business plan,' he said, surprising himself.

Davie thumped his fist on the table, making the plates and Jim jump. 'I've got a fucking proposition for you Jim.' He paused, waiting for Jim to pay proper attention. 'Either you do what I'm going to tell you or you lose all this, and if you tell anyone you're fucking dead and buried Jim.'

His fist banged down again.

'You're a fucking corpse.'

CHAPTER 17

'Couldn't sleep,' Cal wrote in pencil. 'Gone for a walk. Back soon.' He looked in the pickup's window. Violet was curled across the back seat, the top of her head poking from the sleeping bag. Cal prised the page from his notebook and secured it to the windscreen with the wiper blade before taking the coastal path to Boyd's Farm. When he arrived at the steading it had the same odd atmosphere as the beach the night before, of something missing, of something untoward having happened. Cal shouted Duncan's name and waited for a reply, for any sign of life. He peered into the shed into which he had previously been ushered like a courtier. Nothing had changed apart from Duncan's absence. The Neptune Scroll was still nailed to a beam. The Cuvier's whale skull and the barnacled post were exactly where Cal had left them. He shouted Duncan's name again. The barn deadened his voice. 'Duncan, it's Cal, Cal McGill.'

He crossed the steading yard to the back door of the house. To his surprise it was shut. It had been open the previous times he'd been there and he remembered Violet saying it had also been open when she found the room Duncan had filled with Megan Bates's possessions. He tried the handle. It was stiff but the door sprung free and his nostrils filled with the stench of cats and an unpleasant mustiness. The inside door was also closed. Knocking on it, he called out 'Duncan it's Cal' if only to reassure him that it was someone he knew and not a stranger or one of BRC's money-men trying to bully him into selling. He recalled Violet telling him how the open door and the emptiness of the house seemed to draw her in, as though it wanted her to discover the secrets of Megan's room and he felt a similar impulse to go further, to inspect the room for himself.

Walking along the dark passageway towards the front of the house, he continued to call for Duncan, adding by way of explanation, 'I thought you might like some help clearing the beach.' He stopped, as Violet had, where the passageway met the hall. He looked from one scene of dilapidation to another: from an explosion of plaster scattered across the hall floor to the water-stained paper hanging like a partly-sloughed skin from the wall. Like Violet, he found it hard to imagine a human being living there, even one as idiosyncratic as Duncan. The house had an aura of terminal decay and a temperature to match. Crossing the hall to the bottom of the stairs, Cal gave up shouting for Duncan because it struck him as futile. Nothing living was within earshot, with the exception perhaps of a cat, a rat or a mouse. Nothing human; of that Cal was certain. The same feeling of absence and death assailed him when he opened the door to Megan's room. Cal put himself in Violet's position, to imagine what he would be feeling if these were his mother's possessions, if he had been separated from her at birth and this, to all intents and purposes, was the closest he would ever come to her. Even for him it was a peculiar and unsettling feeling: this pristine room in a house that was falling down; everything present and correct apart from the woman herself.

He crossed to the bed and picked up the teddy bear. Holding it, he examined the room's arte-facts, wondering if all they signified was Duncan's enduring attraction to Megan Bates and, of course, his eccentricity. He went to the wardrobe, opening the door and letting his eye track along the clothes rail. Like Violet, he stood on the dressing table stool to find the two boxes. Unlike her, he opened them where they were, lifting one lid then the other, checking their contents, confirming his view that two such different objects were most unlikely to have gone into sea at the same time and later to have been washed ashore together. Their shapes and weights would have sent them on different courses. A small dissimilarity was all it would take. Cal replaced the lids, returned the stool and went to inspect the cot. Once again he considered Violet's reaction, what a powerful symbol this would have been of her lost childhood, indeed of everything she had lost. He touched the wooden frame and went back to the door.

Opening it slowly, he emerged onto the landing. The main staircase lay ahead of him, descending, but another smaller, ascending, flight lay to his left. It was at the far end of the landing and spilling down its bare wooden steps was a length of nylon rope. The colour, a faded orange, caught Cal's eye. There were others like it in Duncan's rope pile outside the steading. Approaching the stairs, Cal saw they led to a short corridor at the far end of which appeared to be an attic room. The door into it was half-open and through the gap Cal could see the slope of the ceiling and a skylight. As far as he could tell, the room was empty. At least there was no movement that he could see, nor sound he could hear. At the foot of the stairs he bent to pick up the rope. It was a coil about three metres long, and it was damp. Cal ran it through his hands, concluding it had been carried indoors sometime during the night or early morning. He glanced again at the attic room. Although much of it was still hidden from him by the door, he had a clearer view of the back wall. What he assumed from further away to be stained or grimy wallpaper, or a combination of both, he realised was graffiti. Then it dawned on him what this room was. Violet had mentioned it: how it was a rite of passage for teenagers from Poltown to run through Duncan's house, how those who signed the back wall of the attic, the room furthest away, were regarded as having shown the most daring. It was the means by which the village had come to know of Duncan's continuing obsession with Megan Bates.

A stair creaked when Cal put his weight on it, making him start. How many of Poltown's teenagers had taken fright at the same place and had gone no further? In two more strides Cal was in the passageway. The rope made him hurry. Despite appearances, the house could not be quite as abandoned as it felt. Duncan or someone else had been there not many hours before. Cal nudged at the door with his left toe, letting it swing slowly open, revealing the back wall to be a jumble of signatures, hearts with arrows through them; a romantic and social history of Poltown over three decades. He stepped into the room and let out a gasp. Duncan, his face leathery and vacant, was hanging from a hook in the ceiling. The rope around his neck was orange, like the piece Cal had found on the steps. A chair lay on its side, where Duncan had kicked it. His boots lay below him, discarded in his death throes by the involuntary thrashing of his legs. His eyes stared sightlessly. His mouth was locked open as though in the act of speaking. Cal was overcome by shock and sadness for this creature, half child, half man, who had chosen to die in this room of all places.

Had he done it there to let his tormentors know they had won?

★   ★   ★

On her way into Poltown for her weekly surgery, Dr Fiona Bell noticed a police car turning down the single-track road to Boyd's Farm and South Bay. She slowed as she passed the turn-off and wondered if it had anything to do with the public meeting two nights before, whether there had been any spill-over of unpleasantness against Duncan Boyd. Fiona had attended the gathering and even before punches started to fly she'd become concerned for his safety. Some of the people sitting around her, patients of hers among them, had been making threatening comments about Duncan whenever Boyd's Farm was mentioned, about his refusal to sell-up putting in jeopardy the windfarm development. As she'd been sitting at the back of the community hall, she'd been able to escape the ensuing fracas but she spent the next half an hour patching cuts and bruises, using her emergency bag from the boot of her car, and offering comfort.

Afterwards, driving home to Ullapool, she had an uneasy feeling about Duncan. She wondered whether someone should warn him about the passions being stirred up, about the personal risk for him. What stuck in her mind was a tweedy man behind her describing Duncan scornfully as a 'useful fool' for the alliance of incomers, white settlers and second home owners opposing the windfarm plan. Back at home, she told Nick, her partner, about the violence and her concerns for Duncan whom she'd encountered a few times at South Bay. She'd taken to walking Pepe, her terrier, there after surgery and sometimes at weekends too. In her short acquaintance, Duncan didn't seem to be as weird as his reputation implied. Indeed, she found Duncan's shyness rather endearing, especially on those occasions when she was close enough to say hello and he'd responded by going off and finding a piece of flotsam to show to her, rather like Pepe bringing back a crab or mussel and dropping it at her feet, expecting a pat and some praise for being so clever.

Maybe someone should have a quiet word with Duncan, she suggested to Nick. So he could take some precautions. It was one of those conversations to which Nick hardly paid attention. She persevered because it helped her work it all out. At the meeting, she told him, she'd seen a community pushed close to boiling point. Until then, she hadn't imagined there was any threat to Duncan, not really. Now she had changed her view.

'He's such an odd man that he's probably not aware how intense the hostility has become,' she said.

Nick cautioned her against interfering: 'Which is really what you're asking isn't it?'

She agreed it was. She didn't like to stand by when she might be able to prevent something horrible happening, but she knew there were other considerations, such as her patients thinking she was taking sides, which was why she was asking Nick's opinion. He had grown up in Ullapool and had a better understanding of the area's customs and taboos than a newcomer like her, who'd only been in residence eight months and still needed a map to find her way about the roads let alone the twists and turns of the communities she visited on her rounds of weekly surgeries. Would there be a risk of her patients getting to know about it if she did speak to Duncan? If there was, of course she wouldn't interfere.

Nick laughed. 'In that case, stay out of it. Nothing stays secret in Ullapool for more than two days. Somewhere like Poltown, you're talking two hours. At the most . . .'

At the time she'd known he was right. She had patients who supported each side of the argument. On the evidence of the public meeting, some of them did so with a passion bordering on fanaticism. Apart from applying witch hazel or antiseptic to their bruises and scrapes, she couldn't afford to become involved. But seeing the police car she felt a twinge of conscience. 'God, Pepe,' she said to the dog lying asleep on the passenger seat, 'I hope nothing's happened.'

She made a silent promise to listen to her instincts more and to Nick's cautions less. Ever since she had come with him to Ullapool – he was following his guiding star to set up a furniture-making business in the town – she'd been aware of swallowing her tongue more than she was used to. Perhaps it was the difference between a city practice – she'd met and fallen in love with Nick in Norwich – and being a community practitioner working among scattered villages and townships. Still, it was a matter of concern.

As she drove on into Poltown, she took her left hand off the steering wheel and ruffled Pepe's wiry coat. The dog stirred and opened his eyes. 'Well, would Pepe like a walk on the beach at lunch-time?' Pepe gave her that intelligent, longing look he always managed to conjure up whenever he heard the word walk. 'You would, wouldn't you?' She ruffled his hair again. 'Good boy.'

She parked in front of the surgery – a converted ground floor flat in Sir Harry Lauder Gardens. Her space had been marked 'Reserved for Doctor', unnecessarily as she had learnt since most of her patients were too destitute to afford a car.

Already she was feeling better for the decision she had made. If Duncan was on the beach at lunchtime she'd say something about the atmosphere in the meeting, about the hostility and anger, just in case no-one had told him. She wouldn't mention it to Nick.

Her first two appointments were in the waiting room. Mr Mackie was standing by the window as usual and Mrs Simons was perched upright on the hard chair while her boy Tom bounced on the old sofa. All the waiting room furniture had been a legacy from a Mrs Keane who had died a few months before Fiona's arrival. In Fiona's opinion, the sofa and its two matching arm chairs would have been better buried with Mrs Keane, or set alight on a memorial bonfire. However, on this as

295

on other things she had to keep her thoughts to herself and to tolerate their presence, at least for the time being, until she was certain of the sensitivities involved. A framed notice pinned askew in the waiting room offered posthumous thanks to Mrs Katherine Keane for her generous gift. One of these days, Fiona thought, she'd swab the chairs to discover whether they were as un-hygienic as they looked. 'Give me a couple of minutes,' she said, bidding good morning to Mrs Simons and Mr Mackie, 'and I'll be with you.' She carried on along the passage to the kitchenette where Janice McGhee, the caretaker-cleaner, was boiling the kettle and dropping tea bags into a pot.

'Morning, Janice.'

'How are you, Dr Bell?'

In Fiona's opinion, Janice was a frustrated nurse. Every time she greeted someone she asked how they were, or whether they were keeping well. 'Good, thanks Janice,' Fiona answered. 'Ooh, can I have tea, please?'

'It's for you, Dr Bell. I'll bring it in.'

Since Janice was older by twenty years, Fiona found it odd to be addressed so respectfully. Generally she corrected Janice by saying 'Fiona, you must call me Fiona' but today she let it pass. 'Janice?'

'Yes Dr Bell?'

'Is there something going on at South Bay?'

'No that I've heard.' A look of puzzlement accompanied her answer.

'I saw a police car there, that's all.' Fiona shrugged and went into her 'consulting room' as Janice liked to call it. Fiona hoped she'd started a hare running. If anyone could find out what was going on, it was Janice. As it happened Fiona herself discovered the first piece of information. As she prodded circumspectly at a weeping sore on Mr Mackie's big toe and mused aloud at its stubbornness to heal, her mobile phone rang. Apologising for forgetting to put it on silent, she fished it from her bag and apologised again because it was the group practice ringing. She would have to answer. Fiona was still mouthing 'I'm sorry' when Mrs Findlay, the practice receptionist began speaking. As normal, she was brusque and rather disapproving (whether of new, female doctors or from habit, Fiona had yet to work out).

'Dr Turner,' Mrs Findlay said, 'has asked if you could take his appointments this afternoon.'

Dr Alexander Turner was the senior doctor in the practice. By her tone Mrs Findlay made clear her opinion that Fiona was ill-equipped for the task.

'Why, what's happened?' Fiona was deliberately breezy.

'Well if you must know he's been asked by the police to attend a death.' Again her tone spoke volumes. It let Fiona know that a 27-year old upstart like her had a long way to go before she could be trusted with such work.

'Where?'

'Near Poltown,' Mrs Findlay said, relishing the opportunity to deliver another slight. 'Of course,' she said, 'if there had been a sufficiently experienced doctor available nearby Dr Turner wouldn't have had to go.'

'Where near Poltown?'

Mrs Findlay sounded taken aback by Dr Bell's abruptness. 'A place called Boyd's Farm.'

Fiona's face turned ashen as she ended the call. Even Mr Mackie noticed it and unusually for him spoke without being spoken to. 'All right, doctor?'

'Yes.' She nodded. 'A bit of a shock but I'm fine now. Right where was I?" She returned to his infected toe, cleaned it, dressed it and left him to put on his sock and shoe after suggesting he made another appointment for the following Wednesday. She found Janice coming out of the waiting room into the hall.

'You'll never guess, Dr Bell,' she said, 'the police are at Boyd's Farm. There's been a death. Apparently it's Duncan Boyd. He hanged himself.' She pursed her lips as though a tragedy like that had been inevitable sooner or later. Janice, as Fiona knew, was a supporter of the windfarm for the jobs it would bring to Poltown. 'It doesn't do to speak ill of the dead, Dr Bell,' Janice said, 'But that one wasn't right, not at all he wasn't. Never was.'

'I wouldn't know,' Fiona said diplomatically but feeling sick. Back in her room she rang Nick to tell him what had happened and that she felt guilty.

'Well don't,' he replied. 'What could you have said or done that would've stopped him?'

'But I should have done something,' she said feebly.

'How would warning him about the meeting have helped? It might just have put more pressure on him. Imagine Fiona if you'd spoken to him and *then* he'd topped himself. How would you be feeling now?'

'I suppose.' She winced at Nick's language.

For the remainder of the surgery, each patient entered Dr Bell's room with a bulletin of the latest news, and in between appointments Janice provided updates. After the last patient had gone, Janice stood in Fiona's doorway, shaking her head at such a morning. 'The whole story's come out now,' she announced confidently. 'Duncan was there when Megan had her baby. He begged her to stay with him, at the farmhouse. He had prepared a room for them both. He was in love with her but she turned him down and he killed her in a jealous rage. If he couldn't have her, nobody else was going to. Her mistake was letting Duncan see a letter she'd written to the baby's father. She'd threatened to disappear with the child, go somewhere where the father would never be able to find them. Duncan realised it gave him a cover for murder. After he'd killed her he posted the letter.' She paused. Her eyes widened. 'And you'll never believe this bit.' Janice launched into another breathless rush of words. 'Once he had hidden

299

Megan's body and abandoned the baby, he dressed up in Megan's clothes, put on her sun-hat and went swimming so that Mrs Armitage would see him.' Janice checked to see if Fiona was still following this. 'Mrs Armitage is dead now but she used to take her little dachshund for a walk every morning. She'd go to the road end at South Bay before returning home. She'd often see Megan there. Well, anyway that morning, she thought she saw Megan walking into the sea. But really it was Duncan.' Janice took a breath. 'The police got suspicious when Duncan didn't raise the alarm after finding Megan's hat and bag on the beach at North Bay. He was about to be charged when Mrs Armitage came forward and Megan's letter arrived in the post.' Janice's eyes widened. 'You'd never have thought it of him, would you, being cunning like that?'

The sound of Janice's mobile phone ringing brought a grin of excitement at the prospect of more news to come. 'Do you mind if I take it?'

Janice retreated into the corridor and Fiona heard her say, 'Really . . . Really . . . uh-huh . . . Oh,' as some new revelation circulated the Poltown grapevine. Fiona went to the window and looked towards South Bay. If she had time she would still take Pepe there for a walk. She would like to remember Duncan as she had known him.

Janice returned. 'Guess what? Duncan hid Megan Bates's body under one of those piles of rubbish he collected from the beach.' Janice waited for

Fiona to look impressed, or at least interested. She tried again, with the titbit she'd been keeping till last. 'And . . . you'll never believe this . . .' Still no reaction apart from a polite expression of dutiful attention. 'Duncan told Jim Carmichael . . . do you know him? The little fat man in the blue van that does deliveries for the shop . . . him. Well, apparently, Duncan told Jim last night that he'd murdered Megan Bates. Jim says he was crying and all sorts, kind of baring his soul, but Jim thought it was just Duncan having one of his funny turns until first thing this morning when he heard the news about Duncan being dead. Then he rang the police.'

'I'm sorry Janice,' Fiona said. 'I've got to go.' She made her escape before Janice's phone rang again, and she had to listen to another bulletin.

Pepe had found a dead gull. The bird's body had been covered with sand. Only its black beak protruded. It was at an angle of 45 degrees and slightly open. In death as in life the gull appeared prepared for a fight. The dog was circling suspiciously, growling and barking by turns, sometimes darting towards the beak, hackles raised, before retreating to safety.

'Oh come on Pepe, we have to go.'

Pepe dashed in one last time, retreated, barked and trotted nonchalantly towards Fiona who was by her car at the road end. 'Come on Pepe. Patients are waiting . . . Dr Turner's patients.' She mimicked

Mrs Findlay's ability to make Dr Turner's patients sound as though they were the most important in medical history. While she waited for the dog, she surveyed the beach, wishing she had the time to remove every piece of flotsam, as Duncan would if he were still alive. Still, she'd gathered up all the big pieces – buoys, rope, plastic containers, drift wood – and put them into a pile and drawn in the wet sand 'In memory of Duncan Boyd who was kind to me'. Looking at it from a distance she liked the idea of the next tide washing away the words and possibly the memorial too, of it being impermanent, even fleeting, like her own acquaintance of Duncan.

CHAPTER 18

Police Constable Buchanan was walking Cal through the house again, double-checking his route to the attic. 'And you're sure you didn't go in there, sir?' The constable indicated the open door to a room which by its dimensions and fire-place if not its furnishings – a clutter of broken chairs and tables – appeared to be the original sitting room.

'I've told you already . . .' Cal broke off because Violet appeared in the hall, a policewoman leading her, another following. She looked dazed, as though she wasn't sure whether she was still asleep and this was a nightmare.

PC Buchanan nudged Cal. 'Hey, you're paying attention to me.'

'No, I didn't go into that room,' Cal replied, still watching Violet as she was led upstairs to the inspector, wondering if she would be treated with the same hostility. Cal had answered question after question: how he'd come to be in Poltown; how he'd met Duncan and Violet; what he knew of her; why she hadn't gone to the police. It had taken him a while to realise why the inspector and now

PC Buchanan were so antagonistic. The body hanging in the attic room would lead to more than one post-mortem: Duncan's and another into the police investigation 26 years ago. Why had the police let a murderer go; why had they allowed a letter to distract them; why had they closed a case without a body? A reporter and photographer from the local newspaper had already been to the farmhouse. Others were on the way. The police seemed to blame Cal and Violet for the media interest, for causing trouble by disturbing the past.

After all, didn't Cal have form as a trouble-maker? The inspector had alluded to him 'making a habit of this'. Someone must have Googled his name and discovered other cases he'd worked on where he had fallen out with the police, usually because he found evidence they had overlooked. Cal had snapped back at the inspector. 'That's not the point really.' It was as though Cal had committed a crime instead of being the one who had raised the alarm about Duncan's death. 'Is it?'

The inspector had ignored Cal and suggested to Constable Buchanan that Mr McGill – he'd said it with distaste, like a dog baring its teeth before biting a rat – might like to go through his story again, how he'd come to be at Boyd's Farm when a man was hanging dead upstairs, why he considered it appropriate to enter a private dwelling without permission, and where he went, step by step.

Constable Buchanan seemed to be a man who obeyed orders to the letter. He'd escorted Cal from room to room upstairs, making him detail his movements again and again, before going downstairs and doing the same. After the question about the sitting room, he made Cal retrace his steps along the back corridor to the porch and to stand exactly where in the steading yard he'd made his phone call to the police and afterwards to Violet. 'Why,' he asked, 'did you go outside before ringing?'

'I just wanted to get out of the house, I suppose.'

His answer provoked a sceptical look from the constable, who said Cal was being allowed to go for now. However, he was warned he would have to make himself available for further questioning as the inquiry progressed.

Cal waited for Violet by the big barn until he was moved on for 'operational reasons'. As he was crossing the field, it became clear what they were. Two trucks and a digger passed him on the track to the farm, followed by a police van carrying a dozen officers. It had been another hour before Violet appeared. By then the officers had cleared one pile of flotsam – the collection of orange buoys – and had filled one of the trucks. The digger had started to excavate the ground underneath.

'They're looking for her aren't they?' Violet said.

Cal nodded. 'Looks like it.' He touched her arm. 'I'm sorry.' It seemed the only thing to say. She flashed him a smile but he could see how wounded she was, how upset.

'The inspector implied Duncan taking his life like that was my fault.'

Cal had expected as much. 'He's wrong. You were looking for your mother, doing the job the police should have done years ago.'

'That's not how he put it. He seemed to be saying even the guilty shouldn't be hounded – that's why countries have systems of justice, juries, judges and courts.'

'Did he actually say that?'

She didn't seem to hear him. Her focus was on the field. A digger dumped another load of topsoil into a truck. Police moved in to examine the newly opened ground. 'I just can't bear to think of her suffering,' she said. 'What he might have done to her . . .' She crouched, watching another truck reverse to be loaded up. 'Do you think he hid her there?'

He made no attempt to reply but she didn't seem to mind or notice.

'I don't want her to be there.' She shivered. 'Cal.' Her eyes were wide with shock. 'I thought he was sweet too.' Until she had gone into the house, until she had seen him watching her. She'd been fooled just like her mother. 'Duncan said she loved me . . . How could he have killed her knowing that? How could he have separated us?'

'Jealousy, maybe; seeing her loving another man, another man's child . . . it's possible, at least that's what the police think.'

There was hesitancy in Cal's answer. Violet looked at him. 'But you don't?' She sounded puzzled, as if there was nothing to doubt.

He shook his head. 'I don't know.'

306

'Don't know what . . . about Duncan being jealous?'

'Don't know about any of it, about Duncan being a murderer.'

'He's admitted killing her.' Violet studied his face. She was trying to work him out. Why was he still taking sides with the creep?

Cal sighed. 'Last time the police took the obvious line. Mother-to-be kills herself and her baby after being let down by her married lover. They wanted a solution that wouldn't involve detectives from headquarters descending on Poltown, turning the place upside down. Now, they're doing the same. It's all so neat and tidy again. I'm sorry.' He gave her a regretful glance. He didn't mean to be difficult, but his training taught him to be suspicious of obvious explanations especially when there were questions without answers.

'Like what?' she asked.

'Why were you brought here? Who wrote the letter and why now?' He paused. 'I keep coming back to that. Whoever wrote that letter knows what happened. And I'm pretty sure it wasn't Duncan.'

He swore, wishing he could make himself clear. 'I'm sorry, Violet but everything you've told me about Duncan, and what I've seen for myself . . .' He paused. 'I know this is going to sound strange, but I don't think he knew your mother was dead, not until you turned up looking for her.'

★   ★   ★

For once Mrs Anderson didn't have to tolerate snide remarks. Usually when she visited the shop, a group of villagers would be hanging around the counter. 'Idle bletherers' she had taken to calling them, grumbling it under her breath as well as to their faces when the occasion warranted. There were more of them today, a dozen at least, but instead of passing the time making comments about Mrs Anderson (how stuck-up she was; how demeaning it must be for her to do her own shopping) they paid her no attention at all, so engrossed were they by Duncan Boyd's death. Mrs Anderson took advantage of her invisibility by going from display to display, picking up items, returning them, selecting one or two for her basket – a packet of rice, a tin of tomatoes, milk – and taking her time. If anyone had paid her attention, they would have seen how she dithered by the shelves closest to the 'bletherers', how she seemed to concentrate as much on what was being said as on the packets and tins she was examining and how, after being in the shop a while, she left it again hurriedly and on the way out abandoned her basket by the door, the rice, the tin of tomatoes and the milk still in it.

If anyone in the shop had gone to the window and looked out they would also have seen Mrs Anderson sitting in her car. They would have noticed her talking to herself and, if they'd watched for long enough, they'd have seen how flustered she seemed to be. They might have called the others over to enjoy the spectacle: the dour and disapproving Mrs Anderson discomfited for a change.

The possibility of being observed was one factor in Mrs Anderson's unease. Another was the way she had already drawn attention to herself by leaving her shopping behind. But mostly her disquiet stemmed from the conversation she had just overheard: how Jim Carmichael had visited Boyd's Farm the previous evening; how he'd found Duncan to be tearful and distressed and wanting to unburden himself 'about a darkness in his life which had become too difficult to bear'; how between sobs and howls Duncan had confessed to Megan Bates's murder; how he'd kept on repeating 'she knows, she knows' and when Jim had asked who *she* was he'd replied Violet Wells. Jim had thought Duncan 'was just being Duncan' and having one of his emotional turns. He'd stayed on at Boyd's Farm until Duncan had calmed down again and then he'd returned to his small-holding. He'd rung the police as soon as he heard about the hanging. He blamed himself, according to the bletherers. Duncan would still be alive and facing trial for murder if only Jim had realised he was telling the truth.

Mrs Anderson's head was left spinning at the turn of events.

When the postman gave her the news about Duncan's death, she gasped with surprise, 'Oh my goodness,' she said. 'Poor Duncan . . .' She must have appeared upset because the postman asked if he could make her a cup of tea with sugar in it before he carried on with his rounds. 'Sugar is good for shock,' he said. He'd learned the tip watching Holby City the night before. Had she seen it, he asked. She said she hadn't and declined his offer. She'd gone back to her kitchen, where she did as he suggested; made herself sugary tea. After all she was a little shocked, as much by Duncan hanging himself – *that* she hadn't expected – as by the postman linking it so definitely to the murder 'a long time ago to some woman called Bates'. After the revivifying tea, she decided on a visit to the shop to discover what else was being said.

So thrown was she by her eavesdropping that instead of returning to Gardener's Cottage (as she knew she should) she decided to take a chance on visiting Jim to find out what was going on. As she had never been to his small-holding before, she fretted about drawing attention to herself again. She started the car in a tizzy of indecision and let it roll towards the road. Left for Jim; right for Gardener's Cottage. She chose left and berated herself for making the wrong decision. She called herself 'idiot' and 'fool' in the vague hope she'd come to her senses, turn the car around and go home. Still, she drove on. A compulsion had overtaken her. She had to find out why Jim had been inventing things, whether he was just being Jim – making himself the centre of attention – or if something else was afoot, something that could spoil her plan.

On the southern shore of Poltown Loch, the road narrowed at a cattle grid. Mrs Anderson stopped the car to compose herself (it would never do to let Jim think she was in a flap) and to rehearse her explanation for dropping by. After checking her face in the mirror and adjusting her hair, she released the brake and let out the clutch. The car progressed slowly along a winding road sheltered by birch and alder trees. Then emerging on to more open ground, Mrs Anderson spied Jim's small-holding ahead of her. It amounted to a patchwork of small fields around a house and outbuildings set back from the shore of the sea loch. She stopped the car to take it all in and noticed sheep spilling from a trailer into a pasture beside the house. A man was banging on the trailer sides as the animals careered down the ramp. Jim, she thought. At least he looked like Jim: small, round and wearing blue overalls. Mrs Anderson released the brake and drove on only to regret her impetuosity. What concerned her was the Land Rover attached to the trailer. She knew it wasn't Jim's. Someone else had to be there: the thought hadn't occurred to her earlier so distracted had she been.

She scolded herself again – *idiot, fool!* If only she had gone home and rung Jim. Why hadn't she thought of it earlier? There was nothing she could say to his face that she couldn't have mentioned on the phone. But it was too late to turn back now. Jim, or the figure she thought was Jim, had noticed her car. He was looking towards it. Although she was still a distance away, too far for her face to be identifiable, the chances were he recognised her car. Being the obliging sort, Jim had a habit of inquiring whether she needed the oil or tyres checked, and sometimes she let him tinker. Even so, Mrs Anderson considered turning round and going home. She could always ring later and spin him a story about not wanting to bother him when he was busy. She looked at the road ahead but couldn't see anywhere to turn; nor, she realised after glancing in the mirror, was there anywhere behind so thick was the bracken growing at the edge of the tarmac. In desperation she considered reversing all the way to the cattle grid. But her neck was far too stiff to carry it off with any degree of safety. She made a muffled exclamation of frustration and resigned herself to the inevitable.

Once she'd parked beside the stone wall in front of the house, Jim came hurrying towards her. He seemed agitated. She wondered if her unannounced (and unprecedented) visit was the cause or if he was aghast at the thought of someone like Mrs Anderson seeing inside his house. As soon as she got out of the car she attempted to reassure him, complimenting him on his home. A little paradise, she called it, and remarked with feigned exasperation at her unadventurous nature that had prevented her from paying a visit until today.

'I'm so glad I made the effort,' she said, gawping at the buildings and the scenery with exaggerated appreciation. 'It's perfect here Jim. You've been keeping this a secret.'

Jim, meanwhile, gave a good impression of being appalled at Mrs Anderson's appearance. He stood in front of her with a pleading expression and as he did so the door of the Land Rover opened and a thuggish-looking man with tattooed arms got out. Jim started talking to Mrs Anderson rather too loudly and in a most peculiar way. He called her Mary, something he had never done before, and made out that she visited his small-holding on a weekly basis; indeed had done so for many years to pick up an order of eggs. Unfortunately, he added with an apologetic shake of his head, his ducks had stopped laying for the moment. 'But it could be they'll have started again by next week . . .'

She watched his performance without saying a word and saw that his pleading look had become even more pronounced. It was clear that something was amiss and that she had to play along. As luck would have it, she remembered she had two empty egg boxes on the back seat of her car. She put the fingers of her right hand against her forehead and complained about her forgetfulness. It'd be her name next, she said. While she was at the car she kept an eye on the driver of the Land Rover who had sauntered over to join Jim. Mrs Anderson recognised the man's face and the name that went with it: Davie White. She knew him to

313

be one of Turnbull's men and he looked the part too: muscled, with dark stubble over his head and sharp face, as well as an unpleasant swagger. It was also obvious that Jim was uncomfortable in the man's company. Remembering Jim's debt to Turnbull, his odd behaviour started to make a little more sense. Perhaps he'd been alarmed at the possibility of Mrs Anderson being her usual outspoken self, of her taking Davie White to task for preying on unfortunates like Jim, of making Jim's difficulties with Turnbull even worse. She had been so wrapped up in her own concerns that she had forgotten Jim's.

Returning from the car with an egg box in each hand, she bid good morning to the unpleasant-looking man, who didn't respond, and otherwise held to the script Jim has outlined for her.

She inquired whether she might have bantam eggs if he didn't have duck and to have six medium sized hen eggs – the browner the better, as usual. 'They do taste so much better.' She smiled as though this was a continuing but good-humoured dispute between them.

She was relieved to see Jim relax. He blinked once, then again, which she interpreted as encouragement to continue in the same vein before going off to fill her egg boxes. 'If I had a place like this I'd have hens too, and geese. I've always had a soft spot for geese.' She addressed herself to Davie.

'Is that right?' His tone was mocking and was accompanied by a smirk as well as a contemptuous shrug. He walked away, waving and shouting after Jim, 'Be good now. Make sure you're only giving her eggs.' The Land Rover's engine clattered into life and the vehicle, pulling its trailer, drove slowly past. The thug nodded at Jim who was coming back with the full egg boxes but ignored Mrs Anderson.

'Not a nice man,' Mrs Anderson said.

Jim looked embarrassed. 'I'm sorry Mrs A.' He pressed the eggs on her.

'There's no need . . .'

But Jim insisted. So she took the full boxes with a mild protest: 'I'm the one who owes you a favour because you're always helping me out when I've trouble with the car or the boiler.'

The mention of trouble set Jim off again. He started to gabble on about Davie having done him a good turn, rescuing his sheep from the road where they'd wandered during the night, and about the unresolved puzzle of who had left open the gate into the field. It couldn't have been him because he had trained Tommy, his collie, to run round last thing in the evening, before the light faded, and if he found a gate open he'd wait by it barking until Jim came to close it. Bright as a button was Tommy, Jim said. So bright it wouldn't surprise Jim if Tommy could be taught to close gates on his own. Maybe Jim would give it a try in the winter months when he had more time.

'Talking of Tommy,' Jim said, 'Where is the lad?' He whistled and a few seconds later the dog appeared in the open gateway to the pasture where the sheep had been unloaded. And sure enough he stopped and barked.

'See there he goes, calling for me to shut the gate,' Jim remarked. 'He keeps me right, he does. Sometimes I wonder whether he's the master and I'm the one who does the bidding. Well, I'd better go and do as I'm told, hadn't I?'

'Indeed you had,' Mrs Anderson replied. 'It wouldn't do to keep the master waiting.'

Jim muttered another apology, this time about leaving her standing all this time. He'd be quick, he promised.

'No need to hurry,' she said, intending to put him more at ease, 'I'm enjoying the view.'

She made a point of looking admiringly at the loch, a shiver of a ripple on its surface, and at the hills around. But as soon as Jim departed to appease Tommy, she went to the stone wall enclosing the garden and looked over it in the hope Jim would take the hint and maybe, after showing her around his meagre borders, would offer her a cup of tea or coffee. It was her best chance of having a sensible conversation with him.

When Jim returned, Tommy at his heel, she steered him away from another discussion about the dog by saying 'I've just been admiring your garden, Jim, and your house'. She needn't have bothered because the Jim who addressed her now was a different character to the one who had gone to shut the gate. What *is* going on, she wondered.

Instead of Jim's face being a mobile display of tics, flushes and evasiveness – he hadn't once looked Mrs Anderson in the eye before going to close the gate – it had become one of settled grimness with his flesh the colour grey to match his mood.

'You'll have heard about Duncan,' he said.

'I have.' She was watching for Jim's reaction. 'And I've heard what you've been saying.'

Jim rubbed his hands around each other, a display of guilt. 'If only I'd stayed with him a bit longer. He talked about Megan, what he'd done to her. It was eating away at him.' He sighed. 'Who'd have thought Duncan capable of murder?'

'Who, indeed?' Mrs Anderson's features matched Jim's for severity. 'Since I know Duncan didn't kill Megan Bates. And,' she said, 'what's more to the point, so should you.'

Jim stared blankly at the loch.

'Tell me Jim,' Mrs Anderson continued, 'how many times has Duncan told you about keeping the beach clean for Megan, about keeping her room neat and tidy? About being ready for her when she came back?'

Jim shrugged. 'He must have been lying.'

'He thought Megan was still alive, so why would he confess to her murder?'

Jim said nothing.

Mrs Anderson's eyes formed little hoods. 'Jim,' she snapped. 'Well?' She studied the returning tic in Jim's cheek and slowly her mouth fell open at the thought that had just occurred to her. 'Jim, you haven't . . .'

'Haven't what?' Jim said.

'Made up this cock and bull story about Duncan because Turnbull told you to?' Her head shook slowly at the dawning realisation, at a Jim she hadn't encountered before. 'Is that why Davie White was here? Is that why he was bringing back your sheep – because you'd done Turnbull's dirty work?'

Then something happened that Mrs Anderson hadn't thought possible. Jim became defiant – with *her*.

'No-one put me up to anything. Duncan murdered Megan Bates. He said so last night. He fooled everyone, you too. Now if you don't mind I've got my sheep to attend to.'

CHAPTER 19

The egg boxes lay where she threw them. One was the right way up; the other splayed open after falling on its side. Jim's bantam eggs were cracked and broken. Albumen and yolk oozed from the ruptured shells and membranes. Mrs Anderson watched the liquid slipping and sliding while her hands searched out the edge of the kitchen table, its wooden reliability a reassurance after the tremors of the day. From having been the person in control of events she found they were now spinning away beyond her reach. The thought of Turnbull being behind Jim's intervention added another and worrying consideration. Why had Turnbull done it? What did he know?

The sound of an engine and the bang of a car door made her jump, at first with surprise – she hadn't noticed the vehicle's approach – then fright. What new shock awaited her? She remembered too late she hadn't locked the door, hadn't even closed it properly in her rush to reach sanctuary.

'Mary,' a man's voice called out. It was followed by knocking. 'Mary Anderson, are you there? It's Hamish. Hamish Boyd.'

To stop him finding her in the kitchen and her having to explain the broken eggs, she went to the hall before attempting a reply. Duncan's older brother was looking through the gap in the door when they saw each other. 'It's you is it?' she said coldly.

Hamish was thick-set and weathered; his frame and features shaped by a life-time of physical work and exposure to the elements. His face was ruddy-brown and his cheeks latticed with broken veins. His eyes were small, blue and darting below a ragged dome of home-cut greying hair and overgrown black eyebrows.

'You'd better come in, I suppose.' Her umbrage at being disturbed, at his failure to call her first, was evident and eloquent though left unsaid.

'You'll know why I'm here,' he said, stepping from the porch after going through the motions of brushing his shoes against the coconut door mat. He had the lumbering heaviness of a man burdened by sadness.

'Yes, I imagine I do.' She preceded him into the sitting room, or thought she had, but he held back in the hallway. Seeing him hovering there, she said, 'Well, do you want to come in or don't you?'

He mumbled his appreciation at being invited into her house, then stopped in the doorway. It was a reminder of the previous times he had called and she had kept him standing outside, like a salesman or itinerant.

'This is about Duncan I assume.'

Hamish pulled at the lapel of his tweed jacket and glanced down at grey flannel trousers. Usually he wore overalls and two or three shirts, the number of layers depending on the temperature. 'I've been to identify the body,' he said, 'Thought I should be decent.'

'I see.' Mrs Anderson's mouth hardly opened so locked was it in disapproval.

Hamish paid attention to Mrs Anderson's furniture, the window, his feet, anything but meet her gaze. 'Duncan brought disgrace to a good name,' he said eventually.

'He ruined my father's farm, my farm.' Her tart reply made clear the family name was a lesser consideration for her.

Hamish nodded. 'I won't keep you, Mary.'

'What would keep you?'

'Well then, I'll tell you why I'm here,' he went on uncertainly. 'I've decided that Duncan should be cremated when the police release his body . . .' The sentence trailed away, as if he expected an interjection from Mrs Anderson, her approval or otherwise. 'We'll scatter his ashes away from here . . .' He paused again. A frown line creased his forehead. 'As for the house and farm . . .'

If he had been expecting Mrs Anderson to put aside her grudges and hurts because he had lost his only brother he realised now his miscalculation. She glowered at him waiting for what was coming next.

'The house and the farm,' he repeated. 'Duncan left his majority share to me.'

'I see,' she said.

'I would keep it for the boy Graeme if I thought he wanted it.'

'Not Margaret?' Margaret was the older of his two children.

'What would she want with a farm when she can go off to the city, get a nice clean job and get married?'

'What indeed,' Mrs Anderson said tersely.

'No life for a girl.' Hamish realised too late his explanation had only propelled him further into the family minefield, 'No, no.' He shuffled from foot to foot. 'No. It'll be sold . . . that's for the best.'

'To BRC?' Mrs Anderson inquired.

Hamish nodded. 'No-one else will want the house. The police think the woman might have been murdered there.' Hamish shook his head again at the shame of it. 'And the land has been ruined. Pulling down the buildings and covering the place with concrete – what else is it good for?'

Mrs Anderson reminded him of her 15% shareholding, pointing out that a man with any decency in him would seek to correct that wrong when it came to dividing up the sale proceeds. And then she asked him to leave, without saying goodbye, without going to the door to see him off. Being confronted again with the Boyd tradition of passing land to male heirs threw her back to her father's betrayal, where this all began.

★   ★   ★

322

The sight and sound of the digger unnerved Violet. She hated the way the boom moved, how it jerked like a bony finger, and she loathed the squeal of the engine as the bucket met the rock-like resistance of undisturbed soil. 'Are they sure she's buried there Cal?' she asked for the umpteenth time.

'I don't know,' he replied again

Watching and waiting like this was agony. Though she longed for her mother's body to be found so she could take possession of her, she dreaded the moment of discovery. She couldn't help but recall television programmes, documentaries as well as dramas, where skeletons had been unearthed and the skull or ribs had been fractured by an axe or some other weapon. Is that what they would find?

Cal said nothing. There was nothing he could say.

After a while she asked, 'Where did she die, Cal?'

'I don't know.'

'The police didn't tell you?'

'No.'

'Nothing,' she said turning to him, 'is worse than not knowing.' She studied him for evasion. 'Nothing . . .' She left it hanging, the implication clear. Her imagination churned with all the bloodiest possibilities so she might as well be told the truth.

'I don't think the police know,' Cal said.

The noise of the digger's engine drew her back to the spectacle which had kept her mesmerised for the past hour and half.

'From what they said to me,' Cal carried on, 'Duncan didn't say anything about how she died or where he hid her. Not in his confession to Jim Carmichael . . .'

The last of these omissions puzzled Cal. If Duncan was guilty wouldn't he have left behind an explanatory note to guide the police to the woman's remains? Cal would. Wasn't it the only redemption available to a self-confessed murderer on the edge of hanging himself: to allow a daughter to bury her mother? Despite Violet's plea to be told everything, he kept this thought to himself. After all, he was only guessing. Perhaps Duncan judged himself past redemption when he slipped his head into his orange noose. Or perhaps he wasn't guilty.

Violet interrupted his thoughts. 'Would you do something for me?'

'Of course.'

'Would you go to Orasaigh? Get my things from the house, and bring the tent?' She found the key in the pocket of her jeans and handed it to him. 'I can't go back.' She looked at him, her eyes filling with alarm. 'The atmosphere there . . .' She shuddered. 'I can't.'

Should he try to reassure her it was like a thousand other properties in the West Highlands without damp proof courses and windows too small for sunshine to penetrate the morbid chill? He decided against. Perhaps the cottage had the atmosphere of a crypt because Duncan did kill Megan Bates there, as Violet seemed to fear.

324

He touched her on the arm. 'You'll be ok?'

'Yes.'

'I won't be long.'

As it happened he was away the best part of an hour waiting for the tide. On his return, he found her sitting exactly where he had left her. 'This had been put through the door.' He held out a postcard, one side of which was a photograph of Brae House. She stared at it and then at him as if she had forgotten he'd been away or that she'd asked him to go.

'I found it at Orasaigh Cottage,' he explained. 'It's for you.'

She looked away, at the digger, at the restless searching for her mother's remains: the trucks, vans and a score of police in white or blue overalls.

'Shall I read it?' Cal asked. Violet nodded, a little movement of her head, her focus remaining on the hunt. 'It's from Alexandra Hamilton,' Cal said. 'She wants to meet. She says, would Brae House 5pm tomorrow be convenient?'

'Anna is coming tomorrow.' Violet flashed him a brief smile. While he'd been away she had rung Hilary. There was a 6am bus from Glasgow with a connection in Ullapool. They – Hilary, Hilary's daughter Izzy and Anna – should arrive early afternoon. Hilary was bringing another tent. They could all camp at South Bay, couldn't they?

After a moment Violet asked Cal if his mother had taken him to the beach as a child, and he said she had.

'I wish I'd had that,' Violet said with feeling. 'Right now I wish it more than anything else.' She'd never done it with Anna. Never paddled in the sea. Never made sandcastles. Never collected shells. Never picked up seaweed and looked for sand-hoppers. Never fished in rock pools for crabs.

Hilary had often told her about a beach on the east coast, near St Andrews. It was a mile or two from Hilary's family home. Hilary played there when she was a child. So did her father, and her grandmother. Now Izzy played there too. Violet wished she had that continuity, the simple pleasures of one generation being handed down to the next. It was too late for her. She saw her life as one loss building on another: first her mother, then Anna's father. But she could break the pattern for Anna. Playing on the beach her grandmother loved: it was a small thing but important. For the first time in her life Anna would know she was following in her grandmother's footsteps. For the first time, she would have something to remember her by which wasn't about loss, or death, or now murder.

At dusk, Cal brought Violet a sleeping bag. He expected her to be stiff and unaccommodating, but she was the opposite, allowing him to wrap it around her without protest or resistance whilst remaining mute. Otherwise, he kept his distance, observing her from across the beach road where he'd parked the pickup. He alternated between leaning against the bonnet and sitting in the driver's seat with the door open. When the police abandoned their search for the evening he stood behind her, in readiness to intervene should any of the officers try to move her on. The vans trundled past in convoy without stopping. Each policeman had the same expression of sombre respect that funeral mourners reserve for a relative of the deceased who remains beside the grave as the crowd departs.

As night fell, he found the scene more affecting than ever with darkness creating the illusion of threat, of looming shapes emerging from the land and sea, of Violet defying monsters. Of all the thoughts he had about her, one impressed itself on him more than others. At times of crisis she preferred solitude to company and silence to conversation. In this, Violet and he shared a characteristic. His inclination was to turn in upon himself and so, it seemed, was hers.

At one o'clock, he retired to the pickup and pulled the door shut. He dozed restlessly, his sense of duty preventing him from dropping off, or so he imagined until he was awoken by the sound of the passenger door opening. He pretended still to be asleep as Violet settled beside him.

CHAPTER 20

They were leaning against the back of the pickup, Cal and Violet side by side, watching out for the Ullapool bus. Hilary had phoned to say it was running ten minutes late. While they waited, Violet asked about Cal's childhood, about his parents, whether they were alive, what relationship he had with them. It was on her mind.

'You know families, parents and stuff . . . whether they always fuck you up.'

Because she was serious, his answer was serious too. He had been a single but not a lonely child, he said. His mother's death, when he was seventeen, from cancer, had been the event that changed everything.

'I'm sorry, I didn't know.' She sounded awkward at having prised such a detail from him.

'Don't worry,' he replied. 'I didn't realise it at the time, but yes, it was the turning point, thinking about it now.' His father's breakdown, his new life in Africa then his new family, and 'even,' Cal smiled to lighten things, 'why a five year old pickup with 102,000 miles on the clock seems to double up as my home.'

He had avoided making any comparison between himself and Violet, though one occurred to him. The death of a mother was formative for each of them, neither really belonging anywhere because of it, the 'pin in the map' thing he called it. He sensed Violet arriving at the same conclusion because she glanced at him, quickly, as if deciding to let him further into her confidence because of it but finding her habit of reticence hard to overcome.

'Go on,' he encouraged.

She looked again for the bus. 'It's funny,' she said slowly, still deciding how much to reveal. 'Sitting last night watching the diggers and the police . . .' She breathed out, a little rush of self-deprecation to pre-empt any reaction from Cal. 'I can't describe it because I've never experienced it before . . . not in my adult life . . . of being a daughter, I suppose.'

She glanced at him again, a silent apology for the right words being hard to find. 'Of having a responsibility to a parent . . . do you know what I mean? That's it . . . of feeling her pulling at me.' She let out a laugh. 'If the police hadn't been there with their diggers and trucks I'd have used my bare hands to find her.'

He nodded. He understood, or thought he did. If she had asked him two, maybe three, years ago who he was or what he was, he could have produced a short list of definitions. The top three would have been 'husband, son, oceanographer' even if he wasn't sure about the order. Perhaps that was why his marriage hadn't exactly been successful. Now *husband* no longer applied and though still a son, he didn't feel like one anymore because his father had 'shed' him, emotionally, had replaced him with another family. At least that was how it seemed to Cal.

'Until last night, I hadn't considered myself a daughter,' Violet said. 'Because I always thought my mother abandoned me.'

Now she knew she hadn't. That had made all the difference.

She picked at her nails. He said nothing.

'Thank you,' she said after a moment.

'For what?'

'For listening.'

He shrugged. *Who says he did?* She flicked the back of her hand against his thigh just as the bus appeared round the side of the hill. 'Today,' she said, setting off towards it, 'is going to be a good day. Don't you think?'

Cal stayed where he was, watching the reunion of mother and daughter. When Violet started back towards him, a child in each hand, she called out to him. 'I should have warned you.'

'What?'

'How alike the girls are.'

'Twins,' he said. One was milky pale with straight white-blonde hair and the other brown-skinned with wide brown eyes and dark curls.

'I'd be guessing now, but that one,' he pointed at the darker girl, 'is yours.'

'How do you know?'

He looked from the blonde child holding Violet's other hand to the blonde woman who followed behind, one a smaller version of the other. 'Luck, I guess.'

'You must be Hilary,' he said, offering to take her rucksack and the extra tent. As he put them in the pickup he noticed Hilary giving Violet an inquiring look and Violet deliberately ignoring her. Something similar happened at the turn-off to South Bay. Cal caught it in his mirror: Hilary's silent inquiry and Violet shaking her head and mouthing 'stop it'. He wondered if that was why Violet had asked Anna and Izzy to tell her everything they'd seen on their journey. Was she trying to stall Hilary's curiosity about Cal, about whether anything had happened between Violet and him? Approaching Boyd's Farm, he realised Violet had another, more urgent concern. The girls had listed buzzard, seal, mountain, heather, river, sea, bus, rook, seagull and forests and Anna was looking out of the window for other ideas. 'Now,' Violet said, turning her back to the door and covering the window so that Anna couldn't see past her, 'why don't you ask Cal what he found in the shop for you?'

'What?' Both girls glanced shyly at the back of Cal's head.

'Nets for fishing in rock pools and,' Violet enthused, 'buckets *and* spades.' She mentioned the different creatures Anna and Izzy might catch, 'starfish, crab, winkle, shrimp, prawn . . .' The girls listened and stretched their arms wide to show how big their catch would be. Having worked out why Violet was behaving as she was, Cal joined in by announcing he'd caught a 'whale' in a rock pool when he'd been a boy, about the same age as Anna and Izzy.

'Could we *really* catch a whale?' Izzy asked Hilary.

'Maybe a small one,' Hilary suggested.

Anna adopted a know-it-all look. 'There aren't small whales.'

By then the pickup had passed the stone pillars to Boyd's Farm and was approaching the road-end by the beach. 'Here we are.' Violet sounded relieved. As far as Cal could tell, Anna and Izzy hadn't noticed a thing, not the police, the trucks or the diggers.

Anna was cleaning her beach apartment, patting the sand smooth with her hands, discarding seaweed and gathering up her collection of shells. 'Really . . . honestly . . . how many times do I have to tell you?' Anna greeted each new example of Violet's untidiness with an exclamation. One by one she picked up the shells and placed them on a flat rock beside which was a puddle of seawater. She scolded each one in turn.

'*You* need to be washed.'

'You *need* to be washed.'

'You need to be *washed*.'

With every change of emphasis she raised her voice. In between times she complained about the state of her new kitchen. 'It's a mess, worse than before. Really I don't know what to do.'

Then she checked to see whether Violet was listening, whether she was sorry.

'How often have I told you about tidying up after parties?'

Violet still wasn't paying sufficient attention. So Anna pulled at her arm. 'Mummy, I'm cross with you. I won't let you stay here again if you don't help.' Violet glanced down at her daughter. Whenever Anna called her 'Mummy' she knew she was upset.

'I'm sorry, sweetheart.'

Anna found a broken shell. 'You'll have to buy another one,' she said, tugging at her, making her play beach apartments. They were among rocks by the bottom of the steep path which Megan Bates used to take to the beach. At Anna's request, Violet had made a notice out of cardboard and put it at the entrance. 'Anna's Beach Apartment. Please remove your shoes,' it said.

'Please . . . pleeeaaase . . . Mummy, help me.' Pulling on Violet's arm wasn't working anymore. So Anna slumped into a sulk. Her shoulders drooped. 'There's so much to do, pleeeaaase.' She stood up, hands on hips, head at one side. 'If you don't help now (she stamped her foot) . . . this minute (again) . . . I'll just have to ask you to leave.'

Violet pulled the little girl to her, hugged her and kissed her head as Anna gave up her struggles of protest. 'Why won't you help with the dishes?' She twisted and turned until she was looking into Violet's face which was puffy from crying. Anna was suddenly solicitous and attentive. She'd do the dishes. She liked doing dishes. Of course Violet mustn't leave the apartment. Where else would she have to go, and anyway who else but Anna would put up with Violet's partying and untidiness? 'Please stay,' she tugged at her mother, trying to persuade her. 'If you don't stay, I'll be very lonely.' Anna reached up to her mother's face and wiped it, leaving grains of sand on her cheeks. 'I wasn't really cross.'

Violet said, 'It's not you silly.'

Anna was now pulling at her mother's lips, making her kiss her finger tips one by one. 'What is it then?'

'Oh it's nothing. It's just being with you . . . here.'

Anna curled up between her mother's legs. 'How many floors will our proper beach house have?' she asked.

'Two,' Violet replied.

'Bigger than this beach apartment . . . ?'

'Yes.'

'And we'll have a bedroom each, and one for Izzy to come and stay?'

'Yes.'

'And a separate kitchen?' A separate kitchen was

important to Anna. The flat in Glasgow had one room with a bathroom off.

'Yes.'

'And someone to do the dishes?'

'Yes.'

Anna reviewed her mother's answers, testing them for truthfulness, checking everything important had been covered. 'All right,' she said, adding, 'I suppose' as a warning against later revisions.

They lay together until Violet said, 'Anna, if I help you with the dishes, will you come for a walk?'

'I might,' she replied. 'Where to?'

'Just along the beach, and then we'll join the others. In fact,' Violet suggested, 'Why don't you put your feet up and I'll do the dishes.' Violet reached for the shells and made splashing noises in the rock pool. 'There,' she said, 'Finished.'

Anna sat and inspected the shells. She pointed at one, claiming it still to be dirty and set about washing it. 'It's always the same,' she said, 'if you want a job done properly you have to do it yourself.' Violet smiled at Anna copying her nursery school teacher. It was one of Mrs Semple's favourite complaints.

'Do you know what?' Violet asked, standing up and lifting Anna over the surrounding rocks and planting her on the sand.

'What?'

'Do you know what your grandmother did every day?'

'No.'

Violet held out her hand for Anna. Their fingers interlocked and Violet walked her to the water's edge. 'She used to come here every morning.'

'Did she paddle?' Anna let the water approach the tips of her toes before jumping back.

'She did. She used to do this, just like we're doing.'

A black Audi with tinted windows was parked at the stone pillars to Boyd's Farm. The car was clean, shiny and, in Cal's opinion, out of place. It belonged to a swanky city street not this back of beyond. He walked towards it, his attention on the progress of the search. The scene was little changed. Teams of police sifted through the piles of flotsam and the numerous small mounds of earth the digger had scooped from the four shallow pits it had excavated so far. Even at a distance Cal could see how little topsoil there was, barely enough to cover a body. He would tell Violet that was why the police were concentrating their search on Duncan's flotsam piles: a body in such a shallow grave would need to have another layer covering it for a guarantee of concealment. Something else was also obvious: by the numbers of police and the level of activity – there were half a dozen vans as well as two diggers and three trucks – the body had not been found.

By then Cal was almost at the parked car. As he drew alongside it, intending to carry on to the Poltown road before returning to the beach a different way, the driver's window opened with an expensive swish. A man in dark glasses, Mediterranean blue shirt open at the neck and a supercilious smile, asked, 'Don't suppose they've found anything?'

'Who wants to know?' Cal said, bending down and looking in. There was another man in the passenger seat. Cal recognised Ross Turnbull. He nodded acknowledgement and Turnbull returned the gesture. Dark Glasses flashed another bright white smile and his card: *Don Saxby, Executive Director, Development, BRC* was written across the base of a drawing of a wind turbine. 'Just wondering what delay to factor in.'

Cal snorted and shook his head. 'Don't you guys ever give up – a man's dead for God's sake.' The window closed.

When Cal returned to South Bay Hilary and Izzy were splashing at the water's edge, and Violet was sitting higher up the beach beside Anna. The girl was turning the pages of her painting book and telling Violet about each picture.

'That's Granny's house. That's her front door, and that's,' Anna pointed again, 'her bedroom window.'

Violet glanced at Cal. He shook his head. *No, nothing, they're still searching.*

'And here's Granny paddling.' Anna turned another page.

'So it is, Anna. You are clever. Just as I asked you. Will you paint some more while you're here?'

'Hilary only let me bring crayons,' Anna said crossly.

'Well, draw something for me in crayons. I'd love that.'

Violet glanced again at Cal. 'Alexandra Hamilton's invitation?' he reminded her. 'What are you going to do?'

After a late picnic lunch of tomato sandwiches, crisps and cans of Fanta, Violet warned the girls they had work to do. It was a rule of camping, she said; everyone pitching in together, children and adults; each having a task. Izzy and Anna drowned out Violet by shouting, and Violet told Cal he wouldn't have any young assistants after all. Anna and Izzy would be accompanying their mothers on a long walk, and he'd have to put up the tents and collect driftwood for the fire by himself. She suggested the girls put on their shoes because they'd be climbing uphill and the path would be stony and rough. Izzy and Anna looked at each other before Izzy announced she had a sore foot and should probably remain behind to help Cal. 'So it'll just be you walking, will it Anna?' Violet inquired while busying herself with her backpack. 'Hilary,' Violet asked, 'have you got any of those plasters for blisters . . . oh, and an insect spray because we'll be eaten alive by midges once we're away from the beach and that nice breeze from the sea?'

Anna pulled at her mother's sleeve.

'Can't I stay here, with Izzy?'

'If Cal lets you,' Violet replied as a small, blue car appeared at the road end drawing her attention way. 'Come on,' she said to Hilary, 'I'll introduce you.' They started across the sand and Mrs Anderson appeared at the open driver's door. She was barely taller than the car. 'You must think me very rude,' Violet said when they were close, 'running out of your house like that, leaving you with all the clearing up after all the trouble you'd gone to.'

Mrs Anderson shielded her eyes from the sun with one hand and held on to the door with the other, as if she needed the support. Violet thought how frail, how shrunken, how different Mrs Anderson looked.

'I don't at all. Not a bit of it,' Mrs Anderson replied. 'I should be apologising to you.'

'Why?'

'I should have realised the effect it would have . . . to hear that Duncan had your mother's possessions. It was thoughtless of me.'

Mrs Anderson looked back over her shoulder in the direction of Boyd's Farm. 'Now this terrible thing and my own flesh and blood too. I don't know what to say to you. It's terrible, just terrible.'

Violet rubbed the older woman's arm. 'You're not to blame.'

'No,' Mrs Anderson replied in the same troubled manner. 'I suppose not, but still, I can't help but feel responsible.'

Violet introduced Hilary and pointed out the children, telling Mrs Anderson which was which. 'Just in case they come over,' Violet warned Mrs Anderson, 'Anna knows about her grandmother being dead, but not how she died, nor about the police search.'

'Well, I won't say anything.' Mrs Anderson seemed to approve of Violet's restraint. 'Far better she doesn't know the details,' she said with the certainty of age. Although she was tactful enough to say 'what lovely children', Violet noticed Mrs Anderson's eye remaining on Anna.

'I just want her to enjoy the feeling of having a grandmother,' Violet said, 'of spending time on the beach where she loved to be.'

'Well,' Mrs Anderson said, 'if there are things you have to do, the police and so on, leave them with me . . . or if the weather changes and they need a hot bath. It's been too long since Gardener's Cottage has heard the sound of children.' As an afterthought, she asked, 'Do small girls still like baking?'

'They do,' Violet replied.

The conversation moved on to Alexandra's invitation to Brae, Violet asking Mrs Anderson's advice on whether she should go. Hilary thought she should but Violet wasn't sure. 'Of course you must go,' Mrs Anderson replied, 'and let me have the children. Then Hilary can accompany you.'

Later, as she was showing Hilary her father's gravestone, Violet said she was pleased the girls would be going to Mrs Anderson because she'd seemed somehow diminished. Duncan's death and the police searching her old home must have hit her hard. Having Anna and Izzy would be good for her.

CHAPTER 21

Alexandra Hamilton wore a silk print dress belted at the waist and a style of shoe that Anna liked to call 'properly'. They were black patent with heels which elevated Alexandra above her visitors. 'Oh, there you are,' she said, her manner as overbearing as her height. 'I suppose you'd better follow me.' Leaving Violet to close the back door, she went briskly from the kitchen to the front of the house; one pantry opening on to another followed by a wood-panelled corridor. Violet and Hilary lagged half a dozen steps behind, their different progress marked by the noise of footwear on polished floors; the squeak of trainers from Violet and Hilary, the emphatic tattoo of Alexandra's heels.

'Queen Bitch,' Hilary whispered to Violet before they found themselves in a large wood-panelled hall with twin leather sofas either side of a fireplace. Above it hung the portrait of a young woman, her blonde hair cascading artfully on to one shoulder, her face tilted upwards and glowing with the hungry expectation of a charmed life. 'A present from William Ritchie, my father,'

Alexandra said, watching for Violet's reaction. 'He commissioned it for my 21st birthday.' Alexandra's fingers played with the string of pearls at her neck. The young woman in the painting wore them too. Alexandra saw Violet make the connection. 'Another present,' she simpered, 'for my 18th.'

Hilary mouthed at Violet, '*Whose* father?' as Alexandra set off again, this time through an open door into what turned out to be the dining room. A man with wire-rimmed glasses and a crust of white hair sat at the far end of a long mahogany table around which were a dozen chairs with matching tapestry seats. 'I'm sorry, Gordon, for abandoning you.' Alexandra addressed him as if speaking to a crowd. 'I had to go looking for them – they'd gone to the *back* door.'

He raised a sympathetic eye-brow at such odd behaviour.

'This . . .' Alexandra pulled a chair away from the table for Violet, 'is Miss Wells.' She gave Hilary a dismissive look. 'And friend . . .' She carried on to the head of the table without pulling out another chair for Hilary. 'And this . . .' She stopped beside Gordon and placed her hand lightly on his shoulder, 'is Mr Campbell.'

He inclined his head at Violet and Hilary before sliding a document across the table to Alexandra.

Violet watched it. 'What's going on? Who is he?'

'Sit down please.' Alexandra turned a page and studied it, like a schoolmistress checking up on the record of a pupil brought before her for a disciplinary misdemeanour.

'No, not until I know what's happening.'

A bored expression crossed Alexandra's face. 'Mr Campbell is a solicitor, and,' she gave Violet a contemptuous look, 'a very old family friend.' She slapped her open hands on the table, indicating the start of proceedings. 'Now, Miss Wells, don't you think it's time you did some listening? This might not be what you want to hear but my father died regretting his affair with Megan Bates.' Alexandra lifted her nose, attempting to rise above a bad smell.

'Excuse me, *whose* father?' blurted Hilary.

The lawyer cleared his throat. 'Who exactly *are* you?'

'I'm Violet's friend, Hilary Reston.'

'Well, Miss Reston you may not realise this but Mrs Hamilton's biological father abandoned her when she was four. So William Ritchie was really the only father she had, and Mrs Hamilton was the only daughter, the only *child*, he acknowledged.' He allowed his left eyebrow to rise again. 'Indeed,' he glanced at Alexandra, 'with Mr Ritchie's encouragement and support she adopted his surname and she used it until her marriage to Matthew Hamilton.'

'Don't listen to him,' Hilary advised Violet before returning to glower at Mr Campbell. 'Why are you being so horrible?'

Mr Campbell cleared his throat again in lawyerly

affectation. 'Because it is important that Miss Wells doesn't harbour any illusions about what were and are the facts of Mr William Ritchie's short-lived affair with Megan Bates.' He drew back his lips to reveal worn-away, sharp little teeth and turned to examine Violet. 'It is quite clear he did not love Miss Bates, nor by the end of the affair did he have any feelings for her or for her unborn child.' His lips stretched again, as if attempting to demonstrate his sympathy for Violet's predicament. 'Indeed, given Miss Bates's reputation there is no reason why he should have formed an attachment for the child since it was far from certain that it was his.'

'Well, that's easily resolved,' Hilary snapped.

'Not as easily as you or Miss Wells might think.' Mr Campbell regarded Hilary over his glasses with a considered and concerned stare. 'I assume you are referring to the possibility of a DNA procedure?'

'Yes, I am.'

'That would require the disinterment of William Ritchie's coffin.' He paused and looked from Hilary to Violet. 'I imagine you realise that, since no other sources of DNA would be available.'

'I hadn't thought about it, but yes,' Hilary replied, glancing at Violet to check whether her friend was in agreement.

'Well, if that is the course of action Miss Wells plans, it would have to be resolved in a court of law. My client, of course, would oppose any interference with her father's grave.' His eyebrow arched. 'I'm sure you realise that going to court would be very expensive, especially for the losing side.' He dropped his chin and stared over his glasses. 'Even more so if there were appeals and the usual costly delays . . . costs that my clients can easily afford.' He directed a pitying frown at Violet. 'And that also applies should you decide to pursue an action for any of the property Mrs Hamilton inherited from her father.'

Violet frowned in return. 'Is that why you think I'm here?'

'Frankly,' Mr Campbell said, 'I have no idea why you are here, but in case it's to try to enrich yourself at Mrs Hamilton's expense . . .' He stopped and referred to the document in front of him. 'There are two issues to be resolved. The first is whether you are indeed Mr Ritchie's daughter, which my client disputes. The second, and the issue of greater significance, is whether, had Mr Ritchie imagined himself to be the father, he would have made any provision for you in his will. Of course, if you *were* his child, under Scots law, you could well have a claim for a share of what we call his moveable property – furniture and so on – but again you would have to establish that claim in court with all the risk and expense that might involve.

'In case of any confusion,' he glanced now at Alexandra, 'Mrs Hamilton thought you should be made aware of her father's, Mr Ritchie's, attitude

346

towards Miss Bates. Before his death, he wrote a letter to his wife, my client's mother, expressing his regret at the affair and the hurt it caused. He is silent on the subject of Miss Bates's child but goes on to make specific reference to his paternal love for my client.' He indicated he was talking about Alexandra Hamilton. 'He refers to her as "our darling daughter".'

He let his words have their effect before continuing. 'The difficulty for you Miss Wells is this: if you were to pursue the legal route my client would give evidence that William Ritchie not only regretted his entanglement with Megan Bates but never accepted the child as his own.' He managed to sound perplexed on Violet's behalf. 'As far as I am aware, there is no witness available to you with more intimate access to William Ritchie or knowledge of his feelings at that time than my client.'

'Stop this – what are you saying?' Hilary shouted. 'Her mother has been murdered and the police are still looking for her body.'

'None of which is my client's concern.' Mr Campbell coughed. 'However, she is concerned at the disruptive effect of Miss Wells's presence here on her family.'

'Meaning what?' Hilary asked.

'Meaning that she is prepared to offer Miss Wells some small recompense.' Mr Campbell searched for the appropriate word. 'Shall we say for her . . . trouble?' He smirked in satisfaction at his eventual choice.

'What?' Violet said.

'My client,' he indicated Alexandra again, 'is prepared to offer you £1,000 in full and final settlement of any future claim you may bring on the basis of your unproven relationship to William Ritchie.'

He looked at Violet, as if inviting a question. 'There are two conditions, that you agree to take no steps to establish his paternity, and that you agree to remove yourself from Poltown and to stay away.'

'What,' Hilary exclaimed, 'for £1,000?'

'Miss Wells would then return to the life she was leading a few days ago, before she'd heard of Mr William Ritchie, before she knew Poltown existed,' Mr Campbell said. Money for nothing, his eyebrow suggested.

Hilary and Violet exchanged glances.

'I would advise you to consider it with care.' Mr Campbell removed his glasses and his lips pulled back into a sneer. 'When you consider the alternative . . .'

The sentence was left hanging, along with the implication of unspecified consequences. 'Of course,' he added, 'we will require a signature from you, Miss Wells, at the places marked.'

With that he slid a document across the table towards Violet. It had yellow tabs at the pages where Violet was expected to sign. 'Your friend too, as the witness.' A pen was lying on the top sheet. 'Mrs Hamilton and I will be waiting outside should you have any questions.'

He picked up his briefcase and snapped it shut. 'To avoid misunderstanding, there will be no repeat of this offer.' He waited for Alexandra to rise and followed her from the room.

After the door closed they heard Alexandra's heels striking against the wooden floor of the hall. Violet stretched across the table and tore the document in half and again into quarters. The pieces of paper fluttered from her hands. Taking the key to Orasaigh Cottage from her jeans' pocket, she placed it among the fragments on the polished mahogany table.

'I was wrong,' Hilary said. 'What an EMPRESS of a bitch.' She hugged Violet. 'Are you ok?'

'I'm fine.'

Hilary surveyed the dining room with its gilt mirrors and a sideboard crowded with a menagerie of animals in silver. 'I know what this is about,' she said. 'She's showing off. That's what she's doing. Don't you see? The house, the painting in the hall, the pearls, all this . . . she's letting you see what she's got, her inheritance, the 'moveable property'. She's daring you to take her on.'

Violet looked around the room too, wondering how she belonged here, *if* she belonged here, how these *possessions* had anything to do with her.

'What are you going to do?' Hilary asked.

'Nothing.' Violet moved towards the door. 'Nothing at all.'

She waited for Hilary before turning the handle. In the hall Alexandra looked up and Mr Campbell studied Violet over the top of his glasses. 'I presume,' he said, 'that you have been sensible.' There was an unspoken 'or else'.

'I wish you'd stop making assumptions about me,' Violet said.

'Come on.' Hilary pulled at her arm. 'Let's go.'

They went along the corridor to the kitchen and the back door. Outside in the yard, Hilary said, 'Did you see the way they were looking at us?' She glanced behind her, as if expecting to find Alexandra and the lawyer in pursuit. Violet walked on without speaking. As they skirted the walled garden on their way to pick up Anna and Izzy from Mrs Anderson, Hilary forced her to stop. 'You weren't supposed to do that. Were you?'

'No,' Violet said.

Izzy's pink tongue darted in and out between her lips in concentration as she guided the knife through the layers of sponge cake. 'That's it,' Mrs Anderson said. 'Hard enough to cut but not so hard the chocolate and raspberry filling spills out.'

The knife hit the plate with a clunk.

'Do the same again here.' Mrs Anderson took the knife and scored the icing with the blade. 'Now press down.'

The first slice was larger than the second and Violet said she 'definitely' wanted the big bit. Mrs Anderson put it on a plate and Anna delivered it by walking stiffly round the table and announcing: 'your order'. She curtseyed and Violet kissed her on the top of her head eliciting an indignant protest: 'Customers shouldn't kiss the waitress'.

Mrs Anderson handed Anna another plate. 'It looks amazing,' Hilary said as Anna put it on the table in front of her without the curtsey. 'Mm, perfect,' she said, taking a bite.

Anna and Izzy grinned at each other and then in anticipation at Mrs Anderson who was cutting two more pieces. 'Now girls,' she said, 'What about your mothers enjoying their cups of tea in peace?' Handing a plate to each child, she asked Violet and Hilary whether they minded Anna and Izzy watching television next door. She'd promised they could, a reward for helping her to lay the table and clear up the dishes.

'Of course not,' Hilary said. Mrs Anderson herded the girls ahead of her. 'Come on then.' She pulled the kitchen door to. 'Let's see what's on?'

In the sitting room, Anna and Izzy knelt on the rug, their cake in front of them. Mrs Anderson turned on the television, apologising for having so few channels. 'That, that,' Anna shouted as Mrs Anderson switched from one to the next.

That was a wildlife programme about a mother monkey and her sick baby. 'It's going to die isn't it?' Izzy complained to Anna.

'It can't,' Anna insisted. 'I won't let it.'

As soon as they were engrossed, Mrs Anderson remembered she had to shut the window in her bedroom. 'Be sure now to tell me everything when I get back.' The girls looked up before the monkey claimed their attention again and Mrs Anderson went from the room across the hall. She lingered at the foot of the stairs, close enough to the kitchen door to hear Violet and Hilary.

Hilary was saying, 'It's meaningless, don't you see?'

Violet replied, 'I told you, it doesn't matter.' Mrs Anderson heard the hurt in her voice.

'So what if he wrote a letter to his wife just before he died,' Hilary continued. 'What was he supposed to say? That he'd loved another woman? Of course he wouldn't. It doesn't prove anything. Your mother had been dead 20 years; as far as he was concerned so had you. Of course he'd say he regretted the affair. Of course he wouldn't mention whether he'd had feelings for you, for the child.'

'Really, it doesn't matter,' Violet insisted.

'Well,' Hilary said. 'Don't let it get to you. That bitch is just frightened of you, that's all. Nobody can tell what would have happened if your father had known you were alive; nobody.'

Changing the subject, Violet said she should check whether Anna and Izzy were exhausting Mrs Anderson. 'She's been so good with them.' A chair scraped and Mrs Anderson retreated into the sitting room. Her entrance barely disturbed the children who were still gripped by the unfolding tragedy of the sick monkey. Its condition had worsened and Anna and Izzy were discussing whether it was still breathing. Mrs Anderson settled into her chair just as Violet looked round the door and saw the girls fixed on an apparently lifeless and almost hairless body.

'Is the poor little thing dead?' she asked and Anna and Izzy explained what had happened, taking it in turns to relate the litany of disaster that had befallen the unfortunate creature. Anna waved her mother closer and Mrs Anderson took the opportunity to excuse herself to put the kettle on.

As she hoped, Hilary was still at the kitchen table. Closing the door, Mrs Anderson wondered whether she would like another cup of tea. 'I don't suppose *Miss* Alexandra offered you very much.'

'Certainly not tea,' Hilary answered with similar disapproval to Mrs Anderson's.

Mrs Anderson replied with a series of tuts. 'In Mr William's time it was always a very welcoming house. Not like it is now.'

'You worked for William Ritchie didn't you?'

'I did, for many years, when he was a bachelor and then after his marriage to Alexandra's mother.'

'What sort of man was he?'

Mrs Anderson considered the question and Hilary mistook her slowness for offence. 'I hope you don't mind me asking?'

'Not at all,' Mrs Anderson reassured her. Her mouth flinched as if in pain. 'Not after the way Alexandra and that husband of hers have treated me.'

'I'm sorry. I didn't know.'

'They wouldn't have dared if Mr William had

353

been alive.' Mrs Anderson managed to look appropriately indignant. 'A gentleman he was *and* he had good manners.' In contrast to Alexandra was the implication. 'Even if he did prefer his own company.'

'You liked him?' Hilary thought it safer territory than a question about Alexandra.

'It wasn't my place to like him.' She corrected Hilary in her precise way. 'I was his house-keeper. I respected him.'

'Did he respect you?'

'I like to think so.' Mrs Anderson saw Hilary's puzzlement at her uncertainty. 'It was the way of things then. Mr William was someone who liked rules and formalities, everything in its proper place.'

'He sounds like a cold man.'

Mrs Anderson considered Hilary's criticism before answering. 'He wasn't an easy man to get to know, that's certainly true. And he could be cold and distant. Emotions frightened him. He wasn't comfortable with them, like a lot of men I suppose. But you could always rely on him to be fair. You could trust him.' Once again the comparison with Alexandra was left unsaid.

'Stop me if I'm prying but did you know Megan Bates?'

'I did.'

'You didn't approve?'

'Indeed, I did not.' Mrs Anderson had become clipped.

'Alexandra had a lawyer with her. A man called Gordon Campbell. Do you know him?'

'I know of him.' She didn't elaborate. Mr Campbell had signed the warning letters she had received about the rent for Gardener's Cottage.

'Well, he said, the lawyer that is . . .' Hilary dropped her voice and glanced at the door in case Violet was about to return. 'He said that even William Ritchie wasn't convinced that Megan Bates's child was his.'

'Mr Campbell said that?'

'Yes.'

'The nerve of some people,' Mrs Anderson muttered.

'William Ritchie thought he *was* the father?'

'That was my impression at the time.'

'Mr Campbell tried to make out that William Ritchie had no wish for any other child but Alexandra. He mentioned Alexandra changing her surname to his as evidence of that.'

'She did change her name, yes.' Mrs Anderson pursed her lips tight together.

'What did her step-father think?'

'I can't say at the beginning,' Mrs Anderson replied. 'It wasn't long after Megan Bates's death.'

Hilary gasped. 'You mean she tried to replace his dead child?'

Mrs Anderson's eyes flicked to the ceiling inviting Hilary to draw her own conclusions. 'At that time I don't think Mr William would have noticed whether she called herself Ritchie or any other name.'

'Why not?'

'He locked himself away. I hardly saw him for months.'

'He was upset at Megan's death?'

'That, and the baby, and the hurt he'd caused Diana, the shame of being exposed like that, everyone talking about it, the disgrace. It was all of those together.'

'He mourned the baby too?'

'Mr William had his differences with Megan Bates before her death but . . .' She chose her words with care. 'It would be a mistake to think he had no feelings for the child.'

'Go on,' Hilary said.

'He would have been torn in two, between Diana and Megan Bates, between his marriage and the child. Diana was threatening him with a divorce if he continued the affair. Megan Bates was using the child to pressure him to live with her.'

'She threatened to disappear with the baby?'

'Apparently so,' Mrs Anderson replied. 'Mr William wouldn't have known what to do and then it was too late. Megan was dead. Afterwards he blamed himself for everything.'

The sound of Anna and Izzy chattering in the hall penetrated the kitchen door. Hilary turned as the girls entered the room. Violet followed with their dirty plates. 'I think it's time we left you in peace,' she said to Mrs Anderson. 'You've been so kind.'

After saying farewells at the front door, Violet

suggested a race to the end of the garden wall. She and Izzy had started running when Anna reached up to Mrs Anderson. 'Thank you,' she said as the old woman bent towards her. Anna planted a sticky kiss on her cheek and ran off, shouting 'wait for me' to Violet and Izzy.

Hilary hung back.

'Don't let Violet know I've told you this,' she said.

Mrs Anderson attempted to conceal the effect Anna's display of affection had had on her. 'What dear?'

'Alexandra made Violet an offer to settle any claim she has against William Ritchie's estate.'

'Did she?'

'It was laughable really, only £1000.'

'What did Violet say?'

'She didn't say anything. She tore up the document.' Hilary looked at Mrs Anderson. 'I've told her to fight for what's hers.'

'Of course, she must,' Mrs Anderson snapped. Her right hand gripped Hilary's arm. 'She must. Tell her she must.'

'I will.'

Mrs Anderson seemed to struggle for words. 'She can't . . . she can't . . . let that *cuckoo* have it all.'

Hilary remembered the portrait in the hall, the way Alexandra's head tilted upwards, just like a baby cuckoo waiting to be fed after it has evicted all the other fledglings from the nest.

★   ★   ★

Mrs Anderson felt the warmth and sugary stickiness of Anna's goodbye kiss, the innocent simplicity of it provoking a storm of recriminations. How daft she was for allowing a child's touch to affect her so. What an old fool she had become. She slumped into her chair in the kitchen to mourn what she had lost, what might have been. The forefinger and thumb of her right hand stroked the edge of the table where Violet had lain as a new-born baby, where earlier that day Violet had eaten chocolate and raspberry sponge cake.

One gust subsided and another of indignation blew in, at the humiliations Mrs Anderson had had to bear, at Alexandra's ill-deserved good fortune to have children and money, at the injustice being done to Violet and Anna. She imagined Violet and Anna living at Brae. How different it would be. Mrs Anderson would be a cherished and frequent visitor. Anna would drop by to make cakes at Gardener's Cottage. For righting the wrong in which she was complicit, had Mrs Anderson found salvation as well as a new family? 'Violet must. Of course she must.'

CHAPTER 22

The speed of the flames enthralled Anna and Izzy. One moment delicate tongues of pale yellows and pinks played around the bleached driftwood, the next a roaring brush-fire of livid red devoured a tangle of fishing nets. The noise reminded Hilary of a breaker crashing on to a beach in a storm.

'Do you think,' she asked the girls, 'that nets and driftwood store the sound of sea until it's released by fire . . . and do you think the sound returns to the waves?' She was kneeling between Anna and Izzy, an arm around each, pulling one then the other back whenever their fascination with the flames drew them unconsciously closer. 'Oh look, Mummy's coming back,' she said to Anna. The fire continued to hold the child rapt and she didn't see Violet's troubled expression after her walk along the beach with Cal or Cal's signal for Hilary to accompany him to the pickup to collect the food for the barbecue.

'What's happened?' she asked Cal as soon as they were out of earshot. 'What's wrong with Violet?'

'The police have suspended the search.'

'Why?' Violet and Hilary had noticed the lack of activity at Boyd's Farm on their way back from Mrs Anderson's. They hadn't really discussed it because of the children but they'd assumed the stoppage was temporary, just for the evening, and would start again in the morning. 'Have they found the body?'

Cal shook his head. 'No.' He'd gone to Boyd's Farm after collecting driftwood for the bonfire, 'Just to check'. He'd arrived as the digger, trucks and police vehicles were driving away. A constable left behind on guard duty told him the search had been suspended. The obvious places to bury a body had been excavated, he'd said. So far they'd found 'nada, zilch, nothing apart from a sheep's jaw bone and some rusting farm tools.' Which left the barns, but they were in imminent danger of collapse, and they took the view it wasn't worth risking an officer's life for a body that was a quarter of a century old. According to the constable, a plan was being drawn up, involving the windfarm consortium. BRC was in the throes of buying Boyd's Farm. Once the purchase had been completed, it would dismantle the buildings under police supervision and the search would continue hand in hand with the demolition. BRC would pay for everything including the cost of trans-porting the barns' contents to a police warehouse where they would be sorted, sifted and searched. According to the constable, there would be a delay

360

of two or three weeks before work resumed at the site, though BRC was in a hurry to get things moving.

Hilary blew out her cheeks, imagining her friend's reaction. 'How did Violet take it?'

'How do you think? She's angry.' Cal had mentioned to Violet the 'flash car' he'd encountered on the beach road by entrance to Boyd's Farm, how the driver had been 'a wheeler-dealer type' working for BRC and the passenger had been Ross Turnbull. Cal said, 'Violet thinks it's happening again – the original inquiry into her mother's disappearance was wrapped up quickly because the Turnbulls didn't want police crawling over Poltown for weeks, disrupting their operations. Now this . . .'

After a barbecue of grilled sausages and tomatoes, Cal suggested a foraging trip to Anna and Izzy. He'd identified a place for collecting mussels, another for winkles and he'd seen some 'good-looking' tidal pools. While Izzy fetched the nets and buckets and Anna her painting book and crayons, Hilary thanked Cal. With the girls occupied, she would have an opportunity to talk to Violet, to persuade her to 'stick with it and fight'.

Walking along the beach, Cal described some of the creatures Anna and Izzy might encounter: limpets, starfish, blenny, whelks, periwinkles as well as crabs. Arriving at the first rock pool, Cal peered into the still water and pointed out a prawn that was backing away towards a sheltering curtain of seaweed. Under his instruction, Izzy slid her net behind the retreating creature and Anna put hers in front. The two girls brought their nets together and lifted them to search for the captive prawn. Despite Cal warning about its agility, it leapt through Izzy's fingers and splashed back into the water. The next hour or so passed with similar scenes of capture and escape, though increasingly of capture, with Izzy proving to be the more dextrous of the girls.

Eventually, Anna abandoned her 'stupid net' with a flash of temper and took her painting book and crayons to a raised ledge.

When Cal asked her what she was doing, she replied sulkily, 'Drawing mummy.'

'What's she doing in your drawing?' he asked.

'She's doing nothing,' Anna said, her sulkiness turning to mild contempt for Cal's ignorance. 'Because she's a baby and babies can't do anything.'

'They can cry,' Cal said.

'I suppose,' Anna conceded reluctantly. 'But I can't draw crying.'

Cal glanced back at Violet and Hilary expecting them to be in conversation by the fire but he spotted them at the road end talking to a visitor. Mrs Anderson, Cal guessed, because her car, or a car very like hers, was parked beside his.

Noticing that Cal's attention had drifted to the other end of the beach, Anna asked, 'What are you looking at?'

'Just checking the fire.' he replied before diverting Anna by suggesting they looked for a crab. 'And then we could collect mussels.'

Having become rivals at catching prawns, Izzy and Anna reverted to being allies against the large crab which Cal had seen scuttling away in a deep pool closer to the point of the headland. Despite prodding and poking, the crab remained hidden. At one stage Cal pretended it had the cane of his fishing net in its powerful claws and was dragging him into the pool. The girls helped to pull him back. After they'd stopped laughing Izzy said, 'What's mummy doing?'

Cal looked up. Hilary was running towards them.

Izzy had a confused expression, caught between happiness at the thought of showing off her catch of sea creatures to her mother and worry at her urgency.

'Just wait here a moment,' Cal said. 'And watch out that crab doesn't get you,' he added, trying to make light of what was happening. He loped towards Hilary, hoping his casual manner would reassure the girls. When Hilary was a few metres from him, she stopped, put her hands on her hips and gasped for breath.

'What's going on?' he asked, walking up to her.

She gulped a lungful of air. 'Mrs Anderson,' she gulped again, 'has got some letters from Violet's father.' She managed a long, deep breath. 'He wrote them to Megan Bates. Mrs Anderson has had them for years.'

It seemed Mrs Anderson had given a hurried explanation about discovering them in William Ritchie's drawers after his death and somehow never finding the right moment to ask Diana whether they should be burnt. Now Diana was dead too, Mrs Anderson thought Violet should decide what happened to them.

There were seven letters, each one hand-written in black ink, and each contained within a single sheet of blue writing paper. Hilary remarked on the turmoil caused by an affair which warranted so slight a correspondence, a mere seven pieces of paper and about a hundred lines of text.

'I wonder why there's none from Megan,' she said, studying Cal as he read the letters for the first time. She waited impatiently for his reaction, any reaction. 'Perhaps she didn't write any,' she suggested, still watching his face. 'After all, William Ritchie was a married man. In her position would I have risked writing a letter which Diana could have intercepted?'

Cal turned a page and carried on reading.

Hilary looked at Violet who had taken Anna and Izzy paddling. They were holding hands and jumping over the waves as they rolled in. 'I wonder what she'll decide,' she said wistfully, observing her friend. 'If I was Violet I'd grab as much as I could. I'd wipe the smile off Alexandra's smug little face. Queen Bitch. I've told her that's what she should do. With these letters she can't lose.'

Still Cal said nothing.

'Or,' she said, having another thought about the absence of letters written by Megan, 'possibly she *did* write and William Ritchie destroyed them because he was worried about Diana finding them.' She sighed at another question without an answer. 'Though why did he keep these ones?' Her face furrowed in frustration. 'I think,' she decided, 'that he kept these letters because the affair had been exposed by the time the police handed them back to him.' Her face brightened, a light going on. 'I know!' She examined Cal, hoping for an equivalent flicker of reaction. 'He couldn't bear to part with them because they were all he had left. That would help Violet's case, wouldn't it?'

Cal turned another page, the second last. 'We know she wrote one letter,' he remarked, continuing to read.

'The one that was posted around the time of her death,' Hilary added quickly, pleased to have a response at last, hoping for another. 'The one the police thought was a suicide note? The one that Duncan used to cover what he'd done?'

Cal didn't answer.

'I've been thinking about that too. Maybe she wrote it in desperation, without intending to post it. Maybe that's why she showed it to Duncan, because she wasn't sure about it.'

She had lost Cal again. She checked the letter he was reading. 'Dear Megan' it began. The last two opened in this way, indicative of the affair having cooled. The earlier letters started 'My Dear Megan'.

'I can't help liking him for that,' Hilary remarked. 'Dear Megan, even when he was probably thinking she was anything but. Though,' she reflected, 'it can't be easy falling in love with a man who starts letters 'My Dear Megan' when he's in the grip of passion, or what passed for it in William Ritchie's case, and 'Dear Megan' when he's backing away and telling her he's going to stick with his wife.'

Cal turned to the last letter in the sequence. It was short. Like the others, it was signed 'Sincerely yours, William'. Hilary read it too, upside down, trying to judge when Cal would be finished. 'Well?'

'Well,' Cal answered. 'He couldn't be clearer. Violet would have been his heir.' Cal referred again to the last letter. 'Megan would have been given a house and an allowance. Diana would have remained at Brae and their home in Edinburgh for her life-time, but the properties would have been put in trust for Violet. She would have gained possession of them on Diana's death.'

'Alexandra isn't even mentioned.'

'It doesn't mean he wouldn't have provided for her in some other way.'

'I guess.'

'Having read these . . .' Cal looked through them again. 'I don't think Megan did send letters to him.'

'Why?'

'Because he never makes any reference to

anything she's written. The first four . . .' Cal read the fifth again. 'Yes. The first four are him making up for his reticence when they've been together, or as he puts it in this one . . .' He held up the second letter. 'Yes here it is . . . where he apologises for his "lawyer's preference for measured judgement over emotional fireworks". By the fifth letter she must have told him about the pregnancy because he describes the "desperate and difficult decision" he's been forced to make, how "for reasons of duty and morality" he cannot contemplate divorce. Then, these last two, he's confirming the details of the settlement he's already proposed to her at a meeting. See here.' Cal showed the passage to Hilary. 'He's trying to reassure her that he'll look after her and the baby. He's committing it to paper so that she'll believe him.' He checked the last two letters again. 'That's it, yes. So the letter she composed just before she died, threatening to disappear, the baby too, might have been her only one, because William Ritchie doesn't make any reference to another.'

Hilary drew Cal's attention to Violet and the children. They were walking back up the beach.

'What do you think she'll do?' Hilary asked.

'I don't know.'

'She must fight. She's got to. You tell her.'

Cal and Hilary sat by the fire and listened to the rise and fall of Violet's voice, now a dragon, now a pleading child, now a booming giant. They heard

367

the protests of the children as their bed-time story ended and they waited for Violet's decision. Hilary was impatient for an answer. As soon as Violet joined them, she asked, 'Well, are you going to ring her?'

'Do you think I should?'

'God, yes.'

Violet took out her phone and scrolled through her call register to locate the number she had first rung to inquire about renting Orasaigh Cottage.

'A bed-time story for Alexandra.' Hilary looked smug with anticipation.

'I'm still not sure,' Violet said.

'Don't think twice about it,' Hilary said.

Violet pressed the call button and Hilary said, 'Good girl.'

Alexandra's imperious voice answered.

'Hi, it's Violet Wells.'

'So you've changed your mind?'

'There's something I'd like you to hear.' Violet held the letter so the glow of the fire illuminated it.

'What is it now?'

'Dear Megan,' Violet started reading, 'I wish another resolution were possible.'

'What is this?' Alexandra demanded.

Hilary shouted, 'It's a letter from *your* father.'

Violet waited for quiet before continuing. 'Dear Megan, I wish another resolution were possible.' She glanced at Hilary who mouthed 'go on'. 'All that is left to me is to honour the commitments that I have already made verbally.

To reiterate: I will treat the child as my own because it is. The child will be my heir and will inherit the bulk of my estate, including my properties in Edinburgh as well as here, in Poltown. I will change my will accordingly.'

'Where did you get this?' Alexandra barked.

Violet shook her head and appeared unable to carry on. Hilary took the letter and phone from her.

'Should I predecease my wife,' she continued in a more triumphal tone than Violet's, 'the use of my properties will be rightfully hers for her lifetime. On her death, they will be the child's to dispose of as he or she wishes.' Hilary interjected, 'that's Violet, by the way,' before carrying on to the conclusion. 'I will provide you with a house for you to choose within the financial limits I mentioned and a monthly allowance of £1,000. I apologise for the distress I have caused you. Sincerely yours, William.'

'So what do you think of *your* father now?' Hilary sneered.

'Don't.' Violet snatched back the phone.

'What's wrong?'

Violet cut the call. 'I don't want this.'

The children were in their sleeping bags chattering, and Hilary was going to join them since Izzy wouldn't settle without her.

'And anyway Violet will stay out all night.' Hilary looked beyond the fading glow of the fire into the darkness. 'If she thinks I'm waiting up to give her a talking to . . .' She sighed. Of course she wouldn't. She was sorry about the flare-up. It was the first they'd had. 'But I don't want her to regret anything. Do you know what I mean?' She made Cal promise to talk to Violet. 'Just what I've said to you. Tell her I'm worried about her making the wrong decision. That's all.'

Once Hilary had gone Cal went to fetch more planks from the driftwood pile. On his return, Violet was standing at the edge of the fire's glow. 'So, not a good day,' he said, putting the planks into the embers.

'No.'

'Would you like coffee or anything? The fire's still hot enough.'

'What should I do?' She folded her arms.

'You don't have to do anything.'

'I just want her to be found. That's all.' She glanced at Cal hoping he would understand.

He nodded. 'I know.'

The driftwood began to burn and crackle. They watched the flames until Cal said, 'Hilary thinks you're planning to go back to Glasgow, to your flat, your waitressing job.' He glanced at her. 'She's worried you'll wake up one morning and realise how much more you could have given Anna, if only you'd fought for it.'

Violet kicked at the sand. 'I know.' It had been playing on her mind too. 'But it's wrong. My mother didn't want William Ritchie's money, she wanted him and, at the end, she told him she would go away, make it impossible for him to find her. She didn't choose his money. Why should I?'

'He's your father, I guess.'

'He's a name on a gravestone. I don't have a father.' She sounded hurt and angry.

'Yeah.'

The fire again held their attention, until Violet touched his arm brushing the back of her fingers against the sleeve of his shirt. 'I'm sorry.'

He nodded. 'Yeah, I know.' Should he say more? He looked at her again. Her skin had turned rosy with the fire. He thought about kissing her. Instead, he said, 'Hilary thinks you should go for a long walk in the morning. Climb to the ridge above Brae. Go to Orasaigh. Walk round the loch. Explore. Take your time. Then come back and tell her you and Anna are better off in Glasgow.'

'She doesn't want me to say that.'

'No, but she won't mention it again if you do.'

Violet closed her eyes. She was tired. She would sleep on it. She kissed him on the cheek and walked towards her tent. 'Good night.'

Cal said, 'And if you do go . . .' She looked round. 'Take your backpack. I've put a bottle of water in it and some chocolate. The phone I gave you is there too. In case . . .' he shrugged, 'you get lost. Stick it in your pocket.'

CHAPTER 23

Hilary struck a bargain with Anna and Izzy. If they would entertain themselves while she slept for a little while longer, she *might* make sandcastles with them later. She said it so longingly that they'd said 'oh, all right' in bored voices and went to sit by Cal who was building up the fire and boiling water for coffee. At his suggestion, the girls rested against a log he'd found and stretched out their legs, making a table on which to rest Anna's painting book.

'That's Violet, when she was tired,' Izzy said, turning a page.

'That's our flat in Glasgow,' Anna said wistfully, turning another. 'Lovely flat . . .' She patted at the picture with the open palm of her hand. 'How long is Mummy going to be?' Anna looked perplexed. She was gazing along the beach road.

'I don't really know,' Cal replied, looking too. 'Couple of hours, I imagine, maybe more. She's just gone for a walk.'

'Why did she go without telling me?'

'You were asleep.'

Izzy raised her hand to Anna's face, forcing her to look at the book again. 'That's me,' Izzy said, 'sitting at Mummy's mirror.'

'And that's Ginger,' Anna said.

Ginger was the cat Izzy had adopted, or Izzy was the child Ginger had adopted. Anna wasn't sure which way round it was.

'That's your granny's house,' Izzy said.

'And that's the beach house mummy and me are going to have,' Anna said.

Izzy frowned, jealous. She turned the page quickly.

'That's Violet when she was a baby.'

Izzy glanced at Cal to check he was paying attention. 'Did you know that Violet had fair hair like me when she was a baby?'

Cal considered Izzy's question with a doubtful expression. 'She has dark hair now.'

'But she *was* fair wasn't she?' Izzy called for Anna's support.

'Mrs Anderson said so.' Anna said it in her most definite voice.

Cal leaned over and looked at the picture, a pink baby with a big round body, short legs and arms, a small face on top of which was a scribble of yellow crayon. 'When did she say that?'

'Yesterday, when we were doing the dishes,' Izzy said.

'What did Mrs Anderson say?' Cal asked. 'Can you remember? Her exact words?'

Anna and Izzy looked at each other and then at

Cal, detecting the difference in his tone, wondering what they'd done wrong.

'I got some soap in my hair,' Anna said uncertainly.

'Some bubbles from the washing up,' Izzy explained.

'And *she* said . . .' Anna continued.

'Mrs Anderson, you mean?' Cal asked.

Anna nodded. '*She* said it was funny my hair being so curly and dark because Violet's was the opposite when she was a baby. Hers had been blonde and fine, like silk.'

'She said that? Are you sure?'

Anna and Izzy looked at each other. They nodded in unison. 'Like silk,' they echoed.

'Did she say anything else?'

The girls shook their head.

'Are you sure? Nothing about *when* she'd seen her, *how* she had?'

In the blurry transition from unconsciousness Mrs Anderson thought she had been in the past again, remembering the baby and Diana banging on the door. She reached for her clock, expecting it to be almost 7.15, the time for her alarm to go off. To her surprise it was later, 7.50. She couldn't decide what had happened, whether she'd omitted to set it or whether she'd woken as usual and had gone back to sleep. She chided herself for being so forgetful when the banging started again; the pounding of a fist on the door; someone calling her name. Her hands went to her mouth. Not a dream. Not Diana. A man's voice. 'Mrs Anderson? Mrs Anderson?' The voice boomed in the stillness of early morning.

'Who is that?' she croaked. 'What do you want?' The sound she made was feeble, hardly loud enough to escape her bedroom, let alone travel downstairs to the front door. Yet, it was as if he had heard her. 'Open the door. It's Cal McGill, I'm Violet's friend.'

She found herself standing by her bed, her feet seeking slippers, the visitor, no, the *drama*, drawing her on. 'I've got to speak to you,' he shouted and struck the door a single heavy blow. Mrs Anderson felt the shock of it as she shuffled from her bedroom. She carried on down the stairs and across the hall, until only the thickness of the front door separated them.

Did he sense her? His sudden quiet made her think so. 'Go away,' she croaked, the silence unnerving her. And again, 'Go away.'

'Not until you open the door,' Cal replied. 'Not until you speak to me.'

She felt the air stir, as if the door was no barrier at all. 'Go away, or I'll ring for the police.'

'Why don't you?'

Mrs Anderson backed away, her slippered feet retreating silently on the hall floor. Cal banged again and swore, as if he knew he was losing her. 'What colour was Violet's hair when she was a baby?' he shouted. 'Was it fair or dark Mrs Anderson? Was it blonde or brown?'

'Mrs Anderson.' He banged on the door. 'Mrs Anderson, what colour was it?'

'Blonde,' she whispered. Her finger tips pressed at the place where she still felt the sticky imprint of Anna lips, her cheeks turning alabaster white as she realised the error she had made.

A progression of tiny red dots led from the beach to the road and along the track to Boyd's Farm. At the steading and farm-house the dotted line became circular and jumbled. Cal enlarged the aerial map on his laptop screen until he had a clearer view of the buildings, until he could see which dots fell on the farmhouse. The first, inside the back porch, was timed at 06.53, ten minutes after Violet had left the beach. The last was at 08.14, two minutes ago. To begin with Violet had been moving around, probably going from the ground floor to the first, Cal guessed. Then she had spent 16 minutes towards the front of the house, roughly where Megan's room would be. But for the last 23 minutes, since 07.53, she had been in the same place, towards the back of the house, and she hadn't moved.

He stared at the last dot. She ought to be told about Mrs Anderson. Should he ring her? Should he go to the farmhouse? Or should he leave her undisturbed, let her work things out on her own as Hilary suggested the night before? A thought nagged at him. The last dot was more or less where the attic room would be. Why would Violet go there, to the place where her mother's killer had

376

died? Why would she stay there for so long? He'd heard of one suicide leading to another but no sooner had he reassured himself of the impossibility of Violet doing the same – she would never abandon Anna – the worry returned. She had been distressed. Who knows what she might do, what she might have done? He stared at the dot. He called the phone. 'Pick up, Violet, pick up.' It went to answer, Cal's voice. Then he tried Violet's own phone. It rang out.

Accelerating along Brae's back drive, he shouted 'fuck, fuck, fuck.' His foot was flat to the floor, but the pickup's response was sluggish. Suddenly every second, every fraction of a second, counted. From the beach road, he went along the track to Boyd's Farm, swerving left and right to avoid the grooves and gouges left by the trucks and police vehicles. He stopped by the steading entrance, at the blue and white police tape with 'Do Not Cross' on it. Ducking underneath, he ran into the steading courtyard and to the back door. He pushed it open and a cat ran past him into the house. Going along the corridor to the hall, Cal recalled Duncan's hanging body, only it changed to Violet's in his imagination. Spurred on by it, he ran through the hallway, up the staircase and across the landing, stopping at the small flight up to the attic.

'Violet, are you there?'

The door to the room was as open as it had been before. Enough to see in. Not enough to see if a body was hanging from the hook Duncan had used.

'Violet, are you there?'

He climbed the stairs and went along the short passageway. He pushed open the door with his foot. There was no hanging body; there was nobody at all. Propped against the skirting board on the far wall, below the graffiti left by Poltown's teenagers on their night-time forays, was his own phone. He crossed the room to pick it up and suddenly saw his name on the wall. It was written in sparkly nail varnish, a message beside it. 'Forgive me. I thought you might try to stop me. Love Violet.' An arrow pointed to the right, to a heart with two names and a date inside it. Ross + Alexandra. September 9 1983. The day that Violet was born. Cal looked from one name to the other. Who would she have gone to first?

Maybe he should have separated Mrs A from the rest of the flock. If he had, Jim could have driven slowly along the road, Mrs A bleating in the trailer, the other blackface sheep following on and Tommy, the collie, bringing up the rear. He took a swig from the bottle, and another. The whisky dropped into his stomach and he waited for the hit; the sensation of bobbing around above a sea of worry and depression instead of sinking into it.

'Aah,' he sighed. 'That's grand.'

He wiped his hand across his mouth and propped the bottle against the passenger seat. 'Better get moving,' he mumbled. 'Tommy will be waiting on me.' A grin creased Jim's face as he imagined the dog lying flat, his ears pricked, his flanks quivering in anticipation of Jim's whistle. The sheep would be milling about in front of him, Mrs A stamping her feet in truculence, the others taking their cue from her. Jim grabbed his stick and hauled himself out of the van, leaving the engine running in case of trouble. He checked whether his parking had blocked off the culvert, where Mrs A had led the blackies astray the last time. 'Good enough,' he reckoned and wandered the fifty metres back to the bend to watch for Tommy bringing the flock. He whistled, a long blast. Tommy barked in response. 'Good lad,' Jim said, his habit of talking to the dog so ingrained it made no difference whether Tommy was within earshot or not. 'Good lad. Nice and slow now.'

Jim heard the rattle of hooves on the tarmac, his ears telling him that everything was under control. Rounding the corner and coming into view, the sheep also seemed to be nicely bunched, Tommy showing restraint, hanging ten or fifteen metres behind, working from one side of the road to the other, letting Mrs A know where he was. As Jim expected, she was at the front but trotting calmly in the middle of the road.

'Good lad,' he shouted and the dog pricked its ears. 'Easy now . . .'

Jim let the sheep come close. Then he walked ahead of them until he was by the van and the culvert. When he stopped to deter another attempted break-out that way, they halted too.

'Bring them on,' Jim shouted to Tommy. The dog chivvied the sheep as Jim had asked but Mrs A refused to budge. Her nostrils flared and her eyes had that wild look which Jim recognised, a look that signalled trouble.

'Damn, damn.'

As soon as Jim had seen the danger Mrs A took off, her hooves slipping and sliding on the road. She leapt the far ditch and started to climb the bank, the rest of the flock in noisy pursuit. On Jim's command, the dog raced uphill to stop Mrs A from doubling back to the field the sheep had just left, which was what she had done the last time. But Mrs A appeared to have a different plan. She wheeled round and started off in the opposite direction.

'Damn,' Jim repeated. If Mrs A made it to the forestry high up on the hill, he and Tommy would be spending the rest of the day rounding them up. The deer fence had long since fallen down. The place was a jumble of fallen timber; every winter the wind dropped some more trees. If the sheep got in there, there'd be no easy way of getting them out again. Damn, Jim said again. He should have put Mrs A in the trailer after all.

As the last of the sheep disappeared from view, Tommy in pursuit, Jim jumped in the van. Swallowing a mouthful of whisky, he went through the gears, first, second, third: if he was smart about it he should be able to reach the top of the hill track before Mrs A and cut her off. Changing up to fourth, he gulped another swig of whisky and tucked the bottle between his thighs. The road swung left and entered a tunnel of overhanging trees. Crossing from bright sunlight into shadow, Jim was temporarily blinded. The van hit something, a glancing blow. He gripped at the wheel and braked. Whisky spilt on his trousers. He swore and checked in his mirror, expecting to see a stone which the sheep had sent rolling down the bank on to the road, or a fallen branch. But the bend was now between him and whatever he'd hit. The noise of the impact rankled too: it reminded him of the time he'd collided with a deer. Flesh and bone against metal made a different thud. Perhaps one of the sheep had toppled from the bank and he'd hit it, not a stone. 'Damn.'

He retrieved the bottle of whisky from the floor by his seat. Most of it had spilled out. He gulped what was left and got out unsteadily to check the damage. There was a dent on the van's front offside, a curved impression made by something softer than stone or wood. A sheep after all, Jim thought, or a deer flushed on to the road by all the commotion. At the speed he was going – less than 40mph – the impact of a glancing blow might not have killed it. More than likely it'd have crawled away somewhere.

'Damn.'

Tommy yelped in pursuit of the runaways. He was some distance off, half way at least to the forestry. As Jim feared, Mrs A was heading for the high hill.

He had no chance of cutting her off now. Leaving the empty whisky bottle on the roof of the van, he walked back along the road. At the bend, he was alarmed to see the contents of a backpack strewn across the tarmac: alarmed as well as suddenly apprehensive.

'Damn,' he said again under his breath, becoming more agitated as he drew closer. He went from object to object, picking up each one; a pair of sunglasses, a packet of hair-clips, keys, a receipt, roller-ball pen, a bottle of nail varnish, a packet of tissues. As he bent to gather up the backpack he heard a noise.

And again.

It came from the direction of the birch trees below the road. Fearing the worst Jim followed a trail of broken and bent bracken stems downhill. Where the ground flattened, a bare expanse of moss, he came across the body of a woman. She was on her side, her right leg at an unnatural angle and there was blood on her jeans. Her head had also taken a blow. More blood was seeping into her hair. For a second, Jim didn't know what to do. The taste of whisky was fresh in his mouth; an empty bottle on the roof of his van. Another that he'd finished a few hours before was in his kitchen.

Just as he was wondering whether there was any way out of this mess for him, she moaned again. 'Help . . . please.'

'Hold on there,' Jim answered. 'I'm almost with you.'

Resigning himself to losing his licence and worse, he knelt by her side. 'What happened?' he said, and when she didn't answer he decided to tell her a lie, his last hope of avoiding punishment. He had been driving along, he said, and he'd seen her bag on the road. Had she slipped and fallen? Had a car hit her? He'd passed one on the road. He touched her clenched right hand. 'Can you speak to me? Can you tell me what hurts?' He looked at her broken leg, at the odd angle of it. He wondered if he should try to straighten it, whether a make-shift tourniquet above the break would stop it bleeding, whether he should move her. What did he know about it? When any of his sheep broke a leg, his only other experience of something like that, he cut their throats.

He checked the wound on the back of her head. It seemed to be a graze rather than a deep cut; the blood oozing rather than flowing. He leant over her body so that she could see him. The right half of her face was pressing into the moss. 'It's ok Violet,' he said. 'You'll be all right. I'll get you out of here.' He squeezed her clenched hand to reassure her.

'Is it just your leg?'

She tried to speak, the corner of her mouth opening. Sounds, not words. 'It's ok,' Jim said. Her open left eye watched him. Although bloodshot, it seemed to be able to follow his movement. A good sign, he thought. 'Can you do something for me?' Jim remembered a scene from Casualty on the television. 'Can you flex your fingers?' He touched Violet's clenched hand to prompt her. The index finger started to open, the others slowly followed. 'That's good,' he said. 'Can you go all the way?' As the fingers stretched out, a small box fell from her hand. The lid sprang open spilling a brooch, the violet of the flowers framed by the bright green of the moss. Jim grunted as if he'd been winded. His expression altered too; shock, guilt and fright, one reflex after another. He glanced at Violet. Now her bloodshot eye watched him coldly and accusingly. *You've seen it before*. Jim wiped the back of his hand across his face. 'Damn,' he said. 'What'll I do with you now?'

Not the first entrance. Not the second. At the third, Cal turned left. The sign on the corner house said William Wallace Drive. Someone had spray-painted a line through William Wallace and had scrawled above it Alec Turnbull. At the far end of the cul-de-sac were three bungalows. A woman pushing a pram told Cal which was whose. The one on the left, 'the posh one with a conservatory', was Alec's. The middle one was where Alec's sister-in-law Marjorie lived. The one he wanted was on the right, with the fresh render around the window. Cal parked outside as Ross Turnbull appeared at the side door. He was tucking in a blue shirt. A patterned tie was hanging undone around his collar. He threw a suit jacket on to the roof of

384

his car while he opened the passenger door and put an executive case on to the seat. Then he noticed Cal.

'I haven't got time for this.' He watched Cal walking up to the gates. 'Whatever it is. Sorry but I just don't.'

Ross shut the door with his knee and picked up the jacket. Walking round the car, he pulled it on.

'Has Violet Wells been to see you?' Cal demanded.

Ross stopped. 'And that's why I don't have time for this. I've lost too much time already.' Opening the driver's door, he said, 'Come and see me later. Whenever. Happy to chat. But I've got to go.'

'What did you tell her?'

Ross raised his eyebrows and sighed. 'Why don't you ask her?' He straightened his jacket and pulled at the cuffs. The sleeves were too short. 'Sorry, but I've got to be at a meeting, and if I'm late Poltown's going to lose a big opportunity.'

He got into the car, shut the door and opened the window. Reversing down the short driveway, he said, 'By the way I owe you an apology.'

'What for?'

'Some of my guys trying to frighten you off . . . They thought you were doing work for Boyd, feeding him data on how the windfarm would interfere with the currents. Someone Googled you, they put two and two together and made five. They thought you should be warned off. It's the way things used to be done around here. Not now. Not on my watch.'

'Did you apologise to Violet?'

'Why?'

'Because one of your people had a go at her too.'

Ross shook his head. 'Nope, not as far as I know. Look, I wish I could stay and talk but I have to go. This afternoon, this evening, whenever. Just ring the bell.'

Walking back to the pickup, Cal rang Hilary. He told her about Anna's picture, what happened at Mrs Anderson's, about Violet going to Boyd's Farm, finding the names on the wall and then her disappearing act. 'Listen,' he said, interrupting her complaint that Cal should have told her earlier, 'has Violet got her own phone with her?'

Hilary said she thought so. In fact she remembered seeing it in the backpack.

'She's not answering,' Cal said.

CHAPTER 24

The hill track became steeper and rougher. It was gouged and gashed by the streams of rainwater that poured down it nine months of the year. Fiona Bell had already banged the car's underside three times and the next stretch looked even worse. The doctor and her dog peered through the windscreen; Pepe in his usual pose, back legs on the passenger seat, front paws resting on the dashboard, his body spanning a relative chasm. To Fiona's amusement, dog and driver seemed to be adopting similar strategies. The car's front left wheel was balancing on the remnants of the ridge that ran down the centre of the track, the front right on the sloping verge, one or other threatening to slip into an abyss. The canine and motoring equivalents of a high wire act, Fiona told Pepe. 'At any moment we could plunge to our doom.'

As she rubbed the dog's head she noticed a stone shed with a tin roof coming into view around the left of the hill, the direction in which the track was veering. Wisps of smoke drifted from the single chimney and cut peat was stacked in a lean-to by the gable. 'Aggie's Croft' was painted in white on a stone by the door. 'This *is* it,' Fiona exclaimed, hardly believing a woman in her eighties lived on her own in so remote a place. Parking the car, she instructed Pepe to stay where he was and reached into the back for her bag. Through the window she glimpsed a sheep with corkscrew horns standing inside the low stone wall around what appeared to be Aggie's vegetable garden. It saw her too and stamped its left foot with increasing frequency as Fiona proceeded from the car to the croft's door. The animal's recalcitrance brought to mind Aggie's mood on her last visit to the surgery. Difficult hardly described it, Fiona recalled gloomily as she lifted the old-fashioned latch. 'It's only the doctor,' she called out, letting herself in, as Aggie had instructed in her message.

An impatient 'what took you?' issued from the fug of peat smoke and drying clothes. No wonder Aggie complained of rheumy eyes, Fiona thought, but she replied cheerfully, 'Oh, just the landslip and the track being half washed away. No excuse really.'

Once her eyes had acclimatised to the murk, Fiona saw Aggie McPherson in a chair by the small window, the only one in a large rectangular room which seemed to be where she spent her days and nights. There was a bed along the opposite wall, pans above the stove in the fireplace and long-johns and grimy vests were hanging out to dry on a length of farmer's twine.

'How are you Aggie?'

The old woman barely acknowledged Fiona, except to display irritation at having to pay attention to anything else apart from what she described as 'that beast eating my garden'.

'Isn't it one of yours?' Fiona put down her bag and taking Aggie by the wrist felt for her pulse.

'Of course it isn't.' Aggie's beaky little face turned towards Fiona. Even with corkscrew horns, the sheep in question could hardly have looked fiercer.

'Is it your eyes again?'

Aggie bridled. 'There's nothing wrong with my eyes apart from what they're seeing.'

'What's that Aggie?'

'That animal . . .'

Fiona looked from the sheep to Aggie and back again. 'Aggie, you haven't called me out because a sheep is eating your garden?'

Aggie's shoulders slumped. 'You said I could.' She glanced at Fiona to see whether this new doctor was more gullible than the last. 'Anything, you said. Just ring and you'd come.' Her eyes had become dull. 'You said it wasn't right someone old like me having to travel all that way.' She sounded alone and defeated.

Fiona sighed and regretted being so sharp. She patted Aggie's hand. 'I do remember saying something like that.' Resignation seeped into the admission. 'But in future . . .' Fiona tried to look stern. 'Not sheep. Never again. Promise.'

Aggie mumbled something inaudible and turned again to stare at the creature. It was moving from her cabbages to her sprouts, its progress marked by the old woman's renewed complaints.

'If it's not yours,' Fiona said, watching it too, 'whose is it?'

'It's Jim's.'

'Have you rung him?'

Aggie shrugged, managing to look weak and helpless again.

'All right Aggie, just this time.' Fiona stood up and looked from patient to sheep. She wasn't sure which was worse, and said so, hoping her pretence at grumpiness would deter Aggie from pulling the same trick twice.

After saying goodbye, Fiona closed the front door, and advanced on the animal. Despite her shouts, it seemed determined to stay exactly where it was. It stamped its front legs alternately and with such rapidity they reminded Fiona of pistons. She imagined a Yukon gold prospector defending a claim with less resolve.

'I'll go and get Jim,' she shouted at Aggie's ghostly face peering through the window. Doubting she'd be able to hear, Fiona waved, indicating the direction of Jim's small-holding. 'I'll get Jim,' she tried again.

Back in the car, she told Pepe he was in for a treat: he was going to visit Tommy. The two dogs had met a few times, usually when Jim and Fiona passed in the road, each on their rounds. But, as it happened, Pepe had already seen Tommy. The little dog was transfixed by the sight of Jim's collie circling a group of sheep higher up the hill, close to the forestry. There was no sign of Jim and anyway no prospect of getting nearer in the car to check if he was there. Fiona decided instead to leave a note at his small-holding and take Pepe for a walk. She could leave the car by the cattle grid, go along the road to Jim's and return by the path which ran along the loch-side.

It took her ten minutes to reach the bottom of the hill and another minute or two before she was at the cattle grid. Soon she and Pepe were striding along the road, the dog darting into the bracken, sniffing out the scents of deer and pine marten. Fiona relished being alone in such a wild place. Not for the first time, she doubted she would ever be able to go back to England's domestic landscape, pretty and comfortable though it was. Where in England could she go for a walk and be among such wildness, so many changing vistas: now loch, now mountain under a magical September blue sky; so pale it looked ethereal?

Snapping back from her daydream she wondered where Pepe was. She swivelled around and spotted him behind her at the edge of the road, nosing excitedly at some bracken.

'Pepe, stop that,' she shouted. 'What are you eating?' She hurried back to deter him from rolling in whatever foul-smelling corpse or excrement he had uncovered. Scattered sheep droppings were on the tarmac, shiny black and fresh. 'Ugh, Pepe leave it.' She hoped she wasn't too late. 'Pepe.'

Unlike the sheep in Aggie's garden, the dog responded as though he had been falsely accused. His plaintive expression tugged at Fiona, much as Aggie's charade had done. Ruffling his head, she slipped the lead around his neck and promised to let him off again as soon as they were at Jim's. Then she parted the bracken with her foot where Pepe had been sniffing and something shiny caught her eye. A mobile phone. Silver. A model similar to hers. She picked it up and checked it was still working. The screen lit up and she saw there had been a missed call. After unlocking the phone with the pad of her thumb, she returned the call. A man answered. 'Hi Violet,' he said, sounding relieved. 'Have you had a good walk?'

'Who's speaking?' Fiona inquired hesitantly.

'Violet?'

'No, I'm sorry. My name is Fiona Bell . . . Dr Bell,' she added without thinking.

'*Dr* Bell . . . Has something happened to Violet?'

'Let me explain,' she replied hastily, realising her error. 'I'm walking my dog and I found this phone lying in a ditch beside the road.'

'Where?'

'On the road to Jim Carmichael's small-holding,' she said. 'Beyond Poltown, at the loch-side. Do you know where that is?'

'You haven't seen Violet?'

'No. That's why I'm ringing you. You'd called her.'

'Where is she?'

'You said Violet.' Fiona thought there couldn't be many women with such an old-fashioned name even in Poltown. 'Would that be Violet Wells?'

Someone was talking, a man's voice. Was there more than one? Violet thought so. A wild cry was followed by an angry rumble of complaint, only the change in pitch and volume penetrating her delirium, not the words. Now there was another voice: it was self-pitying and close-by. Inside her head the kaleidoscope of shapes and colours changed again. A pinhead of brilliant white light expanded and became lips which contorted and spat as words came from them. She was to blame. He'd saved her once. Hadn't he warned her too? After the public meeting. She'd had her chance. Why had she done this to him? What was he supposed to do with her? The lips faded. The light drew away. The sputter of his saliva on her lips and face accompanied her return to unconsciousness.

As Fiona Bell expected, there was no sign of Jim at the small-holding or of his little van. He'd be on the hill somewhere, because Jim and Tommy were never far apart. By now it was even possible he could be at Aggie McPherson's. She wrote a brief message anyway, letting Jim know about his stubborn ewe as well as the mobile she'd found where the road looped close to the loch shore. She added her phone number 'just in case the owner comes looking for it', and she debated letting Jim know the phone belonged to Violet Wells. Would it be a kindness to warn him she might be dropping by, or would it alarm him? Given his walk-on role in the drama of Duncan Boyd's death, she decided to leave it out, erring on the side of caution. She folded the paper and slid it under the door when someone yelled, 'Hey, what do you think you're doing?'

She didn't recognise the voice but looking up she realised it was Jim. Not only was she surprised to see him but she was taken aback by how aggressive he sounded. This was not the mild, obliging, chatty man she often passed on the road. Jim was still thirty metres away, but even without his angry bellow she could tell something was wrong. It was the hurried way he was walking and the blotchy red of his face under his denim cap. She waved, calling out 'hi' in case he hadn't recognised her, and waited for him to draw closer. If she thought recognition would soften his mood, he proved her wrong. Stopping by the garden gate, he demanded, 'What the devil are you doing Dr Bell?' The red of his cheeks had spread to his throat.

Fiona bristled in return. 'Well since you've asked so nicely Jim I was just leaving a message under your door. One of your sheep is chewing its way through Aggie McPherson's garden.' Then she regretted taking umbrage because she smelt the whisky – Jim reeked of it – and he seemed suddenly to be lost for words, a poor soul if ever she'd seen one. She wondered if Tommy had taken advantage of Jim's drunkenness to sneak away and find some sheep. Tommy was always herding something, chickens, ducks, even children given the chance. Perhaps Jim didn't know where the dog had gone. *And* there had been all the upset about Duncan's death. Did Jim blame himself for not preventing it? In her experience, men became fractious and short-tempered with worry. And they drank. Her father had and her male patients were the same. She had gathered from Jim's medical records that he had stopped drinking. Obviously not.

'Have you lost Tommy?' she asked, trying to sound sympathetic.

The question seemed to startle him.

'Why?'

'I saw him on the hill. He was rounding up some sheep,' she added unnecessarily. Would Tommy do anything else?

His reply was slurred. 'I know where he is.'

'Oh, ok.' Suddenly she noticed Pepe. He was licking a wet stain at the bottom of Jim's dungarees. She called the dog to heel but too late. Jim kicked out, catching Pepe in the ribs. The dog let out a yelp.

'Jim, what's got into you?' Fiona knelt to comfort the retreating animal. 'For God's sake, you're like a bear with a sore head.'

'Ach . . .' Jim took off his cap and rubbed it over his face. 'It's been a day.'

'Why, what's happened?' Fiona's tone suggested his explanation would have to be good.

'A walker left a gate open.' He looked around, as if he was still searching for the culprit.

'Is that why your sheep are up on the hill?'

'Aye, it is. Tommy's gone after them. He'll get them all right.' He shook his head, as if there was more to it than that. 'I lost one – it broke its leg on some wire. Been skinning it.' He showed her his hands.

Fiona noticed how grimy and bloody they were. 'I thought it was blood.'

'What was?'

'That,' she pointed to the bottom of his dungarees, at the stain which had attracted Pepe.

He looked too. 'Aye, it'll be blood all right. The wire tore a hole in her, broke a leg as well. Had to put her out of her misery.' Again he rubbed the cap across his face.

'In that case, we'd better let you get on.' Fiona couldn't bring herself to excuse Jim even though he'd had a trying experience.

As she passed him on the path, Jim reached out and patted Pepe's head. 'I shouldn't have done that, Dr Bell.'

'What?'

'Taken it out on the dog.'

'It's done now.' An uncomfortable lull followed: Fiona anxious to be going; Jim fidgeting and making grunts of remorse. Eventually the smell of whisky and sweat was too strong a mix for her. 'I'll be off then,' she said.

By the loch, reflecting on Jim's temper and commiserating with Pepe, it occurred to Fiona she should ring Cal McGill. Might it have been Violet who let the sheep escape? Perhaps they'd taken off down the road and she'd run after them to bring them back. Was that how she had lost her phone? There had been fresh droppings on the road where she'd found it.

Cal listened impatiently, trying to interrupt. 'Where are you?' he broke in once Fiona stalled. 'I've been waiting for you, by your car.'

Fiona stared at Pepe after Cal ended the call. 'Is it me,' she asked the dog, 'or is everyone bad tempered today? I mean couldn't he have *mentioned* he'd get here so quickly?' The more she thought about it, the more she felt a mug. First Aggie, then Jim shouting at her, now a complete stranger getting stroppy when they'd already arranged to meet in another twenty minutes to hand over Violet's phone. Heading back inland from the loch shore towards the road, she saw an old red pickup parked beside her car. A man – McGill she assumed – was pacing backwards and forwards on the road. She resented the way his restlessness made her hurry: typical of her, she thought, always the one putting herself out and trying to make things right. However, on meeting him, she found her pique beginning to fade. He was quite good looking with a squint nose (if he was her patient, she'd advise him to get it fixed) and he was apologetic for being short-tempered and thanked her when she handed over Violet's mobile. Could she show him where she found it?

'Beyond that bend.' Fiona pointed along the road which was shaded by the cover of trees. 'On the left hand side of the road, about two or three hundred metres round the corner.'

Cal looked there too. 'Where does the road go?'

'To Jim Carmichael's place,' she replied. 'The guy I was telling you about, who lost the sheep.'

'So if she was walking from this direction,' Cal said, 'that's where she would have gone.'

Fiona picked up the concern in his voice – he didn't appear to think Violet had dropped the phone by accident. 'You're worried about her?'

'Yes,' he said. 'I think I'll have a word with this Jim Carmichael, ask him if he's seen Violet.'

'In that case,' Fiona said, 'I'll come too and show you where I found her phone. We can stop on the way.' She omitted to mention the real reason for accompanying him. She hoped her presence would deter Jim from another display of drunken temper. She thought she'd save Cal from that.

In the event, she needn't have fussed. As the two vehicles pulled up at the house, Jim appeared from a shed beside the big barn and Fiona was relieved at the change in his demeanour. The bull-headed aggression had gone. Trepidation had replaced it, or so it seemed. Perhaps he'd sobered up a bit. She hoped that was it. 'Me again, Jim,' she called over, stopping short of him, keeping a distance in case of another flare-up. Pepe, she was pleased to see, was of the same mind. He sat obediently at her feet. 'This is Cal McGill,' Fiona said. 'He's looking for a friend of his and wondered if you'd seen her.'

'Haven't seen anybody apart from the doctor here,' Jim replied, and Fiona realised she had mistaken his mood. Rather than trepidation, she picked up a wary watchfulness.

'She lost her phone on the road,' Fiona continued. 'I found it when I was walking Pepe, or rather Pepe found it. I mentioned it in the note I left you.'

Obviously, he hadn't bothered to read it because he shook his head and closed and opened his eyes evasively. 'Not a soul's been here,' he said. 'Apart from the person who let my sheep out between eight and nine.' He gave Cal a hostile look. 'Would your friend have been here then?'

Cal said, 'It's possible.'

'Oh, I can't imagine it was her,' Fiona blurted trying to keep Jim's attention, praying he wouldn't notice what Pepe was up to. While she'd been watching Jim, the dog had wandered off and was now crawling under the door of the barn. She hated to think what he'd find to eat in there but she didn't dare call him back in case Jim had another of his fits and lashed out again.

*   *   *

One moment Violet welcomed the pain which radiated from her leg because it signified life and the possibility of holding Anna again. The next she begged to be spared its torture. Through her agony she heard voices. One was familiar: Cal. Hope at last. She screamed. The sound filled her head yet her mouth hadn't moved. Had she made any sound at all? She listened for Cal again and heard a rustling noise close by. She strained to escape the whisky spit that would soon be spraying across her face. From somewhere she found the strength to strike out and rake at him with her nails, before falling into unconsciousness again.

Fiona knelt at the bottom of the barn doors where they'd splintered and broken. It was where Pepe had disappeared, where the whimpering seemed to be loudest. 'He's hurt.' Fiona glanced back at Jim then put her face close to the gap. 'Pepe,' she shouted, 'Pepe, love.' When she looked at Jim again, he had a peculiar and abject expression. Beads of sweat were running down his face which had become pale and oily. A tic pulsed at the side of his mouth. Fiona rattled the chain and padlock which held the doors closed. 'Jim, the key, where's the key?'

Jim's head sagged and his clenched right hand opened. A key dropped at his boots. It hit a stone with a tinny sound. Cal picked it up. 'In case you hadn't guessed,' she whispered as Cal opened the padlock, 'he's been drinking. A lot by the smell of it.'

Fiona untied the chain and Cal pulled it free. The wooden doors opened a metre or two before sticking on rubble. A shaft of sunlight penetrated the gloom falling on a woman's body. She was lying on compacted earth, one of her legs splayed below the knee, her jeans bloody, her face bruised and swollen and her right hand gripping Pepe. The dog squirmed and whined.

'It's Violet,' Cal said.

Fiona knelt and eased Violet's fingers from the dog. She handed him to Cal. 'Put him in my car and get my bag.' She crouched over Violet feeling at her neck for a pulse, checking on her leg, at the loss of blood. 'Can you hear me Violet? I'm Dr Bell.' She glanced at Cal. 'And call for an ambulance, hurry.'

Outside, Jim hadn't moved but instead of looking at the ground he was staring across the loch, at the hills which extended into one another like drawn curtains, light and dark catching in the folds.

'What happened? What did you do to her?' Cal studied Jim's face, his mottled skin, his stubborn, stupid muteness. He clenched his fist and swung it. The crack of knuckle on bone made Fiona turn round.

'For God's sake, *hurry.*'

CHAPTER 25

The police arrived within minutes of Cal speaking to the emergency operator. One car with two officers was followed soon after by another. Cal answered questions about Violet and Jim Carmichael, and volunteered information about Mrs Anderson knowing about the baby's hair. Only later, once Jim had been led into the house, a policeman at each arm, did Cal inquire how they'd managed to get there so quickly. There'd been another call, a constable told him, a tip-off, about 'another matter', not something he could discuss except to say the first two cars had been responding to that. More were now on the way. So was a detective inspector from Inverness. He would take charge of the operation. 'If you'd just wait in your vehicle until Mr Macrae arrives, sir.'

Mr Macrae was the detective inspector.

'Can't I see Violet?' he asked.

'There's nothing you can do, sir,' the constable said, walking towards Cal, holding his arms wide and guiding him towards the pickup, as though

402

practising for marshalling a crowd. 'The doctor's got everything under control.'

Just before the ambulance arrived, the constable moved in again, standing by the door of Cal's pickup, providing an intermittent commentary on what was going to happen. Dr Bell would be travelling with the patient. Another doctor would join the ambulance on its journey, a consultant who specialised in road accident injuries. 'Miss Wells doesn't seem to be in danger.'

'What about Anna?' Cal asked, after the ambulance had departed under police escort, blue lights flashing.

Another vehicle was being despatched to pick her up with Hilary and Izzy, the constable said. It would take them to the hospital.

'Which hospital?'

'Raigmore.'

Cal smiled ruefully at the tricks fate played. The constable regarded him with a puzzled expression. 'Did I say something, sir?'

'It's where Violet was abandoned as a baby,' Cal explained as a police van arrived and parked close to his pickup. Ten officers disgorged from it. A uniformed sergeant divided them into three groups. Cal overheard him relaying DI Macrae's orders: three to search the barns, another three to search the house and outbuildings, and four to fan out across the fields. What were they looking for, asked one of the field quartet? The sergeant looked sideways at his questioner before shaking his head in wonder at recruits nowadays. *What do you think you're looking for?*

Four sheep skulls were arranged in a row, their empty eye sockets staring sightlessly onto a crime scene. They lay on black plastic sheeting which covered the grass near where the police had been digging. Around them was a scattered collection of other bones – all ovine as far as Detective Inspector John Macrae could tell: legs, ribs and spinal vertebrae – and six packages wrapped in bin-bags and waterproof tape. One packet had split open, ruptured accidentally by a spade. An assortment of different coloured tablets and capsules had spilled out, pinks, greens, browns and blues, some in packets, some not. A drugs officer was on his way to collect the haul for laboratory analysis. Other police had been despatched to detain Davie White.

'And that'll all need to be bagged and taken away too.' Macrae indicated a mound of dug over earth from which more sheep bones were protruding. Then they'd have to wait for the forensic team to expose the rest of the skeleton. Once they'd done that, the pit would have to be dug out, the soil and animal remains removed for sieving and sifting. As a precaution, Macrae said, in case any human material was mixed up in it. A scavenger might have burrowed down, might have displaced a bone. Twenty-six years had passed. This time they were going to be thorough. No stone unturned. He winced at his unintended bad joke.

'So this is where nice old Jim Carmichael used to bury the carcases of his sheep is it?' The detective inspector surveyed the packages, the skulls and the dug-up bones until the horror of the pit drew him back. A shadow seemed to pass across his face, greyness on the white skin which accompanied his slick of red hair: dismay at man's inhumanity to man. He turned away and glared at the loch and mountains, as if they too were culpable, their magnificence nothing but a shimmering distraction for the unwary in their dealings with cold-hearted country folk.

'Get him up here.' Macrae barked, starting off across the field, as if he had to put distance between himself and what had happened there. 'Show him what we've got. See if it'll loosen his tongue.' Then, an afterthought: 'And *make* him look at it.' Macrae stopped by a stone wall and smoked one cigarette after another. All the time he examined his shoes. Scenery had never held much charm for him, or fields, or wide-open spaces. Give him a dingy pub, an ugly street and people he knew he couldn't trust. Not this pretence at something natural and finer.

By now Jim was standing at the edge of the pit, staring down into it. Staring into his rotten soul, Macrae hoped too, glancing over at him. The scene reminded him of a film he'd watched recently. An

Iraqi had dug a grave for the victim of a car-bombing and his reward had been summary execution with a militia bullet to the back of his head. Macrae held up his hand, shaped it like a gun and pointed it at Jim. An exploding sound came from the back of his throat. His hand jerked up with the recoil. He imagined Jim toppling, just as the Iraqi had done.

'Right . . .' He dropped his smoking cigarette into the grass, stamped on it and walked slowly back to the pit. He gestured to the constables to move away before taking his place beside Jim, bowing his head like him. Macrae looked at Jim, at the set of his jaw, at the bruise from the punch turning purple by his mouth. Jim's eyes were fixed on the arm, pelvis and leg that had been exposed. Macrae waited for a moment. When Jim began to shuffle uneasily, he said, 'The way she's holding her hand, do you see it?' Macrae held up his own hand, the fingers and thumb bent, the palm still exposed, adjusting them until they were the same as hers. 'It makes you wonder. Well, it makes *me* wonder.' His hand clawed at the air, and again, and again. 'Whether Megan Bates was dead when you put her in there . . . you or Mrs Anderson, or whoever else was involved.'

The walk had exhausted her, and the upset. By the wall, she hardly had the energy to open the gate let alone to carry on to the intersection of the paths, to the wooden bench. Yet on she went, propelled by the worry which had pursued her from Gardener's Cottage all the way along the moor path; the thought of being prevented from spending her last evening in the tranquillity of the graveyard. Finally, taking her seat on the right of the bench, her place of silent contemplation, she gazed at the panorama of hills and water and surrendered her life. Occasionally she turned her head to glimpse the flat meadow by Boyd's Farm or the canopy of leaves which concealed Brae but mostly she sat as she always did: her knees together; her hands folded one on top of the other, looking straight ahead, observing the coming and goings on the road, and wishing for death to take her away before the police did. The sun set and darkness fell. The autumn chill of a September night turned Mrs Anderson's skin as cold as the gravestones as the breath went from her.

The headlights of Ross Turnbull's car blazed across the beach. Leaving his engine running and his door open he walked over the sand to the water's edge where Cal was standing. 'The police told me where I could find you,' he said. Cal didn't move, didn't reply. Ross tried again. He'd been upset to hear about Violet. This time Cal said 'Yeah.'

'You're not going to make this easy for me are you?'

'No.'

Ross put up his hands. The shadow of his arms

extended over the sea. 'I'm sorry. Is that what you want?'

Cal shrugged. *It's something.*

Ok, Ross said, he should have realised the significance of Violet's visit but he hadn't. He'd been living and breathing the BRC deal every minute of every day, making the case for Poltown, arranging with Duncan's brother for the sale of Boyd's Farm rather than worrying about some woman who had died a quarter of a century ago. He sighed, resignation, regret and apology in a single exhalation. 'Ok, Violet turning up at my door should have rung a few alarm bells.'

So should her questions, when she came to see him.

When had he and Alexandra written their names on Duncan's attic wall, what time of day?

Early evening, he had told her.

Had he seen Duncan later?

Yes, he had. Duncan had been on the beach until late at night.

How late, close to midnight?

Yes, around midnight, and later too. Duncan had been collecting flotsam using a helmet with a torch, like miners used. Ross had seen him.

Then Violet had left.

Ross's head had been so full of worrying about what could go wrong at the meeting he hadn't fully realised what he had told her. Half way to Ullapool he got it, *boom*. The night he and Alexandra went to Duncan Boyd's attic Violet must already have been a few hours old. So Duncan couldn't have driven the baby to Inverness, as Jim Carmichael said, couldn't have abandoned her at Raigmore Hospital. Ross paused. 'Couldn't have had anything to do with Megan Bates's death either, come to think of it.'

Ross had watched Duncan write a message to Megan below the tide line a long time after midnight. 'Stay with me LOVE you Duncan'. Ross remembered the capitals in particular. 'He wrote it so that Megan would read it when she went for her early morning walk on the beach, before the next high tide washed it away.' Ross looked at Cal. 'Why would Duncan be writing luvvy little messages to Megan Bates if he'd already killed her as he's supposed to have told Jim? Or am I missing something?'

Ross had been there because he had broken up with Alexandra. After going to Duncan's attic, they had a row, 'something about nothing'. She had been drinking and typically she'd shouted and screamed at him before disappearing into the night.

'God knows where,' he said. 'I spent the night on the beach to avoid running into her but also to make a big decision. It was only Alexandra keeping me in Poltown.'

He realised he had no future there apart from following in his father's footsteps. But father and son didn't get on: too similar in some ways, too different in others, like night and day, and his old pa was definitely night, a bad man.

'The only way I could escape was just to go without telling anyone. It took me an hour or six to pluck up the courage. I stayed on the beach until daylight then I hitched to Inverness and caught the train to London.'

He hadn't returned for four or five years and then only for a weekend. He couldn't remember when he'd heard about Megan Bates's death but it was some time later.

'And I couldn't have told you what week or month it happened so there was no reason for me to connect it to that night.

'Then after Violet asked me all those questions, I got it. I made the connections. I knew there was something wrong with Jim Carmichael saying Duncan had confessed.'

He had pulled off the road because he was early for his meeting and called one of his guys, someone he trusted. He had asked him about Jim, whether there was anything going on he should know about. The answer was one he'd been half expecting.

'Nothing about Duncan Boyd or his confession but a whisper about Jim borrowing money, and being leaned on to hide stuff while the police were about the place.'

Stuff meant drugs, Ross told Cal.

'Which one of the boys,' he had asked. 'Davie?' His guy hadn't said no, hadn't said anything. That was the way it worked. Silence meant yes.

'Davie White worked for my old pa,' Ross explained, 'and I inherited him.' He shook his head at another oversight. 'When I returned to Poltown I told them all there were new rules.'

He didn't want to know what had gone on before but if he heard of anything illegal he'd call in the police, whatever it was, whoever was doing it.

'Because I've been offshore, Africa, other rough places, they know I can look after myself.' He showed Cal a long ragged scar on the underside of his right forearm. 'I've been in a few scraps. They know I'm not kidding them.'

When his meeting in Ullapool ended, he told the police they might find a stash of drugs at Jim's small-holding. They had too, heroin, marijuana and a 'load of pills'. He also gave them the nod about having a chat with Davie White.

'Stupid,' Ross said, thinking again of Violet, how he could have stopped her if only he had been quicker off the mark. 'Of course she would have gone to Jim's next, after what I told her. Thank God she's going to be OK.'

'Yeah.'

He shot Cal an angry look. 'Give me a break for Christ's sake. I've said sorry.'

In Ullapool Police Station DI Macrae was explaining why he had asked to see Cal. Violet had refused to see the police. He understood the reason. The force hadn't acquitted itself well. They had been too slow and sloppy to mount a proper investigation twenty-six years ago, and too quick to lodge an official complaint about Mr Anwar. Would Cal be an intermediary? Would he reassure Violet that everything was proceeding to a prosecution of Jim Carmichael?

'Someone has to tell her how her mother died,' Macrae said, 'and under the circumstances that probably shouldn't be a police officer.'

'You want me to do it?'

Macrae deflected the question. 'It's been long enough already.'

Cal nodded, and Macrae did too, acknowledgement as well as gratitude. He tapped his keyboard and turned his computer screen towards Cal. 'I want you to hear it for yourself so you can tell Violet that nothing's being kept from her. There's no conspiracy, not this time.'

The scene which began to play was one Cal had seen in various guises before, in films, or a thousand television crime dramas.

A guilty man was slumped disconsolately at a table, picking at his stubby fingers, a smart young female lawyer sitting erect beside him. Her demeanour spoke of prospects and achievements; his of disappointment and failure. Jim Carmichael looked a broken man as he started mumbling, telling of the terrible things he'd seen, his father dying of cancer, ravens hopping across a bog to peck out the terrified eyes of a floundering horse, and the evening he drove to Orasaigh Island with Megan Bates's weekly grocery order.

Jim glanced up, full of self-pity.

'Go on,' a voice off camera said. It was Macrae.

412

The delivery had been his last of the day, Jim said. He had put it into the tin box on the mainland shore as he usually did, but when he looked across the causeway he saw Megan over by the island, lying on the sand. He had run to help her and saw blood coming out of her. The baby was beside her, 'still attached'.

Jim glanced up, the bewilderment of that evening on his face again. What could he have done? He'd never even held a baby before.

'Was anyone else there?' Macrae again.

'No.'

'What did you think had happened?'

'She'd gone into labour waiting for the tide and in the end she couldn't wait.' Jim shook his head. 'Half dead she was, she'd lost that much blood.' All she'd been able to do before losing consciousness was throw her cardigan over the child.

He hadn't known what to do – that look of bewilderment once more – whether to move her and risk making the haemorrhage worse, or leave her and the baby and go for help. He sighed heavily.

'What did you do?'

'The only thing I could.'

He had wrapped Megan's cardigan tight around the baby and secured it with her brooch – 'flowering violets'. He always remembered them because everything else that night had been so ugly. Then he drove to Brae, the nearest house with a phone in those days. He had hoped for Mr William, but

413

Mrs Ritchie had come to the door. He was uncom-fortable telling her because everyone in the village had heard the rumours about Mr William's affair. He was worried about her reaction, but she was calm and practical, going back into the house to ring for an ambulance and returning with towels, a flask of water and scissors.

'What happened next?'

They drove to the causeway.

Jim paused, as if he needed to summon up strength for what was to follow.

After he parked the van, she ran ahead of him. He followed with the towels and water. When he caught up with her, she was already kneeling beside Megan. He thought she must be comforting her. But she wasn't. 'She was saying Megan was a slut, a bitch who deserved to die.'

Jim still looked shocked.

'What did you do?'

'I asked her to stop but she went on and on saying terrible things.'

The baby was crying and Jim wrapped it in a towel. Afterwards, Mrs Ritchie turned away from Megan and started talking about all she'd done for him.

'She said she'd paid off my debts as well as giving me work at Brae. She'd stuck by me and now I had to stick by her.'

Jim lifted his eyes to the camera, his lids seeming heavy with the burden of guilt.

'Mrs Ritchie said Megan would be dead soon,

and I had to dispose of her body, as if she was ordering me to do some job for her at the house.'

When she said the best place for burying bones was with other bones he knew she meant his sheep pit. He'd disposed of diseased livestock carcases from Brae in the past so Mrs Ritchie was aware of it.

He tried to resist her, to make her see sense.

Jim glanced again at Macrae and the camera, pleading. *Believe me.*

'So what did you say to her, Jim?'

'I told her she wasn't thinking straight and anyway the ambulance would be arriving soon. But she smiled again. "Poor Jim, there you go again, never quite understanding how things work".'

There wouldn't be an ambulance, she said. She hadn't called one. She told him to look after the baby 'while the slut dies'.

If he did as he was told she'd help him out again, as often as he needed, stop him falling into Turnbull's clutches again, keep him from getting another beating or worse.

'Did she help you after that?'

Jim dropped his head. 'Aye, a few times, what with the drink and everything else. I was never that good with money.'

'How much Jim?'

He mumbled.

'I can't hear you Jim.'

'A few thousand, six or seven.'

'What happened next?'

He had tried to comfort the baby. He cut the

cord and cleaned her up a bit. Mrs Ritchie kept talking about Megan, things he would never forget. How her baby would have no father because he would never know she had been born. How Alexandra was the only child William Ritchie would ever have and ever wanted. Then she looked over at Jim and said, 'She's dead, the slut's dead.' Then, a few moments later: 'You let it happen too, Jim. Never forget that.' And again: 'You owe me.'

'And you did as you were told. You got rid of the body?'

Jim nodded. He had carried Megan to his van and buried her that night.

'Was she dead?'

He believed so. He hadn't liked to touch her skin. He had wrapped her up in a blanket he kept in the back of the van. 'She wasn't moving. She never moved.'

'What happened to the baby?'

Jim rubbed the back of his hand across his mouth, again and again, as if trying to wipe away a bloody stain. Mrs Ritchie had taken her, he said. He hadn't known where.

'Did she go to Mrs Anderson?'

She might have. He didn't know.

'Mrs Anderson never said anything to you?'

'No.'

'Nor Mrs Ritchie?'

Jim shook his head. She'd instructed him never to talk about it. She had never spoken of it again. Not to him. Not a word.

'When you heard that someone dressed in Megan Bates's clothes had walked into the sea the next morning didn't you wonder who it was?'

Jim looked sullen. 'Who else could it have been but Mrs Ritchie?' She must have collected Megan's things from Orasaigh Cottage during the night. The door was usually left unlocked but even if it hadn't been Mrs Ritchie had a key.

'Mrs Ritchie could swim?'

Jim nodded. Before Megan Bates's arrival at Poltown, she used to swim at South Bay, Mrs Anderson joining her on the beach with a picnic. Jim had seen them there often in the summer months. He remembered Mrs Anderson saying she was a strong swimmer.

'Strong enough to swim from South Bay to North Bay?'

From what Mrs Anderson had told him, yes.

'Wasn't there a danger of her running into Duncan or someone else?'

Jim shrugged as if he didn't think so. Duncan's habit was to collect flotsam straight after high tide so that by the time Megan was able to cross the Orasaigh causeway the beach at South Bay would be clean. No-one else went there at that time in the morning, apart from Mrs Armitage who kept to the beach road walking her dog.

'Mrs Ritchie would have known that?'

'What?'

'That Mrs Armitage would be a witness and could report what she had seen to the police?'

417

Jim nodded. 'Mrs Armitage walked past the Brae driveway every morning before eight.'

Macrae waited before asking another question. Jim's head sagged and he picked at his fingers. After the sound of pages turning, Macrae said, 'Did Duncan Boyd confess to killing Megan Bates?'

'No.'

'Why did you say he had?'

Violet Wells was asking questions. He'd been worried where they would lead. When Duncan hanged himself he had the idea of passing on the blame. Wasn't it what the police had thought anyway?

Macrae said nothing, and Jim began to mumble, working himself up into a last attempt at self-justification. Suddenly he looked up, his eyes shining with indignation. Jim Carmichael had given his loyalty, he told Macrae as though reading a citation from a roll of honour. And Mrs Ritchie had taken advantage of him so that Alexandra would get an inheritance she didn't deserve.

'*Given* your loyalty?' Macrae snorted. 'You sold it, Jim.'

The screen went blank and Macrae said, 'Some things we're never going to know.' His voice and expression said he wished it wasn't so. He knew it would be harder for Violet to accept the police had done all they could if there were loose ends. For what they were worth, Macrae had a few theories

418

about what happened but with Diana Ritchie and Mrs Anderson both dead there was now no possibility of proving them. He was as good as certain that Diana Ritchie had taken the baby to Mrs Anderson after Jim had removed Megan's body as that was the only way she could have known its hair colour. His hunch was that Mrs Anderson drove the baby to Raigmore Hospital because she was the one who had written the anonymous letter, perhaps out of guilt at what she had done. Everything else was informed guesswork, apart from the identity of the woman who walked into the sea. That must have been Mrs Ritchie but he was sure she must have had help from Mrs Anderson.

'There's an estate road through the forestry which runs close to North Bay. Mrs Anderson could have gone there in her car with a change of clothes.' The lack of footprints on the beach, apart from Duncan's, was easy to explain. Diana Ritchie was a strong swimmer and more likely than not she had swum in from South Bay to maintain the illusion of Megan Bates being swept round

the headland. She put the hat and bag at the high water mark and went back into the sea, coming ashore again among the rocks. That way she would have left no footprints because high tide was soon after and it would have washed them away. As for Megan's letter, it had probably been intercepted by Diana Ritchie. Since Orasaigh was close to Brae, Megan would have hand-delivered it to the mailbox at the end of the Brae drive. All Diana Ritchie had to do was seal it again, put on a stamp and post it. 'More likely than not Mrs Anderson took it to the Poltown post box for her.'

CHAPTER 26

Violet was talking about Mr Anwar, how he
had visited her in hospital, how pleased
she had been to see him, how worried she
was about him still. In his self-effacing way he had
deflected all her questions, so she didn't know
whether he was all right or not. Hilary had lent
her £200 so she could repay his gift and although
he had refused the money he did take the card
Anna had made inviting him to visit them in
Glasgow. Violet hoped he would.

'If he doesn't Anna and I will just have to go
and see him in Inverness.'

She was sitting in the back of Cal's pickup, her
leg stretched out across the seat, as her consultant
had instructed. She had fallen quiet when Cal
pulled in at the side of the road high up on the
ridge above Poltown. He asked what she felt being
back there again. Violet stared through the window,
at the spectacle of an October storm hurtling
ashore, a tumult of blacks and greys. 'Nothing,'
she said. 'I don't feel anything.'

The landmarks of her mother's life and death
lay below her: Brae, Orasaigh Island, the coastal

path, Boyd's Farm, South Bay, North Bay, all blurry in the squalls of rain.

'No, that's not right,' she corrected herself, everywhere her eye fell stirring an emotion. 'I do feel something. I hate it, the way it can be like this, you know, wonderful and extraordinary when you're up here. But when you're down there, it's different. It's why I wanted to see it again, just to be sure.'

She looked away to the left, towards the church, the green of the mound on which it sat appearing dull and drab in the rain in contrast to the vivid rush of feelings the graveyard now evoked – her father's last resting place, and now Mrs Anderson's. On the drive to Poltown, Cal told how she had been found dead, slumped on a graveyard bench. Violet heard the news in silence. After staring at the distant church, she said, 'It must have been her, mustn't it?' Violet said. 'Mrs Anderson must have written the letter, the one Mr Anwar brought to me.'

'Yes,' Cal replied. DI Macrae had told him the same. The police had found identical writing paper in Gardener's Cottage. The theory was that Mrs Anderson had abandoned Violet at Raigmore Hospital.

'Why would she write after so many years?'

'Guilt maybe? Perhaps she felt she couldn't while Diana Ritchie was alive, but after she was dead, well . . . Perhaps your birthday was the reminder.'

'I guess.' A shaft of sun slanting through a break

in the clouds claimed Violet's attention. It lit up the hillside above the sheep pit where her mother had been buried and painted it briefly with vibrant russets and greens. The intensity of the colours affected her. 'Cal . . .' Her voice caught with emotion. 'How could Jim Carmichael put her in a place like that? How could anyone?'

'I don't know,' Cal replied. Only a partial skeleton had been found: the remainder probably scavenged over the years by foxes or badgers. Cal hadn't told Violet. Nor had he mentioned DI Macrae's comment that Megan Bates might still have been alive. It was unproven and likely to remain that way, though the remains were still being analysed. He glanced in his rear-view mirror, hoping she hadn't detected concealment in the brevity of his response, and found she was looking at him.

'It does matter,' she said, their eyes meeting.

'What?'

'Having a body, even half a body.' She held his gaze.

'I don't feel . . .' She hesitated, uncertain of finding the word. 'That *responsibility* any more. Not closure. Something else.' She was anxious he understood what she was trying to tell him.

'Your work – finding bodies for the families – does matter.'

'Yeah' was all he said, looking away, keeping to himself the email received two days before. It was from the parents of the five-year old boy who had been swept off the pier by a freak wave. Could

Cal McGill help them find 'our missing boy?' Cal's reply? He was busy, regrettably, and would be for a while, the draw-back of a one man operation. He'd email again when his workload allowed him to commit to another investigation.

Violet allowed the view to preoccupy her for a while. 'That's what I dislike about Poltown,' she said eventually. 'Everyone and everything is like Jim Carmichael, seeming to be benign but really being the opposite.' She found Cal's eyes again in the mirror. 'There's nothing for Anna and me here. Nothing.'

'Ok,' he said. 'That's why you wanted to see it again, before BRC's bulldozers changed it forever. To be sure that's how you felt.'

'It is,' she replied. 'Can we go to Glasgow now? I'd like to go home.'